W9-AQO-338

COLD WIND

ALSO BY C. J. BOX

THE JOE PICKETT NOVELS

Nowhere to Run

Below Zero

Blood Trail

Free Fire

In Plain Sight

Out of Range

Trophy Hunt

Winterkill

Savage Run

Open Season

THE STAND-ALONE NOVELS

Three Weeks to Say Goodbye

Blue Heaven

COLD WIND

C. J. BOX

G. P. PUTNAM'S SONS
NEW YORK

G. P. PUTNAM'S SONS
Publishers Since 1838
Published by the Penguin Group
Penguin Group (USA) Inc., 375 Hudson Street, New York, New York 10014, USA •
Penguin Group (Canada), 90 Eglinton Avenue East, Suite 700, Toronto, Ontario M4P 2Y3, Canada
(a division of Pearson Penguin Canada Inc.) • Penguin Books Ltd, 80 Strand, London WC2R 0RL, England •
Penguin Ireland, 25 St Stephen's Green, Dublin 2, Ireland (a division of Penguin Books Ltd) •
Penguin Group (Australia), 250 Camberwell Road, Camberwell, Victoria 3124, Australia
(a division of Pearson Australia Group Pty Ltd) • Penguin Books India Pvt Ltd, 11 Community Centre,
Panchsheel Park, New Delhi–110 017, India • Penguin Group (NZ), 67 Apollo Drive, Rosedale,
North Shore 0632, New Zealand (a division of Pearson New Zealand Ltd) •
Penguin Books (South Africa) (Pty) Ltd, 24 Sturdee Avenue, Rosebank, Johannesburg 2196, South Africa

Penguin Books Ltd, Registered Offices: 80 Strand, London WC2R 0RL, England

Published simultaneously in Canada

Library of Congress Cataloging-in-Publication Data

Box, C. J.
Cold wind / C. J. Box
p. cm.
ISBN 978-0-399-15735-6
1. Pickett, Joe (Fictitious character)—Fiction. 2. Game wardens—Fiction.
3. Wyoming—Fiction. I. Title.
PS3552.O87658C65 2011 2010048029
813'.54—dc22

Printed in the United States of America
1 3 5 7 9 10 8 6 4 2

BOOK DESIGN BY MEIGHAN CAVANAUGH

To the memory of David Thompson

. . . and Laurie, always

AUGUST 21

When you hear hoofbeats, think horses, not zebras.

—Age-old medical school admonition

1

He set out after breakfast on what would be his last day on earth.

He was an old man, but like many men of his generation with his wealth and station, he refused to think of himself that way. Deep in his heart, he honestly entertained the possibility he would never break down and perhaps live forever, while those less driven and less successful around him dropped away.

In fact, he'd recently taken to riding a horse over vast stretches of his landholdings when the weather was good. He rode a leggy black Tennessee walker; sixteen and a half hands in height, tall enough that he called for a mounting block in order to climb into the saddle. The horse seemed to glide over the sagebrush flats and wooded Rocky Mountain juniper-dotted foothills like a ghost, as if the gelding strode on a cushion of air. The gait spared his knees and lower back, and it allowed him to appreciate the ranch itself without constantly being interrupted by the stabs of pain that came from six and a half decades of not sitting a horse.

Riding got him closer to the land, which, like the horse, was *his.* He owned the sandy and chalky soil itself and the thousands of Black Angus that ate the same grass as herds of buffalo had once grazed. He owned the water that flowed through it and the minerals beneath it and the air that coursed over it. *The very air.*

Although he was a man who'd always owned big things—homes,

boats, aircraft, cars, buildings, large and small corporations, race horses, oil wells, and for a while a small island off the coast of North Carolina—he loved this land most of all because unlike everything else in his life, it would not submit to him (well, that and his woman, but that was a different story). Therefore, he didn't hold it in contempt.

So he rode over his ranch and beheld it and talked to it out loud, saying, *"How about if we compromise and agree that, for the time being, we own each other?"*

As the old man rode, he wore a 40X beaver silverbelly short-brimmed Stetson, a long-sleeved yoked shirt with snap buttons, relaxed-fit Wranglers, and cowboy boots. He wasn't stupid and he always packed a cell phone and a satellite phone for those locations on his ranch where there was no signal. Just in case.

He'd asked one of his employees, an Ecuadoran named José Maria, to go to town and buy him an iPod and load it up with a playlist he'd entitled "Ranch Music." It consisted largely of film scores. Cuts from Ennio Morricone like "The Good, the Bad, and the Ugly," the theme from *A Fistful of Dollars*, "L'Estasi Dell'oro (The Ecstasy of Gold)," and "La Resa dei Conti (For a Few Dollars More)," Elmer Bernstein's theme from *The Magnificent Seven*, "The Journey," and "Calvera's Return," and Jerome Moross' theme from *The Big Country*. Big, wonderful, rousing, swelling, sweeping, *triumphalist* music from another era. It was music that simply wasn't made anymore. The pieces were about tough (but fair) men under big skies on horseback, their women waiting for them at home, and bad guys—usually Mexicans—to be vanquished.

In fact, they'd vanquished some Mexicans of their own off the ranch in the last two months, the result of a surreptitious phone call to ICE placed by his wife. Although the Mexican ranch hands worked hard and were great stockmen, she could document how many times they'd refused to show her respect. She blamed their ingrained macho culture. So the immigration folks rounded them up and shipped them away. Their jobs had recently been filled by Ecuadorans like José Maria who were not as accomplished with cattle but were more deferential to his wife.

He threaded his horse up through gnarled bell-shaped stands of juniper. The trees were heavy with clusters of green buds, and the scent within the stand was sweet and heavy and it reminded him of a gin martini. His horse spooked rabbits that shot out from bunches of tall grass like squeezed grapefruit seeds, and he pushed a small herd of mule deer out ahead of him. It had warmed to the mid-seventies, and as the temperature raised so did the insect hum from the ankle-high grass. He hummed, too, along with the theme from *The Big Country.* He tried to remember the movie itself—Gregory Peck or William Holden?—but that was beyond his recollection. He made a note to himself to ask José Maria to order it from Netflix.

He paused the iPod and stuffed the earbuds and cord into his breast pocket as he urged his horse up the gentle slope. The thrumming of insects gave way to the watery sound of wind in the tops of the trees. The transition from an earth sound to the sounds of the sky thrilled him every time, but not nearly as much as what he knew he'd see when he crested the hill.

Clamping his Stetson tight on his head with his free right hand as he cleared the timber, the old man urged his horse to step lively to the top. Now the only sound was the full-throated Class Five wind, but there was something folded inside it, almost on another auditory level, that was high-pitched, rhythmic, and purposeful. He had once heard José Maria describe the sound as similar to a mallard drake in flight along the surface of a river: a furious beating of wings punctuated by a high-pitched but breathy *squeak-squeak-squeak* that meant the bird was getting closer.

From the crown of the hill, he looked down at the sagebrush prairie that stretched out as far as his eyes could see until it bumped up against the Bighorn Mountains of Wyoming. And it was all his.

From the gray and gold of the prairie floor, across five thousand acres, on a high ridge, sprung a hundred wind turbines in various stages of construction where just a year ago there had been nothing but wind-sculpted rock poking out of the surface like dry land coral. A fresh network of straight-line dirt roads connected them all. The finished turbines—and there were only ten of them operational—climbed two hundred fifty feet into the sky. He loved the fact that each tower was a hundred feet higher than the Statue of Liberty. And they were lined up tall and white and perfect in a straight line along the humpbacked spine of a ridge in the basin. All ten working turbines had blades attached. The blades spun, slicing through the Wyoming sky, making that unique whistling sound that was . . . the sound of money.

And he thought: *Ninety more to go.*

Behind the row of turbines was another row of towers only, and another, then seven more rows of ten each in different stages of construction. The rows were miles apart from each other, but he was far enough away on the top of the hill to see the whole of it, from the gaping drill-holes at the rear where the hundreds of tons of concrete would be poured into the ground to the bolted foundations of the towers and finally to the turbines and blades that would be built on top. They reminded him of perfectly white shoots of grass in various stages of growth, sprouting from the dirt straight into the sky.

The blades on the completed turbines had a diameter of forty-four meters or one hundred forty-four feet each. They would spin at close to one hundred miles per hour. Semi-trucks had delivered huge stacks of the blades and they lay on the sagebrush surface like long white whale bones left by ships.

He was so far away from his wind farm that the construction equipment, the pickups and cranes and earth-moving equipment, looked like miniatures.

That first line of almost-completed turbines stood like soldiers, *his* soldiers, facing straight into the teeth of the wind. They spun with defiance and strength, transforming the wind that had denuded the basin of humans and homesteads more than a hundred years ago into power and wealth.

And he waved his hat and whooped at the sheer massive scale of it.

Meeting the supplier-slash-general-contractor for the project the year before had been a spectacular stroke of luck, one of many in his life. Here was a man, a desperate man, with a dream and connections and, most of all, a line on a supply of turbines at a time when the manufacturers couldn't turn out enough of them. This desperate man appeared at the right place and right time and had been literally days away from ruin. And the old man stumbled upon him and seized the opportunity, as he'd seized opportunities before, while those around him dithered and stuttered and consulted their attorneys, chief financial officers, and legislators. That chance meeting and the opportunity that came because of it had saved the old man a million dollars a turbine, or $100 million total. The old man had gone with his gut and made the deal, and here in front of him was the result of his unerring instinct.

Funny thing was, the old man thought, it wasn't the wind farm that would really make him the big money. For that, he would look eastward toward Washington, D.C. That was the epicenter of the breached dam that was sending cash flooding west across the country like waves from a tsunami.

When he heard a rumble of a vehicle motor, he instinctively swept his eyes over the wind farm for the source of the noise, but he quickly decided he was too far away to discern individual sounds.

Since there weren't any cows to move or fences to fix behind him, he doubted it was José Maria or his fellow Ecuadorans coming out his way. He turned in the saddle and squinted back down the hill he had come, but could see nothing.

The old man clicked his tongue and turned his horse back down the hill. As he rode down through the junipers, the harsh winds from on top began to mute, although they didn't quell into silence. They never would.

Again, he heard a motor coming, and he rode right toward it.

When he emerged from the heavy-scented timber, he smiled when he recognized the vehicle and the driver. The four-wheel drive was on an ancient two-track coming in his direction. He could hear the grinding of the motor as well as the spiny high-pitched scraping of sagebrush from beneath the undercarriage. Twin plumes of dust from the tires were snatched away by the wind.

He waved when he was a hundred feet from the vehicle, and was still waving when the driver braked and got out holding a rifle.

"Oh, come on," the old man said, but suddenly he could see everything in absolute gut-wrenching clarity.

The first bullet hit him square in the chest with the impact of a hitter swinging for the upper deck. Shattered his iPod.

AUGUST 22

If a man does not know what port he is steering for, no wind is favorable to him.

—Seneca

2

An hour before dawn broke on Monday, Wyoming game warden Joe Pickett backed his green Ford pickup down his driveway and called dispatch in Cheyenne.

"This is GF53 heading out," he said. The pickup was less than a year old but the new-car feel of the suspension had long been pounded out of it on rugged two-track roads, through grille-high sagebrush, and another hard winter's worth of snowdrifts. As always, he was crowded inside the cab by clothing, maps, gear, weapons, and electronics. The department refused to buy or provide standard crew-cab trucks for the fifty-four wardens in Wyoming for fear taxpayers would object to the showy extravagance, even though new single-cab pickups were so rare they needed to be special-ordered. Inside the cab it smelled of fresh coffee from his travel mug and an unusually flatulent Tube, his male corgi/Labrador mix, who was already curling up on the passenger seat. The newest addition to his standard arsenal was the Ruger .204 rifle mounted to the top of his cab for dispatching wounded or maimed game animals with a minimum of sound or impact. Since Joe's record with departmental vehicles was by far the worst in the agency, he'd vowed to baby this pickup until it hit maximum mileage, something that had not yet happened in his career.

"Good morning, Joe," the dispatcher said, with a lilt. The dispatchers found that phrase amusing and never got tired of saying it.

"Morning," he said. "I'll be in the east break lands in areas twenty-one and twenty-two this morning, checking antelope hunters."

"Ten-four." She paused, no doubt checking her manual. Then: "That would be the Middle Fork and Crazy Woman areas?"

"Affirmative."

As he began to sign off, she asked, "How are you doing? You had to take your daughter to college yesterday, right? How did it go?"

"Don't ask. GF53 out."

The day before, Sunday, Joe had been out of uniform, out of sorts, and nearly out of gas as he approached Laramie from the north in his wife Marybeth's aging minivan. It was the last week of August, but a front had moved in from the northwest, and thin waves of snow buffeted the van and shoved it toward the shoulder of the two-lane highway.

"Oh my *God*, is that *snow*?" sixteen-year-old foster daughter April said with contemptuous incredulity in a speech pattern she'd mastered that emphasized every third or fourth word. "It can't *snow* in friggin' *August*!" April was slight but tough, and she had a hard edge to her look and style that seemed provocative even when it likely wasn't intended to be. As she matured, she looked frighteningly like her mother Jeannie, who had never made it to forty. Same light blonde hair. Same accusing narrow eyes.

Joe and Marybeth exchanged glances. They'd had a discussion with no conclusion about whether *frigging* was an acceptable word in their family.

April said, "When I go to *college*, I want someplace *warm*. Someplace *way* far away from *here*."

"What makes you think you'll go to college?" Lucy, their fourteen-year-old said just soft enough that perhaps her parents in the front seat wouldn't hear. Joe thought Lucy's mutter had been below the belt, even if possibly true. Lucy was usually more diplomatic and nonconfrontational, so when she did unleash a zinger, it hit twice as hard as if one of the other girls had said it. Lucy was small herself, but not angular like April. Lucy was rounded in perfect proportion, and had blonde hair and striking features and the grace of a cat. Strangers were beginning to stare, Joe had noticed. He didn't like that.

Marybeth heard everything going on in the backseat, and turned to try to head off what could come next. Joe checked his rearview mirror for April's reaction and saw she was coiled and close to violence. Her face was drawn and red, her nostrils flared, and she was focused completely on Lucy sitting next to her.

"Girls, please," Marybeth said.

"Did you *hear* what she friggin' *said*?" April hissed.

"Yes, and it was inappropriate," Marybeth said. "Wasn't it, Lucy?"

A beat, then Lucy said, "Yes."

"So apologize already," April said. "I always have to friggin' *apologize* when I say something *stupid*."

"Sorry," Lucy whispered.

"This is an emotional day," Marybeth said, turning back around in her seat.

Joe shifted his gaze in the mirror and caught Lucy silently mouthing, *"But it's true."*

And April leaned into Lucy and ran a finger across her throat as if it were a knife. Lucy shrugged it away, but Joe felt a chill go up his back from the gesture.

"I hope we can get through this day without fireworks," Marybeth said, missing what was going on in the backseat. "Waterworks is another thing."

Her phone rang in her purse, and she retrieved it and looked at the display and put it back. “My mother,” she said. “She has a knack for calling me at just the wrong time.”

“We need to get some gas,” Joe said. “We’re running on empty.”

A gas station, announced by a green sign that read:

ROCK RIVER
POPULATION 235
ELEVATION 6892

. . . was just ahead.

Sheridan, their nineteen-year-old daughter, was going to college. The University of Wyoming in Laramie was forty-five minutes to the south on the hump of the high plains. She followed them on the exit ramp in their newly acquired fifteen-year-old Ford Ranger pickup with the bed filled with cardboard boxes of everything she owned. Joe had lashed a tarp over the load before they left Saddlestring four hours before, but the wind had ripped long rents into it. Luckily, the rope held the shards down. He’d spent most of the trip worrying about it.

Marybeth either didn’t notice the ruined tarp or more likely didn’t think about it while staring out the window and dabbing her eyes with dozens of tissues that were now crumpled near her shoes on the floorboards like a bird’s nest.

Joe wished he’d brought his winter coat against the wind and cold. This was a place where the wind always blew. The trees, as sparse as they were on top, were gnarled and twisted like high country gargoyles. Both sides of the highway were bordered with a long ten-foot-high snow fence. It howled from the north, rocking both the van and Sheridan’s pickup as he filled the tanks with gasoline.

He tightened the ropes across the bed of her pickup and checked to make sure none of her boxes had opened. Joe imagined her clothes blowing out and rocketing across the terrain until they snagged on bits of sagebrush.

Joe Pickett was in his mid-forties, slim, of medium height and build, with brown eyes and a perpetual squint, as if he was always assessing even the simplest things. He wore old Cinch jeans, worn Ariat cowboy boots, a long-sleeved yoked collar shirt with snap buttons, and a tooled belt that read JOE. Under the seat of the van were his holstered .40 Glock 23 semi-automatic service weapon, bear spray, cuffs, and a citation book. There had been a time when mixing his family and his weapons had struck him as discordant. But over the years, he'd made some enemies and he'd come to accept, if not embrace, his innate ability to so often find himself in the wrong place at the wrong time. He'd learned to accept suspicion and not feel guilty about checking over his shoulder. Even on freshman move-in day at the University of Wyoming in Laramie.

Sheridan watched him fill her tank and secure the load and gave him a little wave of thanks from inside the cab. He tried to grin back. Sheridan had blonde hair and green eyes like Marybeth and Lucy. She was mature beyond her years, but to Joe she looked vulnerable and frail, like a little girl. She wore a gray SADDLESTRING LADY WRANGLERS hoodie and had her hair tied back. When he looked at her behind the steering wheel, he saw her at seven years old, trying again and again with skinned knees and epic determination to ride her bike more than ten feet down the road without crashing. Until that moment, that very moment when they exchanged glances, it hadn't hit him she was leaving them.

Sheridan, after all, was his buddy. Apprentice falconer, struggling athlete, first child, big sister. She was the one who would come out into the garage and hand him tools while he tried to repair his pickup or snow machine. She was the one who really wanted to ride along with him on patrol, and she made valiant, if vain, attempts to try to get him interested in new music and social media. She wouldn't go far away, he hoped. She'd be back for summer and the holidays.

Joe swung into the van and struggled to close the door against the wind. When it latched, there was a charged silence inside. Marybeth took him in and said, "Are you all right?"

He wiped his eyes dry with his sleeve. "The wind," he said.

Four hours later, having gotten Sheridan settled in at her dorm room in Laramie, met her roommate, had a final meal together at Washakie Center, shed more tears, and dodged two more phone calls from Marybeth's mother, they were on their way back to Saddlestring. No words were spoken in the van. Everyone was consumed with his or her own thoughts, and the situation reminded Joe of the ride home from a memorial service. Well, maybe not that bad . . .

Marybeth's phone burred again in her purse, and she grabbed it. Joe could tell from her expression she was both hopeful and fearful that it would be Sheridan calling.

Marybeth sighed deeply. "Mom again," she sighed. "Maybe I ought to take it."

After a moment, Marybeth said, "What do you mean, he's gone?"

Marybeth's mother, Missy, was back on the ranch near Saddlestring she shared with her new husband, the multi-millionaire developer and media mogul Earl Alden. He was known as The Earl of Lexington, because that's where he'd originally come from when he was a mere millionaire. Between them, Marybeth's mother—*Missy Vankueren Longbrake Alden*—and The Earl were the largest landholders in northern Wyoming now that they'd married and combined ranches. Missy had acquired her spread by divorcing a third-generation landowner named Bud Longbrake, who'd discovered during the divorce proceedings what the pre-nup she had him sign actually said.

The Earl was Missy's fifth husband. She'd traded up with each one after her first (and Marybeth's realtor father) died young in a car wreck. After a five-month mourning period, Missy married a doctor the day his divorce papers were finalized, then an Arizona developer and U.S. Congressman who was later convicted of fraud, then rancher Bud Longbrake. The Earl was her greatest triumph. Joe couldn't imagine a sixth wedding. Missy was in her mid-sixties. Although she was still a stunner—given the right light and enough time to prepare—she'd met The Earl as her string was running out. Luckily for Missy, she took—and made—her last desperate shot just as her biological buzzer went off. Joe and Missy had a complicated relationship, as she put it. Joe couldn't stand her, and she still wondered out loud why her favorite daughter—the one with pluck and promise—had stuck with that game warden all these years.

Marybeth said to her mother, "I'll ask Joe what he thinks and call you back, okay?" Then, after a pause, she said irritably, "Well, *I* care. Good-bye."

Joe snorted, but kept his eyes on the road.

"Mom says Earl went out riding this morning and hasn't come back. He was supposed to be home for lunch. She's worried something happened to him—an accident or something."

He glanced at his wristwatch. "So he's three hours late."

"Yes."

"Has she done anything about it besides call you over and over?"

Marybeth sighed. "She asked José Maria to take a truck out and look for him."

Joe nodded.

"She says Earl isn't a very good rider, even though he thinks he is. She's worried the horse took off on him or bucked him off somewhere."

"As you know, that can happen with horses," Joe said.

"She's getting really worked up. He's supposed to have his phone with him, but he hasn't called, and when she tries him, he doesn't pick up. I can tell from her voice she's starting to panic."

Joe said, "Maybe he got clear of her and just kept riding to freedom. I could understand that."

"I don't find that very funny."

The small house was on two levels, with three bedrooms and a detached garage and a loafing shed barn in the back. Joe sighed with relief when they pulled up in front of it, but if he thought he was done with drama for the day, he was mistaken. The House of Feelings, as Joe called it, had been percolating at a rolling boil ever since. First, April moved into Sheridan's old bedroom—she'd been sharing a room with Lucy the same way rival armies "shared" a battlefield. Lucy, giddy with pent-up gratitude, helped move April out, and Marybeth showed up just in time to spot the corner of a bag of marijuana in April's near-empty dresser drawer. Marybeth was stunned and angry at the revelation, April was defensive and even more angry she'd been found out, and Lucy managed to slip away and vanish somewhere in the small house to avoid the fight.

Joe was disappointed by the discovery, but not surprised. April's return from the dead two years before had rocked them all, and the situation since then had been far from storybook. For the years she'd been away, April had bounced from foster family to foster family, and she'd had seen and done things that were just now dribbling out in her two-times-a-week therapy sessions. April had been damaged by both neglect and untoward attention, depending on the family she was with, but neither Joe nor Marybeth was convinced she was beyond repair. Marybeth had made it a life goal to save the girl. But April's moods and rages made it tough on Sheridan and Lucy, who had expected a smoother—and more grateful—reconciliation.

After the discovery of the marijuana, there was yelling, crying, and recriminations late into the night. Whether April would be grounded for two months or three was a major point of contention. They settled on two and a half months. Joe did his best to support Marybeth, but as always he felt out of his depth.

Then, at two-thirty in the morning, shortly after Marybeth and April retired to their separate bedrooms, the telephone rang.

Joe immediately thought: *Sheridan.* She wants to come home.

But it was Missy again, and she was beside herself, and asked Marybeth to implore Joe to put out an all-points alert for her husband. She wanted him to contact the governor's people immediately—apparently Governor Spencer Rulon had taken his phone off the hook after three calls from Missy, and her insistence that he call out the National Guard to look for The Earl.

Joe was slightly impressed Missy seemed to finally grasp what he did for a living. He took the phone long enough to confirm that she'd already reported her husband's absence to County Sheriff Kyle McLanahan, the police chief in Saddlestring, and had left messages with the FBI office in Cheyenne and Wyoming's two U.S. senators and lone congresswoman. She had all her ranch hands out searching for him, despite the hour.

Joe assured her he would follow up in the morning, all the time thinking The Earl had probably tied his horse to a fence at the airport and escaped to one of his other homes in Lexington, Aspen, New York, or Chamonix.

3

Now it was Monday, and it felt good to be heading out. The front had passed through, and the morning was warm and sultry, which brought out the sweet smell of sage as Joe rolled down the gravel of Bighorn Road. He sipped his coffee and was grateful he was going to work. Bighorn Road was the primary access into the mountains, and it passed by the front of his house. The Bighorns loomed like slump-shouldered giants, dominating the skyline. The view from his front porch and picture window was of a vast angled landscape that dipped into a willow-choked draw where the Twelve Sleep River formed from six different creek fingers and gained strength and volume before its muscular rush through and past the Town of Saddlestring eight miles away. Beyond the nascent river to the south, the terrain rose sharply into several saddle slopes that bowed around a precipitous mountain known as Wolf Mountain. He had never tired of seeing the colors of the sun at dawn and at dusk on the naked granite face of the mountain, and doubted he ever would. But it was too early for sun.

It had been a tough and eventful summer, and it was continuing into the fall.

Marybeth's small business consulting firm, MBP, had all but dissolved. A larger firm had been in the long process of purchasing the assets when the recession finally came to Wyoming and three of four of MBP's largest clients ceased operations. Within months, MBP's assets were nothing like what they'd been when negotiations began, and both parties agreed to call off the sale. While Marybeth still worked for several small local firms on her own, the protracted deal had taken the steam out of her. She'd recently resumed her part-time job in the Twelve Sleep County Library while she looked for new business opportunities. It had been an unexpected and unusual defeat because Marybeth was the toughest and most pragmatic woman Joe'd ever met. Joe had no doubt she—and they—would be back.

The lack of MBP income had caused them to cancel their plans to purchase a new home outside of town. The development was disappointing to Joe, who desperately wanted to live without neighbors several feet away—especially his next-door neighbor, lawn and maintenance nemesis Ed Nedny.

In July, however, the other game warden in the district, Phil Kiner, had retired unexpectedly due to poor health, and the department in Cheyenne had given Joe the opportunity to move his family back to the state-owned house they'd once occupied on Bighorn Road, eight miles outside of Saddlestring. Kiner's departure meant Joe's numerical designation climbed a notch from 54 to 53. At one time, before he'd been fired, he'd reached 24, and he wondered if he'd ever get back there. Their former house in town was on the market, and until it sold, things would continue to be tight. Joe reveled in being back in the shadow of Wolf Mountain where his children had grown up. But there was no denying the fact that after all they'd been through, they were essentially back where they'd started ten years before: in the original House of Feelings. Without Sheridan.

"Don't fret," Marybeth had said, "backwards is the new normal."

He passed through the town of Saddlestring as it woke up and the single traffic light switched over from flashing amber, and he drove five miles to the interstate highway. As he merged onto the westbound two-lane, he paused for a convoy of tractor-trailers laden with the long, sleek, twenty-one-and-a-half-meter white blades for wind turbines. They came from manufacturing facilities to the south and east, and were no longer a curiosity on the highway. Massive parts for turbines and wind farms coursed down the highway bound for construction sites throughout Wyoming and the mountain west. Joe remembered seeing the first ones two years before, and he'd been intrigued and followed the convoy for a while to behold the sheer size and grace of the equipment, which reminded him of buffoonishly large parts for a massive toy. But now the frequency of the convoys was routine, as turbines sprouted in perfect white rows throughout the state and the region.

The sudden emergence of wind farms had added another dimension to his day-to-day responsibilities as well. He sighed and eased out onto the highway for areas twenty-one and twenty-two.

He turned from the highway onto the ranch owned by Bob and Dode Lee, a checkerboard of public and private land that contained a vast herd of pronghorn antelope.

He ground his truck up the side of a flat-topped bench that overlooked the vast sagebrush flats of the Lee Ranch. The top sliver of sun winked over the eastern horizon as he positioned his pickup on the top so he could look out over dozens of square miles. The sunlight was orange and intense and lit up the side of the bench, and it was at the perfect angle and intensity to reveal hundreds of tiny American Indian arrowhead and tool chips that still clung to the surface of the rise. Like so many off-road locations he'd found over the years, Joe was struck by the fact that he wasn't the first to use this dramatic geography for the purpose of work. In his mind's eye, he envisioned a small band of Cheyenne or Pawnee on the same bench hundreds of years before, making weapons and tools, looking out at the landscape for friends and enemies.

But as the sun rose, it also lit up row after row of wind turbines to the south. They looked like spindly white toothpicks. Shafts of sunlight bounced and sparked on the slowly turning blades. He knew they signified the border of the Lee Ranch where it butted up against the massive holdings of The Earl and, of course, Missy.

Joe slid down the driver's-side window and fitted his Redfield spotting scope to the frame of the door. As the dawn melded into morning, the vista below him came into view. Hundreds of brown-and-white pronghorn antelope grazed amidst knee-high sagebrush. Mule deer descended from windswept grassy flats back into shadowed draws. Eagles and hawks soared above it all in morning thermals, making long-distance loops at his eye level.

He focused on a single blue pickup that was crawling along a two-track, a thin plume of dust giving chase. There was a flash of orange through the windows of the vehicle, as he identified the occupants—a driver and passenger—as hunters. As far as he could tell, they didn't know he was up on the bench watching them.

The blue pickup was too far away to hear, but he slowly swiveled his spotting scope as it passed beneath him traveling left to right. They were headed south, and because of the contours of the land, they had no idea that the huge herd was to their east on the other side of a ridge. Joe wondered if they'd catch a glimpse of the antelope as they drove along, but the vehicle continued on slowly, apparently looking for all the game out their front windshield.

"Road hunters," Joe whispered to himself. If the hunters fired at game from the vehicle, they'd be in violation and Joe would cite them. He hoped they were ethical and law-abiding, and would leave the truck on foot to stalk the antelope—if they even saw them.

He followed the progress of the pickup. He caught a glimpse of a license plate—Wyoming—but was too far away to read the numbers, so he focused in and narrowed his field of vision until the vehicle filled his scope. It was a shaky view at that distance, but he could see the passenger lower his window and extend his arm out of it, pointing toward something ahead of them.

Joe leaned back from the scope and surveyed the basin with his naked eye. He followed the road the hunters were on until it became a thin tan thread in the distance. And where the two-track crested a hill and vanished, he saw the dark form of a big animal. It was too large to be an antelope, and too dark to be a deer. Puzzled, he swung the spotting scope far to the right.

It was a riderless horse. The animal was big and sleek, well groomed, with a saddle hanging upside down under its belly. Joe knew from experience that when the saddle was inverted, it meant the horse had run hard and usually at great distance. The exertion loosened the cinch and the top-heavy configuration of the saddle caused it to slide. The horse was grazing on a strip of grass between the tracks of the road, but it had obviously noted the oncoming pickup by the way it periodically raised its head and noted the approach.

Joe looked back at the truck, expecting it to be closer to the horse by now. But the pickup had stopped in the road, and the occupants—two older men bundled in Carhartt jackets and fluorescent orange headgear—were out of their vehicle and gesturing to each other. The passenger was again pointing ahead, but it wasn't at the horse, but higher. Much higher.

"What?" Joe asked, as he opened up the field of vision on his spotting scope and swung it back to the right.

He scoped the horizon behind the horse and saw nothing worth noting, nothing unusual enough to prompt two lazy road hunters to jump from their vehicle. Then he looked beyond the crest at the long straight line of wind turbines in the distance. They were now bathed in full morning light and framed against the deep clear blue of the cloudless sky.

The blades all spun in the lazy rotation that Joe had come to learn in reality wasn't lazy at all at the blade-tip. At least nine of the ten were spinning swiftly. He concentrated on the one that wasn't. He'd observed enough wind turbines before to know there could sometimes be a marked disparity of wind speed from unit to unit. And he knew that sometimes turbines were damaged or disabled and the blades turned roughly in comparison with the other machines. But there was no doubt there was something strange about this one, because it turned at less than half the speed of the others in the row.

Joe climbed the tower with his scope until he could see the nacelle, a structure on top where the hub held the turning blades. And he could see what was wrong and he whispered, "Jesus."

A form was suspended from a chain or cable that was looped around the shaft of one of the three spinning blades. The form was close to the hub. It hadn't slid down the length of the blade because the tether held fast where the blade widened. Even with the weight, the rotor turned fast enough that the object flew through the air between the blades, circling up and around the hub like a spider held by a web on a rotating fan.

Although the distance was great and Joe's trembling fingers shook the view within the scope as he adjusted it, he caught glimpses of the form as it flashed through his field of vision. Portly, solid, arms cocked out to both sides, legs spread in a V—it certainly *looked* like a body.

Was it a real body? Joe could imagine workers hanging a dummy or mannequin in some kind of prank. How was it possible for someone even to get up there, much less get caught up in a chain attached to the shaft of a blade? How long had it been up there?

Then he linked the area, the horse without a rider, the location of the wind turbines, and Missy's frantic phone calls the day and night before.

"Oh, no," he said aloud, while he plucked the mike from his dashboard and called dispatch in Cheyenne. He'd hold off calling Marybeth, he decided, until he could confirm the flying body belonged to the former Earl of Lexington.

4

En route to the wind turbine with the form spinning on the blade, Joe passed the antelope hunters and exchanged waves with them—they were locals he recognized from town, and ethical hunters who took good care of their game meat—and he bounced along past them on the two-track to the Lee Ranch fence line. As he drove, the towers rose above him into the sky. Tube awoke and strained forward in the cab and peered out the front windshield as well, determining the direction of Joe's interest if not the object of it, and scanned the sky for birds. That was the Lab in him. So was the penchant for sudden salivation, which strung from his tongue and pooled around the air vents on top of the dashboard.

Joe had called in the situation to Cheyenne dispatch, and they'd relayed the message via SALECS (State Assisted Law Enforcement Communication System) to the Twelve Sleep County Sheriff's Department and all relevant law enforcement agencies. As he drove, he heard the exchanges, and he could only imagine what Sheriff Kyle McLanahan was thinking. And he wondered how quickly and how far the word would spread beyond the local law network. Plenty of citizens in Saddlestring monitored the police band, and rumors shot through Twelve Sleep County like rockets. He hoped Marybeth—or Missy, for that matter—wouldn't get hit with speculative phone calls until he knew for sure what the situation was.

He braked at the gate between the Lee and Alden ranches, perplexed at what he found. The Earl had replaced the old chain and lock system with a ten-foot electronic gate. This was one of the issues locals had raised over the last few years, how The Earl had shut off access to and across his holdings to people who had used the roads for generations. Joe knew Alden had every right to secure his property, but questioned the need to do so. It was like rubbing his wealth and power in the nose of those who had short supplies of both. And the gate in front of Joe was a monument to the controversy.

Instead of calling Alden Ranch headquarters for the keypad sequence, since that would alert Missy, Joe simply parked his pickup to the right of the gate where it joined with the four-string barbed wire fence and got out, leaving the motor idling. He climbed into the bed of his pickup and rooted through his metal gearbox until he found his bolt cutters. As he walked toward the fence, he could hear a cacophony of voices from the radio. Dispatchers talked to dispatchers, and sheriff's department deputies, highway patrolmen, and local police officers all weighed in. He ignored them as he clipped through each strand of barbed wire on the fence top to bottom. He wanted to be the first to the scene.

Like the gate itself, the fence was perfect and new, stretched tight. His bolt cutters bit cleanly through the shiny metal wire. Each strand snapped back into a curl until he had clearance for his vehicle. He was surprised what pleasure it gave him to break through the fence.

Joe was familiar with the layout of the wind farm, although he had never approached it from this direction. The rough two-track gave way to a smooth, graded, and banked gravel road that was part of the development, and he was able to switch from four-wheel drive to two and increase his speed. He roared toward the slowest turbine.

The rapid development of the installations across Wyoming and the West had created new wildlife and environmental concerns. Wind turbines required a significant footprint on the land, at least fifty acres per structure, or three rotor distances apart from one to the other. Alden's huge project of one hundred units stretched across five thousand acres of his land, not counting the well-engineered roads connecting them all. As yet, no transmission lines coursed over the horizon to export the electricity to downstream substation transformers.

Because wind companies obviously chose open areas with plenty of wind, they were often located in untrammeled terrain where there had been no previous impact and no person in his or her right mind would want to build a home. Unfortunately for the wind developers, many of these locations brought out concerns regarding impacts on the winter range of big game animals and their migration routes. The impact on the sage grouse population—strutting, flinty native game birds about the size of chickens—was of immediate concern. Since half of all the sage grouse in existence in North America were located in Wyoming and the population of the game birds had been declining for years, the introduction of wind turbines on their habitat was an issue with environmentalists, hunters, and the Game and Fish Department, as well as the U.S. Fish and Wildlife Service.

One of Joe's new directives was to assist in monitoring the sage grouse activity in areas where wind development was occurring and send memos of his findings to Cheyenne. Although he couldn't honestly link one to the other on his forays into the wind farms, he had noted a number of dead birds (not sage grouse) and even more bats crumpled up dead at the base of the towers. Bats, apparently, had their natural radar fouled by the air pressure of the spinning blades and they'd become disoriented (so the theory went) and fly headlong to their death into the steel of the towers.

As he approached the first row of turbines, Joe noted another vehicle coming fast in his direction. He thought it might be the first of the sheriff's deputies to the scene until it got closer and he recognized it as one of several of The Earl's company pickups by the Rope the Wind logo on the door. Rope the Wind was Alden's newest enterprise. He'd shown Joe and Marybeth a mock-up of the logo, expecting their enthusiastic approval at a dinner they'd attended with their girls at the ranch. He said he'd bought the company and the name recently, anticipating the wind energy boom. The logo was a drawing of a large cowboy straddling the nacelle of a three-megawatt turbine. The cowboy's hat was bent back by the oncoming wind, and he was tossing a lariat into it.

"It combines the historical figure of the frontier cowboy with the new frontier of renewable energy in the twenty-first century," The Earl had said with typical bombast. *"I love the hell out of it and it cost me big money to some of the hippest graphic designers in Portland. It's perfect. So, what do you think?"*

Joe had said he liked it just fine, but apparently not with enough enthusiasm. The Earl had huffed and rolled up the design and stomped away. He was a man who valued those who agreed wholeheartedly with him, and discounted those who didn't. Joe had been discounted.

The company pickup arrived at the base of the tower at the same time Joe did. The driver swung out and faced Joe with his hands on his hips. He was in his mid-twenties and beefy, with a full red beard and a crisp new jacket with the Rope the Wind logo on his breast. "You seeing what I'm seeing?" he asked Joe.

"Tell me it's a joke," Joe said, shutting his door gently on slobbering Tube.

"I wish to hell it was," the worker said, leaning back and craning his neck up. "I can't figure what the hell it is or how it got up there."

"It looks like a body."

"Yeah," the worker said, rattling the door latch on the tower to confirm it was locked. "But that's just crazy. You need a key to get inside one of these to access the ladder. There's no way to go up the outside and the only other explanation is it flew through the air and landed on the blade. That ain't likely."

"Nope."

"Well," the worker said, digging into his jacket for his keys. "Let's go see."

While the worker unloaded hard hats and other equipment from his vehicle, Joe grabbed the handheld radio from the cab of his truck. He turned it on and it was instantly alive with voices, and one of them was addressing him directly.

"Joe Pickett, this is Sheriff McLanahan. Do you read me?"

Joe considered ignoring him, but thought better of it. Although the two had clashed repeatedly over the years, it *was* the sheriff's jurisdiction.

"I read you," Joe said.

"Are you on the scene?"

"Affirmative. I called it in."

"Okay, well, hold tight. We're on the way. Under no circumstances are you to climb that tower and compromise the crime scene."

Joe bristled at the command. "How do you know it's a crime scene?"

Silence. Then, from miles away, someone—probably a highway trooper monitoring the exchange—said, "Good point."

"Did you hear my initial command?" McLanahan asked, with the put-on Western drawl he'd adopted since moving west from Virginia ten years before. "Under no circumstances . . ."

Joe clicked the radio off and slipped it into the holder on his belt. McLanahan seemed to know something Joe didn't, and he didn't want to share what it was, which was typical of the sheriff. Joe looked up and said to the worker, "I'm ready if you are."

"Then let's go. Here, let me show you how this works."

"Have you done this a lot?" Joe asked, gesturing toward the tower.

"I've been a turbine monkey half my adult life," the man said.

The worker handed Joe a nylon harness. Joe fed his arms through it and pulled twin buckles up from between his legs and snapped them tight to receivers secured on his chest. The worker clipped a carabiner through a metal loop on Joe's harness that supported a metal fall-arrest mechanism that hung by a steel cable. The man showed Joe how to fit the mechanism around the taut cable inside the tower that ran parallel to the ladder from the top of the tower all the way to the floor. The mechanism was supposed to seize tight and prevent him from falling if he lost his balance or slipped off the rungs.

"It's two hundred fifty feet to the top," the man said. "That's a lot of climbing. Plus, the handholds are kind of slippery in there. You'll see."

Joe nodded and followed the worker through the open hatch door at the base of the tower. It was instantly dark inside except for a bank of glowing green and amber lights from a control panel mounted on the wall. It took a few moments for his eyes to adjust. He looked up and could see the narrow ladder and safety cable disappear up into the darkness.

"I'm guessing you have an idea what we're gonna find up there," the man said. He'd softened his voice because the sound carried with resonance inside.

"I have a theory," Joe said. "But I'm hoping I'm wrong."

"I didn't see any parked trucks out there anywhere besides ours," the man said. "I don't know how this joker even got through the gates. When I checked in this morning, all our guys were accounted for, so it isn't one of us."

"I saw a horse a while back," Joe said.

Even in the dark, Joe could tell the man was staring. "A *horse*?"

"Yup."

"I'm Bob Newman," the worker said.

"Joe Pickett."

"I've heard of you," Newman said, and left it at that. "I didn't ask—are you okay with heights?"

Joe said, "Kind of." Since he'd stepped inside the tower, he could feel basic terror rise inside him, because he *wasn't okay with heights at all.* Some of the worst moments of his life had taken place as he clenched his eyes shut and gripped the hand rests of his seat in a small plane.

"Don't look down and don't look up," Newman said. "Keep staring straight ahead and climb one rung at a time. Even if you aren't scared of heights, you won't like what you see if you look down, believe me."

Joe nodded.

"If you clutch up and freeze halfway up, well, there isn't any pretty way to get you down."

"Right."

"I wonder how it got up there," Newman mumbled as he snapped his fall-arrest mechanism to the safety cable, locked it around the cable, mounted the ladder, and started climbing.

"Give me a few minutes and some distance before you follow," he said over his shoulder. "The ladder vibrates worse if two men are close together on it." He called down further instructions as he rose, telling Joe how to slide the mechanism up the cable, pointing out the metal grate step-outs every fifty feet up the ladder if he needed to catch his breath. Newman's voice receded as he climbed until Joe could barely hear him. Joe had his hand around the first rung, and he could feel Newman's progress due to the vibration. Joe took a deep breath and clipped onto the cable and stepped up on the first rung. Then another. The fall arrest mechanism squeaked as it was pulled up the lifeline. Joe reached out and gave it a rough yank to make sure it would hold tight if he slipped. It worked. He considered keeping his eyes shut as he climbed, wondering if that would help. It didn't.

He got warmer the higher he climbed. He wasn't sure if the temperature inside actually increased or it was from the exertion of the climb itself. His forearms ached from pulling himself up rung by rung and he tried to control the quivering in his thighs that he attributed to a combination of fatigue and terror. There was a thin film of grease on every surface from the working machinery far above and it made the rungs slippery. The sharp odor of machine oil hung in the tower. He tried to think of other subjects to take his mind off falling and how far he had climbed from solid ground.

He was puzzled by McLanahan's reference to the "crime scene," as well as the sheriff's admonishment not to investigate. Since there had been no chatter over the radio about the situation prior to him calling it in, Joe wondered if McLanahan had inside knowledge—or a tip—of what was going on. Or was what Joe had found linked to an ongoing sheriff's department case?

Halfway up, he stole a look down between his knees and the sensation of seeing the very distant sunlight from the open portal on the tower floor—it looked like a pinprick—made him swoon. He gripped the ladder hard and hugged it. His boot soles rattled on the rungs and he breathed hard, in and out, in and out, until his fear eased. There was a step-out within sight, and he climbed the next three feet to get to it, which was the hardest thing he'd done yet. For a moment he couldn't feel his legs, as he swung them one after the other to the grated metal plate. When he was assured the grate was solid and he could stand on it and lean against the inside tower wall for a few moments, he exhaled and tried to calm himself.

"You okay?" Newman called down. He was a long way up.

"Fine."

"Good. I'm almost to the nacelle. Just remember, when you get up here it's all about safety first. The winds up there could blow you right off the top. So make sure you clip your harness hook to one of the eyebolts. Don't even take a step without making sure you're secured, okay?"

"Okay." Then: "Bob?"

"Yeah?"

"Don't touch anything up there. Wait until I'm with you. It's likely going to be a crime scene."

Newman laughed harshly. "Yeah," he said. "I know the drill. I watch them shows."

When Joe's muscles stopped quivering and his breath returned to normal, he stepped back on the ladder and resumed climbing. Fifty feet higher, Joe noticed a round two-inch hole punched through the steel wall of the tower. A shaft of light lit up a larger orb on the opposite wall. When he reached it, he paused. In a strange optical trick, the hole projected a sharp view of the landscape outside on the opposite shaft wall, as if it were a movie lens. He could see the long row of turbines, the roads that connected them, a bird flying by. Joe didn't know enough about physics to explain the phenomenon, but he found it fascinating and bizarre. He could even clearly see a small four-vehicle convoy in the distance bearing down on the wind farm. Three of the units were sheriff's department SUVs and the fourth a white company pickup that could be a twin of Newman's. Although he'd kept his hand-held turned off, he could imagine a red-faced McLanahan hollering into this microphone, trying to raise him. As Joe climbed through the projected scene, he could see sharp images of the convoy slide down his red and now greasy uniform shirt.

He could hear a steel plate hatch being thrown open far above him and the sound echoed down the length of the tower. He glanced up and saw a distant blue square—the sky—that was then filled by Newman as he scrambled from the ladder to the floor of nacelle itself.

Twenty seconds later, Newman called down. His voice was tight. "It's worse than I thought," he called down, words bouncing back and forth down the tube. "I'm not feeling so good all of a sudden. I hope it's been a while since you ate."

5

Joe was breathing hard when he reached the open hatch. The wind was ferocious. Despite it, he could hear the epic slicing of the blades turning and feel the vibration of the turbine motor through the metal of the ladder. Joe looked up as Newman's helmeted head filled the open square.

"You are *not* going to believe this," he shouted. "And don't worry. I haven't touched anything I didn't have to. Besides, I'm wearing gloves."

Joe cleared the hatch and stood shakily on the corrugated metal floor of the nacelle. Newman had unbolted the cover wings and pushed them open to expose the nacelle to the sun and wind. The nacelle itself was deep and long, shaped like a coffin, and filled with the long prone steel body of the turbine. The lines on the outside were clean and purposeful, and inside it was like straddling an engine that was all business. The ledge between the turbine and the inside wall was barely enough for them both to stand shoulder-to-shoulder. Newman gestured to an eyebolt mounted in the side of the nacelle, and Joe unclipped the fall-arrest mechanism and was keenly aware of the few completely untethered seconds it took him to turn and clip the harness hook to the eyebolt so he wouldn't blow away.

When he looked up again, he followed Newman's outstretched arm. Cold wind pummeled his bare face.

The speed of the blades was remarkable up close, almost a blur. But like frames of film being fed through a movie projector, the image appeared in an eerie stop-motion effect. It was a body, all right. One end of a chain had been looped under the arms in a double wrap and around the shaft of the blade on the other. There was about four feet of chain between the blade and the body. The victim flew through the air. It was a man. Joe could make out the face, although there was something off about it. But no doubt it was The Earl.

Earl Alden's eyes were closed and his face looked strangely thin, gaunt, and jowly, as if he'd lost a lot of weight since Joe had seen him last. But as he spun, Joe realized why. The Earl's legs looked huge and fat, like sausage stuffed into the casing of his jeans, which were splitting over the tall black shafts of his cowboy boots. His boots, too, seemed several sizes too large and were misshapen into squared-off blocks. At first glance, Joe thought The Earl was wearing heavy dark gloves until he realized with horror that the swelled blue-black objects protruding from his cuffs were Alden's grossly misshapen hands. The Earl's shirt and jacket were in tatters but hadn't yet been completely removed by the force of the wind. The cloth was soaked with dark blood and lighter-colored liquids. Joe thought he could catch a glimpse of the bruised hole of a gunshot on Alden's left breast.

"Oh, man," Joe moaned.

"Look what the centrifugal force is doing to him," Newman said, and Joe could hear the amazement in his voice. "It's squeezing all his fluids out toward the bottom. Like if you hung a toothpaste tube on a spinning propeller or something. I've never seen anything like it."

"Me, neither," Joe said, feeling his stomach churn. He turned away and covered his mouth. A spout of acid burned in his throat and chest.

"Is it who I think it is?" Newman asked.

"Yup," Joe said, fighting nausea.

Newman said, "I met him a couple times. At the Christmas party and such. He seemed all right to me. I've heard the stories, but he treated me and the guys all right. I guess we know how he had a key to the hatch down there." He paused.

"He's no spring chicken," Newman said. "Why in the hell did he climb up here?"

Joe shook his head. He didn't think The Earl had done any climbing, but he wasn't ready to say.

"He must have come up here for some reason," Newman speculated. "Maybe he brought that chain with him. Maybe he was going to try to loop it around the blade and stop it from spinning or something, and it took off on him and pulled him over the side. Man, what a way to go. What a horrible fucking way to go."

Joe looked around on the nacelle. On the inside of the structure near the front he could see a brown smear on the wall. He tapped Newman's shoulder and pointed at it.

"What's that?" Joe asked.

Newman shrugged. Then a look of recognition passed over his face. "Looks like blood," he said.

Joe said, "Is there any way to get a body up here if he can't climb the ladder on his own?"

Newman nodded. "There's a hoist over there. We use it to bring up tools and parts when we need to work on the turbine. I heard of a guy down in Texas having a heart attack up top and they had to lower him down by the hoist. So I guess you could winch somebody up here. It'll hold two hundred fifty pounds of equipment."

Joe guessed The Earl was about that.

"Who in the hell would do this?" Newman asked. "It's a lot of damned trouble to bring a body up here."

"Unless somebody was making a statement," Joe said. He looked back over his shoulder at The Earl spinning by. He thought, *No one deserves a comical death.* He had once been on a case where two humans had been blown up by a cow. It had been tragic, and horrendous. And people still laughed about it.

Newman whapped the side of his hard hat with the heel of his hand. "Oh, now I get it. Why they didn't want you coming up here. He's your father-in-law. Man, oh man."

Joe thought, *Too bad it wasn't his wife.* He said nothing, but checked to make sure his harness hook hadn't somehow magically come undone before grasping the sidewall of the nacelle. He leaned over and looked down. The convoy surrounded the tower. The vehicles were tiny from his vantage point, and the sheriff and his deputies were scurrying around like ticks. He could see one of the deputies pulling on a climbing harness with help from the Rope the Wind employee who had accompanied them out.

"The sheriff will be sending someone up now," Joe said to Newman. He patted his uniform for his digital camera. "I want to get some evidence shots of my own before they take over the crime scene."

"Sheriff McLanahan?" Newman said.

"Yes."

Newman shook his head. "He's a tool. I've had a couple run-ins with him. Thinks he's some kind of Old West cowboy lawman, when he's just a goddamned ass-hat." Then he realized what he'd said and who'd heard it and quickly added, "I'm sorry. He might be a friend of yours."

"He's no friend," Joe said.

Taylor was visibly relieved. "I see his reelection signs all over the damn county. I hope he loses."

Joe nodded. He didn't want to agree in public. McLanahan had spies everywhere, and he kept a meticulous count of who was with him and who wasn't. The sheriff made it a point to make life hard for those opposed to him, and had turned it into a career when it came to Joe Pickett.

As they waited for the deputy to scale the tower, Joe withdrew his cell and speed-dialed Marybeth. She should just about be at the library to start work, he thought.

When she picked up, he told her where he was—noting that, whatever his location, it didn't seem to shock her anymore—and said, "Tough news, honey. We found The Earl's body."

"Oh, my God."

"I'll drive out to the ranch to tell your mother," Joe said, already dreading it. "It should probably come from me."

"What happened? Did he get bucked off his horse?"

"Worse," Joe said. "Much worse. My first guess is somebody shot him and then they hung his body from one of his own wind turbines."

"Oh, my God, Joe," she said again. "That's awful."

"It is."

"Uh-oh," she said. "I've got another call coming in." Joe could hear the click. "It's my mother." There was panic in her tone, which was out of character.

"I better take it," she said. "What should I tell her, Joe?"

"Tell her that as soon as I can get down off this tower, I'll be there."

"As if that will hold her off," she said. "You know how she is."

"Do I ever," Joe said.

He'd scarcely closed his phone when it lit up again. Marybeth.

"Joe," she said. She was frantic. "She said someone she trusted at the county building just called her in secret to tell her Sheriff McLanahan is sending someone to the ranch now. Not to break the news, but to *arrest* her! For murder, Joe! They think she had something to do with this."

Joe was grateful he was secured to the nacelle by the cable, because he suddenly felt lighter than air.

"That's kind of crazy," he said, turning away from Newman who was eyeing him closely. He was afraid he might be grinning.

"You don't sound very . . . upset," Marybeth said icily.

"I am," he pleaded. "Really. It's just . . . McLanahan is nuts. There's no way a sixty-year-old woman shot the guy, drove him to the wind farm, climbed a two-hundred-fifty-foot tower, hoisted a body to the top, and tied it to a blade. Of course, if any woman was mean enough do such a thing . . ."

"Joe."

"I'm kidding."

"This is not the time," she said, and he realized she was crying.

"I'm sorry," he said. "I feel horrible. I shouldn't have said that."

"No, you shouldn't have. Joe, despite what she is and what she's done, she's my mother. And she's your daughters' grandmother. Do you want them to think their grandmother is a *murderer*, for God's sake?"

"No."

"I've got to go," she said, and he could imagine her wiping at her tears angrily so no one could see her crying. Open displays of emotion in front of co-workers wasn't her style. "Call me when you know something."

"I will," Joe said, closing the phone.

"Sounds like you stepped in it," Newman said.

Before Joe could respond, Deputy Mike Reed's helmeted head poked through the hatch. He was red-faced and breathing hard. Joe extended his hand and helped Reed up into the nacelle. When Reed could catch his breath, he reached out and put both of his hands on Joe's shoulders, looked into his eyes, and said, "The sheriff wants your hide, Joe."

Joe shrugged. "Won't be the first time."

Joe had known and worked with Deputy Reed for a number of years. He liked him. Reed was low-key and dedicated, and had managed to stay out of McLanahan's web of intrigue and influence. He had surprised practically everyone by filing papers to run against the sheriff in the upcoming election. And McLanahan had surprised everyone by not immediately cutting Reed loose from the department.

"I'm surprised he sent *you*," Joe said.

Reed chuckled. "He didn't want to, but he ran out of guys, and he's too fat anymore to even think about climbing that ladder."

"Where are his homeboys?" Joe asked. McLanahan had recruited three young deputies who spent most of their time in the weight room or appreciating McLanahan's original cowboy poetry recitations. Joe had met most of them and saw they aspired to follow in the sheriff's footsteps, and therefore they were to be treated with caution.

The deputy looked hard at Joe. "I think you know."

Reed's radio crackled to life. Because of the proximity to the trucks below, McLanahan's voice was strong and clear. "Deputy Reed, have you reached the top?"

"Almost, sir," Reed said, and winked at Joe and Newman.

"Get a move on," McLanahan ordered.

Reed took a deep breath.

"I'm surprised you're still around," Joe said. "But I'm glad you are."

"He keeps his friends close and his enemies closer," Reed said. "He wants to be able to keep an eye on me. So," he said, looking over Joe's shoulder at the body spinning by, "it's true then. Earl Alden. This is gonna be a big deal."

Joe nodded. He filled Reed in on what little he knew, from the missing person's report to the riderless horse to the climb up the tower with Newman. He pointed out the hoist and the possible smear of blood. The whole time, Reed simply shook his head in disbelief. Then he called down on his radio and repeated the whole thing to the sheriff.

"We'll need the evidence tech," Reed said. "There might be some traces, and we might have some blood."

McLanahan said, "You want me to send Cindy up there? She weighs what, three hundred? How we going to get her up there?"

"I don't know," Reed said.

"Can't you at least stop that damned windmill from turning?"

Reed looked to Newman, who said, "Yeah. We can disengage the rotor. Joe told me not to touch anything."

"He was right," Reed said, and then nodded toward the radio, "but you heard the man."

"And get that son-of-a-bitch Joe Pickett off there," McLanahan said. "He's got a built-in conflict. We can't have him up there."

"I'll tell him," Reed said.

"You'll *ask* me," Joe shot back.

"Please?"

"Okay," Joe said. "But first you have to tell me why McLanahan sent his deputies out to my mother-in-law's ranch. There's nothing I'd like better than to see her in prison just to give her a scare, but come on. She can't really be your suspect."

Reed shrugged. "From what I understand—and nobody really tells me anything directly—the sheriff has been getting calls for a while about the possibility of this"—he gestured toward The Earl's body as it flew by—"happening. He got another one last night, I guess. He didn't act on it because he couldn't believe it, either. But whoever called—all I know is it was a male—gave us enough detail ahead of the discovery to implicate her. I don't know all the details, Joe. McLanahan didn't share them. Maybe he'll tell *you.*"

Joe snorted.

As he unclipped from the nacelle and reattached the fall-arrest mechanism to the cable to prepare his descent, he heard McLanahan tell Reed they were in the process of locating an industrial crane that would go high enough to unhook the body from the blade. And that he'd already contacted the state DCI (Division of Criminal Investigation) to send their best forensics team north.

"I want this thing puncture-proof," McLanahan told Reed. "No mistakes. No cut corners. Now stay up there and secure the crime scene, Reed. I need one of my guys here when the crane shows up. I'm headed out to the Thunderhead Ranch to oversee the arrest and the search. And don't let anyone else up there unless you clear it with me."

"You want me to *stay* up here?" Reed said, frowning. "It could be the rest of the day. Maybe into the night."

"That's why you get paid the big bucks," the sheriff said. "And why I get paid bigger bucks for making these decisions. We need this to be as clean as our mountain streams and as open as our blue skies."

Reed looked up at Joe, who said, "I can already hear that last quote on the news and in his campaign ads."

Reed shook his head and smiled bitterly. "The sheriff's got this whole thing orchestrated pretty damned neatly. He's on his way to make the arrest and I'm sure it won't be a low-profile affair. I'm stuck up here waiting for evidence and forensics folks to somehow get this body down and find any physical evidence they can. If there are any procedural errors in the evidence chain, guess who is responsible? The guy left in charge of the stupidest crime scene in Wyoming history."

Joe shrugged. "Good luck," he said, straddling the hatch. "I'll be checking back with you on what you find here."

"I may not be able to share everything," Reed said. "I hope you understand that."

It was easier getting down the ladder than it had been going up.

But Joe knew as he approached the ground that his life was about to get real complicated.

6

Although between them The Earl of Lexington and Missy Vankueren Longbrake Alden had accumulated and then consolidated six adjacent ranches—including the Longbrake Ranch, where Missy had once lived—they'd chosen the wooded compound of the Thunderhead Ranch as their headquarters. Joe passed under the massive elk antler arches that marked the entrance—the gates had already been flung open, so he didn't need to stop—and drove through a low-hanging cloud of dust obviously kicked up by a stream of vehicles that had arrived just before him. As he approached the headquarters, he could see the wink of metal and glass of law enforcement units parked haphazardly in the ranch yard.

There had been so much traffic ahead of him that even the ranch dogs, who always raised a fuss and ran out to challenge visitors, simply glanced up, exhausted, from their pool of shade underneath an ancient billowing cottonwood on the side of a horse barn.

Joe pulled in next to an unmarked SUV he recognized by the state plates and antennae on the roof as DCI. He swung out, letting Tube follow him, and strode toward the old Victorian mansion that had once belonged to the Aldens, the original owners of the ranch. The renovated block stone home served as the residence of his mother-in-law and father-in-law until their new place was finished. As he skirted the bumper of a highway patrol car on his way to the house, Joe glanced to the west through an opening in the trees and saw a corner portion of The Earl and Missy's new home. It dominated the high bluff on the other side of the Twelve Sleep River, and was a complex design of gables, windows, sharp angles, and peaks. It was to be 15,000 square feet and the construction of it alone was keeping half the contractors and one of Saddlestring's lumberyards open through the recession. Joe wondered if the contractors had paused for the day when they heard the news, wondering if their jobs were now over and if they'd ever get paid for the work they'd done so far.

Deputy Sollis saw Joe coming and stepped out from the lilac bushes next to the front door of the ranch house. Sollis raised his hand to Joe, palm out, and said, "That'll be far enough."

Joe stopped, looking Sollis over. Sollis was square-shaped and his head was a block mounted on a stump of a neck. He was solid and buff, and his uniform looked a deliberate size too small in order to accentuate his pectorals, biceps, and quads. His eyes were black and small and could be seen like spider holes through the lenses of a pair of black wraparound shades. A fresh crop of acne crawled up his neck from his collar, and Joe thought, *Steroids.*

"Sheriff inside?" Joe asked.

"Yes, sir."

"So let me in."

"No, sir. No one goes in. Especially you."

Joe put his hands on his hips and shook his head. "I want to see my mother-in-law. Is she under arrest?"

A slight smile tugged on the edges of Sollis' thick mouth. "I reckon, by now."

"What's the charge?"

"Charges," Sollis corrected. "You can take that all up with the county attorney. My job is to keep everybody out."

Joe stepped back, his hands still on his hips. The day was surreal.

The last time he'd been inside this house was two weeks ago with Marybeth and his daughters. Missy had planned the menu—chile relleños smothered in green chile sauce in honor of Sheridan soon going to college—even though the meal had turned out to be Lucy's favorite and not Sheridan's. Missy favored Lucy over all the children, seeing in her the spark of a kindred spirit, although Lucy no longer welcomed the attention. Despite the mix-up, Missy still supervised the cooking, but never touched the food and didn't eat it. Neither did Sheridan.

And here he was again, Joe thought. Only this time Missy was somewhere inside being placed under arrest for . . . murder?

He snorted.

"Something you find funny?" Sollis asked.

"This whole thing," Joe said, gesturing toward the vehicles in the ranch yard and all the law enforcement personnel standing around. "I knew Sheriff McLanahan needed something to happen to boost his chances of reelection, but even I didn't think he'd go after the wealthiest landowner in the county for this."

Sollis' jaw muscles started working, like he was chewing gum. "You best keep your mouth shut until you find out more about the case against her," he said. "I think you'll be surprised. And I'd advise you to back off and pipe down. You're being observed by the media."

Joe turned. The Saddlestring media consisted of Sissy Skanlon, the twenty-five-year-old editor of the Saddlestring *Roundup*, and Jim Parmenter, the northern Wyoming stringer for the Billings *Gazette*. They stood together under a tree behind a yellow plastic band of crime scene tape where they'd obviously been ordered to stay. Joe nodded toward them. Jim nodded back and Sissy waved.

"There's at least two television trucks on the way," Sollis said with some satisfaction. "From Billings and Casper. Maybe more."

Joe asked Sollis, "So how long has the sheriff been planning this?

It takes a while to get both Jim and Sissy in one place. And I see we've got DCI vehicles here, meaning Cheyenne was called in enough time for these guys to get here. How long has this operation been under way?"

Sollis began to say something, and then caught himself. A slow grin formed. "Naw, that's not going to work. You need to talk to the sheriff. Or better yet, maybe you ought to hold on until you can visit your dear mother-in-law in jail. Seems to me she knows a hell of a lot more about what's going down than anyone else, even if she's not talking to us."

Joe nodded, then turned on his heel and walked up to Sissy and Jim.

"Have you guys been briefed?" Joe asked. He knew them both well and he'd never jerked them around. He always returned their calls and spoke to them plainly. In turn, they'd never burned him.

"We're waiting," Jim said, checking his wristwatch. "McLanahan said he'd be out with a full statement within half an hour. It's been forty-five minutes. I think he's waiting on the cameras," he said with disdain.

Sissy said, "If it's big enough news, like if she's arrested for murder, we might even do a special edition of the paper. I can't remember ever doing one before."

She checked to make sure her recorder was on, then thrust it toward Joe. "Do you think she did it? You probably know her best."

Joe was on thin ice. No matter what he said, it could be perceived wrongly. An immediate "No Way" would make it sound like he was her advocate and guarantee he'd be banned from any aspect of the investigation. A "No Comment" might imply guilt, since it was coming from the accused's son-in-law. After several beats, he mumbled, "You need to direct that question to the county attorney."

"You saw the body?" Jim asked Joe. "Is it true he was hanging off the blade of a wind turbine?"

Joe nodded, grateful Jim had saved him from a follow-up from Sissy. "I did," he said. "It wasn't something I'll be able to get out of my mind for a while. Deputy Mike Reed is on the scene, so you may want to call him."

"Yuck," Sissy said, as she reached into her bag for her cell phone. "Excuse me," she said, "I've gotta make a call."

Jim reached out and touched her hand. "If you're calling a photographer to go out to the wind farm before they bring the body down, I'd like a copy of that shot, if you don't mind."

Sissy contemplated the request for a moment—Joe could tell she realized the photo and the story could get picked up nationally and likely win some awards—then relented. "I know I owe you a few," she said to Jim.

Since Jim had said the sheriff would be out to give a full statement, Joe thought that perhaps he'd given them *something*. So he asked, "Did he tell you the department was tipped? That they'd been told by someone to get ready for this?"

Jim nodded. "You know who it might have been tipping them?"

Joe shook his head. "Nope. So he called you two when? This morning?"

Jim sighed. "Yeah, early. He said get ready for something big, maybe. It was bad timing, because I was going to take my kids fishing today. I had the truck all packed and everything. I was hoping he'd call back and say, 'false alarm,' but instead he said to meet him out here."

"How early?" Joe asked.

"Seven, maybe," Jim said. "I was just getting dressed." Jim read Joe's face, and said, "What's wrong?"

"Nothing," Joe said, shaken. So McLanahan had called Jim Parmenter *before* Joe himself had called in the incident? Behind him he heard several voices and he turned in time to see Missy, head down, being escorted from the front door toward a waiting sheriff's department GMC. She looked tiny between two deputies who had roughly the same build and bulk as Sollis. Except for Mike Reed, McLanahan had staffed his department with hard men.

Missy was slim and dressed in black slacks, a starched, untucked and oversized white shirt with an open collar and rolled-up cuffs, and simple flats. She looked like she was dressed for a day of celebrity gardening, Joe thought. For her small size, she had a large head and a smooth, heart-shaped open face. She *always* looked great in photographs, and the camera tended to trim twenty years off her. Her close-cropped coiffed hair was not as perfect as usual and a few strays stuck out, as if she'd done it in haste. Her over-large and sensual mouth was clamped tight. As she stepped down off the porch—the deputies on both sides physically guided her—she glanced up and locked on Joe.

Missy's eyes were rimmed with red. Without her customary makeup, she looked pale, drawn, small—and her age. They'd handcuffed her in front, and the heavy stainless steel bracelets made her wrists look even thinner. For the first time, Joe noted how the skin on the back of her palms was mottled with age and that her fingers looked skeletal. He'd once heard that no matter what a woman did to fight off the years, her hands revealed all. And Missy's hands were revealing.

Missy kept her eyes on Joe, silently pleading but not groveling, as the deputies marched her across the lawn toward the car. Behind her, Sheriff Kyle McLanahan filled the doorframe, scowling briefly at Joe and then peering over Joe's head at the ranch yard. He carried a lever-action .30-30 Winchester carbine with plastic-gloved hands. Behind him was Dulcie Schalk, the new county attorney who'd replaced Joe's friend Robey Hersig.

Joe looked over his shoulder to see what the sheriff had fixed on, and saw the television satellite truck rumbling up the long driveway. McLanahan had no doubt frittered away time inside until he could make a dramatic appearance before the cameras.

Dulcie Schalk was in her early thirties, with dishwater-blonde hair, dark brown eyes, and a trim, athletic figure. She'd been hired by Robey as his assistant a few months before he was killed three years before, and she'd stepped into the vacuum and filled it so well that when she'd run for the office she was unopposed. Schalk was unmarried except to her job, and Joe had found her to be honest and professional, if very tightly wound. Marybeth and Dulcie Schalk ran in the same circles, and shared a profound interest in horses. They'd gone on trail rides together and Marybeth spoke highly of her, which counted with Joe.

Schalk was driven and passionate and worked long hours. Her record for obtaining convictions was a hundred percent. In Joe's opinion, if she had a weakness as a prosecutor it was her penchant for not going into court unless the case was airtight. Joe had been frustrated by her a few times when he brought her cases—one involving the suspected poaching of an elk and the other an out-of-state hunter who may have falsified his criminal background of game violations on his application for a license—because she thought there might be too much "air" in the case to pursue it further. So when he saw the determined set to her face as she came out of the door behind McLanahan, he knew there was substance behind the arrest. And for the first time that day, he questioned his initial assumption that Missy was innocent.

Even so, Joe said to both McLanahan and Schalk, "Are the handcuffs really necessary? I mean . . . look at her. Does she look like she might resist?"

Missy thanked Joe with a barely perceptible nod. She seemed to need a champion, and Joe felt odd playing the role. He even admired her a little for her dignity and poise, given the situation. The deputies towered over her.

Dulcie Schalk nodded at Joe as if she agreed, and turned to the sheriff for his reaction.

McLanahan lowered his lids and smiled slyly at Joe. "Keep 'em on," he told Sollis, who had moved toward Missy with his cuff key. Sollis retreated.

Missy said nothing, and lowered her eyes to continue her slow walk toward the GMC. But McLanahan chinned a silent command at his deputies to hold her there. Joe realized the sheriff wanted to make sure Missy was caught on camera being escorted to the car.

"Come on, McLanahan," Joe said, feeling his anger rise, and surprised it did. "There's no point in humiliating her even more." He looked to Dulcie Schalk for support, but Schalk had turned away.

Joe saw something remarkable when McLanahan finally gave the go-ahead to his deputies to resume the perp walk with Missy toward the GMC. As the video camera rolled and both Jim Parmenter and Sissy Skanlon snapped photos with their digital cameras, Missy's entire face and demeanor changed. Not just changed, but transformed. Her walk became a shuffle. Her shoulders slumped. The poise she'd shown earlier morphed instantly into pathos. Her eyes moistened, and her mouth trembled as if holding back a wail. She looked suddenly pathetic. A victim. She seemed barely capable of entering the GMC without help. He assumed the cameras captured it all.

McLanahan had missed the show, however, and was clearing his throat so the reporters would look back his way. When they did, he displayed the .30-30 and said, "Although we still need to run it through ballistics to verify it beyond doubt, we believe this is the rifle that was used to murder Earl Alden."

Joe squinted. He'd seen the rifle before, or one that looked a lot like it, in The Earl's antique-gun cabinet.

For the cameras, the sheriff worked the lever of the rifle, ejecting a spent cartridge case that was quickly gathered up by Sollis and placed in a paper evidence bag. Then McLanahan gestured toward the GMC: "And there, we believe, is the woman who pulled the trigger. Missy Alden killed her husband with this rifle."

"Allegedly," Dulcie Schalk corrected.

"Allegedly," McLanahan echoed with slight irritation. "And then she allegedly hoisted her husband's body to the top of one of his new wind turbines and rigged it up to the blade so it would spin around until it was discovered."

With that, McLanahan handed the rifle off to Sollis, who took it away. He put his hands on his hips and rocked back on his heels in his well-practiced *I'm-the-law-in-these-here-parts* stance. "I'd like to publicly recognize and salute the efficiency and professionalism of my team here at the Twelve Sleep County Sheriff's Department for their prompt and thorough investigation, which led to the arrest of . . ."

Joe tuned out as the briefing turned into a "Reelect Sheriff Kyle McLanahan" stump speech. The county attorney approached him and stood there until he noticed her.

"I wish he wasn't so blatant," Schalk whispered to Joe under her breath. "He's grandstanding. Tainting the jury pool . . ."

"Do you have a minute?" Joe asked.

He led her away from the press conference, but noted she didn't want to go so far that she couldn't interject again if McLanahan's statements got out of hand.

"We need to make this short," she said. "I'm not sure I should be talking to you. Don't you have an interest in this case?"

"She's my mother-in-law," Joe said.

"I know. So understand that anything I tell you is purely for public consumption. It's the same thing I'll tell the press. Nothing more, Joe. No inside information, so don't put me on the spot. This is a delicate situation."

"I realize that," he said, glancing over her shoulder. He could see the side of Missy's head through the window of the GMC. Missy stared straight ahead now that the cameras had swiveled to McLanahan. She seemed to have shed her pathetic persona as easily as Joe removed a jacket.

"Where was the rifle found?" Joe asked.

"Under the seat of her car. She drives the Hummer, right? That's her personal vehicle."

Joe nodded. The Hummer was constantly blocking his driveway so he either couldn't get in or out. Usually with the motor running.

She said, "The tracks we found out on the ranch where we think the murder took place appear to match up with the tires on the Hummer. Our team couldn't explain why we couldn't find a spent cartridge on the ground until we found the gun and realized the casing hadn't been ejected but was still in the gun. Plus, her fingerprints were all over the rifle itself."

"So the tipster even knew where the crime took place."

"I'm not going there," she said.

Joe took that in. "McLanahan didn't mention an accomplice."

"That I can't tell you," Schalk said. "Not yet."

"So you've got the tipster secured," Joe said, fishing. "And you've got his statement."

"Joe," she said, exasperated.

"Okay, okay. But this whole thing seems so . . . pat."

"It is what it is, Joe. I have nothing against your mother-in-law, and neither does the sheriff."

"Except she's quite a big prize," Joe said. "And she isn't exactly the most popular woman in the country, that's for sure. Believe me, I know about *that.* Hauling her in like this will give McLanahan a big boost in popularity. Some folks love to see the high and mighty taken down just for being high and mighty."

Schalk nodded, "I've heard some things, and you have my word I'll do what I can to keep this from turning into a circus. But she does have a tendency to rub people the wrong way. So I never had any personal dealings with her."

"Lucky you," Joe said. Then: "So the theory is she shot The Earl and hung his body from that wind turbine?"

Schalk eyed him closely, paused, then said, "That's our working theory right now."

Joe took off his hat and raked his fingers through his hair. "Have you seen a turbine up close? How high it is? And hang his body up in public? What was that supposed to accomplish?"

"Maybe to throw us off the trail," she said. "Alden was a very controversial figure as well. He had plenty of enemies, and you know that wind farm of his hasn't been popular with some of his neighbors."

Joe was aware of some of the complaints, particularly those from ranchers Bob and Dode Lee. They hated Rope the Wind, and especially the new transmission lines planned to be built across their ranch, which Alden had arranged by getting a swath of their land condemned by eminent domain.

"Are you gonna talk to the Lees?" Joe asked.

"Joe, please."

He said, "So the first part of the theory is a crime of passion was committed, probably without premeditation, since she didn't get rid of the rifle or even wipe it down. But the second part is a conspiracy designed to throw everyone off the track."

She nodded her head, but Joe saw a glimmer of doubt in her eyes when he put it like that.

"Okay," he said. "I won't ask anything more about the internal investigation because you can't tell me. But I've got to wonder about motive. I know Missy, believe me. I know what she's like. And it took her a lifetime of trading up to finally hit the jackpot." He gestured toward the mansion-in-progress on the river bluff. "Why would she risk that, and all of this? This is what she always wanted."

Dulcie Schalk's eyebrows arched and she started to answer, then apparently thought better of it.

"So you've got a motive, then?" Joe said, surprised.

"Not that I can speak about yet," she said. "But I'm comfortable enough with what we know so far to press charges."

"Wow," Joe said. "*Wow.* You've got enough that you really think she's guilty."

"I think we better go back to the press conference," Schalk said. She turned away, then stopped, and looked back at Joe.

"If I were you," she said gently, "I would stay away from this and keep your head down. I'm not saying that as a threat, Joe. I'm not like McLanahan. But this is from me, because I like you and I'm close to Marybeth, as you know. This is a solid case, Joe. I'm approaching it with even more caution than usual. I don't want you to go out there and embarrass yourself, and I don't want us to be in a situation where we're butting heads. But so far, and this I *can* say, it doesn't look good for your mother-in-law. Not at all."

Joe said, "I've had a fantasy about this over the years, I have to admit."

Schalk smiled. "I don't know what to say to that."

"And I shouldn't have said it." He felt ashamed. Then: "Did she admit anything?"

"You'll have to take that up with her lawyer."

"She's already lawyered up?"

"Yes. She's retained Marcus Hand, and he advised her not to say a word until he gets here."

Joe was rocked. "Marcus Hand? You're kidding."

"I wish I were," Schalk said.

Marcus Hand was a Wyoming legend, and was known nationally through his years of cable television legal punditry. Tall, white-maned, brilliant, and given to Stetsons and fringed buckskin clothing, Hand had won millions for clients (and himself) in tort cases against pharmaceutical companies and doctors, as well as securing innocent verdicts for scores of notorious, but wealthy, clients in criminal proceedings. Joe had not met Marcus Hand personally, but he'd been in the courtroom for a case in Jackson Hole where Hand had persuaded the jury that the developer Joe was certain had killed his wife was not guilty.

"I'm looking forward to going up against him," Schalk said.

"You are?"

"Like I said, we've got a strong case. And he needs to get knocked down a peg."

Joe thought, *You poor tough, but naïve, girl.*

He could see why Marybeth liked her.

Dulcie Schalk joined McLanahan, who was fielding questions from the press. Joe sauntered over near the GMC where Missy was being held. Sollis came over to intercept him, but not before Missy slid the window down a few inches and turned her head toward him. The air of dignity was back, and coupled with something Joe had seen before—a cold and ruthless defiance.

"I know we've had our differences, Joe," she said, "but for the sake of my daughter and your children—my grandchildren—you've got to help me."

Before he could answer, she rolled the window back up.

"That's enough," Sollis said. "Step aside. We're taking her in."

With shaky hands, Joe fished his cell out and opened it. He texted a message to Marybeth.

PREPARE OUR GIRLS.
IT LOOKS REAL BAD.

Joe closed the phone and folded his arms and leaned back against the grille of his pickup. He wondered what Nate Romanowski would have made of all this, if he'd been around to hear about it. Nate had never liked Missy, either, but he'd always had a special connection with Marybeth. For the fiftieth time in eleven months, Joe wondered where Nate was now and what he was doing. And if they were enemies now or still friends, or something in-between.

As if there could be an in-between with Nate Romanowski.

7

Nate Romanowski woke up worried, and the feeling persisted through the cool August morning. Even his three birds, the peregrine, the red-tailed hawk, and the golden eagle, seemed edgy and bitchy in their mews as he fed them chunks of bloody rabbit for breakfast.

Dawn came two hours late in Hole in the Wall Canyon, as it always did. The sheer walls prevented sunlight from pouring over the rims until mid-morning, but when it did there was a special intensity of light and heat because of the lack of wind to cushion it. As he returned to the cave, he scanned the canyon wall opposite where the trail wound down. The trail was a tan scar against the scrub and brush that switchbacked down from the top and he could see nearly all of it from where he stood. That was one primary reason he'd chosen the location four years before, because it was a natural phenomenon practically designed for hiding out. He could clearly view the only approach into the canyon, but from the trail it was all but impossible to locate his cave without intimate familiarity. On the rare occasions when people appeared—and they were usually fishermen making their way to the Middle Fork of the Powder River down below—he'd never been discovered. That was the way he wanted it.

Because of the fishermen who'd recently come to the area, he'd dismantled the fatal booby traps on the lower half of the trail and replaced them with sensors, motion detectors, and a pair of game cameras that could broadcast an image to his laptop. He'd observed the few people who'd come down into the canyon recently and they had no idea their progress down to the water had been viewed through the crosshairs of a scope.

But he saw nothing out of order. It was quiet and calm, and the early-morning chill in the air was an ally because of how it carried sound. There were no unfamiliar sounds.

He returned to his cave in the rocks and quietly gathered his fly rod, flies, and wide-brimmed hat. Alisha Whiteplume, his lover, was there for the weekend. She was still sleeping in the mass of quilts, and he paused for a moment to admire her face in repose: dark silken hair fanned across the pillow, the smooth high cheekbones of the native Shoshone, long lashes, sweet lips turned down on the ends, as if she were worried, too.

She liked trout for breakfast and he wanted to catch her a couple.

Because of that feeling he had which he couldn't explain, he slipped his leather shoulder holster over his arms and fitted it snugly over his sweatshirt. The butt of his powerful .454 Casull five-shot revolver faced out above his left hip, so he could draw it out with his right hand in less than a second and fire. The handgun was scoped and Nate was an accurate shot within several hundred yards.

He paused for a moment and looked at himself in the mirror he'd slung from a root on the cave wall. Nate was a few inches over six feet tall and had broad shoulders. His long blond hair was tied into a ponytail with a leather falconry jess, and his eyes, even to him, looked sharp and cruel and haunted. His nose was thin and sharp, his jaw prominent. He always wondered if by simply spending so much of his life with falcons—he was a master falconer—that he'd taken on the characteristics of his birds, like a fat man and his pet bulldog or the society fashion doyenne and her poodle.

He slipped back outside. Again, he scanned the canyon wall across from him and slowly studied every foot of the trail. He watched as well as listened, because the natural sounds—birds, the high-pitched whistle of fat marmots in the rocks, the off-chord caws of two chicken-sized ravens cruising the rims—told him as much about the situation as anything he could see. There was no concern expressed in their talking. Worse would have been complete silence, and complete silence meant an intruder had come.

Despite the blue-black cloud of doom that lingered in his consciousness, he discerned nothing out of order.

Still, as he picked his way down to the river between boulders the size of trucks, and the natural music of the creatures was replaced with the burbling and tinkling sound of the river, he knew he wouldn't be long for this place.

He returned an hour later with three twelve-inch rainbow trout, to find Alisha up and dressed and brewing coffee on his camp kitchen. She'd tied back the heavy covers that hung across the opening to facilitate fresh air and morning sunlight, and she'd made the bed. Their clothes, which had been discarded the night before as if they were on fire, had been folded into his and hers. The coffee smelled good.

"I'll fillet these," he said, laying out the fish on the cutting board like three shiny shards of glistening steel.

"Wonderful," she said, smiling. "When did you learn to fish so well? Was it Joe?"

"Yeah," he mumbled. "But anyone could catch these fish. They were easy and hungry and they came right for the fly."

She nodded and he could feel her trying to read his face. She had recently started asking about Joe Pickett, and he always deflected the inquiry.

"You haven't talked much about him recently," she said.

"No, I haven't."

Alisha Whiteplume was a schoolteacher on the Wind River Indian Reservation. Since her return from the outside world, where she'd been a married electrical engineer, she'd plunged into reservation life. She was practical and charismatic and, in addition to being named to the tribal council, was also in charge of a club that encouraged teenage Shoshone and Northern Arapahoe to start up and manage small businesses. She had nothing but disdain for U.S. government paternalism and handouts that, she felt, had held her people back for generations. She was the mentor for a half-dozen young entrepreneurs who had started businesses that included a small local newspaper, the crafts shops, a video rental store, and a sub sandwich franchise. She was also the guardian of a five-year-old girl who stayed with Alisha's mother while she sneaked away to visit Nate. He not only loved Alisha, he admired her strength, stamina, optimism, and loyalty. He felt guilty they couldn't get married because of his problem with the Feds. She was too good a woman to have to sneak around the way she did in order for them to be together, as if they were both cheating.

She said, "So you and Joe—you're still working things out?"

"You're going to keep hammering away, huh?"

"I don't hammer. I just keep asking politely until I get an answer."

He sighed as he cut the fillets. He'd put a dollop of shortening into a cast-iron skillet and it had dissolved and had begun to smoke. After dipping the trout fillets into buttermilk, he'd dredge them in cornmeal and lay them in the skillet.

"Joe's the one who needs to work things out," Nate said. "I'm clear where I'm at."

The year before, in the Sierra Madres of southern Wyoming, Nate and Joe had encountered a set of violent twin brothers who wanted to be left alone. Joe had special orders to go after them and he'd done so, relentlessly, even when the circumstances for their isolation were revealed. Nate wanted to ride away. In Nate's mind, it was a disagreement about what the law said and what was right. Joe chose the law.

"I never thought I'd say this," she said in her musical voice, "but I think maybe you need to make the effort."

"You never liked it when we got together for a case," Nate said. "What changed your mind?"

"He seems like a good man," she said. "And a good friend to you."

Nate grunted.

"You can't just dismiss him as a government man. You know better, and you two have been through a lot. Do you still keep in touch with his daughter? Is she still your falconry apprentice?"

Nate nodded. Sheridan should have gone to college by now, and he knew nothing of her choice of school. He didn't know where she was, which was troubling to him.

"You shouldn't punish her," Alisha said. "It's not her fault."

"I know." He was getting annoyed because she was right.

"Marybeth knows I'm still here," Nate said. "She called a while back to check on me. I even got a call from her *mother*."

"The pretty dragon?"

"Yes, her."

"But not Joe?" she asked.

"Not Joe."

"Phones work two ways, you know," she said.

"Hmmmmph."

"Well?"

"Well, maybe I'll give him a call one of these days."

"No," she said, "Go see him. You two don't talk well on the phone. I've heard you. You're like two apes grunting. You don't *say* anything."

Nate turned the fillets. He liked how angrily they sizzled. When he looked up, she was staring at him, waiting.

"Okay," he said, with a little edge. "But first I have to get the hell out of this canyon. I told you why last night."

She made a face. It had to do with his time working for a branch of Special Forces, a rogue branch. He didn't tell her the name of the organization or what he'd done while he was there. He never would, because she'd be outraged. Even Joe didn't want to know, even though Nate had offered to tell him.

There were things he'd done—that his team had done—that were coming back to haunt him. Because Nate had left abruptly, without clearance, an exit interview, or his pension, there were men who were concerned about exposure. He'd never threatened to reveal them or talk about their work, but they were paranoid by nature. Several of his old team had come to the Rockies at different times to try to take him out. Each had failed, and they no longer walked the earth. But the rotten core of the team—four men and a woman—still survived, and several had moved up in the government within the Department of Homeland Security. He called them The Five.

According to a contact he still trusted in the agency, The Five were alarmed about Nate's work and growing underground reputation. There was no doubt they'd breathe easier if Nate didn't breathe at all.

From what he understood from his contact in Virginia, The Five had not yet deployed. He wondered if telling her about them the night before had caused his uneasy feeling when he woke up that morning, or if it was something else. If The Five deployed, he didn't want Alisha anywhere close to him.

Another source of tension was the increasing numbers in the underground resistance. They looked to him for help and protection. What had originally been a few dozen people who had dropped out of contemporary America because they loathed the direction the country seemed to be headed in had swelled to hundreds and perhaps more. They were located in remote pockets throughout the mountain west. The woman Joe and he had saved a year ago—for what turned out to be different reasons—had been the catalyst for their disagreement. She was now in the Snake River country of Idaho, among her kind. He had no idea what would happen when the movement was either publicized or challenged. But he knew there would be a good chance of violence.

"I've got a lot on my mind," he said, after the fillets were cooked golden brown. He removed them and put them on a towel to drain and cool. He gestured toward the mews. "Plus, that damned eagle still won't fly even though it's fully healed and capable of flight."

"Maybe it's a symbol," she said.

"Maybe. Let's eat."

"Please remove your weapon," she said. "Civilized people don't eat breakfast wearing guns."

"First time you called me civilized."

"You aren't there yet. It's something to aspire to." She looked up and smiled coyly. "Maybe when you don't feel the need to live in a cave."

As they finished breakfast, he thought of something. He said, "You didn't mention seeing Large Merle last night."

Large Merle was a fellow falconer and member of the underground resistance. He was a huge man who had known Nate in the old days but had moved west and had gone to fat. He wore a full beard and stained clothing from his job as a cook in the restaurant in Kaycee. Large Merle rented a ramshackle home up on the south rim of the canyon. The only established road to get to Nate's stretch of the Hole in the Wall passed through Large Merle's property, and his friend would clear or shoo away visitors. Either way, Large Merle would call Nate on his satellite phone and let him know who had been there at his place and who might show up in the canyon. Since Nate had been expecting Alisha, he hadn't realized until now there had been no call.

Alisha took her last bite of the trout and closed her eyes as she chewed it. She loved the fresh fish, and he loved watching her eat it. She said, "Merle wasn't home."

"Maybe he was cooking," Nate said, unsure.

"The restaurant wasn't open when I drove by," she said. "I was thinking of stopping in for a cup of coffee."

Nate sat up. "Large Merle has never left without letting me know," he said.

She shrugged. "Maybe it was an emergency. Doesn't he have a sick dad somewhere?"

He leaned back in his chair and rubbed his eyes.

"He'd let me know if he drove to Casper. He always does." Then, pushing quickly away from the table: "Alisha, I can't explain it, but something's wrong. Let's pack up."

"Where are we going?"

"I don't know yet."

"Are we coming back?"

"No."

8

Nothing spells trouble like two drunk cowboys with a rocket launcher.

That's what Laurie Talich was thinking as she drove them down the rough two-track toward Hole in the Wall Canyon.

Not that they were *real* cowboys, sure enough. They wore the requisite Wranglers, big Montana Silversmith buckles, long-sleeved Cinch shirts, and cowboy hats. Johnny Cook was a silent strapping blond from upstate New York near Albany, and Drennen O'Melia, chunky and chatty and charmingly insincere, was a Delaware boy. But they were young, strong, dim, handsome, and eager to please. Not to mention currently unemployed since that incident on the dude ranch from which they had recently been let go.

The AT4 shoulder-mounted rocket launcher, still in the packing crate in her rented pickup, was as real as it came, though.

The night before, Laurie Talich had found Johnny and Drennen playing pool for drinks in the back of the Stockman's Bar in Saddlestring. The bar was dark, cool, long, narrow, and iconic in a comfortably kitschy Western kind of way. She'd been advised this would be the place to find the right kind of men for the job, and her adviser had been exactly right. She'd sat alone on her stool at the bar for three straight nights, long enough to learn the name of the bartender—Buck Timberman. She was coy and hadn't revealed hers. He'd called her "little lady," as in "What can I get you, little lady?"

"Another one of these, please." Meaning Crown Royal and Coke, even though her husband used to chide her and say she was ruining two good drinks with that combo.

She'd paid in cash so there would be no electronic receipts, sipped her second drink of the night, and shot furtive glances at the two dude ranch cowboys. They chalked their sticks, called the pockets, mowed down all comers—tourists, mainly—and collected their drinks. They noticed her: slim, jet-black short hair with bangs, and light blue eyes the color of a high-noon sky. She dressed the part in form-fitting Cruel Girl jeans, a jeweled cowgirl belt, and a white sleeveless top. Her legs were crossed one over the other, but when she rotated the stool and looked at them, the dagger-like toe of her right boot would twirl in a small tight circle, like a tongue licking open lips. Oh, they noticed, all right.

The more she watched them, hearing snatches of braggadocio and bullshit, knowing they were being observed and playing it up as much as possible, the more she began to believe she'd found the right boys. They'd be perfect for the job. They were role players, too: rent-a-cowboys for the summer. The guest and dude ranches throughout the Bighorns as well as most of Wyoming and Montana were swarming with them. The ranch owners needed seasonal help who looked and acted the part, because their clients expected it, and boys like Johnny and Drennen were perfect for the kind of job she had in mind. Young, handsome (at least Johnny was), Caucasian, nonthreatening to the permanent staff, unambitious in terms of running the guest ranch operation, willing to work the short three- to four-month seasons between snows, and without two nickels to rub together. For the ranch managers, it helped if they knew something about horses, and it was even better if they could play a guitar and sing a cowboy song. Mostly, though, they were required to look and act the part. No backwards baseball caps, street piercings, baggy pants, or shirts two sizes too big. These types would never replace the real wranglers and hands on the ranches, but they'd serve as pleasant enough fantasy eye candy for the wives and daughters, and they'd provide strong arms and backs for menial chores around the ranch.

Unless, of course, they lured the two teenage daughters of a wealthy Massachusetts union boss away from their family cabin while the parents participated in Square Dance Thursday and got the girls drunk on Keystone Light beer and were caught in the horse barn in the act of ripping the tops off the foil-wrapped condoms with their teeth—well, then they'd be fired, like Johnny and Drennen had been.

And they'd wind up playing eight-ball for drinks in the historic Stockman's Bar, overlooked by beer lights hung from chains from the knotty pine ceiling, and generations of local black-and-white rodeo cowboy photos looking down at them from the walls, judging them and no doubt finding these two insufficient. As if Johnny or Drennen would give a rip about *that*.

Once she'd decided they were probably the right fellows, she slid off her stool and slinked by them on the way to the women's. They politely tipped their hats to her, and she paused to talk. She offered to buy them both a drink when they were through playing pool. She said she liked their style. That she was *intrigued* by them. They ate it up.

Laurie Talich settled into one of the dark high-backed booths near the restrooms and waited. Timberman brought her another Crown Royal and Coke, and she ordered two long-necked Coors because that's what Johnny and Drennen were drinking. She'd counted and knew they'd each had six beers already.

They played the last game fast, and lost when Drennen scratched on the eight ball. She watched the shot and determined he'd done it intentionally to speed things up so they could meet her. She suppressed a smile and waited to unleash it when the two faux cowboys joined her in the booth. Drennen asked to sit next to her and she moved over. Johnny slid in straight across the table. Neither removed his hat.

It didn't seem to matter that she was ten years older and without another female friend. She caught Johnny staring at her wedding ring, despite the fact that she'd sprinkled the phrase "my late husband" into the conversation here and there. Since the boys weren't much for nuance, she finally said, "My husband was killed two years ago," and it finally seemed to register with them.

"Uh, sorry about that," Drennen mumbled.

"What happened?" Johnny asked.

"He was shot," Laurie said, keeping her voice low and steady. "And I was kind of hoping you might want to help me locate someone. A man who knows something about what happened because he was there. See, I'm new to the area. I could really use the help from a couple of men who know their way around."

Johnny and Drennen exchanged glances. Drennen broke into a smile, although Johnny seemed either unsure of his own reaction or simply drunk and placid. She could tell they liked being called men as well as the implication they were locals.

Johnny grinned crookedly and held out his hand. "Johnny," he said. "This other's Drennen."

"Walking After Midnight" was playing on the jukebox. "Patsy," she said, knowing they wouldn't get it. She shook Johnny's hand first, and then offered her hand to Drennen, who flinched at first but then shook it.

"Nice to meet you, Patsy," Johnny said, draining his bottle. "I bet Drennen and me could use another one of these while we talk, if you don't mind."

She gestured to Timberman again with two fingers, meaning she was fine but the boys were thirsty.

"I'm willing to pay you boys quite a lot of money," she said. "As long as you keep your mouths closed and we actually find him. You see, I'm quite well off, due to the insurance money and all."

"Shoot," Drennen said. "Who don't need some money these days? Money's like . . . *gold*."

Which made Johnny grin and say to Drennen, "If you've ever said anything stupider than that, I can't remember it."

"I have," Drennen assured him.

"See," Johnny said, "it gets kind of frustrating to be around rich folks all summer long. They don't seem to even know they're rich, which is a pisser. You just want to say to them, 'Give me just a little of what you got. You won't miss it and I could sure use some of it.'"

The new beers arrived, and she sat back. She'd laid it out and now it was up to them. She wouldn't tell them any more until they begged for it. And if the whole deal collapsed, she'd said nothing so far that would implicate her in any way. Not the name of the man she was looking for. Or the name of her adviser.

"It ain't like we're busy right now," Johnny said, drawing little circles with his fingertip through the condensation on his full bottle.

Drennen said, "Hell, we're camping up by Crazy Woman Creek.

And it's starting to get cold at night, and damned if I'm gonna spoon with that guy." He pointed the mouth of his bottle toward Johnny, who grinned.

"Me and Johnny—this ain't no *Brokeback Mountain* kind of deal," Drennen offered.

"Jesus," Johnny groaned at his friend. "Get back to the money part. Don't pay Drennen any mind. He . . . talks."

Drennen agreed, not the least bit offended.

She shook her head and gestured toward the pool table. "You boys are unemployed and living in the mountains, yet you manage to get a ride to town for some leisure activities."

"Yes, ma'am," Drennen said earnestly. "Even the unemployed got a right to a night on the town."

"I couldn't agree more," she said, looking closely at him, wondering how much of his head was solid rock. "That's why it's such a great country. We won't let anyone take our rights away."

"Damn straight," Drennen said, nodding. "I could just kiss you for that." Then he leaned over to her, the weight of him on her, and raised his chin in an effort to peck her on the cheek.

"Ow!" he yelped, and recoiled, snapping his head back so hard his hat bounced off the back of the booth and tumbled to the table. He plunged both of his hands between his thighs. "What was *that*? It was like a snake bit me in the unit."

"No snake," she said, withdrawing the knitting needle from where she'd jabbed him under the table, "and no kissing. No hijinks of any kind. Not until we come to some kind of understanding."

Johnny watched the whole scene without flinching, without expression. He looked at her and said, "But maybe after *that*?"

"Jesus," Drennen said, reclaiming his hat and fitting it back on. "Did you see what she did?"

Laurie looked back at Johnny and said, “It’s always a possibility. But first things first.”

“You mentioned money,” Johnny said in a whisper, leaning forward across the table. “What kind of dollars we talking about here?”

“Ten thousand,” she said. “You can split it even or decide who gets the greater percentage.”

Johnny frowned. “Why would one of us get more than the other?”

“We’d split it right down the middle, right, Johnny?” Drennen said.

“Suit yourself. I was just thinking one of you may have a harder job than the other. But however you want to handle it is fine by me.”

Timberman brought more beers and again she paid in cash. “Last call, little lady,” he said.

“Her name’s Patsy,” Johnny said, as if he were gallantly defending her reputation.

Timberman winked at her. He got it.

“So,” Drennen said, leaning in as well, so the three of them were inches apart. “Who we gotta kill?”

His tone indicated he was half joking.

She said, “Have you ever killed anyone?”

The question hung there for a moment, then Drennen quickly said, “Sure.” But the way his eyes darted to Johnny and back to her after he said it indicated to her he was lying. Trying to impress her. And he knew she probably knew it, so he said to Johnny, “That Mexican,” as if trying to prompt a false memory. He lowered his voice, “That fuckin’ Mexican wrangler they hired. The one with the attitude.”

She nodded.

“Well,” Drennen said, leaning back and puffing out his chest. “Let’s just say he don’t have a bad attitude no more.”

“That Mexican,” Johnny echoed, nodding. “We capped that son-of-a-bitch.”

She said, "His name is Nate Romanowski, but that shouldn't matter to you one way or another. So, where are you boys camped? I'll give you a ride."

It had happened two years before. Chase Talich, her late husband, had gone west from Chicago—where they had fine jobs working for important, if infamous, local men—with his brothers Cory and Nathaniel. The Feds had cracked down in a high-profile show of force that had caused Chase's employers to flee the area. The last time she'd seen him, he was packing a suitcase in the bedroom. He was calm, as always. He said it might be a couple weeks before he came back. He said he'd call, but he couldn't tell her exactly where he was going. He said he'd bring her back a cactus or a saddle.

Since Chase handled all the finances and had given her a murderous stony stare the one time she'd asked about them, she was naturally concerned about his future absence, especially because she was two months pregnant. They lived well on the North Side, she didn't have to work, and her days consisted of shopping, Pilates, and lunching with the other wives whose husbands were involved in the Chicago *infrastructure*, as they put it. Of course, she had seen references to the "Talich Brothers" in the *Tribune*, and she knew Chase had been in prison when he was young. But he took good care of her and gave her a generous cash allowance every month and she was treated very well in clubs and restaurants when she gave her name. She was willing to not think much about it. That was her trade-off.

For five weeks, he didn't call. His only contact was a large padded envelope sent from somewhere called Hulett, Wyoming, with her monthly cash allowance. Not even a note.

Then the Feds showed up. She knew when she opened the door that something had happened to her husband. They told her he'd been shot and killed in a remote part of northeastern Wyoming, practically in the shadow of Devils Tower. Nathaniel, Chase's younger brother, had also been killed. Only Cory, the oldest, had survived. He was in custody and facing federal and state charges.

Desperate, she went to see her brother-in-law in Denver. Through the thick Plexiglas of the federal detention facility, he told her what had happened. How Chase had been bushwhacked by a local redneck who carried the largest handgun he had ever seen. That's when she first heard the name.

She'd desperately quizzed Cory. Where had Chase stashed his money? How could she get access to it? How could she raise another child—Cory's future nephew or niece—on her own with nothing?

Cory didn't help. He said Chase had kept his finances to himself. Besides, Cory said, he had problems of his own and she'd need to learn how to take care of herself.

It was devastating. She was ruined. She wished she could find Chase and kill him all over again for leaving her like that with nothing. So she'd got an abortion, sold the house—which he'd put in her name to avoid scrutiny—and learned to knit to help take her mind off her situation. She'd turned bitter and spent a lot of time imagining what her life would have been like if Chase had come back. If that redneck hadn't killed him.

Laurie Talich's father had spent his life within the Chicago *infrastructure.* Alderman, bookie, and mayoral assistant—he'd held so many jobs, yet never seemed to have an office where he went to work every morning. He was a loving father in a remote way, and seemed to look to her and her brother for solace and comfort and to remind himself he wasn't all bad. He was a slow, doughy man who arrived home at all hours but never returned from a trip without candy and gifts for his children. In his retirement, he grew peppers and onions in his garden and watched a lot of television. But he was still connected, and when she went to him in desperation, he opened his home to her and listened to her troubles.

One night, after a few glasses of after-dinner wine, he told her she must seek vengeance.

"No matter what you think about your ex-husband or what you've learned about him since, you can't let this go unpunished," he said. "When someone hurts a member of your family, no matter what the reason, he's hurt you by proxy. You go after him and get revenge. People need to know there are consequences for their actions, especially when it comes to our loved ones. That's the only way to keep some kind of order in the world because, God knows, these days no one will do it for you. Not the pols, not the cops. I'd do it myself if I could get around, but I'm too damned old and busted up. Revenge is a cleanser, honey. You need to be cleansed."

She'd arrived in Wyoming the month before. It was remarkable—everyone seemed to know everyone else. She asked questions, got answers and leads, and eventually wound up in Saddlestring. It took only three days to find someone who knew Nate Romanowski.

Her adviser had said, "So you want revenge? I'm one of the few people who actually knows where he hangs his hat."

Then her adviser told her he had access to a rocket launcher through some friends in the arms business. Said it could be shipped to her overnight. Her adviser was incredibly helpful, eager even. She never asked about agendas, because she didn't need to know. All she cared about was that they had a common interest and a common purpose.

So now it was payback time. It was time to be cleansed.

Although Johnny and Drennen talked excitedly about what they'd do the next day all the way into the mountains to their camp—especially the prospect of holding and firing the rocket launcher she claimed she had for the job—they weren't nearly as enthusiastic that morning when she returned to pick them up.

She wound through the pine trees through the established sites and took a side road that was clearly marked by the U.S. Forest Service as prohibited to vehicles. It was another full mile through dense lodgepole pines that scratched the paint on her rental before she found the two of them. The camp was a shambles. They each had a stained, thin dome tent and there were empty bottles strewn about, as well as chunks of foil and old bones in the fire pit. Clothes hung from lengths of parachute cord strung between trees.

As Laurie wheeled into the opening, she saw Drennen emerge from the trees zipping up his Wranglers. His face was gray and drawn, his eyes red. She killed the engine and got out. Drennen nodded hello to her and called out to Johnny, who backed out of his tent and stood up. He looked just as bad. She could tell by the way they exchanged looks they had come to some kind of agreement, and she waited to find out who would speak first.

"Me and Johnny," Drennen said, shoving both his dirty hands into his front trouser pockets and staring at a place in the pine needles between his boots. "We had a little talk this morning. We're not so sure this is a good idea."

She leaned back against the grille of her pickup and felt the warmth through the back of her jacket. The mid-morning sun was just then shooting yellow shafts through the trees to the forest floor. The trampled-down grass sparkled with the last of the morning dew. The thin air had a snap to it. "What don't you like today that you liked last night?" she asked calmly.

Silence. Both now looked at the ground. She wanted to slap them both and tell them to act like men, for God's sake. But she waited.

Finally, Johnny mumbled, "Tell her, Drennen."

Drennen cleared his throat. His voice was raw and thick from his hangover. "Me and Johnny don't think ten thousand is enough to risk our lives for."

She held in a grin. They were so . . . *simple.* She said, "Where do you get the idea you're risking your life?"

"Well, Patsy," Drennen said. "We were pretty drunk last night and it all sounded good. Especially that part about the rocket launcher. That sounds pretty damned cool. But we don't even know this guy. We don't know what he did."

"He killed my husband," she said. "What more do you need to know?"

Johnny kicked at some pine needles. "So he's a bad guy?"

"Yes."

"Then why didn't the cops arrest him and throw him in jail?"

"Because they're incompetent," she said crisply.

Drennen said, "I hear *that.*"

"Look," she said, "he's a wanted man. That's why he's hiding out. There is no chance at all he'll call the cops, because if he did, they'd arrest him. This is as safe as anything could be. Law enforcement won't be weeping any crocodile tears if they find out something happened to Nate Romanowski, from what I understand. Hell, if any of us are ever caught, they might want to give us a medal."

Drennen snorted a laugh, but stanched it after Johnny glared at him.

"I'm not going to beg," she said. "You can either do this or not.

You can try to make a living playing pool, or you can run back home and live with your parents for all I care. I'll find someone else to help me."

They stared at her dumbly.

"What about that Mexican?" she said. "You didn't seem to have a problem with this last night."

It took them a moment to recall the lie. Drennen said, "That was personal."

She turned and tap-tap-tapped her fingers along the hood of the pickup as she walked around it. As she reached for the door handle, Drennen said, "We were thinking maybe twenty. Ten each. This is a big deal you're asking, Patsy. If it don't go right . . ."

She turned and smiled. "It has to go right. And if you follow my instructions and do everything to the letter, it will. You can be back here by this afternoon. I'll go fifteen. No more."

She waited.

"We got to discuss this," Drennen said. "Give us a minute."

While they turned their backs to her and talked, she looked at the packing crate in the bed of the pickup. It was four feet long and a foot high. Someone had stenciled the name and address of a Crate and Barrel store on the outside so no one would be suspicious. She remembered what her associate had told her about how the rocket launcher worked. It was accurate within a thousand feet, but it would be best to get much closer than that.

Next to the crate was a case of Coors she'd bought the night before and left in the back to keep cold. She called out to Johnny and Drennen, "You boys want some hair of the dog? It might help you make up your minds."

Drennen said, "That sounds mighty good."

While they ambled over, she lifted the lid off the crate. The weapon was short, fat, and looked lethal just lying there in the packing peanuts.

Johnny reached for a beer, but stopped when he saw it. He whistled in admiration. Drennen saw what he was looking at and whispered, "Fuckin' A. You weren't kidding, were you, Patsy?"

And she knew she had them.

9

Laurie Talich slowed and pulled off the two-track into knee-high sagebrush and turned off the GPS unit that had guided her there. It was nearly noon and heat waves shimmered across the plains. In the distance, the Bighorn Mountains framed the horizon.

"It's an interesting view in that you can't even tell from here there's a canyon between here and those mountains," she said to Johnny and Drennen. "But there is. From what I understand, Butch Cassidy and the Sundance Kid used to hide in the caves down there."

"I heard of them," Drennen said.

"I saw the movie," Johnny added.

Before they got to the canyon rim, she stopped the pickup to show them how to fire the rocket launcher. Her adviser had carefully gone through the procedure and made her repeat it back. She was not well versed in firearms of this size, but was shocked how simple it all sounded. So simple, she thought, even Johnny and Drennen couldn't foul it up.

She climbed into the bed of the pickup and opened the lid of the crate. The boys watched her carefully, looking mainly at her butt, until she unveiled the weapon. Then they switched their interest to that. There was no disguising their visceral fascination with the rocket launcher.

She held it up and brushed clinging packing peanuts from the AT4. She was shocked how light it was. She'd anticipated something much heavier.

She showed them where to remove the safety pin so the sights would pop up automatically. She handed it over to them so they could hoist it on their shoulders and aim through the sights. They were like boys with their first air rifle, and they took to it instantly. Drennen stepped back and aimed it at Johnny and said, *"Ka-pow. Die, rag-head, die."*

Johnny wrenched it away while she looked on in horror, but it didn't go off. Johnny said, "Knock that off, you dimwit," to Drennen. "And don't call me no rag-head." Drennen grinned and shrugged.

She showed them the two remaining safety steps, the repositioning of the cocking lever, then where a thumb could press the red firing button. Her adviser had told her she needed to press on the second safety while aiming. Then when she had the shot, hit the button. She repeated the procedure to them, and watched—again in horror—as Johnny armed the weapon and squinted down the sights toward a tree in the distance. Then he carefully uncocked it and waited for additional instructions.

"Make sure you know what's behind you," she said. "There's back-blast."

Drennen pouted, "So Johnny gets to shoot it, huh?"

"Yes, fool," Johnny said.

"We're still splitting the money," Drennen said to Johnny. Johnny agreed.

"What if I miss?" Johnny asked her.

She shook her head. "You've got only one chance. This is a one-shot weapon, and after it goes off, that's it. Just remember to bring the tube thing back to me. Don't throw it aside because it'll have our prints all over it."

There was a faint footpath through the brush from where they parked to the rim of the canyon. She pointed it out and told them they were to take it. While they cracked the tops off more bottles of beer and watched and listened intently, she showed them the drawing she'd been given. She smoothed it across the hood.

"This is where the opening of the cave is," she said, pointing to an oval marked with an X. "There's a place with some cover on the trail down where you can see the cave entrance, if you know where to look for it. That's where you hide and aim. But like I told you on the way here, don't just blast away. Make sure you actually see him. Make sure he's there."

"How far is the cave from this hiding place?" Drennen asked.

She paused and tried to recall what her adviser had told her. "Five hundred feet. So it's not that far."

"What's he look like?" Johnny said.

"I've never seen him, but he's tall with long hair. He's a big guy. But it's not like there are going to be other people down there in that canyon."

"And we have to actually see him, right?"

"That's why I gave you the binoculars," she said. "We have to confirm he's there. Don't just shoot at the cave and hope you catch him inside."

"And if he ain't there?" Drennen asked.

"Come back after a few hours. We'll have to try again later."

"No one said anything about a later," Drennen said.

"I'm only paying you if the job is done," she said. "That was our deal."

Drennen sighed theatrically. "He better be there, then."

"That's what I was told."

"Who told you?" Johnny asked. "Who else knows about this?"

She shook her head. "Someone who knows the situation, and who knows Nate Romanowski."

Johnny grimaced, but seemed to accept it.

"There's something very important you need to know," she said, looking from Johnny to Drennen and back again, making sure she had their full attention. "You've got to make the shot count. If you miss or screw up, we're all in deep shit."

Drennen sat back against the passenger door, shaking his head. "What are you talking about?"

"This guy we're after," she said. "He's got a reputation. Have you ever heard the line, 'When you strike at a king, you must kill him'? Some guy named Emerson said that."

"Who the fuck is Emerson?" Drennen asked. "Is he somebody big?"

"Never mind," she said, sorry she'd repeated the line from her adviser since she didn't have a clue, either. "Don't worry about it. Just don't miss. It shouldn't be that hard."

They each took another beer with them and stuffed another in the back pockets of their Wranglers. She climbed back into the pickup cab. Her knitting bag was behind the seat and she pulled it out. She'd taken to storing her knitting needles in the shafts of her tall cowboy boots, and she drew them out. She was a piss-poor knitter, but she was nervous and needed something to do with her hands. Since she'd taken up the craft, all she'd managed to complete was a piece that was twelve inches wide and fifteen feet long. It had no purpose. It was the longest scarf in the world, she thought, and she didn't know how to end it.

She watched them walk down the path with the rocket launcher, trading it back and forth to get the feel of it. She'd made them repeat the firing procedure back to her before they left and they seemed to recall it. Men were intuitive when it came to weapons, she thought. Maybe it was the *only* thing they were intuitive about. She recalled how Chase was with his handguns, like they were an extension of him. She got edgy even looking at one, and rarely handled the .38 she kept hidden away in her knitting bag.

She had given them the drawing so they wouldn't fire at the wrong place.

Johnny and Drennen were in view for five minutes before they found the trail that would lead them down into the canyon. She'd been assured that it wouldn't be booby-trapped on the top half of the trail, so she didn't even mention it to them.

When they were out of sight, she knitted furiously, waiting for the explosion.

She was looking forward to feeling cleansed.

10

"Faster, faster," Nate said to Alisha, who was throwing her clothing into her bag.

She looked up with fear in her eyes and swept her arm around the interior of the cave. "What about all this? You can't just leave it." She meant the furniture, gear, books, and electronics he'd amassed in his three years there.

He shrugged as he took his shoulder holster and the .454 down from a peg in the wall and put them on the table. "All I need is this," he said. Then: "And my birds. In fact, I'm going to go get them hooded up so we can take them with us."

She rolled her eyes. "You need more than a gun and your birds."

"And you," he said, misunderstanding.

"No," she said. "You need clothes. And your satellite phone. Here," she said, grabbing an empty duffel bag and placing it on the table. "I'll pack them while you get the birds ready."

He nodded, and turned for the opening. As he did, the receiver for one of his motion detectors chirped. Nate froze and stared at it. It was the uppermost sensor.

"Okay," he said. "We've got to hurry."

Johnny said, "I think I see it."

"Where?"

"Over there. On the other side. Follow my arm."

Drennen stood shoulder-to-shoulder to Johnny and bent so he could rest his cheek on Johnny's bicep. He squinted down the arm, past the pointer, across the canyon.

"It's kinda dark," Johnny said. "It looks like a half-moon behind some bushes. It don't look like one of those caves in the cartoons. It's more like a slash in the rocks."

After a beat, Drennen said, "Okay, I think I see it."

"Keep your eye on it," Johnny said. "Let's move down the trail a ways. If we can see the cave, that guy can see us. So let's move until we can get hid."

Johnny carried the AT4 by a handle that swung up from the top of the barrel. He crouched and picked up his pace, his cowboy boots clicking against loose rocks. Drennen ducked and followed, keeping his hands out in front of him in case he slipped on the loose gravel. He plucked the beer bottle from his back pocket, twisted off the cap, and threw the cap aside.

Johnny didn't slow down until there was a thick wall of sharp-smelling brush on the left side of the trail that obscured the view from the cave entrance. When Drennen caught up and joined him, Johnny put the AT4 down and gently parted two stiff boughs. "See it?" he asked.

"I lost it," Drennen said, then took a long drink that made his eyes water.

"Put that beer down and use your binoculars. That's what they're for."

"Fuck you," Drennen said, but he did as he was told and placed the bottle between his boots. He raised the glasses to his face.

Johnny waited while Drennen adjusted the focus on the binoculars. He watched his friend, trying to read him.

"Okay," Drennen said finally. "I found it again."

"What do you see?"

"Well, it looks like the top of the cave. There's a bunch of brush hiding the lower half, but the hole looks tall enough for a man to walk in and out of without bending over. I can't see inside—it's dark—but it looks like there are blankets or some such thing tied back on each side."

Johnny nodded and drew out the map from his back pocket. He unfolded it and held it out in front of him, matching the features in the drawing to the canyon itself.

"Yeah," Johnny said, "Where we see that opening is where Patsy has the X."

"Hot damn," Drennen said, chuckling. "This is gonna be the easiest fifteen grand we ever made."

"We ain't made it yet," Johnny said. "Keep your eyes on that cave. See if you can see him. I'll get ready, and if you see that son-of-a-bitch, you tell me. We may not get another chance."

The mews for Nate's falcons was eight feet tall and six feet deep and was located twenty yards west of the cave opening. It was constructed of dried willow branches gathered near the river, and although it was in the open, the construction material rendered it almost perfectly camouflaged. Inside, he started with the peregrine while the eagle watched imperiously. He slipped a leather-tasseled hood over the hooked beak of the bird and fastened it in back. The hoods inured the raptors from reacting to outside stimuli and blinded them so they wouldn't try to fly while being transported. Each bird had a custom hood sized for a tight fit.

He paused after the peregrine was hooded to glance through the willow branches toward the opposite cliff face. He could see no movement, and he knew how often a wandering deer or bobcat unknowingly strolled through the motion detector. Unfortunately, there were several dense stands of mountain juniper hiding portions of the trail. He watched for a few seconds to see if anyone—or anything—emerged from them. Nothing. But his sense of urgency didn't diminish and the hairs on the back of his neck were pricked.

Nate turned back to his birds and hooded the red tail. She didn't object and it took less than a minute. He looked at the eagle, who was sizing him up as well, and sighed. The eagle didn't take to a hood, and it was often a struggle. He said, "Cooperate just this once."

The eagle shifted its weight back and forth on the thick dowel it perched on. Its talons were black, long, and diabolical. Even through the thick welding glove Nate wore when he carried the eagle, she was capable of clamping down with power that practically took him to his knees. *Now,* he thought, *is not the time for any foolishness.*

He raised the large hood to her head deliberately, so she could see what he was doing. "Come on," he said gently, "come on . . ."

Outside the mews, Alisha called to him. "Nate, another one of these boxes went off."

Sensor number two, he thought. Jesus. "Get back inside," Nate called back. "I'll be there in a second. Stay out of sight, Alisha, please."

"Okay," she said, chastened.

"Oh shit," Drennen squealed. "I see somebody."

Johnny took a deep breath. He was both excited and more than a little nauseous.

"Make sure," Johnny said, raising the rocket launcher to rest on his right shoulder. He snapped the sights into place and leaned his cheek against the tube. He could see the top of the cave in the distance, and when he fit the scope against his eye, it leapt into view. There was movement, but he couldn't make out what it was. Whoever had been at the opening had gone back inside.

"I saw somebody move," Johnny said.

"I can see better," Drennen said. "He's in the shadow of the cave, but I can make him out. Long hair, Patsy said. Long black hair. It's him."

"Are you sure?" Johnny asked, suddenly getting cold feet. "Are you fucking sure? Didn't Patsy say he had blond hair?"

"That was him, goddamn it," Drennen hissed. "Shoot, shoot, shoot! Now!"

"Fuck," Johnny said. "I forgot the stupid cocking lever."

"I knew I shoulda done it," Drennen said, now hopping from foot to foot, barely able to contain himself. As he hopped, he moved back farther on the trail but kept the binoculars up.

"Okay," Johnny said, raising the AT4 back up.

"Dumb shit," Drennen said, still moving back and inadvertently slipping behind Johnny. "Don't forget those other two switches."

Then Nate realized how quiet it was outside. The birds and rodents seemed to be holding their breath. And almost imperceptibly, he heard a sound, a sharp if distant metallic click.

He knew that sound, it was a sound from his past, and he roared in reaction and wheeled inside the mews and threw open the door as the roar and the whoosh filled the canyon.

For Johnny, the muscular thrust of the rocket was exhilarating, and the flash and roar of the explosion inside the cave took his breath away. The heavy boom echoed back and forth from canyon wall to canyon wall, and the sheer power of it seemed to wash over and engulf him and open his pores. The vapor trail hung in the air as if frozen there, a white snail's-track of smoke that extended from the juniper stand midair over a tumbling river far below and straight into the mouth of the cave.

Nate saw it: a lightning bolt of smoke and light streaking his direction from a thick stand of juniper halfway down the trail.

The rocket vanished into the opening of his cave. The explosion a split second later threw him back into the mews, flattening it, and he crashed to the ground in a sharp tangle of broken willows, broken skin and bones, and panicked falcons.

Johnny jumped to his feet and threw the tube aside and howled, "Jesus! Did you see *that*? I got him, Drennen! I got that son-of-a-bitch with a perfect shot. Did you *see* that?"

His ears rung and his hands shook and white-hot adrenaline shot through his veins and he thought it was better than sex, better than money, better than anything. He wished he had a camera with him to get a snap of that vapor trail and the huge gout of smoke rolling out of the cave. He'd put it on his Facebook page.

Then he turned around and saw Drennen writhing on the trail. Drennen's clothes were on fire, and so was his hair. Acrid black smoke haloed his head. His face was black and swollen and looked like charred meat. He'd stepped right in into the back-blast.

"She told you not to do that," Johnny said.

Drennen squealed like a little girl, the sound coming from inside his throat. Johnny watched as Drennen rolled in the dirt until the flames were out.

Behind him, a golden eagle lifted up from the smoking debris and caught a thermal and rose into the cloudless blue sky. Johnny turned and tracked it as it rose, mesmerized.

11

Nate Romanowski moaned and attempted to roll over to his belly in the debris, but he couldn't make his arms or legs respond. He was on his back and he could see the eagle in the sky above him rising up and out of the canyon. His ears rang with a high whine, and his mind seemed to be disconnected from his body, as if his thoughts were a gas that had been released under pressure to form a cloud around him.

He closed his eyes and tried to pull himself together, to reassert control over his limbs and will his thoughts back into his head. Oh, how his ears screamed.

He wasn't sure how long it took for his faculties to return, but he realized they had—somewhat—when he was able to reach up and rub his face with his hands. His skin was covered with a film of grit. Then, struggling, he managed to flop over to his side. Thin wooden slats from the decimated mews snapped under his weight and his head swooned. He threw up his breakfast and could smell it along with the sharp and familiar stench of the explosives and dust, and the combination made him remember where he was, although he was unsure what had happened.

Through the sound in his ears, he thought he heard a whoop from the other side of the canyon. It was the whoop of a fan whose team had just scored. Painfully, he turned his neck to see, but his vision was fuzzy and he couldn't focus well. What he thought he saw were two distant figures practically melded together on the canyon trail. They were so close together he thought for a moment they were embracing or dancing. But they were moving up the trail together, attached to each other in some way, for some reason.

Even through his injury and confusion, he knew instinctively they'd attacked him and weren't out of range if he had his weapon. A long shot, sure, but not impossible. Unfortunately, he didn't have the hand and eye coordination necessary to make the shot, and he didn't have his .454. He vaguely recalled taking off his shoulder holster and hanging it on a peg, but he couldn't remember why. What he did have, he knew, was a serious concussion that made it difficult to think straight.

And then, like a thunderclap, he remembered the reason he'd taken off his holster: *Alisha.* The sound that came from his throat was unfamiliar, but it sounded vaguely like a woofing bear.

He lurched from smoking tree to smoking tree, burning the flesh on his hands, to the cave entrance. It was eerily quiet; the buzzing in his ears was competing with the pounding of his heart, and he took in the horrible scene with the sound off.

Bits of clothing and hair. Shards of bed covering and chunks of electronic equipment. Her shoe, the foot still in it.

The bear sound came again, low and rumbling, choked off at the end in a yelping sob.

He reached out with a trembling hand and grasped a thick strand of her long black hair that was stuck to the cave wall, and he pulled it into his face and smelled it and it smelled like her.

Nate turned slowly, still holding the hank of hair to his face. The figures he had tracked earlier were nearly to the top of the canyon rim, specks in the distance. The vapor trail of the rocket wasn't entirely dispersed, and arched across the void. It all came back to him with sickening clarity.

He searched in vain for his weapon inside. It was hard to see in the dust and smoke that hung there, and what he did see and touch enraged and nauseated him. Alisha had always been so much more than a sum of her parts, but that's all she was now: parts. He felt hollow, as if they'd killed him as well.

And he decided that if he didn't go after them immediately, they would get away, weapon or not.

He would tear them apart with his hands.

He raced down the canyon. His head pounded and he fought through it as he plunged headlong into the river, splashing through the icy thigh-high current, slipping on slick submerged river rocks, going under, nearly drowning, getting completely turned around by the time he broke through the surface twenty yards downriver from where he went in.

But the cold water served to wake him up a bit, sharpening his senses a few clicks, and when he staggered up the other bank he imagined the two killers close to the top of the canyon now. He imagined them chuckling, high-fiving, patting themselves on the back for the fine shot, oblivious to the fact that he'd soon be on them.

Nate charged up the rough foot trail, his knees pumping, his breath coming in labored honks. He strode through the brush from which he was sure the rocket had been fired and paused to turn and look. He could see the top of his cave from there. A curl of smoke came out of it, like a child's drawing of a chimney. He noted a Coors beer bottle that had been tossed aside, as well as a couple of bottle caps in the dirt.

There would be fingerprints. Even DNA left behind. This confused him, but didn't slow him. It made no sense that any of the people from his past who were after him would be so sloppy. The Five were professionals, as he had once been. They wouldn't leave evidence.

Near the top of the canyon, when he could see the rim and the light blue sky with fat-bellied rain clouds scudding across it, he stopped for a moment to catch his breath. It would do no good to be exhausted when he found them. He'd need all his speed and strength to rip their throats out.

They were gone.

He walked unsteadily on the trail, stepping in their footprints to and from the canyon. He saw a spatter of dark blood from one of them beading on the dust and he ground it into the dirt with his heel. Heat shimmered over the sagebrush flat, and he could see the back bumper of their pickup retreating at least a mile away. Dust from the tires still hung in the air.

Nate stood up tall and straddled the trail. He lifted his right arm and placed his left hand beneath the right fist that still clutched Alisha's hair. He pointed his right index finger and cocked his thumb like a hammer and sighted down his forearm. The thumb fell.

He said, "You're dead."

Halfway back down the canyon, Nate sat and put his head in his hands. One of the lone thunderclouds settled over the canyon and plunged it into shadow, and errant raindrops smacked onto the dry ground and freckled the rocks in the trail. He lifted his face to the rain, knowing nothing would ever wash this day away. To Alisha's spirit, he said, "I'm so sorry."

12

Joe Pickett was finishing his statement across the desk from Deputy Sollis in the County Building when Marcus Hand arrived. Dusk painted the windows and, despite the furious activity that had gone on throughout the day, the squad room was oddly silent. Most of the sheriff's department was at dinner, except for Deputy Reed, who was still at the crime scene assisting the DCI forensics crew as well as the crane operators who, as far as Joe knew, were still trying to figure out how to lower The Earl's body from the windmill without dropping it.

Joe's cell phone was backed up with three messages from Marybeth, no doubt wondering what was going on, and he held the phone in his hand as if to alleviate his guilt at not responding sooner. Sollis was a two-fingered typist, and his fingers were as thick as his neck, and they'd spent most of the previous hour going over the circumstances related to the discovery, the climb up the tower, and the condition of The Earl's body that Joe could recall. Every other word Sollis typed, it seemed, was misspelled or wrong, and he was constantly leaping backwards in the text and correcting his errors. When Joe offered to key it in for him, Sollis shot him a murderous glare.

"You say his boots looked big," Sollis said. "What do you mean by that?"

"Centrifugal force," Joe said. "He'd been up there spinning so long and so fast that the fluids in the body were driven toward his extremities . . ."

"So you're a forensic scientist as well," Sollis sneered, rolling his eyes. "I thought you were just the game warden. Turns out you're an expert on centrifical force, too."

"Centrifugal," Joe corrected. "I'd suggest you look it up, but it would take an hour for you to Google it using your sausage fingers."

"Look, buddy," Sollis said, turning in his chair away from his monitor and thrusting his meaty face halfway across the desk, "that's about enough of that crap from the likes of you . . ."

Joe leaned forward as well, fed up, nearly but not quite wanting Sollis to start something, when he noticed the deputy's attention was elsewhere, his tiny eyes squinting over Joe's shoulder.

"This is the sheriff's department," Sollis said over Joe's shoulder. "Can I help you with something?"

The voice that responded was deep and smooth, like thick syrup: "Sir, I'm well aware of my location. I'm also well aware that you currently have a sweet, beautiful, and innocent woman—my client—sitting like a common criminal in your jail. I wish to speak with her immediately. My name is Marcus Hand."

Joe craned around to the criminal defense attorney filling not only the doorframe but somehow the entire room. Marcus Hand was a big man in every respect. He stood six feet four and a half inches, according to the height scale mounted to the left of the door itself, and he had wide shoulders made wider by the shoulder pads of his thigh-length fringed buckskin jacket. Hand had long silver hair that curled up neatly at his collar, and piercing blue wide-set eyes. His face was broad and smooth, his lips rubbery and downturned, his nose large and bulbous on the tip. He wore coal-black jeans, roach-killer ostrich skin cowboy boots, a large silver buckle, a black mock turtleneck under the leather jacket, and a tall black flat-brimmed cowboy hat adorned with a band of small silver and jade conchos. He carried a worn leather coffee-colored pouch that looked more like a saddlebag than a briefcase.

Joe had heard—but couldn't confirm—that on the wall behind Hand's desk in his law office in Jackson there was a rough barn-wood sign burned with:

RATES (PER HOUR)
INNOCENT WYOMINGITES: $1,500
OUT-OF-STATERS: $2,000

"And you are?" Hand said, taking a few steps into the room.

"Deputy Jake Sollis." The answer was quick and weak and, to Joe's ear, surprisingly submissive.

"Deputy Sollis," Hand said, "I wish to speak to my client immediately. As in right now."

Sollis swallowed, intimidated and flushed, and said, "I need to ask Sheriff McLanahan . . ."

"Ask anyone you wish," Hand said, "as long as you do it in the next ten seconds. Because if you keep me from consulting with my client any longer than that, it's the first of many grounds for immediate dismissal of all charges.

"My God," Hand said, raising his arms and modulating his voice even deeper so it sounded more stentorian and God-like to Joe. "You ridiculous people have actually taken into custody—*into custody!*—the grieving widow of a brutally murdered man—the love of her life—and put her on display in the press as if she possibly had something to do with the crime. I'm personally and morally *outraged.* OUTRAGED. *This will not stand, Mr. Sollis.*" The last words were shouted.

The deputy snatched his phone from its stand and fumbled with the buttons. Joe looked from Sollis to Hand.

"And who are you?" Hand asked, still accusatory but slightly less so.

"Name's Joe Pickett. I'm a Wyoming game warden. I found the body."

Hand quieted for a moment, his eyes taking Joe in the way a wolf assesses a calf elk. "I've heard your name before," Hand said in almost a whisper. Then he snapped his fingers with recollection. "You're the one who arrested Governor Budd for fishing without a license! I don't think I've ever laughed so hard as when I read the story in the newspaper. I determined then you were either naïve or a zealot."

"Neither," Joe said. "Just doing my job."

"Ah," Hand said, "one of *those.* But if I recall, you now work for Governor Spencer Rulon. You're his secret agent, of sorts. An unofficial range rider dispatched to do the governor's bidding."

"Not anymore," Joe said.

He had not spoken with Rulon in a year. The governor had taken a liking to Joe several years before and used the machinations of state government to work outside the lines and assign him to locations and give him directives that would have normally been far beyond his scope of work. He'd been the enigmatic governor's point man, a range rider of sorts. Rulon had been in his corner although he'd always maintained an arm's-length distance from Joe, so if Joe screwed up, Rulon could claim ignorance.

But the nasty business that had taken place in the Sierra Madre with the twin brothers the year before had resulted in total and complete silence from the governor's office. Joe had done what he was assigned to do—sort of—but the end result no doubt angered Rulon. Since then, the governor had neither reached out to help nor to manipulate circumstances so Joe would be hurt. And Joe had moved somewhat comfortably back into his role as game warden for the

Twelve Sleep district. But when the phone rang at home or his cell phone danced, he still felt the tingle of anticipation and dread, wondering if would be the governor on the other end.

"We've tangled a time or two," Hand said. "I can't claim we're the best of friends. But this is Wyoming and there aren't enough people around to avoid anyone, so we put up with each other."

"You've defended some guilty folks I wanted to put in prison," Joe said more calmly than he thought capable. "Remember the name Stella Ennis?"

"Remember her?" Hand said, his mouth forming a slight smile. "Those lips! Those legs! I have *dreams* about her. But her husband was found innocent in a court of law."

"He was guilty."

"That's not what the jury concluded, Joe Pickett."

"Nope," Joe said. "You got him off, even though he did it."

"Water under the bridge," Hand said, dismissing the topic with a wave of his hand. "I have no control over inept law enforcement personnel and prosecutors who can't put forth a solid case despite the enormous coercive power and resources of the state. Not that I'm suggesting you're inept, of course. Just not persuasive enough." Then: "So you found the body? Aren't you related to my client in some way?"

Joe nodded. "She's my mother-in-law."

Hand thought that over, and his smile grew larger. Sollis lowered the phone to the cradle and looked up at the lawyer with a whipped expression on his face. "Sheriff McLanahan will be here as soon as he's done with an interview with CNN."

Marcus Hand made an elaborate show of taking that in. He mouthed, "CNN? *National news?* Whatever could your sheriff be telling them?"

"Don't know," Sollis said, looking away.

"Call him back," Hand said, his voice pure cold steel. "Tell your boss if he spends one more second poisoning the jury pool, I'll be up his ass so far I'll be winking at shapely ladies from behind his molars. Got that, deputy?"

Sollis stammered, and his mouth opened and closed like a fish in a tank.

"Call him back," Hand said. "Tell him what I said. Meanwhile, I'm walking across this room into the jail to see my client."

Hand walked in front of the flustered Sollis as the deputy grabbed the phone. The lawyer put a large hand on Joe's shoulder and squeezed. "Where is the best place to stay in this town? I may be here a few days and nights."

Joe shrugged. "Saddlestring doesn't have the kind of accommodations you might be used to. There's the Holiday Inn."

Hand snorted. "What about the ranch house?"

"The Thunderhead Ranch?"

"Of course. I remember going there for some charitable fund-raiser a year ago where I met Earl and Missy Alden. Lovely people. And the view from the front portico was heavenly and reminded me of my own ranch in Teton County. You see, I'm used to waking up to a mountain view. Horses in the pasture and the plaintive mewling of bovines. In my next life, I want to be in charge of scenic cow placement in any meadow I overlook. I find these corny Western settings quite restful. Much more so than a white-bread hotel room with thin plastic cups wrapped in cellophane."

"I guess you'll have to ask your client about staying at her place," Joe said. "And about arranging her cows."

"I surely will," Hand said, patting Joe's shoulder. "So despite our past differences, Mr. Pickett, in this circumstance we're on the same side."

Joe said, "Don't be so sure of that."

After a beat, Marcus Hand threw his head back and laughed.

13

Joe arrived home long after the dinner dishes had been put away, and he sat at the table and filled in Marybeth while she warmed up the leftover spaghetti she'd saved for him. She listened intently, occasionally shaking her head with worry and disappointment, but waited until he was finished with his introduction to Marcus Hand to say, "She couldn't have done it, Joe. She's mean and ruthless and awful, but she couldn't have done it. I want to know who the sheriff got his inside information from. Then we'll know what's really going on."

"Neither Dulcie nor McLanahan would tell me," Joe said. "But it's got to come out soon. They can't withhold the evidence from discovery. Hand will insist on them turning everything over sooner rather than later, especially since they seem to be rushing to press charges. Dulcie seemed pretty confident, and that makes me think. The rumor in the county building is the charges have been written up to be filed, including murder one, and the arraignment will be tomorrow in front of Judge Hewitt."

Marybeth sat down and rested her chin in her hands. "It makes me think, too. And it makes me worry. From what you've told me, it appears Missy has been framed by someone who wanted Earl dead—or wanted to hurt her in the worst possible way. If she did it, would she keep the rifle in her car? Why would she even use that particular gun, since it was so easy to prove it came from Earl's collection? Somebody stole it, shot Earl, and put it in her car for the sheriff to find."

Joe nodded, urging her to continue.

Marybeth said, "My mother doesn't know anything about guns, I don't think. Are they suggesting she actually fired the shot? Are they thinking she carried The Earl's body up a frigging wind tower and hung him by a chain? It's ridiculous."

Joe didn't comment on his wife's use of the word "frigging," but took it to mean it was now an acceptable word in the household.

"No one's saying that," he said. "I think they're assuming she hired a killer or had an accomplice to do the dirty work."

"Who?" Marybeth asked sharply. "And most of all, why? My mother now has everything she's ever schemed for. Why would she blow it like that? It doesn't make any sense, Joe. It doesn't make any sense that the sheriff and Dulcie could be so sure what they're saying will hold up."

Joe agreed.

"My mother is a lot of things," she said. "But she's not a murderer, for God's sake."

"Yes," Joe said. "She's a lot of things."

"Joe."

He got very interested in eating his plate of spaghetti and wanted to change the subject.

"It's quiet in here," he said. "What's going on?" Meaning: *How is April?*

"She's in her room in a huge snit since I took away her cell phone and told her she could use the computer only to do her homework. She acts like if she can't text her friends it's the same thing as being put into solitary confinement. Like we've cut her off from the rest of the world."

He nodded.

"Lucy is trying out for a school play," Marybeth said. "She said one of her friend's moms would bring her home."

"Do either of them know?"

"About Missy?"

"Yes."

Marybeth sighed and shook her head. "I haven't told either one. I was thinking we would have to do it tonight."

Joe said, "We?"

"We. Coming up with the right words, though . . . that will be tough."

"What about Sheridan?"

Marybeth said she'd sent her a text and asked her to call home as soon as she got a chance, but Sheridan had responded with a text of her own saying, "I know, Mom. Everybody knows. Did she do it?"

"And you told her what?" Joe asked.

Marybeth glared at him. "I told her it was all a big mistake."

Lucy and April sat side by side on the living room couch. April smoldered with her arms crossed in front of her and her chin down, upturned eyes like daggers. Joe was distracted by Lucy. She hadn't removed the makeup from the tryouts, and she looked strikingly mature and beautiful. It was as if she'd turned from a girl into a woman in a single night, and he didn't welcome it because he was sure he wasn't the only one to notice the transformation. Looking at her, he envisioned long nights ahead of sitting on his front porch with his shotgun across his knees, keeping high-school boys at bay. He was happy they'd moved so far out of town.

He wondered how they'd take the news. April had never been close to Missy, and Missy regarded her as an interloper. Slightly higher on the food chain than Joe himself, in fact. It was an alliance they shared.

Although Lucy had distanced herself from Missy in the past year, there was absolutely no doubt that Missy preferred her over all the girls. At one time, when Lucy was still vulnerable to her grandmother's charms, Missy had gone through a period where she bought matching outfits for the two of them and took her favorite granddaughter for shopping and long lunches.

"Something terrible happened today," Marybeth said to the girls on the couch.

"You took my phone," April muttered.

Marybeth closed her eyes, fighting back anger. "Much worse than a phone," she said. "Your Grandmother Missy was accused of murdering Earl. They found his body this morning. In fact, your dad found it."

April's mouth shot open involuntarily, then just as quickly she realized that she was baring her feelings and she shut it again. It was as if the Perpetual Mask of Petulance had slipped momentarily. Joe was relieved to see there was still a girl inside vulnerable to such news.

Lucy's eyes were huge. She said, "I got some texts in school asking me about Grandma Missy, but I didn't know what to answer."

"I got no texts," April hissed, "because you people stole my phone."

"It's all been a terrible misunderstanding," Marybeth said, ignoring April.

"You mean Earl isn't dead?" Lucy asked softly.

"No . . . he's gone," Marybeth said. Then she turned to him. "Joe?"

"He was murdered," Joe said. "No doubt about it. Somebody killed him."

"But it wasn't Grandmother Missy?" Lucy asked, looking back and forth from Joe to Marybeth.

"Of course not," Marybeth said. "But she's been accused of it. We don't have all the facts yet, but we think someone made it look like she had something to do with the crime. We don't know who or why. Once everything's investigated, she'll be back home."

"I can't believe it," Lucy said. "Did she stab him or poison him or what?"

"Neither," Marybeth said heatedly.

Joe thought it interesting Lucy made the leap from Earl's death to how Missy would have likely chosen to kill him.

"He was shot," Joe said. "Then hung from a windmill."

"Eeew," April said, making a face.

"This is like a joke," Lucy said. "What will people say about her? What will people think about *us*?"

Exactly, Joe thought.

April snorted and sat back in the couch, her arms still folded across her like an iron breastplate. "Well," she said, "I guess maybe *I'm* not the only one in this *perfect* little family who makes *mistakes*."

Marybeth recoiled, tears suddenly in her eyes. Joe reached out and pulled Marybeth to him and said to April, "I know you're mad, but that wasn't necessary."

"But it's true," April said, narrowing her eyes, looking mean. "Maybe it's time you people learned how to handle the truth."

"Actually," Joe said, "I think we're pretty good at it."

April rolled her eyes, suddenly bored.

"Meeting's over," Joe said. His tone was hard. And effective, since he rarely used it.

April sprang up and marched to her bedroom, smirking and satisfied with herself, but a quick look back at him indicated she thought she might have gone too far.

Lucy got up and walked behind her, slowly, and before she entered her room she said, "If anyone cares, I got the part."

Joe felt as if he'd been punched. They hadn't even thought to ask her about it. Marybeth pulled away from him and said to Lucy's back, "I'm sorry, honey. I've had so much on my mind . . ."

They lay in bed awake, neither speaking. Joe ran through the events of the day in his head, trying to make sense of them. Trying to come up with alternative scenarios to the one most compelling and obvious. Trying to figure out why an innocent woman would be on the telephone to Marcus Hand within minutes of hearing about the death of her husband.

And wondering who had tipped off the sheriff.

Marybeth no doubt had the same thoughts. But there was more. At one point she sighed and said to Joe, "I hope this doesn't tear our family apart."

"Missy?" Joe asked.

"Her, too," Marybeth answered. Then, after a few moments: "I miss Sheridan. It doesn't feel right to go through this with her gone. I want all my girls around me when something like this happens."

"She's not that far," Joe said.

"Yes, Joe. She is."

The phone rang at two-thirty and Joe snatched it up. He was wide awake. Marybeth rolled to her side and arched her eyebrows in a "Who can that possibly be?" look.

"I can't find the bourbon," Marcus Hand boomed. "A bottle of twenty-year-old Blanton's, to be precise. The best bourbon on the planet is what I'm talking about. I gifted one bottle to Earl and asked him to save the other for me when I visited again. I've turned this house upside down and I can't find it. Where do you suppose he hid it?"

Joe said, "I don't know. He's dead."

"I'll find it before the night is over," Hand said, as if he were talking to himself. Then: "The reason I called. I mean, the other reason. Tonight after consulting with my client, I met with the comely Miss Schalk to review the charges and get a lay of the land. Turns out the bulk of the case revolves around information passed to the sheriff from an informant intimately involved with the planning and execution of the crime."

"I knew that," Joe said, swinging his legs out from beneath the covers and sitting up. He could hear Hand rooting around in what sounded like pots and pans.

Hand said, "Apparently, he started talking to the sheriff a couple months ago, telling him this crime was going to happen. McLanahan is thickheaded, as we know, and sort of entertained the guy without ever believing him. Until this morning, when the guy called the sheriff at home and described the murder and the location of the body. And according to the fetching Miss Schalk, the informant is willing to testify against your mother-in-law."

Hand spoke so loudly his voice carried throughout the bedroom from the phone.

Marybeth whispered, "What's his name?"

"What's his name?"

"Damn. I wrote it down." More clanking and clanging. "Where did he hide my Blanton's? Hiding a man's bourbon. This alone would justify shooting him, if you ask me."

"I didn't ask," Joe said, gripping the phone tight. "Can't you remember his name?"

Hand sighed. "Bud something. Kind of a cowpoke name. Missy's ex-husband."

Marybeth heard and gasped.

"Bud Longbrake?" Joe said. "Bud is McLanahan's informant?"

"Yeah, that's the name."

"I can't believe it," Joe said.

"Believe it. That's the name. Of course, I know nothing of this man's credibility. And the Longbrake name is well known here in Twelve Sleep County, so I should have recalled it right away."

"Oh, my God," Marybeth whispered.

"Missy divorced Bud and got his ranch in the settlement," Joe said. "She's had nothing to do with him for two years. She even got a restraining order on him so he wouldn't try to contact her ever again. He's spent the last two years inside a bottle."

"Kind of where I'd like to be right now," Hand said.

Joe said, "Bud has every reason in the world to frame her. She weaseled his third-generation ranch away from him by making him sign a pre-nup he never bothered to read because he was so madly in love. This might blow the case out of the water."

"Maybe," Hand said. "Maybe not. Bud the informant says she tried to get him to kill Earl for her. For a while, he claims he went along with it to draw her out."

Joe shook his head, even though Hand couldn't see him disagree. If that was the situation, there would be phone records tying Bud and Missy together. Maybe even taped calls if in fact Bud was working with the sheriff for a while beforehand.

"One more thing the lovely Miss Schalk said," Hand continued. "She claims The Earl was about to file divorce papers of his own. Do you know anything about that?"

Joe was speechless.

Suddenly, Hand said, "Eureka! I have found it. The key to everything."

"Which is?" Joe asked hesitantly.

"The Blanton's. Earl hid it on the top shelf of his closet. Good night, Joe."

They went over what Hand had said even deeper into the night. Joe agreed with Marybeth that what had seemed fairly clear-cut just a few hours before—a boneheaded frame-up of Missy—was now even more complicated. On the one hand, there was motive if Hand was correct that Earl Alden had decided to leave. But if Missy believed that and wanted to kill Earl, why the elaborate staging? Why would she plot with Bud? Why would Bud trust her? And why would she leave the rifle in her car?

And if Bud Longbrake was the informant, why would he implicate himself as well as Missy? Did he want them both to go down together? Could he possibly be that vindictive? Or did he have a scheme going on the side?

Marybeth said, "Joe, I don't feel I can trust Marcus Hand completely to exonerate her."

"Have you looked at his track record?"

"I know all about it. But Missy isn't well liked and the jury will be local. Bringing him in could backfire for her. He has a reputation for slickness and jury manipulation. Didn't he even write a book about it?"

Joe said he had. It was called *The Eight Percent Rule: A Top Attorney's Foolproof Method for Defending Your Client.* Hand's strategy was to identify at least one juror of the twelve who was most susceptible to partnering up with him and who would to stick it to the system by holding out and refusing to go along with a guilty verdict. Joe had tossed the book aside in disgust.

"And I sure don't trust McLanahan and his crew," Marybeth continued. "He's got everything riding on a guilty verdict. He's put it all out there for everyone to see. If she goes to prison, he wins. If she gets off, he loses. Not only the case but probably the election as well."

Joe nodded. "What about Dulcie Schalk?"

"She's smart and tough," Marybeth said, "but she's never gone up against somebody like Marcus Hand. She's kind of a control freak, as we know. She wants everything in perfect order to proceed. Marcus Hand will make it his mission to throw her off."

Joe shook his head, confused. "Isn't that what you want?"

"No."

"I don't get it, then."

"Joe," she said, setting her jaw, "I don't want her found innocent because Marcus Hand ran rings around Dulcie in court. I want her found innocent because *she didn't do it.* Don't you understand? I don't want this hanging over the heads of our girls. I don't want it hanging over *my* head."

"Mmmm."

"Tell me you understand, Joe."

He let a long stream of air out. "I understand what you're saying."

"Good. Then you have to do what you can to find out what happened. Who did it, and why. The sheriff and Dulcie have tunnel vision. Everything they're doing is based on Missy's involvement. They're not even considering other factors, I'm sure. Joe, you're the only person I absolutely trust to keep an open mind."

He moaned. "I'm a game warden, honey. I'm not the governor's point man anymore. He wants nothing to do with me. After what happened in the Sierra Madre, I made a promise to myself to just do my job as well as I can. No more freelancing."

A smile formed on her lips and her eyes sparkled in the moonlight from the window. She knew him better than he did, sometimes.

"Okay," he said. "In the midst of my day-to-day activities, I'll find out what I can and push it. I'll do what I do best—blunder around until something hits me in the head."

She chuckled at that, then turned serious again. "Joe, what about getting some help?"

He looked away.

"Joe," she said, putting her hand on his bare shoulder. "It's been nearly a year. It's time you called him again. You two have way too much invested to let it be destroyed."

Joe said, "You know what happened."

"I do. And I realize you two together are better than either one of you alone. I swear, you're acting like a couple of schoolgirls. Neither one wants to make the first move to reconcile."

"Men don't reconcile," he said. "We just pretend it never happened and move on."

She kept looking into his eyes. She knew that would work.

"I don't even know where he is," Joe said, grumpy.

"You know where he *was*," she said. "Maybe you can start there."

He sighed deeply and rubbed his eyes. "If this was to get you out of jail, or save Sheridan or Lucy or April . . ."

"Joe, she's my mother."

"Boy, do I know *that*."

She sat up in bed, excited. "We'll work on separate tracks. I'll use library resources to find out what I can about Earl that we obviously don't know. Maybe I can get a lead on someone who wanted him dead in that particular way. It's strange when I think about it: I met the man fifty times, but I know very little about him before he got here. He's made a lot of money over the years. I bet he's made enemies, too."

"No doubt."

"And you'll do what you do," she said.

"Blunder around until something hits me in the head," Joe said sourly.

"A little more enthusiasm would be nice," she said.

He tried to smile. "How about if we figure out who did it, but we keep quiet and she goes to prison? That way, you'll know in your heart she's innocent and you'll be able to sleep at night—but she isn't around here anymore to cause trouble. That way, everybody wins."

"That's not a good solution. At all."

"Had to try," Joe said, kissing her good night as the eastern sky began to blush with dawn.

AUGUST 23

If the wind will not serve, take to the oars.

—Latin proverb

14

The initial appearance for Missy Alden took place in front of Justice of the Peace Tilden Mouton in his closet-like room in an older section of the City/County Building where the air-conditioning didn't reach.

Joe arrived just as Deputy Sollis escorted Missy into the room. Marcus Hand was two steps behind and towered over both of them. If anything, Joe thought, Missy looked worse than she had the day before. Her skin was white and her hair was stringy. Her eyes looked out from the sockets, and her mouth was thin and wrinkled vertically, which reminded Joe of the stitched mouth of an Amazonian shrunken skull. He thought how humiliated she must feel to be in the county jail without her massive bathroom mirrors and makeup.

There were only a dozen chairs in the chambers, and Joe took one nearest the exit. Sissy Skanlon of the *Roundup* took another. They were the only spectators, which surprised Joe. He'd never been present for an initial appearance before, and was taken aback by the informality of the proceedings.

Twelve Sleep County, like several other small Wyoming counties, had retained the JP position. Joe surmised the main reason the county hadn't modernized to a circuit court procedure was because no one wanted to tell Tilden Mouton he no longer had a job. Mouton ran the largest feed store in Saddlestring from a massive complex built by his father, which had been carried forward and expanded upon to sell hardware, sporting goods, and work wear. The building was on the National Historic Register and the single table and chairs across from the counter was the morning gathering place for ranchers and old-timers. Joe loved Mouton Feed and had told Marybeth more than once that everything he ever wanted or needed could be found there. He delighted in the quantity and variety of tools, flies for fishing, and impressive duct tape selection.

Because of Mouton's good-hearted civic activities—sponsoring practically every team, school trip, celebration, and economic development scheme, buying the prize beef and lambs at the county fair, putting full-page ads in the *Roundup*, which practically kept it afloat—the consensus in town was that removing the man from a part-time job he treasured just wasn't worth it to anyone. Tilden was so good-natured and proud of his side job as JP there was no reason to disappoint him by taking away his title. Everyone assumed the position would go away when Tilden Mouton did.

Mouton was short and bald and pear-shaped and looked like a cartoon character. As his belly grew each year, his beltline rose, so his buckle was just a few inches below his chest. He parked his glasses on the top of his head and Joe couldn't ever remember seeing the man actually use them. His eyes were kind and he had a dry humor suffused with awful puns, like stocking duck decoys in the duct tape section. Mouton still personally waited on customers, and would spend as much time as necessary with them that they left satisfied.

So it was uncharacteristic when the JP scowled at both Missy and Hand with naked antagonism as they took their seats behind a scarred table. Joe wondered whether Mouton's ire was directed at Missy, Hand, or both.

Dulcie Schalk was efficient. She recapped the charges and framed the evidence in a tone that was strident, as if she was holding back her true contempt in respect for the court. While Schalk talked, Missy looked off to the side with her chin down, the way a helpless puppy surrendered wounded domination to a larger and more aggressive dog.

It took less than ten minutes. Tilden Mouton nodded, thanked Dulcie Schalk, and looked to Missy and Hand for a reply.

Hand seemed taken aback. He said, "With all due respect, sir, I am still waiting for more. I anticipated hearing from the sheriff who arrested my client, and especially the testimony of the secret witness Miss Schalk mentioned who is testifying against us. All Miss Schalk has done here could have been accomplished by reading the front page of the newspaper."

Joe was confused as well. He thought there might be something new and revelatory in regard to the charges or the evidence.

"The witness isn't available this morning," Dulcie Schalk said, and Joe caught a bit of trepidation catch in her voice.

"Isn't *available*?" Hand said, faux-astonished. "These charges rest almost completely on the testimony of a mystery man, and he isn't *available*?"

"We have plenty of other evidence," Schalk said quickly. "The murder weapon, for example, which was found in the defendant's Hummer."

"This is ridiculous," Hand said, playing to a jury that wasn't there. "The prosecution has sullied the reputation of a pillar of the community and thrown her in jail, but they don't feel it necessary to produce the witness that put her there?"

Joe thought he had a point. Where was Bud?

"Mr. Hand," Mouton said, "I'm aware of you and your reputation. I know you think you can dictate how things will go, because you're a big man in this state and you appear on national television. But that's not how we do things here. We're not trying the case here and now. We're trying to decide if there *is* a case."

Joe thought, *Tilden doesn't like the guy.* Maybe Missy had made a mistake bringing Hand in to defend her.

Mouton wasn't through. He said, "Mr. Hand, let me give you just a little bit of friendly advice while we're here at this very early stage. Phrases like 'pillar of the community' only work if the defendant is in fact a pillar of the community.

"For example," Mouton said, "if the defendant has made choices over the years to acquire large family ranches in the area and immediately put locks on gates that have been used for years by locals, or all but refuse to participate in any of the civic activities within the county because she looks down her nose at them"—he shot a glance Missy's way while he paused—"or has chosen to obtain all of her groceries, hardware, or agricultural supplies from out-of-town firms because she saves a few pennies, well, it is hard to characterize that person as a pillar of the community."

Joe sat straight up in his seat.

"Yes, sir," Hand said.

Joe thought, *It's both of them.*

Tilden Mouton banged a gavel and turned to his assistant and said, to Marcus Hand and Missy, "You are hereby bound over for a preliminary hearing before me this Friday. I've spoken to Judge Hewitt, and he wants this to move along with all due speed. Bail will be set at one million dollars."

"I object, Your Honor," Hand said. "One million dollars is punitive and unnecessary. It suggests my client, this wonderful woman with roots deep in this place, might actually *run away*."

"You don't have to call me 'Your Honor,'" Mouton said. Then: "Your objection is noted and denied."

"Mr. Mouton, I have problems with the amount, but for a different reason," Dulcie Schalk said. "Given the defendant's ability to simply buy her way out of jail *using her dead husband's money*, the county implores you to detain her rather than grant her bail."

"We accept the bail amount, sir," Hand said sheepishly, after a quick conference with Missy where their foreheads were touching, "and I plan to make the proper arrangements so my client will be able to sleep in her own bed by this very evening." He lowered his voice so Joe and Sissy Skanlon had to lean forward to hear. "So she can properly grieve her murdered husband and try to figure out how she'll ever get her life and her reputation back."

Dulcie Schalk sighed and rolled her eyes while Sissy scribbled.

Joe wondered what it would be like to have access to a million dollars within a single afternoon.

"Until Friday," Tilden Mouton said, nodding at Schalk.

As Joe approached his pickup in the parking lot, he heard his name called out. He looked over his shoulder to see Marcus Hand walking toward him in big loping strides. Hand had a bemused look on his face. "That was interesting," he said. "I wish for our case the Aldens had bought more feed and trinkets in town. But that's water under the bridge at this point." He looked at Joe.

"I know you're an honorable fellow," Hand said. "Even Missy says it."

"Good of her," Joe said.

"My understanding is you know Bud Longbrake quite well—is that right?"

"Yup."

"I'm getting the impression our prosecutor doesn't know where he is right now, unless she's more fiendish than she appears and she's got him hidden away somewhere."

Joe shook his head. "She's not like that. Dulcie is a straight shooter."

"Look," Hand said, "my team will be arriving soon from Jackson and I've got PIs on retainer who can tear this little town apart. But it will take a few days to get them settled in and up to speed. Those are days we can't afford if we hope to get an immediate dismissal. If you can determine Bud's location before that and I can get a chance to interview him, well . . ."

Joe acted as if he didn't understand.

"We might be able to kill this thing before it starts," Hand said.

"I don't know why you're telling me this," Joe said.

Hand put a big paw on Joe's shoulder and gazed at him with warmth and sincerity that gave Joe a chill up his spine. "Let's just say if you can help us, it would mean a lot to everybody you know and love," Hand said. "And it would be the *right* thing. From what Missy tells me, that's important to you."

Joe turned for his pickup, and Hand said, "Not to mention it would be worth a lot to the both of us. Missy and me."

Joe climbed in, slid the window down, and said to Hand, "You almost had me until that last bit."

"Oh, darn," Hand said with a mischievous wink.

AUGUST 26

The wind's in the east. . . . I am always conscious of an uncomfortable sensation now and then when the wind is blowing in the east.

—Charles Dickens, *Bleak House*

15

Groggy from lack of sleep and thinking too hard, Joe drove through light rain and fog the eight miles into Saddlestring. The cool dark morning reflected his outlook, so he hoped the sun would break through. The arraignment of Missy was scheduled for 1:00 p.m. in the county building, and he'd agreed to pick up Marybeth at the library so they could attend together.

A major reason for his discomfort was his unease at being on the other side of the legal proceedings. Usually, he was out in the field or going to court to help put a bad guy away—not to try to figure out ways to circumvent law enforcement procedure or the county attorney's charges. In his uniform shirt and state-owned pickup, he felt like a traitor. He didn't like the feeling.

He'd known Bud Longbrake for years as a solid and influential county citizen and rancher first, father-in-law and employer second, and bitter and pathetic alcoholic most recently. The loss of his ranch had devastated Bud, and even more so the loss of Missy, whom he worshipped. Joe was always taken aback how Bud had revered Missy and was blind to her schemes and manipulations. Once, as they drove back to the ranch headquarters in the middle of a sudden blizzard,

Bud had turned to Joe and said he was the happiest man alive. He cited his productive ranch and his beautiful new wife, and confessed that the only thing—the *only* thing—he still wanted was to get his son or daughter interested enough in the place to take it over and keep it running under the Longbrake name.

That was a problem, though. Bud Longbrake Jr. was a thirty-three-year-old college student at the University of Montana in Missoula whose prime interest was performance art on Higgins Street wearing a jester costume inspired by the French court at Versailles. He went by the name "Shamazz" and had had it legally changed. Shamazz's specialty—and he was quite good at it—was satirical pantomime. He also sold drugs and took them. After his second arrest, the judge agreed to remand him to Bud's custody. Bud had taken Shamazz back on the ranch for a while during Junior's (he'd changed his name back by then) probation and tried to get his son on the right track. Joe was between stints with the state at the time, and served briefly as foreman on the Longbrake Ranch. Bud Jr. was assigned as his project. Joe was not successful in getting Bud Jr. interested in cattle, horses, fences, or legacies. Especially not fences. Bud Jr. lasted six months before vanishing on a cold day in November. Three weeks later, Bud Sr. received a postcard sent from Santa Fe asking for money. It was signed "Shamazz."

Bud just couldn't give up on Bud Jr. The old man continued to hold out hope that his son would one day show up clean-shaven in starched Wranglers, boots, and a Stetson and ask, "What needs to be done today, Dad?" Joe couldn't understand what Bud was thinking, but that was before the past year with April. Giving up on a child was now a subject he couldn't broach.

Bud's daughter, Sally, had been severely injured in a car crash in Portland the year before. Thrice married, she'd been an artist specializing in wrought iron, but her injuries prevented her from resuming her career. The news of his daughter's hospitalization, coming just months after Missy changed the locks on the ranch buildings while Bud was buying cattle in Nebraska, sent the man on a downward spiral that was epic.

Despite her actions, Bud still carried a torch for Missy. The meaner she was to him, the more he missed her. Although the restraining order on him prevented any contact with her, she wanted Bud to move away and stop telling his sad story to anyone who would listen from his stool at the Stockman's Bar. Missy was angered when she found out she couldn't obtain a court order to prevent him from speaking her name in vain to strangers and asked Joe for Nate Romanowski's contact details so she could hire the outlaw falconer to put the fear of God into her ex-husband. Joe hadn't obliged.

The last time Joe had seen Bud was the year before, when Bud had wandered into the backyard of their house in town drunk, armed, and confused. Joe and Nate had taken the old man home, and Bud had wept like a child the whole way. He'd said he was ashamed of what he'd become. Joe believed him, and thought Bud might pull himself together at some point.

Now, based on what Marcus Hand had told them, it looked like he had. And not in a good way for Missy.

As far as Joe knew, Bud Longbrake still resided in a rented a two-bedroom apartment over the Stockman's Bar. At least that's where they'd taken him the year before.

Downtown Saddlestring, all three blocks of it, was still sleeping when Joe arrived. The only shop open was Matt Sandvick's taxidermy studio, which *never* seemed to close. And there were always a few pickups around. Joe heard rumors that Sandvick sponsored a nonstop poker game that helped pay the bills during the summer months when there were no carcasses to stuff, but since Sandvick was a craftsman and took pains to have the right taxidermy licenses, Joe didn't bother him.

He cruised down Main Street, passing up empty parking spaces in front of the Stockman's. There were already a few vehicles in front of the bar. Joe drove around the block and turned up the alley that ran behind the row of storefronts. He parked between two Dumpsters in an alcove where his truck couldn't be seen by passersby on the street.

He swung out of his pickup and clamped his worn gray Stetson on his head and took a narrow passage between the old brick buildings that housed the Saddlestring *Roundup* on his left and the bar on his right. The door Bud had used that night was on the side of the Stockman's. Joe avoided kicking empty beer bottles on the ground that would cause attention, and looked in vain on the wall for a buzzer or doorbell. There was neither. Looking around to see if anyone was watching—there was no one—he reached down and tried the latch. It was unlocked.

The door swung inward on moaning rusty hinges, and he stepped inside and closed it behind him. The staircase was dark and close and smelled musty. He let his eyes adjust for a moment until he could locate and flip a dirty light switch, but the bulb above was gone or burned out.

The stairway was narrow, and his shoulders almost brushed the sides as he climbed. He kept his eyes on the landing at the top and his right hand on the grip of his weapon on his hip. He didn't know if the stairs were part of the apartment. As far as he knew, there was only one residence above the bar.

On the landing, to the left, was another door. There was no indication it was the entrance to an apartment. There was no number on it, or name. The door was solid with no window or peephole and was slightly warped from age. Peeling strips of varnish on the surface of the door looked like dozens of stuck-out tongues. Joe cleared his throat, as much to alleviate his nerves as to signal to anyone inside he was out here. Then he rapped on the door three times, hard and businesslike.

"Bud, it's Joe. Are you in there?"

He heard no response or movement inside.

"Bud? Are you in there?" He knocked again sharply, hurting his knuckles.

Nothing.

Joe put his hands on his hips and stared at the door, as if willing it to open. He'd considered calling ahead to see if Bud was there, but had decided against it. He'd learned in investigations over the years that it was almost always more productive to arrive without warning. Catching a suspect off-guard sometimes resulted in surprise admissions of guilt or bouts of dissembling that contained the truth inside. One of Joe's tricks was simply to knock on a door and introduce himself by saying, "I suppose you know why I'm here?" and let them talk. At least a dozen times over the years, people alluded to crimes Joe hadn't even been aware of until he asked that question.

But he couldn't ask Bud because there was no response.

He started to turn to leave, but couldn't help himself and tried the doorknob. Locked. Meaning it was possible Bud was inside, maybe sleeping off a late night. Maybe sick. Maybe hurt. Maybe . . .

Joe leaned closer to the door. Because of the darkness in the hallway, he could see a ragged line of light between the door and the doorjamb. Although it was locked, the seal wasn't tight and he could see there was no lock bolt, only the dead latch on the knob itself. And because of the gap in the door, the dead latch barely caught the strike plate. Joe wasn't surprised. Ranchers—or ex-ranchers, in Bud's case—didn't think a lot about security and locks. That's why they surrounded themselves with dogs and guns.

In one move, Joe grasped the knob with both hands and jerked up on it and pushed against the door with his shoulder. It opened. He stepped back and to the side to peer through the inch-wide opening. It was light inside, but not bright. He could see the corner of a rug on a hardwood floor, an empty beer bottle on its side under the edge of a couch, and a spatter of dark liquid flecked across the floor.

Thinking *blood*, Joe nudged the door open all the way with his hand on his weapon, ready for anything.

Nothing happened when the door creaked open. Bud wasn't on the floor or on the couch, although Joe could see the sag of the cushions where he'd no doubt spent a lot of time.

He stepped inside the apartment, squinting, all senses turned full on. The place smelled of old grease, dust, sour beer, and Copenhagen chewing tobacco.

The muted light was a result of the morning sun painting the floor through paper-thin yellow blinds that were pulled all the way down. The windows overlooked Main Street. He took a few steps and squatted to get closer to the floor, careful not to let his boot tips touch the spots. As he observed the scene, he let out a long breath. The spots were black and old, maybe paint, oil, or shoe polish.

A coffee table in front of the couch was littered with beer bottles, a spit cup for tobacco juice, and several thick bound manuals stacked one on top of the other. Not books, but bound documents. The top one had several round stains on it where beer bottles had been places. The cover read WIND POWER PROJECT ECONOMICS: SATISFYING THE WORLD'S GROWING DEMAND FOR POWER REQUIRES A BALANCED PORTFOLIO OF ENERGY OPTIONS. Joe nudged it aside to look at the others. A LAND RUSH IN WYOMING SPURRED BY WIND POWER and COMMERCIAL WIND ENERGY DEVELOPMENT IN WYOMING: A GUIDE FOR LANDOWNERS. Written in a shaky longhand scrawl on the cover of the last document was the name *Bob Lee.*

Joe said, "Huh?" Again, he called, "Bud?"

Nothing. Joe checked the kitchen to his left. There was a stack of dirty plates in the sink, and a half piece of toast on the counter. A half-empty carafe of coffee sat inside a Mr. Coffee setup, and Joe reached out and touched the glass. Cold. In the refrigerator there was a half-gallon carton of milk and four bottles of Miller Lite beer. Joe opened the carton and sniffed. Not spoiled yet.

Bud never used to be like this, Joe thought. He recalled Bud's immaculate tool sheds on the ranch, with every tool wiped down and in its proper drawer in the industrial tool chests. Bud didn't even allow oily rags tossed on the garage floor or workbench. And his horse tack was hung neatly and symmetrically in his barn, small saddles to the left, large ones to the right.

Joe entered the bathroom. Dirty gray towels hung from a rod. Joe touched them. Dry. The garbage can overflowed with crumpled tissues. He opened the medicine cabinet. Although there were a half-dozen pill bottles for various ailments and the labels said "LONGBRAKE," there was no toothbrush or toothpaste and the other shelves were empty. Meaning it was likely Bud had packed up his essential medicines and toiletries to take with him.

Joe confirmed his theory as he made his way through the apartment. Although there were still clothes in the closet, there were large gaps in the hanging garments, like he'd taken some. The covers on the bed had been pulled up over the pillows but not tucked in, as if he'd made the bed in haste.

Joe thought about the milk and the coffee. The piece of toast was dry, but not hard. Bud hadn't been gone long. Joe guessed the old rancher had left the day before, after breakfast. At about the time Joe was climbing the wind tower . . .

Outside on the street, Joe heard two car doors slam almost simultaneously in a percussive double-tap. He covered the living room floor in a few steps and carefully pushed the edge of the window shade to the side so he could see out.

A sheriff's department SUV had taken a space recently vacated by one of the early-morning cowboys directly below the window. Sheriff Kyle McLanahan stood on the passenger side of the vehicle, hands on hips, waiting impatiently for Deputy Sollis to adjust his hat and aviator sunglasses in the side mirror on the driver's side. Joe smoothed the shade back before either the sheriff or the deputy glanced up and saw him.

He walked as quietly as he could toward the open door and got to it as a series of heavy knocks shook the ground floor entrance door. Sollis shouted, "Bud Longbrake? You in there?"

They planned to come up.

Joe took another quick look outside in the hallway to make sure there wasn't another door he could escape through. There wasn't. He was trapped in Bud's apartment and the only way out was down the stairs the sheriff and deputy were about to come up.

The uncomfortable feeling he'd had that morning bloomed into full-fledged guilt and dread. Technically, he'd entered a private residence without a warrant, and officially he had no reason to be there. He could even be charged with breaking and entering since he'd forced the door open. Although he didn't know where Bud was or why he was gone, Joe could imagine the sheriff adding on charges and framing the incident as an attempt to hide or destroy evidence, or saying the reason Joe was there in the first place was to intimidate or tamper with the key prosecution witness.

Which wasn't all that far from the truth, he thought. Although from his standpoint, he simply wanted to ask Bud if he'd really been the informant. And why.

Joe hesitated for a second before shutting the door. He considered greeting the sheriff on the way down with a story about trying to find his ex-father-in-law. But why, if it wasn't related to the case? Joe was the lousiest liar he knew, and he just couldn't do it.

At that instant, Sollis opened the door downstairs and Joe started to ease Bud's door closed. The hinges moaned again, but he hoped the sound was drowned out by Sollis himself, who was telling the sheriff, "Damned if it wasn't open. Now where's his place? Top of the stairs?"

Feeling sweat bead beneath his hatband, Joe eased the door shut and prayed the dead latch would spring back and catch again in the switch plate without a sound. He heard a dull click as it locked, and he let out a long ragged breath and stepped back.

He looked around Bud's apartment. Would he try and hide? Did the sheriff have permission to enter? A key?

The voices of the sheriff and deputy rose as they climbed the stairs. Once they made the landing, Joe recognized McLanahan's labored breathing.

"Well, knock, damn it," the sheriff said between gulps of air.

Joe waited, facing the door.

Sollis pounded on the door so hard Joe's heart raced. He wondered if the sheer force of the deputy's blows would open the door again.

"Bud Longbrake?" Sollis shouted. "You in there? This is Deputy Sollis and Sheriff McLanahan from the Twelve Sleep County Sheriff's Department. The county attorney wants you to move to a safe place until you testify."

Joe tried to keep his breath calm and to stay quiet. Did they have a warrant to enter? If so, he was doomed.

"Too much information," McLanahan admonished his employee in a low growl. "Just get him to open the damn door."

More fierce pounding. It rattled the empty bottles on the coffee table. Joe watched the doorknob assembly, just waiting for it to give way.

"Bud, open the door," Sollis boomed. Then, after a beat, his voice not as direct, "I don't think he's in there, boss."

"Then where the hell is he?"

"How would I know?"

"Jesus—if we lost him . . ."

"I could force it," Sollis said. "This lock don't look like much. We could say we heard something inside and thought he might be injured or something."

"That would give us PC," McLanahan said, but by the tone of his voice he wasn't encouraging Sollis to do it. Yet.

"Naw," McLanahan said after a few seconds. "If we damage the door and he isn't in there, it'll look bad. We can be back here with a warrant in an hour and open it up. But I think you're right—he isn't home."

"Then where is he?" Sollis asked.

"You dope," McLanahan said. "I just asked you that question. You think I've got an answer between a minute ago and now?"

"No, boss."

"Holy hell in a handbasket."

Joe took a deep relieved breath and let it out through his nose.

"Tell you what," McLanahan said. "You stay here in case he shows up. I'll call the county attorney and get the warrant going and bring it back."

Joe thought it interesting that Bud had left without informing the sheriff.

The sheriff's boots descended the stairs. After a beat, the sheriff called up to his deputy, "We've got to find that son-of-a-bitch, and fast. Without him, we're up shit creek without a paddle."

"Ten-four," Sollis said.

Joe waited ten minutes. He thought Sollis might disobey orders or let his curiosity get the best of him and force the door open himself. If he did . . . Joe didn't know what the hell he'd do if he did. Remarkably, Sollis stayed out. Joe could hear the deputy sigh with boredom, then tunelessly hum the melody for "I've Got Friends in Low Places." Joe tiptoed back into Bud's bedroom and shut the door. He went to the farthest corner and dug his cell phone out of his pocket and called 9-1-1.

When the emergency dispatcher answered, he mumbled, "Hey, I just left a game at Sandvick's and some old rancher was there raising hell. I think something's wrong with him and you need to send somebody."

"Please identify yourself," the dispatcher said coldly. Joe recognized her voice. He hoped like hell she didn't recognize his.

"Ain't important," Joe said. "Just tell the cops Bud Longbrake is gonna get himself hurt if he doesn't learn to watch his mouth." And with that, he shut the phone.

Joe went back to the door and listened. A minute later, he heard Sollis' radio sputter to life. The dispatcher relayed what he'd told her. She referred to Joe as "an unknown party."

Sollis said, "Sandvick's? That's right up the street from where I am now."

"Should I send backup?"

Sollis snorted. "I can handle that old coot. Just let the sheriff know we've got our man."

With that, Sollis' boots thundered down the stairway.

Joe again crossed the room and parted the blinds. The deputy was crossing Main Street on foot, stopping a car on the street with his outstretched palm while talking on his radio. Sollis reached the sidewalk on the other side of the street and strode purposefully up the block toward Sandvick's Taxidermy. As he did, he watched his own official reflection in the glass of the retail stores.

Joe let himself out and let the door latch behind him.

16

Joe gathered himself up, fitted his hat on tight, and strolled out of the passageway onto the sidewalk. The morning sun was burning off the fog and the clouds were dissipating. Even in town, the air smelled of pine and fragrant sage from the light rain that morning. It would likely be a nice day after all. He wished he didn't feel so proud of himself for his deceptive maneuvers.

Buck Timberman was behind the bar wearing reading glasses and working on a liquor order when Joe walked into the Stockman's. Timberman was in his eighties, but was still an imposing presence. A lean and ropey six-foot, Timberman was a half-blind former basketball and rodeo team coach who took over the bar on retirement twenty-five years before and hadn't missed a day since. The barman was stoic and soft-spoken and was everybody's friend because he never made a public judgment or offered an opinion on anything. When customers rattled on about one thing or another—water rights, guns, dogs, neighbors, politics, sports—Timberman nodded slightly as if he agreed and went about his business. Joe had always admired the man.

"Buck," he said by way of greeting. He sat down on a stool and put his hat crown-down on the bar next to Timberman's order form.

"Joe," Timberman said. "Coffee?"

"Please."

"Black?"

"Yup."

Timberman poured and went back to his order. Joe checked out the early-morning clientele. Ranch hands, mostly, four of them clustered at the far end of the bar sipping red beer. Keith Bailey, an imposing ex–highway patrolman who worked part-time manning the entrance gate to the exclusive Eagle Mountain Club resort up on the hill, eyed Joe with a suspicion born of decades of open-road encounters. Joe nodded toward him and Bailey nodded back. An older couple were in the back in a high-backed booth, talking softly and holding hands across the table, likely making up after an argument. The Stockman's Bar opened at seven in the morning. The tradition had started eighty years before, when local ranchers and cowboys wanted a beer or two after calving all night, or a red beer (tomato juice, Tabasco, and draft) to nurse a hangover.

"How you been, Buck?" Joe asked, after blowing on the coffee. The coffee was hot but weak, little more than tinted water. Timberman didn't want to encourage his customers to drink coffee, particularly.

"Getting on."

"Business good?"

"All right, I guess."

Joe smiled. The rumor was Buck Timberman was one of the wealthiest men in Twelve Sleep County. He worked long hours, spent little, took care of his customers, and bought and stockpiled gold with the profits. Little of his money was spent on new clothing. Timberman wore his usual faded cowboy shirt and frayed red suspenders.

"I'm wondering about my ex-father-in-law, Bud Longbrake," Joe said. "Has he been in recently?"

Timberman gestured toward an empty stool two spaces away from Joe.

Joe waited for more, but Bud went back to his figures. That was it.

"Buck?"

"That's his stool," Timberman said, indicating a space next to Keith Bailey. "He enjoys his bourbon."

Joe nodded. "I was wondering if he'd been in lately."

Timberman shrugged, as if he wasn't sure. Then said, "Most days."

"Was he here yesterday?"

Timberman placed the tip of his finger on a scrawl so he wouldn't lose his place, and looked up. "Don't think so. Day before, maybe."

"When does he come in? I mean, what time of day?"

Timberman's face told Joe nothing beyond what he said, which was, "He's usually here by now."

"So you haven't seen him this morning?"

Timberman shook his head. He nodded toward Bailey, who shrugged as well.

"That's unusual, isn't it?"

"Could be."

Joe sighed and smiled. This is why everyone trusted Buck Timberman.

Joe leaned in toward the barman, speaking very low. "Did Bud talk a lot about his ex-wife Missy?"

Timberman looked away, but nodded almost imperceptibly. He didn't want the cowboys at the end of the bar to see him answering the game warden's questions. Now Joe understood.

"You heard what happened, right?"

Another nod.

"Do you think Bud hated her so much he'd try to pin something on her?"

Timberman shrugged noncommittally.

Joe said, "I'm not asking you to tell me something I'd ask you to repeat in court. I'm just trying to sort things out for myself. I know

Bud to be a kind man, but pretty mule-headed at times. He'd focus on things until they got done. I remember when I worked for him, he'd bring up the same section of loose fence at breakfast every day to his ranch hands until I'd go out and fix it myself just to shut him up. I'm wondering if he was focused on getting back at Missy."

"He did have some choice things to say about her from time to time," Timberman conceded.

"Me, too," Joe said.

Timberman reacted to that with a slight smile—no more than a twin tug up on the corners of his mouth.

"Word is," Joe said, "Bud's the star witness for the prosecution."

Timberman said, "Hmmmm." Then: "Maybe I ought to cut down on my Jim Beam order. I might not be pouring as much in the next few weeks."

Joe finished his coffee. "Did Bud ever talk about wind turbines?"

Timberman looked up, puzzled. "Everybody does these days."

Joe sighed. This was hard work getting anything out of Buck Timberman. "Did he seem to have any opinion of them either way?"

"Not that I can recall. More?" Timberman asked, chinning over his shoulder toward the pot.

"You've got more?" Joe said, not meaning coffee.

"Not really."

"Then I'm fine."

Joe slid off the stool and put a five on the bar.

"Don't worry about it," Timberman said, waving at the bill as if trying to get it out of his sight.

Joe left it, and said, "If you see him, give me a call, will you? My wife is pretty concerned about what's going on."

The slight nod. Then, "He lives upstairs. I've rented the rooms to him for a while. He pays in cash and on time, and there haven't been any complaints."

"Does he entertain guests?" Joe asked.

"Not that I've ever noticed."

"No one recently, then?"

"No, sir."

"Thanks for the coffee, Buck."

"Anytime, Joe."

Joe hesitated before opening the door to go outside. He glanced up the street, to see Deputy Sollis striding back angrily from Sandvick's Taxidermy, barking on his radio.

"One thing," Buck Timberman said softly, and Joe realized he was talking to him.

Joe turned and raised his eyebrows in surprise. Timberman had left his order on the counter and stood in the crook of the bar close to Joe and as far away from the four cowboys as possible.

"Nice-looking lady in here a week ago. She and Bud seemed to get on pretty well. She said her name was Patsy. Don't remember a last name."

Joe shook his head, not following.

"Before she met Bud, she asked me if I knew where she could find your friend."

Joe felt his scalp tighten. "Nate Romanowski?"

"That's the one," Buck said.

"What did you tell her?"

"Nothing. There's nothing to tell as far as I'm concerned."

Joe nodded. Then he got it. "You said she got along with Bud, though. Think she asked him about Nate?"

"Couldn't say for sure," Timberman said, but Joe could read between the lines.

"Interesting," Joe said. "Will you let me know if Patsy comes back?"

Timberman nodded his slight nod before turning and going back to his order form. Cutting down on his order of Jim Beam.

Justice of the Peace Tilden Mouton held the preliminary hearing. After a recap of the charges and the evidentiary testimony by Sheriff McLanahan but without an appearance by Bud Longbrake, Mouton bound Missy over for arraignment before Judge Hewitt on Monday.

AUGUST 27

Funeral by funeral, theory advances.

—Paul A. Samuelson

17

The funeral for Earl Alden took place at the Twelve Sleep County Cemetery on a warm still morning. It was a small affair.

Joe wore his dark suit and stood with Marybeth, April, and Lucy in the sun. As the Rev. Maury Brown read the eulogy about a man he'd never met, Joe felt a drip of sweat snake down his spine beneath his shirt. He looked up and took in the scene around them.

The cemetery took up ten acres on the top of a hill west of Saddlestring. From where they stood, he could see the cottonwood-choked river below them, the town itself, and the Eagle Mountain Club perched on a bluff on the other side of the river. Insects burred in the turf, and while he was looking, a big grasshopper landed on the top of the casket with a thump. The air was ripe with pollen and the dank smell of dug-up dirt. A massive granite monument had been delivered to the site on a pallet. It was nearly as high as the large tarped mound of fresh dirt it sat next to.

Missy stood across from the casket and the hole in the ground. Small and black and veiled, she was flanked by Marcus Hand on one side and Sheriff McLanahan on the other. After the funeral, she'd be returned home on bail. A small knot of ranch hands and construction workers from the Thunderhead Ranch stood together apart from the other mourners. Joe wondered if they were there to pay their respects or to find out when and if they'd get their last paychecks.

He didn't hear much of what Rev. Brown said. Instead, he observed Missy. Her veil hid her face and he couldn't tell if she was crying, she seemed so still.

When the Rev. Brown turned to her and cued her to toss a handful of dirt on the casket that had been poised over the hole, Joe heard Missy say, "No thank you."

On their way down a dirt pathway to the parking lot, Marybeth said how odd it was to attend the funeral for a man she barely knew, and she wondered aloud why members of Earl's extended family hadn't shown up.

Joe shrugged, wondering the same thing himself.

"I'd like to know how much that monument set Missy back," Joe said. "It'll be the tallest thing in the cemetery now."

April and Lucy argued about where they wanted to go eat since it was Saturday and lunch out had been the incentive offered to attend the funeral.

"I couldn't tell," he said. "Was your mother crying?"

"Who knows?"

Joe reached out and found Marybeth's hand and squeezed it. As he did, he heard a motor start up in the parking lot.

He looked up to see a boxy old-model yellow van back out of a space unnecessarily fast and race away.

"Who was that?" Marybeth asked Joe.

"I'm not sure. I thought I saw two people in the front, but I couldn't see their faces."

"I wonder if they were coming to the funeral and got here late. It would have been nice to have a few more mourners."

"Yup," Joe said, watching the van descend over the hill as if it were being chased by bees.

AUGUST 29

You cannot make a wind-mill goe with a paire of bellowes.

—George Herbert

18

Joe escorted Marybeth up the stone steps of the Twelve Sleep County Courthouse for the arraignment of her mother in the courtroom of Wyoming District Judge Hewitt. The building had been erected of rough granite blocks and topped with a marble dome in the 1880s, and it reflected the original grandiosity of what the town was predestined to become but never did. Joe opened the heavy door for her.

"Your mom isn't the first celebrity tried here," he said. "Big Nose Bart was found guilty here back in the range war days. Lots of Old West outlaws were tried here. Most of them found innocent."

"Joe," Marybeth said with exasperation, "my mother is not an outlaw."

"Sorry," he said. "Just trying to provide some historical perspective."

"That doesn't help," she said. "My colleagues at the library tiptoe around me like there was a death in the family."

"There was," Joe said, before he could catch himself.

She turned on him. "You are *not* being helpful. What I mean is, good people don't know how to act around me. I don't know how to act around me, either. Do I go about my business as if my mother wasn't accused of murder, or do I walk around with my head down, ashamed?"

Joe reached out and stroked her cheek. "Keep your chin up," he said. "You've got nothing to be ashamed of."

She nodded and thanked him with her eyes. "Which way?" she said. "I've never been in this building before."

Judge Hewitt was small, dark, and twitchy. He'd been a judge for seventeen years and Joe appreciated Hewitt's lack of pomposity and almost manic insistence on a fast, no-nonsense pace in his courtroom. He was known for cutting off long-winded questions and statements and ordering lawyers to get to the point. He often asked especially verbose attorneys, in front of the jury and their clients, "Are you being paid by the word?"

Joe and Marybeth entered the courtroom. It was narrow and ancient with a high stamped-tin ceiling and the acoustics were hollow and awful. The pine-paneled walls were covered by old paintings depicting 1940s versions of local Western history: politically incorrect renderings of Indian massacres filled with dripping scalps and war paint, cavalry charges, grizzly bear hunts, powwows, covered wagons loaded with cherubic children. Joe was intimately familiar with each and every one of them since he'd spent so much time over the years in the room waiting to testify in game and fish violation cases. Joe disliked being inside courtrooms nearly as much as hospitals, and always felt uncomfortable, constrained, and false when he was inside either.

"There she is," Marybeth whispered, almost to herself.

Joe looked up. Missy sat in the first row on the left side with her back to them, next to the broad buckskin-covered shoulders of Marcus Hand. Missy had her hair up in a matronly bun and was wearing a light print dress. The effect, Joe thought, was that she looked older than her age. He was shocked.

He wondered if Hand had coached her. After all, she'd been at home on the ranch for a week since she made bail, sharing the rambling mansion with Hand and his team of attorneys, paralegals, and investigators. She'd had plenty of time to regroup since the arrest and to work on her appearance, to work her magic. But for those without that knowledge, it looked as though she'd thrown on a dress minutes before court in her jail cell and had been denied makeup or a mirror.

On the other side of the aisle, Dulcie Schalk studied notes on a legal pad. She wore a dark business suit with a skirt and black flats. Sheriff McLanahan lounged next to Schalk, arm flung back over the bench, chin up, and looking smarmy and bored, Joe thought.

Four people stood in front of the bench as Judge Hewitt glared down at them. The two men in the middle were in orange jumpsuits and boat shoes. They had long black hair and dark skin. Joe recognized them as Eddie and Brent Many Horses, Eastern Shoshones from the reservation. They'd been long-distance runners in high school and he'd checked their fishing licenses more than once. Bookending the Many Horses was public defender Duane Patterson on their left, and Dulcie Schalk's deputy county attorney Jack Pym on their right.

"What's going on?" Marybeth whispered to Joe, as they found a seat several rows back from her mother.

"Arraignment day," Joe whispered back. "Judge Hewitt likes to do them one after the other each Monday. The Many Horses brothers are accused of stealing cars and dealing meth. Your mother is next in line."

"My God," Marybeth whispered, shaking her head. "This is too unbelievable."

Joe sat back and took in the scene. Everyone, with the exception of the Many Horses brothers and their counsel, was waiting for the next event. Jim Parmenter and Sissy Skanlon sat amidst a cluster of a half-dozen reporters from various newspapers, radio and television stations. Several of McLanahan's deputies, including Sollis, took over the seats directly behind Dulcie Schalk and the sheriff behind the prosecution table. A dozen or so local busybodies Joe usually saw clustered around coffee cups at the Burg-O-Pardner and the diner were scattered through the court, simply out of curiosity, he assumed. This was certainly a different feel from the initial appearance, and the gravity of the situation struck him. No doubt, he thought, Missy noticed it, too.

"She's looking back," Marybeth whispered.

Missy had turned in her seat to assess the courtroom crowd and her eyes searched slowly through the room until they found Joe and Marybeth. "She sees us," Marybeth said.

There were dark circles under her eyes and her skin looked like parchment. She looked so sad, so small, so . . . *wronged.*

Marybeth clenched her fist in a "stay strong" gesture, and Missy smiled sadly and nodded. When she turned back around, Marybeth said to Joe, "I've never seen her look worse. How can anyone think she was capable of what she's accused of?"

Joe thought, *Exactly.*

Judge Hewitt whacked his gavel and set a trial date for the Many Horses brothers. The brothers and their attorney shuffled out in their boat shoes, throwing suspicious glances at the growing crowd in the courtroom who weren't there for them.

"Next," Hewitt said, glancing down at his schedule. "Twelve Sleep County versus Missy Alden on the charge of conspiracy and first-degree murder."

Marybeth grasped his arm with both of her hands at the words.

"Showtime," Joe muttered to Marybeth.

Dulcie Schalk looked young, sharp, athletic, and competent, Joe thought, as she ran through the charges for Hewitt. She outlined the county's case with devastating brevity.

"Your Honor," she said, standing and holding her legal pad in front of her but barely glancing at it, "the county charges the defendant, Mrs. Alden, of deliberately murdering her fifth husband, Earl Alden. Mr. Alden was about to file divorce proceedings against her, which would have left her without the majority of the financial empire she'd worked so long and hard to obtain. We will prove beyond a reasonable doubt that Mrs. Alden, upon learning of the pending divorce proceedings, actively engaged in the pursuit of hiring a killer to carry out her plan. And we know this, Your Honor, because a man who was asked to pull the trigger will tell us so. He'll also testify that when he was unwilling to commit the murder on the defendant's behalf, the defendant did it herself. Our witness is working closely with the county and he's been fully cooperative. He's agreed to become a state's witness and testify against her. We have phone records to prove communications between Mrs. Alden and the murderer-for-hire. We have the murder weapon and forensic evidence to prove it. And we will establish both motive and opportunity."

Schalk paused to turn and point her finger at Missy at the next table. Joe followed her gesture and found Missy's reaction discordant with the buildup. Missy looked demurely at the county attorney, moisture in her eyes. Her lips trembled. Despite his inclinations, Joe's heart went out to her.

Schalk continued, "The people ask that the defendant"—she looked down at her pad—"Missy Wilson Cunningham Vankueren Longbrake Alden—be tried for these charges and punished to the full extent of the law."

There were several gasps from spectators, as well as a whistle of satisfaction. Joe doubted most of the spectators in the courtroom were fully aware of Missy's track record, and had certainly never heard the names of all of her ex-husbands strung together like that. It was a bit of theater that appeared to have worked. Sheriff McLanahan turned in his seat and glowed, basking in the reaction and by doing so taking credit for it. Marybeth's grip on Joe's arm had become vise-like, and he could no longer feel the fingers on his left hand.

"First things first, Miss Schalk," Hewitt said, showing a cool edge of annoyance. "You seem to be getting ahead of yourself."

He raised his eyebrows and took in Missy and Marcus Hand. Joe noticed a softening in the judge's features when he beheld Missy, and it surprised Joe that Missy's appearance and demeanor had created the desired effect even on the judge.

"Mrs. Alden," he asked softly, "how do you plead to the charges?"

It hung out there for a moment while neither Missy nor Hand responded. Then, as if so filled with disgust that the mere effort of standing seemed to demean him, the attorney rose and slowly swung his shaggy buffalo head at Dulcie Schalk. Joe could see him in profile, and it appeared the skin of his face had been drawn back in pure white rage.

"Mrs. Alden?" Hewitt prompted. "What say you?"

Missy looked up at Hand in expectation. Hand continued to glare at Schalk. Schalk responded by looking away, but Joe could tell she was a little taken aback. He thought, *Marcus Hand starts to earn his money now.*

Finally, after a full minute of tense silence, and as Hewitt craned forward and his eyes narrowed in annoyance, Hand's voice rumbled out low and contemptuous. "We reject this outrageous frame-up and plead not guilty to each and every charge the county attorney has filed and every charge against my client she and Sheriff McLanahan may dream about filing in the future."

Hewitt blinked, then regained his footing. "Mr. Hand, that will be the last of your stage performances for the remainder of this trial."

Hand said defensively, "Your Honor—"

"Can it," Hewitt said. "Save it for the jury. Mrs. Alden, do you concur with your attorney's statement?"

"Yes, Your Honor," Missy said, in a little-girl voice Joe had heard her use addressing his young daughters. "I'm not guilty of anything. I loved Earl."

Hewitt waved the last sentence away and struck his gavel. He narrowed and focused on Dulcie Schalk. "Miss Schalk, the county seems to have its ducks in a row and you appear to be chomping at the bit to proceed. Is there any good reason not to move along to scheduling at this point?"

"Your Honor?" Schalk said, with a catch in her voice.

"You heard me," the judge said. "And I've heard enough from you. You seem to think you've got evidence and witnesses lined up. I see no reason to drag this out, do you?"

"No, Your Honor . . ."

"Pardon the court," Hand said, looking around the room as if he couldn't believe what was happening, "but once again Miss Schalk and the county have made damning allegations against my client based upon a mystery man they've not produced. While I've no doubt Miss Schalk is the most honorable county prosecutor in the land, I find it hard to believe that we will attempt an accelerated schedule when the star witness has yet to show his face and take the oath and attempt to condemn my client to a prison cell in Lusk or a lethal injection with a needle."

Schalk rolled her eyes when he said "needle."

"Miss Schalk?" Hewitt said. "Mr. Hand has a point."

"He'll be here, the witness," she said, faltering for a moment. "He'll be here to testify. And for the record, we haven't announced if we'll seek the death penalty."

"So where is he now?" Hewitt asked.

"Attending to personal matters," she said. "We expect him back within days."

"Personal matters?" Hand said, shooting a glance at Joe, then turning to Hewitt. "This is the first we've heard of this. If one were suspicious or a cynic, one might come to the conclusion that the prosecution is hiding the witness away until they can spring him on the court without notice."

Schalk's face flushed red. "I can assure you that's not the case," she said. "We're ready to proceed."

Hewitt nodded and thumped the heel of his hand on his desk for emphasis. "That's good," he said. "That's what I wanted to hear. The defendant is hereby remanded for trial to begin on September twelfth, two weeks from today. Jury selection will begin that Monday morning."

Marcus Hand quickly folded his arms across his chest as if to prevent his hands from reaching out and throttling Judge Hewitt. He said, "Two weeks, Your Honor? Is this a major murder trial or are we scheduling a track meet?"

Hewitt let that echo through the courtroom—there were a couple of sniggers—then turned his full attention back to Hand.

"No, Mr. Marcus Hand, famed criminal defense attorney and bestselling author, this is not a track meet and this is not Teton County or Denver or Hollywood or Georgetown. This is Twelve Sleep County, and this is my courtroom."

Hand took a deep breath and let his arms drop, fully cognizant of the fact he'd angered the judge. He shuffled his feet, recalcitrant, and looked down at the floor.

"It seems to me, Mr. Hand, if your client is as wrongly accused as you claim and as innocent as you insist, that you'd want to clear her as quickly as possible and let her go home for good. Why you'd want to let her twist in the legal wind for weeks and months is something that doesn't strengthen your position. And if the charges are as shallow and contemptible as you indicate, you should want nothing more than an opportunity to quickly disprove them. Am I missing something?"

"No, Your Honor," Hand said. "It's just that I want to present the best possible defense. We've yet to see all the evidence gathered by the prosecutor, or had a chance to interview their so-called star witness . . ."

"You heard her—you'll have all that," Hewitt said. "Miss Schalk, turn everything over without any further delay and make the statements of your witness available to the defense. Got that?"

Hewitt turned to Hand. "Any motions?"

Hand made a motion to dismiss the case. Hewitt laughed, denied it, and asked if there were any others. Joe expected Hand to open his briefcase and produce a dozen motions to delay the trial or make Dulcie Schalk's life a living hell.

"No motions, Your Honor," Hand said.

Joe sat back, perplexed.

"So we're set," Hewitt said.

Schalk nodded, then followed with a weak "Yes, Your Honor."

Marybeth talked briefly with Missy and Marcus Hand after the proceeding was recessed, while Joe went into the hallway to wait. The bailiff, an ex–rodeo cowboy nicknamed Stovepipe, sauntered from behind the metal detector he manned into the courtroom and grinned at Joe.

"He's something, ain't he?" Stovepipe said.

"Moves things right along," Joe said.

Stovepipe switched a toothpick from the left side of his mouth to the right in a deft move. "I get the impression that celebrity lawyer from Jackson might not know what hit him."

"He knows," Joe said. "He's done this before."

"You think?"

As they approached Joe's pickup, Marybeth said, "What just happened? Mom's in shock."

"He runs a tight ship," Joe said. "Judge Hewitt doesn't screw around. Marcus Hand will have to be amazing. Of course, Hand's specialty is jury manipulation, not judge manipulation."

"Which won't be necessary," Marybeth said, "for an innocent woman."

Joe nodded.

"I'm pretty good at reading people," she said, climbing up into the cab, "but I couldn't read the judge. He seemed to be angry at *everyone.*"

"He's in a hurry," Joe said, starting the engine.

"But why?" Marybeth asked, shaking her head.

"Talked to Stovepipe," Joe said. "Judge Hewitt drew a tag for a Dall sheep in Alaska. If he gets one, he'll complete his grand slam: Stone, Rocky Mountain bighorn, desert bighorn, and Dall. Trophy hunters like Judge Hewitt will do anything to complete their grand slam, and this may be his only chance. The season up there opens and closes next month. I'll check with a couple of buddies I know in the Alaska Fish and Game to get the particulars."

Marybeth moaned aloud. "He's hurrying so he can go *hunting*? When my mother's life is at stake?"

"Man's got priorities," Joe said. "Hand has to realize he needs to work within them. A Dall sheep permit is a once-in-a-lifetime deal."

"She looked so . . . lonely up there," Marybeth said. "For the first time in my life, I realized she has no one to support her. She has no friends, Joe."

He turned toward the library. "Can't blame that on anybody but her," he said.

"But it's so sad. She's truly alone now."

"She's got you," Joe said.

"But not you," Marybeth countered.

"Didn't say that."

"Don't look so glum, pretty lady." Marcus Hand grinned at Marybeth as he approached them across the courthouse lawn.

"Why not?" Marybeth asked. Joe looked on.

Hand said, "'Cause we've got 'em right where we want 'em."

Marybeth looked at Joe for an explanation, and he shrugged back at her.

She said, "I thought you objected to the two weeks? I was surprised you did absolutely *nothing* to gain more time."

Hand chuckled. He looked at Joe, and Joe raised his eyebrows, also curious.

"Okay," Hand said, "but this is the last time I talk strategy with you. Not because I don't trust you two, but because . . . well, just because.

"The news about Bud was unexpected, but wonderful. It means one of two things: they're hiding him away or they don't know where he is. We can work with each of those possibilities. But the important thing is their entire case rests almost entirely on the credibility of their star witness. If they're hiding him, it's for a reason, like they can't trust what he'll say in public or my questioning of him will destroy their case. That's good, too. If they don't know where he is, it means he may not even show up. Or if he does, his credibility is already shot because of his flaky nature. This is all good. So the faster we go to trial, the better for us."

Hand leaned back on his boot heels and smiled.

"One other thing," Marybeth said. "My mom is innocent."

"Of course she is!" Hand said.

AUGUST 30

To be happy at home is the ultimate result of all ambition.

—Samuel Johnson

19

"I *hate* how this has taken over our lives," Marybeth said to Joe, thunking her fork down next to her half-eaten dinner salad on the picnic table outside the Burg-O-Pardner. Joe was finishing his burger with Rocky Mountain oysters on the side. He didn't know why he'd ordered so much and knew he'd feel lethargic later in the afternoon.

"We don't have to let it," he said, after swallowing. They had local grass-fed beef at the Burg-O-Pardner, ground lean, and they broke state law by cooking it medium rare on request. He wished he didn't like the hamburgers so much.

"Our girls are weirded out and neglected," she said. "April is no doubt plotting something while our attention is diverted, and Lucy is miffed how little attention she's gotten from us about that part in the play. Joe, she's the lead. She sings and everything. The girl is talented, but you know what she said to me this morning before she went to school?"

"What?"

"She said, 'Female stars like to say they're actors, not actresses. So if an older woman kills someone, is she a murderer or murderess?' "

Joe put down the rest of his sandwich. "She asked that?"

"Yes. This plays heavily on her mind. No doubt she's heard things at school."

"How is April handling it? At school, I mean. High school kids are the worst."

Marybeth sighed. "They are. And it's even worse in that she said some of popular kids now think she's kind of cool having a grandmother who's accused of murder. Can you imagine that?"

"I can," Joe said sullenly.

"And there's a lot going on we're missing. I almost forgot to tell you, in fact. Eleanor Sees Everything at the library said Alisha Whiteplume didn't show up for work last Monday and no one's heard from her. The folks at the high school are getting worried. Apparently, she's not at her house and her stepdaughter is still with her grandmother. And her grandmother hasn't heard a word from her."

Joe's mouth got suddenly dry. He took a long drink from his iced tea. He said, "Alisha is missing?"

"It's not like her," Marybeth said. "You know how responsible she is."

Joe rubbed his jaw.

"Do you think Nate knows she's missing?" Marybeth asked, trying to act nonchalant. "I think he'd want to know, don't you?"

He grunted.

"I know what you're thinking, that she's with him. But she wouldn't leave that little girl without letting her grandmother know."

"Has anyone called the sheriff?"

Marybeth rolled her eyes. "Eleanor said they called yesterday. She said one of McLanahan's flunkies said Alisha hadn't been missing long enough to do anything yet. He implied keeping track of local Indians wasn't their first priority since they almost always show up eventually."

"He said that?" Joe asked.

"I don't know whether he said it outright. Either way, Eleanor was angry about it. But that doesn't matter. If Alisha is missing, that's a big deal."

She let it hang there.

Joe finally broke the silence. "Honey, I'm not sure whether you're asking me to try to find Bud, clear your mother, try to find Alisha, call Nate, go to the school play, lecture April, or do everything at once. I'm only one guy, and I have a job to do on the side."

Her eyes narrowed and shut him down. He was immediately sorry he'd let his frustration boil to the surface. He reached out and squeezed her hand. The one without the fork in it.

"Sometimes," he said, "I think if we traded minds for an hour there'd be so much going on in yours I'd drive off a cliff because I couldn't take all the voices. You, however, would probably be able to relax because it's so quiet and not much is going on except maybe you'd want to take a little nap."

She simply stared at him for a moment before she burst out laughing.

"That's what I wanted to see," he said, and chanced a smile back.

But on the haphazard list he'd created in his mind, he added another task: Find Alisha.

Joe pulled into the library parking lot and they sat there a minute before Marybeth went in. He could tell she was processing what she'd heard and sorting it out. He told her about Bud's absence the week before, hesitating when he confessed forcing the lock, but she seemed unfazed.

"So they don't know where Bud is, either?" she asked.

"I don't think so. I can only imagine the scene when McLanahan tells Dulcie Schalk he's misplaced the star witness."

"What do they have if they don't have Bud?"

Joe shrugged. "They may not have the airtight case they thought they had. I could see Hand blowing it wide open."

"They still have his statements, though?"

"I assume so. We don't know what he said, but we can assume it's pretty bad for Missy. But without Bud . . ."

"Dulcie wouldn't hide him, would she?" Marybeth asked. "From what you described, it sounds like he packed up for a few days. It's not like someone kidnapped him and took him away?"

"There were no signs of a struggle," Joe said. "I doubt kidnappers would tell him to grab his toothbrush before they took him somewhere."

"I'll bet Dulcie will be in full panic mode," she said. "Same with the sheriff."

Joe agreed.

"What if we find him first?" she asked.

Joe said nothing. He wasn't sure he liked where she seemed to be headed. "What if we did?" he asked.

She shook her head. "I'm not sure. But maybe he ran because he's been making this up all along and his conscience got the best of him? Maybe he'd like a chance to recant his part in the frame-up?"

"Marybeth," Joe said, reaching out and touching her hand. "There's still the rifle. And if Earl really was in the process of divorcing her . . . well, it still doesn't look very good."

"How do they know he was going to leave her?" she asked. "Was that from Bud, too?"

Joe shrugged. He hadn't thought of that.

"Where would Bud go to hide out?" she asked. "We know him pretty well. You know him. Where would he go?"

AUGUST 31

The truth is incontrovertible, malice may attack it, ignorance may deride it, but in the end, there it is.

—Winston Churchill

20

The next day, after checking the licenses and stamps for a group of antelope hunters from Texas, Joe drove across the break lands to the home of Bob and Dode Lee of the Lee Ranch, which bordered Missy and Earl's property. Cumulus clouds scudded across the expanse of sky as a cold front approached, as if fleeing the state for warmer climates. As he approached the ranch headquarters, Joe was cognizant of the tops of the wind turbines peeking over the southern horizon, their tri-blades turning. There was the snap of fall in the air, and he'd had to scrape frost from his windshield that morning before leaving his sleeping house.

After the arraignment and posting of bail, Marcus Hand had driven Missy home. According to Marybeth, Hand had sent for a large team of paralegals and additional lawyers from his Jackson Hole office. Team Missy, as Hand had taken to calling it, would occupy most of the bedrooms of the ranch house to prepare for the next stage of the trial. Cable news satellite trucks rumbled into Saddlestring, and a half-dozen legal reporters from newspapers as far away as New York and Los Angeles booked rooms at the Holiday Inn.

There had been no news in regard to either Bud Longbrake or Alisha Whiteplume. Joe had placed a call to the sheriff's office to check on Alisha and gotten Sollis, who said they were giving it another day or two before opening an inquiry. When Joe asked why, Sollis said he didn't appreciate the implication and hung up on him.

Unlike the spectacular stone headquarters on the adjoining Thunderhead Ranch once occupied by Missy and Earl Alden and now serving as command central for Team Missy, the Lees' place was clapboard, tired, and utilitarian. The once white house needed a coat of paint and the old gray shingles on the roof were warped and cracked from sun and weather. It sat in a wind-whipped grove of Austrian pines—the only standing trees for miles—on the high prairie at the end of a rough two-track. The trees all leaned to the south. The windward sides were flattened and the southern sides were bushy and gnarly as if they'd all been shot in the back and were reaching out with branch-hands to break their fall. Joe thought the word "hardscrabble" would have had to be invented to describe the Lee Ranch if it didn't already exist.

The ranch compound consisted of the house, three battered metal Quonsets that served as garages, an oversized peeling wooden barn, and an intricate set of corrals and chutes built with crooked poles sunk into the hard ground and linked with haphazard railings. Hereford cattle and bony horses fed on piles of hay scattered across the ground within the corrals and looked up at the approaching green pickup.

He didn't know the Lees well. They weren't the kind of ranchers who participated in the community or in public meetings, politics, or even the state livestock organizations. They kept to themselves, making no demands when it came to problem game animals or hunters, for that matter. Joe had heard the rumor that Bob Lee once took care of elk feeding on his hay by mowing them down with a .30-06 rifle and burying the carcasses with his front-end loader, but there'd never been a call or report on him.

Hollow-eyed mixed-breed ranch dogs came boiling out from beneath the front porch as Joe got out. He quickly jumped back in his pickup next to Tube, who was alarmed but not exactly motivated to protect him from the snarling pack. The dogs circled his pickup as if they'd treed it, snapping their teeth in the air and yapping. It was obvious there were people around; the lights were on inside and five vehicles—two battered ranch pickups, a later model Jeep Cherokee, and two low-slung restored muscle cars from the 1970s—were parked around him. Joe waited for someone inside the house to come out and call the dogs back.

Finally, a woman pushed through the front screen door and held it open, as if unsure if she wanted to come all the way out or go back in. She was old and heavy, wore a faded tent-like dress and bright yellow Crocs on her feet and her iron-colored hair was in curlers. She squinted at Joe's pickup with her mouth clamped tight, and Joe slid his window down and said, "Mrs. Lee, can you call off your dogs so I can talk with you and Bob?"

He saw Dode Lee turn to someone inside and mouth "game warden" as if answering a question. To Joe, she said, "They won't hurt you, those dogs. They haven't bit anyone in years."

"I believe you," Joe said cheerfully, not sure if he believed her but reminding himself that one-third of his job description fell under the heading *Landowner Relations*, "but I'd appreciate it if you'd call them back."

Again, Dode Lee turned to address someone inside. "He's scared of the dogs," she said, rolling her eyes. Then back to Joe, "What is it you need?"

"Just to talk to you for a minute," he said. "It won't take long."

"He says he wants to talk to us," Dode reported. Then back to Joe: "What about?"

A large man with shoulder-length black hair and a basketball-sized beer belly shouldered past Dode and yelled angrily at the dogs. He was wearing greasy denim jeans and a black Aerosmith T-shirt. He also wore Crocs, which Joe thought odd. The dogs cringed at his voice, one yelped as if struck, and they crawled back to the house. Joe knew how dogs behaved around someone who had severely beaten them, and this pack was a case study. He swung out and shut his door on Tube, who, now that he was safe and the dogs were gone, started barking at them. That was the corgi part in him, Joe thought with regret.

"Thanks," he said to the man. "They're obviously scared of you."

"Good reason for that," the man said.

The big man was much younger than Dode, although Joe could see some resemblance in his rough wide face and unfriendly manner. He thought he must be her son.

"Are you Wes Lee?"

"Yeah," he said.

"Joe Pickett."

"I know. I heard of you." He said it in a way that suggested Wes wasn't impressed at all.

"Mind if I talk to your folks for a couple minutes?"

Wes glanced at his mother, who looked back without expression. "Make it quick," he said. "We're kind of busy today."

Joe nodded. He didn't question what it was they were busy doing. "Mind if I come in?"

"If it's about Earl Alden," Dode said, "we don't have much good to say."

"It's about him," Joe replied, trying to see past Wes, who hadn't moved his bulk from the top of the porch steps to let Joe by. "Your neighbor."

"Couldn't have happened to a better guy," Dode Lee said.

"Mom," Wes said to Dode, while eyeing Joe suspiciously, "the less you talk to law enforcement, the better. They can twist your words around and use it against you."

"So you've had some experience in that regard," Joe said breezily, stepping around Wes, trying not to show he was wary of the son's bulk, size, and attitude.

"That was years ago," Wes said, fully aware of his effect on Joe and only reluctantly letting him by.

Joe nodded and made a mental note to himself to look up Wes Lee's rap sheet after the interview. Joe had spent years trying to read people the first time he encountered them in the field, and he had the strong impression Wes owned a mean streak a mile wide.

The home was dark and cluttered and smelled of cigarette smoke, motor oil, and dogs. The reason for the oil smell was obvious. An engine block sat on a stained tarp in the middle of the living room. Tools were scattered around it. Joe wondered why the work wasn't being done in one of the three outbuildings, but he didn't ask about it. People's homes were people's homes.

Bob Lee sat in a worn lounge chair at the back of the room next to a tall green oxygen bottle. Despite the yellowed tube that ran from the tank to a respirator that clipped under his nose, Bob held a lit cigarette between two stained fingers. Joe glanced at the decal on the side of the tank that read:

WARNING: NO SMOKING
OXYGEN IN USE
NO OPEN FLAMES

The television was on: *The Price Is Right.* Lee had a large frame but looked sunken in on himself, as if his flesh had collapsed over his skeleton. He had large rheumy eyes, thin lips, and folds of loose skin that lapped over his shirt collar.

"What's the game warden want with us?" Bob asked, his voice both scratchy and challenging.

Joe removed his hat and held it in his hands. Wes came back in and sat on his engine block with his big hands on his knees and looked up at Joe expectantly. Dode hung back, not far from the door, as if she needed to be close to it in case she had to escape.

Joe said, "I was just wondering if all of you were around last week. Sunday and Monday, to be specific. I was wondering if you saw anything unusual on the day Earl Alden was killed, since his place is next to yours."

Bob commenced coughing. It took a moment for Joe to realize the old man had started to laugh, but the phlegm in his throat made him cough instead. Wes looked over at his father, not alarmed by the reaction. Dode tut-tutted from her place near the door. Joe found it interesting that both wife and son deferred completely to the old man and waited for him to speak. Especially Wes.

"Unusual like what?" Bob asked.

"You know," Joe said, "vehicles you didn't recognize on the county roads. Strangers about, or even people you know who were out and about on a Sunday."

"Maybe like equipment trucks and construction vehicles?" Bob asked, sarcasm tainting his tone. "Like hundreds of goddamned wind farm people driving through our ranch raising dust and scattering our cattle? Like engineers and politicians driving through our place like they owned it? Like that?"

Joe said nothing.

"That's just a normal day around here," Bob said. "It's been like that for a year. And now we have *the noise*."

Joe said, "The noise?"

"Open that kitchen window, Dode," Bob commanded.

Mrs. Lee left her place near the door and entered the kitchen. The big window over the sink faced south, and she unlatched it and slid it open.

Joe heard it: the distant but distinct high-frequency whine of the turbine blades slicing through the sky, punctuated by squeaks and moans of metal-on-metal.

"The goddamned noise," Bob said. "It drives the dogs crazy. It drives us crazy. Gives me headaches, I swear, and makes Dode crankier than hell. That odd sound you hear means the bearings are going out on one of the turbines. Eventually, I guess, they'll have to climb up there and replace it. But until they do, we get to listen to it twenty-four hours a goddamned day."

Joe nodded. He was surprised he hadn't noticed the high but constant whine before he entered the house, but concluded it had been drowned out by barking dogs and the gusts of wind.

"That's what we get to listen to all our damned lives, thanks to Earl Alden," Bob said. "And that's not counting all the heavy equipment on our roads. I suppose you saw the start of them transmission lines on the way in?"

"Yup." Tower after tower of gleaming steel coursing across the sagebrush, power cables sagging between them like super-sized clotheslines.

"Earl was behind that. Because he owns the wind energy company, he's somehow considered to be a utility, which means he has the right to condemn that corridor across our ranch so they could put those up. That way, he can ship his power to the grid somewhere."

"You got paid, though, right?" Joe asked. "They have to pay you fair market value."

Bob sneered. "Which is next to nothing. Dry land pasture doesn't have much value, they said. Breaking up the ranch that has been in my family for four generations don't mean nothing when it comes to the state and the Feds on a goddamned crusade for wind power."

"Fucking windmills," Wes said, practically spitting the words out. Joe glanced at Wes and was surprised by his vehemence. Definitely a mean streak, Joe thought. A big guy like that could easily hoist a body up the inside of a wind tower.

Bob said, "This county sits right on top of natural gas, oil, coal, and uranium. I have the mineral rights, but no one's interested because they all think that's dirty and bad these days. But for some damned reason, they think wind power is *good.* So they got all this federal money and tax credits and bullshit. Anything that has to do with wind power just gets steamrolled through. Let me ask you something, Mr. Game Warden."

"Ask away," Joe said, hoping to end the diatribe and get back to his questions.

"When you look at a wind turbine, do you see a thing of beauty? Is it more beautiful than an oil well or a gas rig?"

Joe said, "I see a wind turbine. Nothing more or less."

"Ha!" Bob said, tilting his head. "Then you need to get with the damned program, son. You're supposed to behold the prettiest goddamned thing you ever saw. It's supposed to make you feel all warm and fuzzy inside. The sight of it is supposed to give you a boner."

Wes barked a laugh and slapped his knees. Dode said, *"Bob Lee!"*

Joe shrugged.

"Earl Alden claimed he loved those windmills. He'd always talk up his wind farm while he was getting his government checks and getting the locals to condemn my land for the transmission towers. But you notice where he put 'em, don't you? Right outside my window on that big ol' ridge. He put 'em where he wouldn't have to look at them or hear them all goddamned day, on a ridge where the wind never stops blowing. Right up against my property. They mess up my sky, son, and they mess up the quiet. I can't take it. A man shouldn't *have* to take it just so a gaggle of politicians back east can feel good about themselves."

"I understand," Joe said. "But that's not what I wanted to ask you about."

Bob leaned forward and removed the oxygen tube from his nose with one hand while raising the cigarette with the other in a well-practiced way. He inhaled deeply, sat back, and plugged the oxygen apparatus back in. Joe watched the exchange while holding his own breath, anticipating an explosion and fireball that did not come. Bob said, "So if you want to ask us if we feel bad Earl Alden got killed and hung up from one of his towers like a piece of meat, the answer is hell no."

"Hell no!" Dode chirped from the kitchen while closing and latching the window.

"But you didn't see anything unusual Sunday?" Joe asked again, trying to bring it back. "Anything you told the sheriff, or didn't think of until now?"

"The sheriff?" Bob said. "He ain't been out here. You're the first. And not that it matters, 'cause I don't even look out anymore. I hear them equipment trucks and Rope the Wind vehicles, but I don't even look out at them anymore because it makes me so damned mad."

"What about you, Dode?" Joe asked. "Or Wes? Did you see or hear anything?"

Dode shook her head. "We keep the curtains shut most of the time anymore," she said. "We never used to do that, but we do now. And we keep the windows shut on account of the dust those trucks kick up."

"Wes?"

The son had an odd smile on his face, Joe thought. Almost a smirk. "I guess I was just working on my engine all day," he said, unconvincingly. "I'm trying to get that '69 Pontiac GTO Judge out there to run again. You probably saw it when you drove up. That's from when they made real cars and Americans weren't scared to drive them."

Joe was silent. He stood and let the silence become oppressive, hoping one of them would rush to fill it with something that might prove useful. But Dode stood kneading her hands, Wes stared at a spot on the wall, and Bob did his quick oxygen-for-cigarette move again.

He stood up and said, "Do you have any idea who might have had it in for Earl Alden? Enough to kill him?"

Bob snorted, as if to say, *Who doesn't?*

"Well," Joe said, digging a card out of his uniform shirt, "I thank you for your time. If anyone thinks of anything, feel free to give me a call." He crossed the room and offered the card to Bob, who wouldn't reach out and take it. Humiliated, Joe placed it on a cluttered end table next to the lounge chair.

"I heard Missy Alden did it," Dode said, her eyes lighting up. "I wouldn't put it past that stuck-up . . . well, I can't say the word but it rhymes with 'ditch.'"

Joe stifled a smile, despite himself. He clamped his hat on and headed for the door. As he opened it, he turned back. The three of them hadn't moved. There was something they weren't telling him, he was sure of it.

"I was wondering," Joe said, "why you couldn't take advantage of the wind opportunities you describe. You've got the land and you sure do have the wind, and it sounds like there's big money in it."

Bob said, "You really want to know what's going on?"

"I'm curious."

"Then come back in here and sit yourself down, son. Wes, clear a place on that damned engine block for the game warden."

21

Nate Romanowski stood deep in a grove of aspen on a mountainside in the Salt River Range. It was a cool fall day with a slight breeze that rattled the dry heart-shaped aspen leaves with a sound like a musical shaker. To the north was the town of Alpine and, beyond that, Jackson Hole. To his south was Afton. From where he stood in the shadows, he could see a distant silvery bend of the Grays River, and when he faced west he could see Freedom, Wyoming, just inside the Idaho border. He'd hidden his Jeep in an alcove in the dark timber above and hiked down the weathered two-track to the rendezvous spot.

He was waiting for a man to deliver a gun.

Nate checked his pocket watch. Large Merle was an hour late. Plenty of things could have happened to delay him, Nate knew, but he took a few steps farther back into the aspens and hunkered down just in case Merle had been intercepted by someone who was out there looking for him. Lord knew, he thought, there were enough people after him these days.

The sound of the motor came with a gust of wind. A flock of gold leaves dislodged and fluttered to the ground like wing-shot birds. Within a few minutes, the sound became pronounced. It was punctuated by the grinding of the transmission as the driver missed a gear on the climb. Merle drove like that—badly—and Nate rose.

The toothsome grille of Large Merle's 1978 Dodge Power Wagon thrust through the brush below, and Nate didn't move or blink until he could see there was only one occupant in the cab. One very big occupant.

Nate raised a hand and stepped out from the trees. The dry leaves crunched underfoot like cornflakes. Through the windshield, Merle nodded in recognition and goosed the Dodge up the road. When he reached Nate, Merle killed the engine, jammed on the parking brake, and swung out. Nate watched Merle carefully, looking for the sign of a tell.

Large Merle was seven feet tall and weighed about four hundred and fifty pounds, Nate guessed. Although he could afford a newer vehicle, the Dodge had been adapted to a man of Merle's size by retrofitting the seat flush against the back cab wall and cutting lengths out of the brake and clutch arms. Large Merle left the keys in his Dodge all the time because, he'd once told Nate, no car thief was big enough to steal it.

What Nate was looking for on Merle's face was a nervous twitch or a refusal to make eye contact. Or if Merle started spouting small talk unrelated to the matter at hand. Any of those traits would be a sign of guilt and thus the end of Large Merle.

Nate had always believed in justice even if he didn't believe in many laws. And if Merle revealed anything besides remorse or blind stupidity, Nate would see that justice was done.

"You're a sight," Large Merle said, stepping out of his truck. "Sorry I'm late."

"I was starting to wonder," Nate said, watching Merle closely. So far, so good.

"It took longer than they thought it would to mount the scope. We went with a Leupold 4X in the end."

Nate nodded. "Good scope."

"That's what they said."

Merle was studying his boot tops. Not looking up. Nate felt something begin to swell inside him.

Then Merle said, "I feel so goddamned bad about what happened. I blame myself for those yahoos getting through my place, Nate, and I'm just so sorry."

Nate let the words hang in the air until the breeze floated them away. He *sounded* sincere.

"It was a girl that made me screw up, Nate," Merle said, glancing up, his eyes begging for understanding. "A woman, I should say. She came into the café two nights before. She said she was from East Texas and she was going to visit her sister somewhere in Montana. Ekalaka, I think she said. Damn, she had pretty eyes and a nice figure and she asked me to come along."

Nate watched Merle carefully.

"There ain't that many girls who like a guy like me," Merle said. "It wasn't always like this, you know. Back when I went two hundred twenty, two hundred fifty, I didn't have that many problems. Lots of girls thought I played basketball," he said, chuckling.

"I remember," Nate said. "I was there."

Merle had been in Nate's unit in black ops. They'd served together in Africa, South America, and the Middle East. He'd been there when the whole thing blew up.

Merle still stared at his boots. "Yeah. But it's been a long time since a girl looked at me that way. When she said to come along with her and meet her sister . . . hell, I just took my apron off right there at the grill and followed her out the door. I don't think I even locked up the place and I sure as hell forgot to let you know I was leaving. I hope you can forgive me just a little."

"Hmmm," Nate said.

Large Merle took a deep breath and chanced a smile. He acted as if a huge weight had been lifted from his neck and shoulders. "All I want is a little understanding," he said. "And I swear to you right now I'll help you find them. I'll stick with you until we find those bastards."

Nate shook his head. "Thanks for the offer, Merle, but this is all mine."

"Really, I want to help. Do you think it was The Five? Did they finally get a bead on you?"

Nate reached up and scratched his chin. "It wasn't professional. It wasn't The Five, Merle. They were just sloppy amateurs and they left evidence behind. That only makes it worse. It's just a matter of time before I find them."

"You got names?" Merle asked. "Locations?"

"Not yet, but I've got fingerprints and DNA. I need to get them analyzed and I'll have my boys do that. What I don't know yet is who put them up to it and why. And who gave them my location. That bothers me."

"It wasn't me, Nate," Merle said. "If it was, I sure as hell wouldn't be here now."

Nate nodded.

"Hell, that girl took advantage of me. What a disappointment, you know?" Merle moaned. "Turned out she wanted me around as muscle so she could intimidate her sister into moving off the family ranch so she could move in. It was complicated as hell, but my gal left the place a long time ago and wanted to come back and claim it. Once I found out what the deal was about, I slunk back to Kaycee with my tail between my legs. That's when I saw what happened to your place while I was gone. When I saw the wreckage . . . I thought they'd killed you. I was so damned happy when you called me. Women," Merle said sadly. "Can't live with 'em, can't shoot 'em."

"Not all of them anyway," Nate said.

Merle looked up sharply. "One of them was a woman?"

"That's what my sources tell me," Nate said. "She wasn't the shooter, but she may have put them up to it."

"No name on her, either?"

"I've got a good idea who it is," Nate said.

They drove up the mountainside in Merle's Power Wagon with the box on the bench seat between them. The road leveled on a long plateau of short grass and knuckles of rock that stretched out flat several miles as if the terrain were gathering its strength before thrusting upward into the Salt River Range. An old barbed-wire fence stretched out parallel to the road.

Nate picked up the box and hefted it in his hands. Heavy, and not quite right.

"This isn't a .454 Casull," Nate said, looking over at Merle. "I thought we talked about the right weapon."

"Jesus," Merle said. "You can tell by the *weight*?"

"Couple of ounces different," Nate said. "Lighter."

Merle whistled. Then: "You amaze me. You're right; it's not a .454. Seems Freedom Arms has a new model, and I thought you might want to give it a try."

Nate frowned back, perturbed.

"Tell you what," Merle said. "If you don't like it, I'll take it back for a .454 this afternoon and get the scope swapped. But at least make an informed decision."

"What new model?" Nate asked.

"It's called a .500 Wyoming Express," Merle said. "Stainless steel five-shot revolver, just like what you're used to, only bigger: fifty cal. A little over three pounds without the scope. It's got a Model 83 chassis just like the .454 so it should feel the same in your hand. Seven-and-a-half-inch barrel. Shoots 1.765-inch belted cartridges at 35,000 psi. Twice the power of a .44 magnum. The belted cartridge allows them to cut down a little on the cylinder weight."

Nate raised his eyebrows in appreciation.

"It's not as fast as your .454," Merle said, "but the knockdown power is greater. The .454 has a TKO of 30, while the .500 goes 39. And according to the man who sold it to me, it's like getting hit by a freight train as opposed to a car. It'll knock down a moose or a cape buffalo or a grizzly like nothing else. The penetration is incredible. The bullets just blow through flesh and bone and are rarely ever recovered afterward, which is an attribute I thought you might appreciate."

Nate nodded. He liked that. "Range?"

"Five-hundred-yard capability," Merle said, "but it's most effective within a hundred.

"In the right hands," he winked at Nate, "and with an adjustable scope, accurate one-thousand-yard shots are not impossible. Plus at close range, one could, you know, knock out a bulldozer.

"Hell," Merle said, "you're *Nate Romanowski.* You've got the rep. You've *got* to have the baddest gun known to man or beast."

Nate said, "I'm getting interested."

He liked the way it felt in his hand, loved its balance and weight. Large Merle stood behind him, silent, letting him get acquainted with the weapon. Nate kneaded it with his hands, spun it on his finger through the trigger guard, checked out the scope, then opened the cylinder.

He was well practiced with the model. He loaded one large shell, rotated the cylinder past an empty hole, then loaded the next three rounds. The idea was to leave the firing pin resting on the skipped cylinder for safety. Then he raised it like an extension of his right arm and cupped his left hand under his right. He kept both eyes open and cocked it with his left thumb. The snick-snick sound of rotating steel cylinder was tight and sweet, he thought.

The fence they stood next to had warped wooden posts spaced every ten feet. He counted out fifteen posts from where he stood—fifty yards—and fired. The concussion was tremendous and it seemed like the air around them had been sucked away for a second. Large Merle cried out, "Jesus Christ! My ears . . . give a guy some warning."

The post was split cleanly down the middle. A wisp of smoke and dust rose from the top of the post. The barbed wire strands sang up and down the fence from the impact.

Nate smiled grimly. "A different attitude than the .454," he said more to himself than Merle. "The .454 is snappy compared to this. The .500 pushes straight back like a mule kick."

Then he counted out fifteen more posts and blew the top off one at a hundred yards. He let the gun kick back over his left shoulder near his ear, and as he leveled it, he thumbed the hammer on the down stroke. Another heavy boom, and a post a hundred fifty yards away shattered into splinters. He calculated, aimed down the fence line, and fired his last round.

"My God," Large Merle said, taking his fingers out of his ears. "But you missed the last one."

"No," Nate said, "look farther down. At two-fifty."

The post at two hundred fifty yards was blown cleanly in two, and the top half sagged near the bottom half, held aloft by the strands of wire stapled to it.

"It doesn't need to be said, but that's some shooting."

"Then why say it?" Nate asked. "You did well, Merle. This will do the job. How much?"

"The .500 WE retails for twenty-three hundred dollars without the scope," Large Merle said. "The shells alone cost three dollars each, so keep that in mind. But given the circumstances, you owe me exactly nothing."

Nate said, "I don't like being obligated."

"Given the circumstances," Merle said again, "it's the least I can do. I really liked Alisha, you know. I know how you felt about her."

Nate said, "Let's not talk about her, please." And he raised the weapon and aimed it between Merle's eyes.

"Tell me again you didn't know a thing about the people who killed her," Nate said without inflection.

Merle's eyes got huge. He was close enough he could no doubt see the half-inch round of bronzed lead seated in the long, dark end of the barrel and no doubt envisioned what it would do to his head.

"I didn't know a thing," Merle whispered.

"Okay," Nate said, letting the hammer down easy and slipping the weapon into his new shoulder holster. "Just needed to make sure."

Large Merle collapsed back on the grille of his pickup as if his legs had lost their strength. He put a big paw over his heart. He said, "I wish you wouldn't do things like that."

Before they left the grassy plateau, Nate withdrew two one-hundred-dollar bills from his wallet, rolled them into a tight tube, and shoved it into one of the empty .500 brass cartridges. He jammed the brass into a crack in the first shattered target.

"So the rancher can buy some new posts," he explained to Merle.

As they drove slowly down the mountain, Nate said, "Have you heard how Diane Shober is doing in Idaho?"

Shober had been relocated via the growing underground network after what had happened the year before in the Sierra Madre with Joe Pickett. Nate hadn't kept in contact with her, or with his friends who took her in.

Merle said, "Changed her name and her hair color. She's gained a little weight since she's not running anymore. But from what I can tell, she's settled in."

Nate grunted approvingly.

"Learned to shoot," Merle said. "She's just waiting for the revolution, from what they tell me. Nate, what do you think? Will there be one? Will they come and try to take away our guns and our freedom?"

"Don't know," Nate said. "I've only got one thing on my mind right now and it's not that."

"I'm worried," Large Merle said. "Everybody's worried. But we ain't gonna let it happen without a fight. What the bastards don't really understand is what it *means* to have an armed citizenry."

Nate grunted again.

"How you gonna get the fingerprint and DNA identification you mentioned?" Merle asked as they neared Nate's Jeep.

"I know a guy in law enforcement," Nate said, looking away. "I'm pretty sure he'll help."

"Is it the guy I'm thinking about? The one you had the falling out with over Diane Shober? The game warden?"

Nate looked over and silenced Merle with a look.

After a few beats, Merle said, "You want me to go down in the canyon and clean it up a little? Make it habitable again?"

"No."

"So you aren't coming back?"

Nate shook his head. "If an angry woman and two yahoos can

figure out where I am, The Five wouldn't have any problem. No, I'm gone from there."

"Where are you gonna be?"

"For now," Nate said, patting the holster and the weapon, "I'm going hunting."

"Let me know if you need anything," Merle said, pulling up next to the Jeep. "Money, ammunition, a home-cooked meal. Anything. Just let me know. And keep in touch."

Nate looked over. "Why?"

Merle said, "In case we need you. If things turn real ugly, you know? Or if The Five decide to start taking out everybody from our old unit who're still around. I know there aren't many of us left, but as long as we breathe, we're a threat to them."

Nate nodded, said good-bye with his eyes, and climbed out of Merle's Power Wagon.

As Large Merle rolled away, Nate got out of his shoulder holster and placed it on the hood of his Jeep. He withdrew the .500 WE and reached into his jeans pocket.

He'd braided the three-inch length of Alisha's hair into a stiff bolt and tied one end of it to a supple leather jess he'd last used on his murdered peregrine. Nate took the loose ends of the jess and knotted them to the end of the muzzle of his weapon, just behind the front blade site.

He lifted the revolver and aimed it. The length of hair tilted slightly in the breeze. It would help when it came to gauging wind velocity for long-range shots. And it would remind him—as if he needed it—of the only thing he cared about right now.

SEPTEMBER 2

Speak not evil one of another, brethren . . . There is one lawgiver, who is able to save and to destroy: who art thou that judgest another?

—James 4:11–12

22

Friday evening, Joe and Marybeth took Joe's pickup to dinner at the Thunderhead Ranch. Missy had invited them, and Joe had been dreading the event all week. Lucy couldn't join them because of play practice, and when they raised it with April, she said, "If I'm grounded, I'm friggin' *grounded*."

"Family events can be an exception," Marybeth said.

"One of the problems with you people is you keep changing the rules," April said, stalking back to her room and slamming the door.

Her favorite new phrase, besides "frigging" was now the accusatory *you people.*

Joe held the front door open for his wife. As she passed him, she said, "Marcus Hand better be as good as they say, because if he isn't, April gains in power."

"Ouch," Joe said, flinching.

"I don't want to do this," Joe said, as they turned onto the highway.

"I know," Marybeth said. "I can't say I'm very excited myself. But my mother needs to know she's got some support, Joe. Can you imagine how she feels?"

He bit his tongue and drove. If the woman had made any effort at all to befriend the locals or even show some respect for them, he thought, she might have a few allies.

"I know what you're thinking," Marybeth said.

"Can't help it."

He'd taken a shower and changed into jeans and a Cinch shirt, but his face still burned from being outside in the wind and sun all day. Mourning dove season had opened on the first, and he'd spent the last two days in the field checking hunters and limits. There was no other season where all a successful hunter had to show for himself was a small bag of the soft gray birds that would barely make a single meal—even though it was a tasty one. But because mourning doves migrated out of the area as quickly as they arrived, it was a furious few days of hunting and work and he'd not been able to pursue his investigation further.

Joe and Marybeth had not caught up because they'd been missing each other at home with his long days and her evening shift at the library.

As they turned off the highway and passed under the magnificent elk antler arches that marked the entrance to the Thunderhead Ranch, he said, "I guess this will give me the chance to ask Missy a couple of questions that have been nagging me since my talk with Bob Lee."

"Like what?" she asked.

Joe chinned toward the north in the direction of the Rope the Wind turbine project. "The wind," he said. "It blows."

Dinner was served at the regal long table in the rarely used dining room. José Maria had been pulled from duty with the cows and dressed in a black jacket to serve ranch-raised beef tenderloin, asparagus with hollandaise, garlic-roasted sharp-tail grouse, and red-skinned new potatoes. Missy sat at one end picking, as usual, at tiny bits of food. She wore pearls and a black cocktail dress that showed off her trim figure and youthful legs, and Joe wondered if she could possibly be the same wan person he had seen in the courtroom.

Marcus Hand occupied the other end of the table. He wore a loose guayabera shirt over jeans and cowboy boots. His reading glasses hung from a chain around his neck. He ate huge portions and loudly enjoyed them and washed down each bite with alternate gulps of either red or white wine. Hand was well known as a gourmand, and he'd penned dozens of unapologetic essays about eating large quantities of rich food. In one piece Joe had read in a national magazine, Hand lamented that fried chicken was rarely offered in local restaurants and that elites should stop looking down on big eaters who enjoyed their food in quantity. Hand dismembered a grouse by pulling it apart and gnawed the meat off the carcass. Then he snapped the thighbones in two and sucked out the marrow.

Joe and Marybeth faced each other in the middle, shooting glances toward either end and exchanging puzzlement to each other when their eyes met. Joe had expected angst and gravity to accompany the meal, but not this. He couldn't help but stare at the lawyer, who enjoyed his food with a kind of moaning passion that nearly made Joe feel like a voyeur.

"This grouse," Hand swooned, sitting back and letting his eyes roll back into his head while a half-eaten thigh jutted out of his mouth like a fat cigar, "may be one of the most succulent dishes I've ever had. And I've eaten well all over the world, as you know."

"It *is* good," Missy said from the other end of the table. Her face beamed, and she seemed oddly relaxed. Marybeth obviously thought the same thing, and she had trouble hiding her agitation.

"Fresh grouse," Hand said, "is like fine wine. You can taste the pine nuts and the sage they eat in the meat itself, as if master chefs infused it. Few culinary artists in the world can come close to replicating the savory flavor of freshly roasted grouse no matter how many fancy sauces they cover the fowl with, or what they stuff it with."

"All these years," Missy said, talking softly and directly to Hand as if Joe and Marybeth weren't in the room, "I didn't know how wonderful these birds could be. There they were, just flying around the place. I didn't even know they were *grouse.* I thought they were just fat little birds."

Hand laughed and shook his woolly head. He was charmed by her, or doing a very good impression of it.

"It's like this dining room," Missy said. "Earl never wanted to eat in here. He said it was too dark and he never liked to linger over fine food and wine. To Earl, food was just fuel. But it's lovely, isn't it? A lovely room to eat wonderful fresh grouse in."

"Mom," Marybeth said sharply, "are you okay?"

"I'm *wonderful,* honey," Missy said, inflecting a slight Southern accent Joe had never heard before. He noted how the lilt made Hand smile in appreciation, as if she'd triggered something from his youth just the two of them understood.

Joe felt his scalp crawl. She was *flirting* with him.

"Marcus shot them," Missy said. "He brought them to me this afternoon and said they would be as magnificent as they turned out to be."

"I find upland shooting relaxing," Hand said, still looking at Missy. "I take my Purdey side-by-side shotgun with me everywhere I go, just in case. Hunting and shooting helps me clear my mind and focus only on the things that matter."

Missy turned her head slightly to hide her blush and her smile.

Joe said, "Grouse season doesn't open for two weeks."

"Excuse me?" Hand said.

"You're poaching."

It was suddenly very silent in the room. In his peripheral vision, Joe could see José Maria step backwards from Missy's side into a dark corner.

"Those are *my* birds," Missy said. "They're on *my* ranch."

"Nope," Joe said. "They're wild and managed by the state."

"I didn't realize we lived in Communist China," Missy said.

Joe shrugged.

"Marybeth," Missy said, an edge in her voice, "your husband is a kill-buzz."

"That would be 'buzzkill,'" Joe corrected. To Hand, he said, "I'll drop off the citation later. Don't worry. You can afford the fine."

Marcus Hand grinned at Joe, but his eyes couldn't completely hide his anger and resentment.

The rest of dinner proceeded awkwardly. Joe pretended not to notice. The grouse *was* delicious. Marybeth and Missy filled the vacuum with small talk about the girls, the library, the weather. Anything but the case.

Marcus Hand studied his wineglasses and filled them often. Joe could hear the rest of Hand's Jackson Hole legal team in the small dining area beyond the door. He thought there must be six or seven people eating dinner in the other room, like the kids' table at Thanksgiving. He doubted they were being treated to grouse.

As José Maria brought out small dishes of vanilla ice cream with bourbon sauce, Joe turned to Missy.

"How involved were you with The Earl's wind project?"

Missy's smile turned hard. "Why do you ask?"

"It's one of the biggest in the state and it cost tens of millions to build," Joe said. "It's not like a new corral. I'm sure it was discussed."

"What about it?" she asked, looking down the length of the table for her lawyer to step in. Since he was wrapped up with opening another bottle of rare red wine he'd found in the cellar, he didn't respond. Neither did Marybeth.

"You asked me to help investigate the murder," Joe said to Missy. "I'm on thin ice as it is, since I'm technically on the other team. So if I'm going to help at all, I need to have some things cleared up. I can't be flying blind."

"I thought that was your specialty," she said. Then she noted Marybeth glaring at her and quickly added, "Not that I don't appreciate what you're doing, Joe. I know you've been spending quite a bit of extra time establishing that I had nothing to do with this."

Missy filled the end of her spoon with a tiny bit of ice cream and stabbed the tip of her tongue at it. Her eyes closed slightly as she did, like her more delicate version of Hand's food swooning. She seemed to know it would get his attention. It worked and he looked up, saw her, and appeared enchanted.

"He wants to know how involved I was in Earl's business dealings," she said.

"Why is it important?" Hand asked Joe.

"Because I talked to Bob Lee on the next place," Joe said, thumbing over his shoulder in the general direction of the Lee Ranch. "He said The Earl approached him two years ago to buy his holdings outright, but Bob wouldn't sell it all. So Earl negotiated a price for just the adjoining ridge. Bob didn't mind selling that, since it was worthless for livestock or hay, and he thought he'd get the best of Earl since the price was twice what it had been appraised for. Then less than a week after the closing, Earl met some guy from Cheyenne and bought his company—Rope the Wind."

Joe let that sink in. He checked Missy for a reaction, but she wore her best porcelain mask.

"Now Bob realizes the windy ridge was all Earl ever really wanted," Joe said.

Missy said, "You are asking me about things that happened before we were married."

"Right about the time you started sneaking around with him behind Bud Longbrake's back," Joe said. "I thought maybe he'd talked to you about his entry into the wind business."

Her eyes became cold and hard, and she barely moved her mouth when she said, "We had other things to talk about."

Joe nodded and said, "Rope the Wind was an established company at the time, from what Bob Lee told me. They'd gotten going before the current administration came into power and created the big boom in renewable energy. But apparently Earl could look ahead and see it coming, so he put everything into place before it did. He bought the company since they were up and running and he could move fast."

Hand said, "Earl Alden was a kind of genius that way. He bought up depressed Iowa farms before the Feds started handing out ethanol subsidies, and it sounds like he had the same instinct when it came to wind.

"That's something I've learned about the genius of Earl Alden," Hand said, nodding his head, "and one of the three common categories of wealthy clients I've served over the years. The people who exist in a stratosphere outside of ours, although one could say thanks to them I'm now in it," he chuckled. "But I digress. I've learned over the years there are three kinds of rich men, and only three. The first are those who had their wealth given to them. Those types generally get in trouble because they haven't earned their wealth, although they certainly enjoy it. It gives them a skewed kind of entitlement, and they often step over the line because they think the rules don't apply to them, alas. I've been hired by many of them. Even if they avoid prison—which they do thanks to me—they eventually spiral out. Many of them have such self-loathing that it's contagious."

Joe sat back, listening. While Hand talked, the thighbone bounced up and down in his mouth.

Hand said, "The second type is what I call the 'makers-of-things.' These are your entrepreneurs, the risk-takers. Most of them started out humble and figured out a way to make a product or a service that customers want to buy. These are the truly creative, mad geniuses. They're quintessentially *American.* They produce real things—widgets, ideas, devices, inventions, you name it. Many of them started out at the lowest level of their fields and rose up. Although they aren't self-destructive like the trust-fund babies, they're fighters for what they've earned. They'd rather go to court to prove their innocence than take a plea and pay a fine or go home. I usually end up in arguments about my fee with them, for example," he said, smiling.

Hand paused. "Earl Alden is a charter member of the third type. Earl is—was—a skimmer. He's like many of the Wall Street and Big Business types we've heard so much of in recent years. Earl started with some money, but he learned early on to work the system and take a cut. He produced nothing of record and made nothing of note. But he worked the politics and figured out ways to be there when the money flowed. He didn't care if the gusher of cash made sense or if it was moral or ethical. He just concentrated on the gusher itself. And apparently Earl saw the value of ethanol before the farmers did. Ethanol uses more energy to produce than it generates, and it deprives the Third World of corn to eat, but the politicians and the agribusiness firms benefit. And he foresaw wind power before the ignorant ranchers could. Earl was the best skimmer I ever studied."

"I find that repugnant," Marybeth said softly.

"If it wasn't Earl," Hand said, "it would have been someone else.

At least Earl was here to take care of your mother, and your family to some degree. And for once he was actually building something himself instead of skimming only."

Missy didn't weigh in. The method of wealth had never interested her, Joe thought, only that her man had it. She was similar to her ex-husband in that she couldn't see past the gusher.

Joe said, "I learned a lot from Bob Lee and I've got some leads to track down. Bob is a bitter man. He doesn't exactly mourn the untimely death of Earl Alden. He thinks Earl cheated him out of that windy ridge—which he didn't. Earl had a better use for the ridge than grazing cows."

"When you say he's bitter," Hand said, learning forward and plucking the thigh out of his mouth and tossing it aside, "the question is how bitter? Bitter enough that maybe I should send my investigators over to have a talk with him as well?"

Joe shrugged. "He's a tough old bird. That might not work out in your favor. Plus, he's not in good shape. He's on oxygen and can barely move around. There's no way he hoisted Earl's body to the top of that turbine."

"Is there anyone around who could have done it?" Hand asked, arching his eyebrows.

"Well," Joe said, "he has a son."

"Wes," Missy said, as she narrowed her eyes. "He's a big guy. He's some kind of biker or hot-rod type. I think we've run that redneck off our land more than once."

Joe held up his hands. "Don't get me wrong. I'm making no accusations here. The Lees are solid folks and don't you dare smear them without solid proof, which we don't have. My point is Earl had enemies other than his lovely wife."

"Shame on you," Missy hissed toward Joe. "Of course he did."

"Have the sheriff and the comely Miss Schalk interviewed the Lee family?" Hand asked, gently sweeping his plates aside with his arm so he could steeple his fingers on the table and think aloud.

"No," Joe said, nodding toward Missy. "They've had blinders on. They've got one suspect and they're bound to convict her come hell or high water."

"Thanks to Bud," Marybeth said.

Missy said, "Yes, thanks to Bud."

Joe turned to his mother-in-law. "How did the rifle end up in your car?"

Her eyes flared, and she took a breath to speak. Joe expected Marybeth to intervene, but she didn't. She was just as interested in the answer.

"Never mind that," Hand interjected. "Missy, don't answer. It's water under the bridge. Obviously," he said to Joe, "whoever framed her put it there."

"Don't you want to hear from your client?" Joe asked.

Hand sat back, incredulous. "No," he said finally, as if Joe had asked the most ridiculous question in the world. Then with a wipe of his hand through the air, he changed subjects.

"This is all getting very interesting," Marcus Hand said. His eyes were lit up. "Do you realize what you've just done, Mr. Pickett?"

Joe and Marybeth looked over. "What?"

"You've established another theory," Hand said, resting his chin on the top of his steepled fingers. "You've introduced a reasonable doubt in the prosecution narrative.

"Joe!" Marybeth said, surprised. Then to Hand: "But that doesn't prove anything. It doesn't prove Mom is innocent."

"Doesn't have to," Hand said to Marybeth, suddenly professorial. "Our job here isn't to out the killer. That's the job of law enforcement and the prosecution. This isn't Perry Mason. Confessions on the stand just don't happen. All we need—and what your clever husband

Joe might have given us—is the eight percent of doubt I need to build on."

Missy said nothing. Joe didn't expect her to shower him with gratitude. She simply leaned back in her chair with her most pleasant face. As if she'd been anticipating this and it was all her due.

Joe and Marybeth went outside toward Joe's pickup as Marcus Hand stayed behind to give a new set of marching orders to his team. Joe heard enough to know Hand was building on the new theory, and dispatching personnel to blanket Twelve Sleep County and others to start collecting affidavits and interviews.

Marybeth walked with Joe in silence. As Joe opened the door for her, she said, "I was hoping this would all be a matter of proving her innocence. Something clean."

Joe said, "It's rarely like that in a high-profile murder case or when money and ambition are involved on both sides. Or when the defendant . . ." He bit his lip.

"I'm going to check on Lucy and April to make sure they haven't killed each other," she said, digging her phone out of her purse. Joe reached across her lap and found his citation booklet in the box of documents and regulation books he kept on the floorboards. "Back in a second," he said.

Missy met him at the front door. Over the years, both had made conscious efforts not to be anywhere alone with the other for fear of what would be said. Joe saw her standing in the shadow and he paused for a moment before continuing. She waited for him in silence. He realized she was sneaking a cigarette, and the cherry glowed red in the dark.

He said, "Here's Marcus Hand's ticket for poaching those grouse. See he gets it."

She took it without a glance. "You never fail to disappoint," she said, blowing smoke and keeping her voice down so her daughter couldn't overhear her across the ranch yard.

"Thanks for the reminder," Joe said.

"I know you're doing what you're doing more for your wife and daughters than for me. I understand that."

Joe didn't argue with her.

"You think I'm a heartless bitch," she said. "I can see it in your eyes. You've nothing but contempt for me. Look around you," she said. "Then think about it later. You think this has been easy, don't you?"

Before he could respond, she said, "I was the last of eleven children and my parents never failed to remind me I was their *mistake*, as they put it. We moved every year to a new farm in Missouri or Arkansas, wherever my father could get hired. I never had a home. We slept two or three to a bed. The clothes I wore had been handed down through six different girls, so by the time I got them they were rags. I once was forced to go to school wearing boots my brother made of *duct tape*."

She paused, and Joe shuffled his feet and looked down.

"I didn't own a new dress until I was two years out of high school," she said. "And I bought it myself. By then my parents were so old and broken they could barely remember my name. My older brothers and sisters all scattered and I don't know—or care—where a single one of them is or if they're even alive. You think I'm kidding, but I'm *not*."

"I gotta get going," Joe said.

"You've only seen me as your wife's gold-digger mother," she said. "You've never seen or even thought about what made me this way, or how I clawed my way out of it. And you never give a thought to how tough that was to raise Marybeth right—with the right values—from the hole I crawled out of."

"No," Joe said, "I guess I haven't given it much thought."

She smiled triumphantly, but it morphed into a sneer. "If anyone thinks they're going to take away all this, they don't know me, either."

"Did you do it, Missy?" Joe asked suddenly.

The sneer remained. There was no flinch. She took a long drag on the cigarette and blew the smoke at him and said, "What do *you* think?"

Then she turned on her heel and went back into her house. The citation Joe had given her fluttered to the ground.

"What was *that* about?" Marybeth asked, when Joe climbed into the pickup.

"She told me about her childhood," he said. "Some details I hadn't heard before."

Marybeth sat back in her seat and looked over at Joe, puzzled. "What about her childhood?"

"About growing up moving around, all her siblings, her parents, the poverty and all that. Like it sort of explains the way she is, I guess."

Marybeth was stunned. "She said *that*?"

"Yup."

"She didn't tell you about shoes made out of duct tape, did she?"

"Yes. I hadn't heard that one before."

"Joe, you know my grandfather owned a dozen car dealerships in Southern California and my grandmother was an actress. Mom was an only child who grew up with everything she ever wanted. She was spoiled and *she makes things up.*"

Joe said, "I know all that. She lies without blinking an eye."

"And the way she was flirting with Marcus Hand at dinner," Marybeth said, "it was disgusting. Earl Alden is barely cold."

"He'll never be as cold as your mother," Joe said.

On the way home, they divided up duties. Even if Hand and his people developed the new theory, Marybeth thought it imperative that she know for sure what had happened, who had killed Earl even if Hand didn't care as long as reasonable doubt could be established.

Joe agreed. He said, "I'm curious about what you'll find out about Rope the Wind. How they came to be. Who they are—or were."

"I'll find out what I can about them," she said.

"Also," Joe said, "if Earl was such a big-time skimmer as Hand described him, why would he invest so much of his own money into actually building a wind farm? It seems out of character. Since Missy didn't seem to know much about the initial financing—and I think she would—I wonder if maybe someone else was putting up the money? That seems more like Earl's style. And if so, who?"

"I never thought of that," Marybeth said. "I'll find out what I can. The state has corporation filings, things like that. They're all public documents."

"I'm going to keep looking for Bud," Joe said. "I have a feeling he's not far. And despite what we talked about tonight, Hand knows Bud is still the key. If Bud takes the stand and comes across as credible, the rest is history. So I want to talk to Dulcie. She's got to have more on Missy than we realize or she wouldn't have pushed it as hard as she has. She can't have based everything on Bud's testimony."

"Maybe she wants to beat Marcus Hand," Marybeth said.

"Maybe."

"Or maybe she wants to put my mother away."

"Could be."

"We know what Sheriff McLanahan's motivation is," Marybeth said. "He wants to get reelected."

"Yup."

"Joe?" Marybeth asked as they drove under the archway. "Do you really think the Lees had something to do with it?"

Joe drove five minutes before answering. "No, I don't."

"Then why are we doing this? Is it just to help Marcus Hand create enough doubt?"

"Yup."

She said, "If nothing else, I want to be assured Bob Lee had nothing to do with it so we can look elsewhere. Since Earl left a lifetime of deals behind him, he could have enemies we don't know anything about. I can't just sit here and let Hand get her off under a cloud. It makes me feel kind of dirty. Isn't there another way?" she asked.

He shrugged. "Didn't you ask me to do what I could to help her out? To help *us* out?"

Sighing, she said, "Yes, but I meant we should help prove her innocence. Not just muck up the water so badly the judge and jurors can't decide. There's a difference between innocence and being found not guilty."

"Not to Marcus Hand," Joe said. "Maybe not to your mother, either."

"But we're different," Marybeth said.

Joe couldn't think of a response that wouldn't get him in trouble.

"Joe," she said, "now would be the time we need more help with this. The trial starts in ten days."

He nodded.

"Joe?"

"I tried to call him today," he confessed. "The call didn't go through and there wasn't any way to leave a message. He might have switched phones. So I might have to go where I know he was last and try to find him in person."

She said, "Then go, Joe. Put the rest behind you."

SEPTEMBER 5

All truths are easy to understand once they are discovered; the point is to discover them.

—Galileo

23

Joe spent the Labor Day weekend in the field, patrolling his district from the banks of the Twelve Sleep River through the main streets of Saddlestring and Winchester to the high mountain roads in the Bighorns. As was his custom on the two busiest weekends of the summer, Memorial Day and Labor Day, he made himself as conspicuous as possible in his red shirt and green pickup truck. He noted the philosophical difference in the fishermen, hunters, hikers, and campers from the first three-day holiday of the season. On Memorial Day weekend, it was often still chilly, but the mood of the citizens he encountered was bursting with optimism and anticipation for the warm weather ahead. The Labor Day weekend, although nearly always blessed with pleasant weather and good conditions, was fused with a sense of loss and dread that the summer was over. More fights and violations occurred on Labor Day weekend, and citizens seemed to be walking around with shorter fuses.

He'd ticketed several fishermen for not having licenses as they got out of their drift boats at a river takeout, and he'd issued a warning to a raftful of floaters for forgetting their personal flotation devices. Although he was doing his duty and enforcing the law, he was immeasurably distracted because his head was swimming with thoughts of

Missy, Earl, Bud, Marcus Hand . . . and what he'd discovered about Nate Romanowski.

He'd been alarmed on Saturday to find Large Merle's house abandoned on the two-track to Hole in the Wall Canyon. It was a hot and windy day, and dust devils swirled across the mesa that fronted the canyon. Sandy grit washed across the hood of his pickup like rain and filtered through the air vents on the dashboard. The closer he drove to the trailhead that led into the canyon, the worse his feeling of dread.

The feeling was confirmed even before he trekked down the trail to the caves. There was a palpable emptiness in the air, and when he saw the horrible gaping mouth of the cave marked by black tongues of soot that licked upward, it was as if he'd been hit hard in the chest.

Joe nudged his boot tip through the debris inside the cave, recognizing items he'd seen there before. Nate's radios and monitors were shattered, table and chairs practically vaporized, his satellite phone disemboweled. Panic set in as Joe rooted through the wreckage. If Nate had been caught in the explosion—*What the hell had happened?*—there was no sign of a body. Which meant whoever had done this had taken the body. Or *somehow* his friend had survived. But when Joe surveyed the scorched walls of the cave and kicked through the shards that remained, he couldn't imagine anyone living through it.

Joe had never anticipated this. Nate was security-conscious to the point of paranoia, and he had the ability to track anyone venturing into the canyon. Which meant that whoever had attacked had slipped by the wires, sensors, and cameras on the trail and gotten close enough to lob a grenade or explosive into the mouth of the cave. Either that, or it had been done from long distance. A missile?

And then he saw a blackened and cracked object within the pile. His first thought was: *burned flesh.* Swallowing hard to keep from retching, Joe used a broken stave to flick debris away from the object. To his horror, he saw it wasn't skin or a body part, but the bottom half of Alisha Whiteplume's black leather boot.

He said, "Oh, no."

Knowing more than most how Nate thought, Joe exited the cave and hiked up above the shattered mews to a wooded alcove his friend had once showed him. The clearing was small but pastoral. Nate said he liked to sit naked on a lone rounded boulder in the clearing to read or think. Nate found it spiritual, and invited Joe to use it any time he needed it. Joe declined.

And here she was, or what was left of her body, anyway. Nate had placed her remains on hastily built scaffolding so it lay exposed to the sun and birds in the traditional Native way, before the Jesuits had banned the practice. Bits of her clothing and hair had been tied to the corner posts and they wafted in the slight breeze. Her skull was tilted to the side and Joe recognized her large white teeth grinning at him in a manic forced smile. Ravens that had been feeding on the body had nearly stripped it clean. They watched Joe from overhanging branches with tiny black soulless eyes, waiting for him to leave.

Nate hated ravens, Joe knew.

So in homage to his friend, he blew one out of a tree with his shotgun. Black feathers filtered down through the branches to settle on the pine needle floor. The surviving ravens scattered with rude *caws* and heavy wing-beats.

He knew they'd come back after he left to finish the job. But he knew *he'd* never come back, and he doubted Nate would.

If his friend was somehow still alive.

And if Nate had somehow survived an attack that killed his lover and wiped out his sanctuary . . . there would be hell to pay.

When Marybeth heard the story on Saturday night, she sat back on the couch and closed her eyes. She said, "Poor, poor Alisha. She always knew if she stayed with Nate, something could happen. But she didn't deserve *this.* Her poor family. Her students and everyone who knew her . . ." Marybeth's voice trailed off.

After a minute, she opened her eyes and looked up at Joe. "We'll never know for sure what happened, will we?"

"Maybe not," Joe said. "Unless Nate comes back and tells us. Or whoever did it brags."

"This is the price for living outside of society," she said. "When horrible things happen, no one knows. This is the price for living the way Nate lives."

"Either that," Joe said, "or marking time in prison. Nate made his choice."

"And you helped him," Marybeth said, not without sympathy.

"I did," Joe said.

"Do you have any idea where he is?"

"Nope."

"But you think he's alive?"

Joe nodded. "Someone built that scaffold. I'm sure it wasn't the guy who attacked him. There's Large Merle, but he seems to be missing also."

She hugged herself, thinking that over. She said, "Poor Nate. He fell hard for Alisha. What do you think he'll do?"

Joe didn't hesitate. He said, "My guess is things are going to get real Western."

He was surprised when she didn't ask him to try to stop it.

Early the next morning, Joe drove out of town into the heart of the Wind River Indian Reservation. His green Ford game warden truck always got plenty of looks from those outside, and he could guess most of them were speculating who had done something wrong on the outside this time, since Joe had no jurisdiction within the sovereign borders of the reservation. He tipped his hat to a pair of large short women padding along the roadside, and at a group of boys playing pickup basketball at the school playground. He noted the pronghorn antelope carcasses hanging from tree branches and especially from basketball hoops hung over most garages. Three men in the process of skinning a pronghorn squinted at him as he drove by, wondering if he was going to stop.

Alice Thunder's home was a neat ranch-style pre-fab plopped down in the center of a postage-stamp lot. Her car was parked outside on the driveway to the garage. Joe wondered why American Indians never used their garages for parking their cars, but let it remain a mystery.

On the res, Joe had learned, bloodlines ran deep and far and everyone was connected in some way. Alice Thunder was the receptionist at Wyoming Indian High School. She and Alisha had been close friends and possible relations of some kind. Alice was oval-faced and kindly-looking, a Native whose eyes showed she'd seen a lot over the years in that school. She was an anchor within the community whom everyone confessed to and relied upon, the Woman Who Knew All and Was Not a Gossip.

Joe parked pulled behind Alice Thunder's car and took a deep breath before opening his door. He told Tube to stay inside. He removed his hat as he walked across the dew-sparkled lawn to her front door.

She opened it as he raised his hand to knock.

"Mrs. Thunder," he said.

She didn't smile or grin with greeting or recognition. Her face was still, stoic. He followed her gaze from his pickup to his hat in his hands to his expression, and she said, "She's gone, isn't she?"

Joe said, "I'm sorry."

There was the slightest flicker of her eyes, but her mouth didn't pucker and there were no tears.

"I knew the second I saw you drive up," she said. "I've had a feeling about Alisha for several days that she was gone."

He looked at his boots.

She asked, "How?"

He said, "I'm not exactly sure how it happened. She was with Nate when someone went after him. I don't know who it was or how they got to them. I'm sure she wasn't targeted."

Alice Thunder nodded slightly, as if she wasn't surprised. "Is Nate alive?"

Joe said, "I hope so, but I don't know that, either. I haven't heard from him. By the way," he said, looking up, "law enforcement in Johnson County doesn't know about this. I didn't report it. You and my wife are the only people who know. I can give you the location of her body if you want to bring her back or pay your respects."

Alice said, "I'll have to think about that. Was her body treated with respect?"

Joe nodded.

"Then it isn't necessary right now."

"Thank you for coming and telling me," she said. "I appreciate that, Joe."

"Yup."

"You'll find out who did it and punish them?"

Joe said, "I think Nate's on the hunt right now. If I can catch up with him, I'll do what I can."

She nodded approvingly. "I hope you don't mind if I close this door on you right now. I need some time for myself." And she closed the door.

Joe stood on the porch for a moment, then turned and walked back to his pickup.

For a woman like Alice Thunder, who had seen so much tragedy over the years due to the crime rate on the reservation and so many young people taken away, Joe thought, death was a part of life.

For the next two days while Joe patrolled, the scene in the cave—and especially Alisha's body on the scaffold—stayed burned into his mind and was there when he closed his eyes at night. His theory, based on the layout of the canyon and Nate's security system, leaned toward an explosive fired from a distance. Maybe so far away Nate never knew someone had found him.

Which led Joe to wonder who, besides Large Merle and Joe himself, knew where his friend could be found. Sheridan knew because she'd once been there. Marybeth was vaguely aware of Nate's hideout, but had never been there and couldn't find it on a map. Joe, of course, had no idea who Nate was in contact with who might have be aware of his location. There was so much about Nate that Joe didn't know and didn't want to know that he now wished he did.

While Joe was out on patrol, Marybeth used the long holiday weekend at the library to do research. As she learned specifics about the wind energy industry, she called Joe on his cell. The more she learned, the more agitated she became.

She said, "I always thought all these windmills were going up because the energy they produced was clean and cost-effective. But that's not the case at all. The reason they're going up is political, and the demand for the power they generate is because of mandates by states and cities that a certain percentage of their electricity come from renewables like wind or solar."

"Down, girl," Joe said. "One thing this state has is wind."

"I know," she said. "I'm all worked up. Too much coffee and too much information I never knew before. And, yes, there are places where the wind blows hard enough where some of those turbines actually do make enough electricity to be profitable. Nearly all of the older turbines were put in places where they could actually do some good. But there isn't anywhere in the state or the country where the wind blows all the time. According to what I found, a good wind project produces at forty-five percent of capacity. That's all. And there's nowhere to store the energy if the power grid doesn't need it when the wind *is* blowing. There aren't big batteries anywhere, I mean. A lot of that energy is just wasted."

"Okay," Joe said, "but what does this have to do with Earl Alden's project?"

"I'm not exactly sure yet," she said, "but this whole thing might fall right into what Marcus Hand said about him, that he's a skimmer and not a 'maker-of-things.'"

"That's what I don't get," Joe said. "How much does a wind turbine cost to put up?"

She said she'd found the figures, and read them off. The installed cost of a turbine was roughly three million to six million dollars per including the equipment, roadwork, and overhead. The disparity in cost depended on whether the turbine was a 1.5-megawatt machine or one of the newer, bigger 3-megawatt generators.

"Wow," Joe said. "So a hundred turbines at Earl's farm . . ."

"I figured it out," she said, reading, "and came up with an investment of four hundred million dollars."

Joe whistled.

"For a farm the size of Earl's," she said, "Bob Lee would have received at minimum one point five million dollars per year. With all the considerations, he could have generated forty-five million dollars over the first thirty-year lease."

"Oh, man," Joe said.

"Lots of people would kill for that," she said. "Or kill if they were swindled out of it."

"He doesn't seem like the killing type," Joe said. "So tell me about Rope the Wind," Joe said.

"I'm still researching," she said. "What I've found is pretty interesting. Give me a little more time to dig."

As if he'd somehow been pulled there, Joe wound up on the two-track public easement that led to the windy ridge and the wind farm on the Thunderhead Ranch. He retraced his route from two weeks before when he'd seen the antelope hunters and later found The Earl's body. The blades of the turbines cut through the cloudless sky like scythes, whistling, and he drove to the edge of the Lee Ranch and pulled off the road onto a promontory.

He was surprised to find another vehicle on top, a red Subaru wagon. County Attorney Dulcie Schalk's car.

She apparently didn't hear him coming, because she didn't turn around as he drove up behind her. She was out of her car, leaning back against the hood, looking out at the wind farm with her arms crossed below her breasts. She wore a red tank top, snug white shorts, and a ponytail cascaded from the back opening of a King Ropes ball cap.

Joe had never seen her on her day off before. Her long tan legs were crossed one over the other. She looked young, athletic, and undeniably attractive.

So that he wouldn't scare her by suddenly appearing by her side, he tapped his horn as he pulled his truck in behind her car. The sound startled her and she wheeled around, fear and anger in her eyes until she recognized him. She acted as if she'd been caught doing something she was ashamed of, and he wondered what it was.

Joe told Tube to stay inside and climbed out.

"I didn't expect to find you out here," he said, fitting his Stetson on his head and ambling up to her. "I'm sorry I surprised you."

"I was focused on the windmills," she said, "and that high-pitched sound they make. It's like you can't hear anything else except that *sound*."

"You should hear 'em when the wind is really blowing," Joe said. "You'll think there's a truck coming at you."

"There's always a downside, I guess," she said, turning around and assuming the pose she'd had when he arrived.

Joe leaned back against the grille of the Subaru next to her and looked out, trying to see what she was focused on. "Downside to what?"

"Every kind of energy development, I guess," she said.

He thought about what he'd learned from Marybeth, but decided it wasn't the time to go there.

"I'm just getting it all straight in my mind," she said by way of explanation, "since things were pretty crazy that day you found the body. I want to make sure it's clear in my mind where Earl Alden was shot, how far the body was transported, and which turbine he was hoisted up."

"The one not turning," Joe said. "They disabled it so the forensics boys could do their thing."

She looked over, slightly miffed. "I know *that*," she said. "I just wonder why Missy chose that particular windmill. It isn't the closest one from where he was shot. There are eight towers in between."

Joe rubbed his chin. "I never thought of that. Maybe because the one he was hung from was the most visible from out here. So the body would be sure to be seen."

"But why?"

"That I couldn't tell you," he said.

After a moment, she said, "We really shouldn't be talking like this. What if someone sees us?"

Joe shrugged. He was wondering that himself.

"I mean, you've got a built-in conflict in regard to this case. I've told you I can't confide in you."

"I know," Joe said. "And I honor that."

"I knew you would," she said. "But I'd rather you were on our side."

"I'm not on a side," Joe said. "I'm trying to figure out what happened. What's true. That doesn't put me on a side."

She shook her head and frowned. "I disagree, Joe. I'm the county attorney and I'm presenting a case based on the evidence. You're trying to prove me wrong."

He started to argue, but folded his arms across his chest and looked out. He realized they were both standing in the exact same posture now.

He said, "This reminds of a question Bob Lee asked me. What do you see when you look out at that wind farm?"

She started to answer flippantly, but decided it was a serious question. "I see the future of America," she said. "For better or worse. I know that sounds corny."

Joe pursed his lips, looked out, considered what she said.

"Do you think they're beautiful?" he asked.

"The wind turbines?"

"Yup."

"I guess so. They're graceful-looking. They gleam in the sun, even if they make that annoying sound."

He nodded. "If those same machines out there were pumping out oil or gas or if they were nuclear generators, would they still be as beautiful in your eyes?"

"Joe, what's your point?" she asked, slightly exasperated.

"Like you," he said, "I'm trying to get things straight in my mind. I wonder if things are beautiful because of where a person sits."

She glared at him. "I don't want to get distracted right now, Joe. I've got a murder case to win and I don't want to have this discussion."

"I know," he said. "I'm just suggesting that it's easy to look at something and see what you want to see when somebody else, say, could look at the same thing and see something else."

"What's your point?" she asked again.

He shrugged.

"Are you talking about windmills, or are you saying I might have blinders on concerning your mother-in-law's guilt? That maybe we should be looking elsewhere for Earl Alden's killer?"

Joe didn't answer directly but nodded toward the wind farm. "A little of both, I guess."

"No," she said heatedly. "This is why you shouldn't have come up here. This is why we shouldn't have talked. You're trying to steer me somewhere I don't want to go."

He said, "Dulcie, I'm just trying to figure out what happened."

"You're making me a little uncomfortable," she said. "We should go."

He said, "Yup."

In the early evening, as Joe worked his way back home via back roads and two-tracks, he cruised up Main Street in Saddlestring toward the river bridge. The air was still and sultry, and a few revelers poured out of the Stockman's as he passed by, beer bottles in their hands. He glanced over to see who they were but didn't identify them as locals.

They were thirty-somethings, three men and two women. The men had facial hair and baggy pants, and the women wore cargo shorts with river sandals.

One of the men, in a black oversized polo shirt with a ball cap pulled down low over his eyes, looked up as Joe drove by, and for a moment their eyes locked.

A bolt of recognition shot through Joe, and he tapped on his brakes.

The man broke off and quickly looked down. His companions called after him as he turned abruptly and walked stiff-legged back in the bar.

"Shamazz, what the fuck?" one of the women said. "You look like you've seen a ghost!"

24

Johnny Cook and Drennen O'Melia were outside of Farson and Eden in west central Wyoming doing meth and getting their ashes hauled. They'd been there most of the week. Their plan, for a while, was to go west to California or at least as far as Las Vegas. But they hadn't even made it to the Utah border.

It was that green sign saying they'd entered the tiny town of Eden that held them up. Who, Johnny had asked, wouldn't want to stop and have a beer in a place called Eden?

Johnny was taking a break. He slumped in a director's chair someone had set up outside between clumps of sagebrush about fifty yards from the trailers and smoked a cigarette and drank a can of beer. Although the sun was moving in on the top of the Wind River Mountains in the distance, it was still warm out and Johnny didn't know where his shirt or pants were, which trailer, so he sat there in his straw cowboy hat, boxers, and boots with a pistol across his bare knees. He knew he looked awesome without a shirt, so he didn't mind.

Occasionally, he would raise and fire a Ruger Mark III .22 pistol at gophers that raised their heads up out of a hole. He'd hit a couple. When he did he'd shout *"Red mist!"* to the sky. He'd watch as other gophers rushed over to feed on the remains, and when they did,

Johnny shot them for being such lousy friends. At one point he'd had a revelation about the nature of friendship in the cruel, cruel world, but he couldn't remember now what it had been.

Johnny shivered, despite the heat. The tremor ran through his entire body and raised goose bumps on his forearms. Immediately afterwards, he was flush and felt sweat prickle beneath his scalp. Damn meth, he thought, trying to remember the last time he'd eaten something. Two days ago, maybe. He had a vague recollection of eating an entire package of cold hot dogs dipped one-by-one into a warm jar of mayonnaise. But he might have dreamed that, he conceded.

He heard a whoop from behind him and he turned his head to see Drennen emerging from one of the trailers. Drennen was telling one of the girls inside something, and he heard her laugh.

"Don't go anywhere or get too comfortable," Drennen said to the girl. "I'll be coming right back after I reload."

As he shambled toward Johnny in the dust, Drennen said, "Jesus, what a wildcat. Cute, too. I can't get enough of that one. Lisa, I think her name is. Lisa."

Johnny nodded. "Brunette? Kinda Indian?"

"That's her," Drennen said. "Like to burn me down."

Johnny thought Drennen was lucky *any* girl would spend time with him, even for money. The burns on his face and neck from the back-blast of the rocket launcher on his face and neck looked hideous, Johnny thought. All red and raw and oozing. Drennen forgot how crappy he looked because he was high all the time, but no one else could possibly forget. He'd be fine after a while—the damage wasn't permanent—but getting there was not sightly.

Drennen collapsed into the dirt next to Johnny, then propped himself up with his elbow. He reached up and plucked the pistol from Johnny's lap and fired a wild and harmless shot at a gopher before handing it back. "Missed," he said. "Where'd you put that pipe?"

"You weren't even close." Johnny gestured toward their pickup. "In there, I think. Let me know if you see my shirt or my pants anywhere."

"I was wondering about that," Drennen said, slowly getting up to his hands and knees. "We still got plenty of rock?"

"I think so," Johnny said, distracted. "I can't remember a damn thing, so don't hold me to it."

Drennen laughed, got to his feet, and lurched toward the pickup to reload. Drennen said, "Man, I love this Western living."

The collection of double-wide trailers hadn't been out there for very long. They weren't laid out in any kind of logical pattern and looked to Johnny as if they'd been dropped into the high desert from the air. The dirt roads to get to the trailers were poor and old, and there wasn't a single sign designating the name of the place. An ex–energy worker named Gasbag Jim was in charge of the operation, and he had a small office in one of the double-wides where he collected money, assigned girls, and passed out from time to time from drinking too much Stoli or smoking too much meth.

Drennen and Johnny had learned about the place from a natural gas wildcatter at the Eden Saloon. They'd stopped for a beer or nine at the edge of the massive Jonah gas field before continuing on to California. When they found out Gasbag Jim's operation was less than twenty miles out of Farson and Eden in the sagebrush, they thought, *What the hell.*

That was four days ago. Or at least Johnny thought it had been four days. He'd have to ask Drennen.

Gasbag Jim's was an all-cash enterprise, which suited them just fine. That meant there would be no paper trail—no credit card receipts, no IDs, and no need for real names. They'd decided to call each other "Marshall" and "Mathers" because Drennen was a fan of the rapper Eminem, and Marshall Mathers was his real name, but Johnny had slipped and called Drennen "Drennen" when they were in bed with three women at once. One of the girls, Lisa Rich, the raven-haired beauty with heavy breasts, had coaxed their real names out of them the night before. She seemed very interested in their real names, for some reason.

"Fuck," Drennen said as he staggered back from the pickup holding the crack pipe. "We've been burning through cash like it was . . . money."

"I know," Johnny moaned, and rubbed hard at his face. He'd been noticing that his face didn't feel like it was his, like someone had stitched it over his real face to fool him. "Does my face look normal to you?" he asked.

Drennen squinted at Johnny. "You look normal," he said, "for an over-sexed tweaker with no pants."

They shared a good laugh over that one. But Johnny still distrusted his face. He probed his jawline with his fingertips, expecting to find a seam.

Then Drennen said, "I was talking to Gasbag Jim a while ago. I can see where this is headed and we're going to be broke on our asses in no time flat. So I made him a proposal."

"Yeah?"

"Yeah," Drennen said, pulling the top off a cold Coors. He lowered the lid of the cooler and sat down on it so he was facing Johnny. He was so close their knees almost touched. "See, all his business except for you and me comes from Jonah field workers between here and Pinedale. You seen 'em this last weekend."

Johnny had. Dozens of men, a parade of them, in new model four-wheel-drive pickups. Many of the customers lived in man camps put up by the energy companies. There were few women around. They talked of three things mostly: the prostitutes, hunting, and how the price of natural gas was dropping like a rock and might endanger their jobs and then they'd be out of work like everybody else. They wanted to spend their money while they had it.

"A bunch more layoffs coming," Drennen said. "This place is going to look like a ghost town pretty soon. Those guys'll get their pink slips and head home to wherever they came from. Gasbag Jim will have to send those girls away and sell his trailers, is what I'm thinking."

"So what?" Johnny said, shifting his weight so he could see the prairie over Drennen's shoulder. A gopher popped up twenty yards away and Johnny raised the pistol and fired. Missed. The pistol had gone off just a few inches from Drennen's ear and Drennen flinched, said, "Jesus, you almost hit me, you ass hat."

"Sorry," Johnny said, looking past Drennen for more gophers.

"Anyway," Drennen said, rubbing his ear and regaining his momentum. "So there's always a need for whores somewhere. Maybe just not here in a few months. So what I was talking about to Gasbag Jim was you and me get an RV and load in a half-dozen whores and take 'em to wherever there's action. Like that big oil discovery up in North Dakota. Gasbag Jim says they found oil and gas down in southern Wyoming, too. Southern Wyoming and northern Colorado someplace. And all those fucking windmills going up everywhere. Somebody's got to be building them. That means there'll be plenty of desperate men in lonely-ass places like this."

Johnny rubbed his eyes. They burned and he imagined they looked like glowing charcoal briquettes, because they felt that way. He'd need to go to the pickup and reload soon as well, and avoid the crash that was coming. It felt like there were a million spiders crawling through his body just beneath the skin. The rock would put them back to sleep. Johnny said, "Like a whorehouse on wheels?"

"Exactly," Drennen said. "*Exactly.* We drive up to the well, get the word out among the workers, go set up somewhere on public land or some dumbass rancher's place, and take our cut. Of course, we have to protect the whores and keep them productive, so we've got to be on-site and be alert and all that. I'll handle the accounting and paperwork, and all you'll have to do is stand around and look jumpy and menacing. I know you can do that."

"I can," Johnny said, pointing at the cooler. Drennen stood up and got him another beer.

"We need to make some money," Drennen said. "We're just about out and there is *no* work out there. We couldn't even get on at a dude ranch since it's September and the end of their season. Man, we burned through the whole wad in a couple a weeks."

"Maybe we can kill somebody else," Johnny said, patting his pistol and dropping his voice. "That's easier than hitting the road in an RV."

Drennen grunted. "Nobody we know needs anyone whacked," he said. "So there's no business there, either."

Johnny said, "Maybe we can get unemployment from the government. I heard one of those gas guys saying you can collect for something like two years now before you have to even look for a job. That sounds like a sweet deal to me."

Drennen rolled his eyes. "That's subsistence level, man. We can't do *that.* We've got to live higher on the food chain."

"So where do we get an RV?" Johnny asked. "Those mothers are expensive."

"I haven't figured that one out yet," Drennen said, dismissing Johnny's concern.

"And if we do somehow get one, why would Gasbag Jim trust us to lend us his whores and give him his cut? He don't know us from Adam. And along the same lines, if this is such a great idea, why won't Gasbag and his buddies just do it? Why do they need us?"

Gasbag Jim was always shadowed by two large Mexicans named Luis and Jesus. Luis openly wore a shoulder holster. Luis had a tricked-out tactical AR-15 he sometimes used to shoot at gophers using his laser sight. The Ruger also belonged to Luis.

Drennen had a blank expression on his face that eventually melded into petulance. "I didn't say I had the whole fuckin' thing figured out," he pouted. "I said I had a concept that I'm working through. One of us has to think ahead farther than the tip of our dick, you know."

Johnny looked down at his lap and smiled. At least *that* felt like his. "Wish I could figure out where I left my pants," he said. Then: "I've been thinking, too. What about that Patsy? I bet she'd part with a whole bunch more if we got to her and said we might have to talk. Hell, she got that bag of cash from somewhere. I bet there's a hell of a lot more where that came from."

Drennen shook his head and said, "I'm ahead of you on that one. But all we know is she's from Chicago. We don't have an address, and we don't really even know if that was her real name. It's not like she gave us a business card, bud."

"I went to Chicago once," Johnny said. "You're right, it's big. And I think Patsy knows people, if you know what I mean."

When Drennen didn't respond, he looked back at his friend. Drennen was sitting in the dirt, legs crossed Indian fashion, head tilted back. He was squinting at something in the sky.

"What?" Johnny said. "You're not gonna ask me what animal a cloud looks like again, are you? Because I'm not interested."

"Look," Drennen said, gesturing skyward with this beer can.

Johnny sighed and looked up. It seemed like a lot of effort.

"See it?" Drennen asked.

"What?"

"That bird. An eagle or whatever, going around in circles?"

Johnny squinted and finally found it. It was a long way up there.

"Remember when we got that job done in the canyon? Remember we saw a bird like that?"

"Yeah."

They both got the same thought at the same time, and they looked at each other.

"No waaaay," Drennen said, forcing a smile.

"Hell no," Johnny said, feeling a little sick after looking at Drennen square in the face.

25

Joe entered the dark and windowless Stockman's Bar. After he had spent all day outside in the bright September sunshine, the sudden gloom required a momentary hitch just inside the front door. As he waited for his eyes to adjust, his other senses took over: he heard the click of pool balls from the tables in back, the thud of a beer mug being put down for a refill after the ranch hand ordered a "re-ride," and smelled the piquant combination of sweat, dust, and cigarette smoke. The sound track for the emerging scene was the jukebox playing Lucinda Williams' "Can't Let Go."

Neither can I, Joe thought.

Most of the stools were filled. Half by regulars deep into the last stages of a three-day bender before going into extra innings of the holiday blues. Keith Bailey, the part-time Eagle Mountain Club security guard, was there again at his usual place, cradling a cup of coffee between his big hands. There were a few tourists Joe didn't recognize, mixed in with the locals but still standing out from them, and a bumptious gaggle of college-age cowboy and cowgirl wannabes clogging up the far end of the bar. But not the man he wanted to find. Joe felt sorry for these people who chose the dark solace of a cave when a bright, crisp, and multi-colored almost-fall day was exploding outside all around them in every direction.

Buck Timberman appeared out of the dark when Joe could see.

Timberman towered over the seated customers with both his hands flat on the glass and his head tilted forward with a "What can I get you?" eyebrow arch toward Joe.

Joe said, "Did anyone just come running through here? A male, mid-thirties? Thin, with fashionista stubble on his face? Black shirt and ball cap? Goofy look in his eyes?"

Timberman said, "Sorry, I can't help you, Joe" with his mouth, but his eyes darted down the length of the bar toward the back as he said it. He did it in a way that none of his customers could have picked up. Joe nodded his appreciation, and meandered down the ancient pine-stave floor that was sticky with beer spillage as if it were his own idea. He excused himself as he shouldered through the wannabes, past the wall of booths, and around the pool tables. When one of the shooters looked up, Joe said, "He go this way?" as if they knew each other. The man gestured with the tip of his cue and said, "Out that door in the back."

"Thank you kindly."

The door between the Cowboys and Cowgirls led through a cramped storeroom to a back door that opened up in the alley. It was used for deliveries. Beer crates and kegs were stacked to the ceiling, but there was an aisle through them to a steel back door. Electrical boxes, valves, and water pipes cluttered the wall next to the exit. Joe searched for a light switch, but couldn't find it and gave up.

He pushed out into the alley and quickly looked both ways. No Shamazz.

He put his hands on his hips and tried to think. Where would he go?

Joe jogged around the building to the sidewalk to see if the small knot of Bud Jr.'s colleagues were still out front so he could ask them for a confirmation. But they were gone, too.

Joe wished he could call for backup, but once again he was operating completely on his own. Was Bud Jr. in town for the trial? If so, why had he run when Joe recognized him? There was nothing wrong with attending a trial where his father was the featured player.

Since Bud Jr. wasn't on the street or in the alley and Joe hadn't heard a car start up or a door slam, Joe was befuddled. Then he recalled seeing a rusty ladder in the alley to the roof of the building, and cursed himself for not looking up when he came out of the bar. Maybe Shamazz had clambered up and watched Joe run around below him like an aimless rabbit?

And was he sure it was really Shamazz? If so, Bud Jr. was in what he'd consider his civilian gear. No puffy white shirt or jester hat for street performance, no white mime pancake makeup. He was even wearing his ball cap as a ball cap should be worn with the bill rounded and to the front and not backwards, sideways, or unbent with the label still showing on the bill in street fashion. And he was walking around without bouncing a Hacky Sack on the top of his foot, which for Shamazz was a trademark. But Joe remembered those vacant eyes because he'd seen them so many times. Pale blue eyes that saw the world in a different way than Joe did, as a place that oppressed him and other free spirits like him. And not just because the pupils were nearly always dilated. Eyes that said, *"Why the hell me?"* as a response to any request Joe ever made on the ranch, like, "Could you please go get the post-hole digger?"

That ladder was a no-go, Joe realized, when he returned to the alley, looked up, and saw it was detached from the brick at the top. If anyone had tried to use it, the ladder would have fallen back away from the building and crashed into the alley. Joe wished Bud Jr. had used it because then he'd be on him.

Then he pursed his lips and realized exactly where Shamazz was hiding.

The door to the stairs up to Bud Sr.'s empty apartment was open as it had been before. Joe took the steps slowly, being as quiet as he could. He listened for movement on the second level, and for Bud Jr.'s humming. Shamazz was *always* humming, or singing snatches of lyrics from songs from bands Joe had never heard of and was pretty sure he wouldn't like. Songs about angst and doom and loss and lack of diversity.

Joe mounted the landing. The light was out as it had been before, but he could see that the seal the sheriff's department had taped along the doorframe had been breached. Breathing softly, he removed his hat and leaned forward so he could press his ear against the door. There was a low-frequency vibration coming from inside, either the refrigerator or . . . an air-conditioning unit. No doubt it got very warm on the top floor of the old building with all those windows and what was likely poor insulation.

And he heard it: the hum. Then bad singing:

You gotta spend some time, love . . .

And Joe rolled his eyes and said to himself, *I have found you, Shamazz.*

He couldn't simply knock and expect Bud Jr. to let him in. Bud Jr. had run away for a reason, whatever it was. Because Joe had no jurisdiction or probable cause, he couldn't smash the door down, either. He knew Shamazz well enough to know he would quickly assert his constitutional rights even though he had nothing but contempt for the country. As Bud Jr. had once explained to Joe, The Man was always hassling him or putting him in jail, after all, simply for selling drugs that made people happy or doing street theater to loosen up the tight-ass types.

So how to get him to come out voluntarily?

He recalled the layout of the Stockman's storeroom below, where the breaker boxes and water pipes were located, and smiled.

It took twenty minutes of no electricity or water for Shamazz to come out. Joe stood just outside the door in the walkway between the Stockman's and the drugstore. He heard the door open upstairs, then counted a full two minutes while Bud Jr. fumbled around for a breaker box or water valve in the stairwell.

Finally, Joe heard a string of curses and heavy clomps coming down the stairs. Shamazz was cursing out Timberman for the loss of power and water. Joe stepped aside.

The door opened, and Bud Jr. came out without looking over his shoulder, where Joe was leaning against the bricks.

Joe said, "Shamazz."

Bud Jr. froze, then cried out and wheeled around so quickly he lost his footing and fell to the dirty cement. "You fucking *scared* me," he said to Joe. "Did you shut off my AC?"

"It's been a while," Joe said, extending a hand to help him up.

Bud Jr. didn't accept it at first. Then he sighed and let Joe pull him to his feet. As always, he looked resentful and petulant. Bud Jr. was four inches taller than Joe, and solidly built. Despite that, Joe now stood between Bud Jr. and the street. The passageway was so narrow it would be difficult for Bud to get around him toward the sidewalk.

"How have you been?" Joe asked.

"Fine. I'm just fine. Hey, it's great to see you again, Joe, but I've got to run." He took a step toward Joe to see if Joe would stand aside, but he didn't. Bud Jr. glared and set his mouth.

Joe said, "Where did you get the key to your dad's place?"

"Where do you think? I didn't break in, if that's what you're accusing me of," he said, defensive. "And what gives you the right to shut off the utilities? That's just cruel, man."

Joe said, "So Bud gave you a key, did he?"

Bud Jr. brushed dirt off his pants and shirt from the fall. He said, "Why wouldn't he? I'm his son, after all."

"I thought you hated him," Joe said. "You told me that, oh, a thousand times."

Bud Jr. had no response.

"Was that you at the funeral in the yellow van?" Joe asked.

"Maybe," Shamazz said, not meeting Joe's eyes.

"I can't believe you went there to show your respects."

"I'd rather spit on his grave."

"Where's Bud?"

"Who?"

"I'm looking for him," Joe said. "Just to talk. You probably know about the case against Missy and the fact that your dad is the star witness. Can you tell me where he is? Where you got the key?"

Bud Jr. looked past Joe toward Main Street. "I've really got to go," he said. "I'm sorry I can't stay around and, you know, relive old times with you."

Joe didn't like the way Bud Jr. was brushing him off, or the way he wouldn't meet his eye. As Bud Jr. tried to shoulder past, Joe stepped in front.

"You're annoying me," Joe said. "What are you trying to hide?"

"Nothing. You need to get out of the way. I've got my rights. Either arrest me or get the hell out of my way."

"You hated your dad. You hated the ranch. You hate this town. You hate the state. So why are you here?"

"People change," he said.

"You don't," Joe said.

"Really," Bud Jr. said, a note of whimper in his voice, "I have to go. I know my rights. I know you can't hold me here or make me answer your damned questions."

"Why are you in disguise?" Joe asked. "Why do you sort of look like a normal person?"

"That's fucking cold, man. Just cold." Then he leveled his eyes at Joe. "I hated you, too, man. Dudley Do-Right cracker and your white-bread cookie-cutter family. Guys like you . . ." He paused, his lips trembling.

"Go on," Joe said flatly. Joe had heard Bud Jr. say so many thoughtless and vile things before that he was shocked that he wasn't shocked. Bud Longbrake's son seemed to have no internal brake mechanism installed between his emotions and his mouth. Anything he thought came out in words. Joe had learned to tune him out, not engage, and pay no attention. Bud Jr.'s inability to put a sock in it had caused him much heartache over the years, but he'd never seemed able to connect what he said to the reaction his words elicited from others. He still couldn't, Joe thought . . .

"You people living out there on my family's ranch, taking advantage of him just like that old bitch Missy. Freezing me and my sister out like that, keeping me away . . ."

"I tried to *help* you," Joe said through clenched teeth. "I did a favor for your dad and tried to teach you how to work for a living."

"Duh," Shamazz said, bugging his eyes out. "It didn't take."

It was hard for Joe to see through the filter of rage that had descended over him like a red hood when he looked at Shamazz. "Who does that song you were singing up there?" Joe asked.

"What—you mean Death Cab for Cutie?"

"Death Cab for Cutie?"

"Yeah."

"I knew I didn't like them," Joe said, and reached out and grasped Bud Jr.'s ear.

"Tell me why you're here," Joe said, twisting hard. In the back of his mind, he listed the charges he could be brought up on. There were a lot of them. But he had the impression Bud Jr. would do all he could to avoid talking to the police for any reason.

"That *hurts,*" Bud Jr. cried, and reached up for Joe's hand. Joe kicked Shamazz hard in the shin with the toe of his boot. Bud Jr. squealed and dropped to his knees.

"I learned this from a friend," Joe said. "Remember Nate Romanowski? Now tell me what I want to know or I'll twist your ear off. I've seen a couple of ears come off. They make a kind of popping sound, like when you break a chicken wing apart. You know that sound? I'd guess it's even worse from the inside, you know?"

"Please . . . Joe, this isn't like you." There were tears of pain in his eyes.

Joe nodded. It wasn't. Whatever. He twisted. Bud Jr. opened his mouth to scream.

"No yelling," Joe said. "If you yell, you lose the ear. And if that happens, you've got another ear I can pull off. Then it will be real hard to listen to Death Cab for Cutie."

Shamazz closed his mouth, but there were guttural sounds coming out from deep in his chest.

"Tell me why you're here."

"I wanted to come home," Bud Jr. said, spitting out the words. *"I just wanted to come home."*

Joe was taken aback. He said, "But you don't *have* a home. Bud Sr. lost the ranch. You knew that."

"Ow-ow-ow-ow-ow," Bud Jr. said.

"We never took advantage of your dad," Joe said. "Missy did. You did. But I *worked* for him."

"Ow-ow-ow-ow-ow."

"Now where can I find your dad?" Joe asked, keeping the pressure on.

"You really don't know? *You really don't?*"

"Tell me why you're here."

He yelped, "I'm here to reclaim what's mine."

Joe said, "Nothing's yours anymore." But when he saw the wild-eyed passion in Bud Jr.'s eyes—passion he'd never seen before—Joe wondered if Shamazz was capable of murder, or at least willing to help out his father. He'd never thought of the kid that way before.

After he said to Bud Jr., "Tell me everything," Joe noted movement in his peripheral vision and glanced up to see a sheriff's department SUV cruise through the opening between the drugstore and the bar. Sollis was at the wheel. Had he been seen?

Joe involuntarily eased up on the ear, and Shamazz took full advantage of the sudden release of pressure. From where he sat on the garbage-covered pathway, he was able to reach back and fire a roundhouse punch that caught Joe full force in the temple. The blow made Joe let go, and staggered him. Bud Jr. scrambled to his feet and punched again, clipping Joe across the jaw and dropping him. Joe tried to protect his face against a fury of Hacky Sack–conditioned feet, but Bud Jr. was fueled by anger and desperation, and several hard kicks hit home. Joe rolled away, felt two sharp thumps in his back along his spine and one near his kidneys, and by the time he was able to right himself and struggle to his hands and knees, Shamazz had run away.

Joe stayed like that for a long time. His head and face ached sharply, and as his shock wore off, the kicks to his arms, shoulders, neck, and back began to pound.

Moaning, he managed to lean against the brick wall and vertically crabwalk up until he could balance on his feet again. He probed at his head for blood, but didn't find any. He hoped like hell Sollis wouldn't drive by again and see him. He wanted no one to see him.

As he limped to his pickup, Joe looked at his right hand—the one that had twisted Bud Jr.'s ear nearly off—as if it belonged to someone else. Like Nate, maybe.

Bud Jr. had fought like a wild man. Partly out of self-defense and partly out of something inside him that was of greater intensity than Joe's urge to protect himself. In a way, he admired Bud Jr., while he felt ashamed of himself both for the pressure he'd applied and for opening himself up for the attack.

Angry with himself, Joe climbed into his pickup. He looked into his own eyes in the rearview mirror, wondering who was looking back.

Ten minutes later, when he thought he'd recovered enough to find his voice again, he dug his phone out of his pocket—it was undamaged—and it rang before he could call Marybeth. The display indicated it was his wife calling *him*.

"Hi," he croaked.

She paused. "Joe, are you all right?"

"Dandy," he said.

"Your voice sounds different."

He grunted.

"Look," she said, "I had to call you right away. There're some things about the company Rope the Wind that I find really fishy. I've been on the Internet all afternoon, and I can't find the answer to some questions that just pop right out at me."

"Like what?" he said. He shifted in his seat because the places on his back where Shamazz had kicked him were sore. He'd had his ribs broken before, and he knew they'd not been fractured. Overall, he was okay, but it would be a while before he knew if anything was bruised or damaged.

"I located the original articles of incorporation application online at the secretary of state's office," she said. "Earl wasn't originally on the board five years ago. Five years is an eternity as far as wind energy companies go. Five years is *ancient.*

"The chairman and CEO was a man named Orin Smith," she said. "He listed his address as a post office box in Cheyenne. So of course the next step was to find out what I could about Orin Smith and see if I could connect him to Earl."

Joe *hmmmmmmm'd* to keep her going.

She said, "I came back with thousands of hits. And this is where it gets strange. Orin Smith is apparently the chairman and CEO of *hundreds* of companies incorporated in Wyoming. They run the gamut from energy companies like Rope the Wind to crazy ones like 'Prairie Enterprises,' 'Bighorn Manufacturing,' 'Rocky Mountain Internet,' 'Cowboy Cookies' . . . all kinds of companies."

Joe grunted, and said, "A couple of those sound sort of familiar."

"I thought so, too," she said, "but that's the really weird thing. They're just names. They sound like companies you hear about, but they don't really exist."

Joe shook his head, "What?"

"None of them seem to produce anything. There's no record of them after incorporation. Beyond the name itself, these companies just seem to be sitting there."

"I'm lost," he said.

"I am, too. I don't get it. And I don't understand at all how Earl Alden came into the picture."

Joe said, "We might be really going the wrong direction here. This doesn't seem to fit any kind of scheme I can think of."

"I know."

Then she said, "But I found one thing of interest."

"Yes?"

"I think I know where we can find Orin Smith."

"Fire away," he said.

"He's in federal custody in Cheyenne. It's amazing what one can find with a simple Google search of a name."

"What are the charges?"

"Let's see," she said, and Joe could hear her tapping keys. "Securities fraud, investment adviser fraud, mail fraud, wire fraud, international money laundering to promote specified unlawful activity, money laundering . . . on and on. Eleven counts in all."

"Which agency's got him?"

"FBI."

"Good," he said, putting his pen down. "Someone owes me a favor there."

Before he punched off, Joe said, "Ask your mother what she knows about Bud Jr. being back in town. I think she's hiding something."

"Bud Jr.? You mean Shamazz?"

"Yeah. I just had a run-in with him in town. I didn't get the best of it and I lost him."

He resolved to tell more her about the encounter later. Much later.

"Call me with what she says," Joe said.

"When will you be home?"

"I won't," he replied, looking into the visor mirror at the swelling and bruises beginning to show on his cheekbone and jaw. "I'm driving all night to Cheyenne to talk to Orin Smith."

As he drove south out of Saddlestring, he scrolled through the contact list on his phone until he found the name for Special Agent Chuck Coon.

26

"Now, *run,*" Nate Romanowski said to Johnny Cook and Drennen O'Melia.

"Man," Drennen said, "you can't make us do this. It's cruel."

"You can't," Johnny echoed.

Nate arched his eyebrows and said low and breathy, "I can't?"

He'd silently marched them a mile east from Gasbag Jim's place, in the direction of the Wind River Range, with the informant, Lisa, the dark-haired girl who'd learned their names and made the identification, in tow. She was coffee-and-cream color with dark eyes and high cheekbones. Her large breasts swelled against her white tank top. Short, muscular but shapely legs powered her through the sagebrush. She dangled a pair of strappy high heels from her finger because they hurt to walk in.

Nate guided Johnny and Drennen's progress by gesturing at them with the muzzle of the .500 Wyoming Express the way a trainer instructs bird dogs with hand signals. The sun was behind them at eye level, minutes before dusk, and the four of them cast long shadows across the sagebrush and dried cheat grass. Johnny Cook was still in his underwear and boots.

"What do you mean, run?" Drennen asked. "You gonna shoot us in the back?"

Nate shrugged. He said, "I'm giving you more of a chance than you deserve. It's an old Indian trick. You ever heard of Colter's Run?"

"Colter's what?" Johnny said.

"I have," Lisa offered. "Blackfeet, right?"

"Right," Nate said to her over his shoulder. Then he turned his attention back to the two men. "Eighteen-oh-eight, at the site of the present day Three Forks, Montana. The Blackfeet captured John Colter, the first white man to discover Yellowstone Park. They didn't know what to do with him: kill him like they'd just done to his partner John Potts, or strip him naked and let him run. They decided on the old Indian trick, and gave him a few feet head start before they chased him down. What they didn't know was that Colter was *fast.* He managed to outrun all the warriors except one. As he got close to the river, the Blackfoot who kept up threw his spear at Colter but missed, and Colter snatched it up and used it on the poor guy, killing him.

"Then Colter jumped into a river," Nate said, "and over the next few days managed to elude the entire band by hiding in driftwood snarls along the banks while the Blackfeet searched for him. Eventually, Colter got away and worked his way back east over the next few years. In the end, he married a woman named Sallie.

"So," Nate said, "a happy ending for John Colter."

"Nice story," Drennen said. "But this is stupid. I ain't running nowhere."

Nate grinned at him and said nothing.

"Oh, shit," Johnny lamented, reading the malevolence in Nate's cruel smile. He glanced up in the dusk sky that was deep powder blue except for the fiery puffball clouds lit by the evening sun. "I knew when I saw that damned bird . . ."

Nate said, "Not my bird. But it worked out kind of nice, didn't it?"

"*I* thought that was your bird," Lisa said. "Like it was your spirit or something. We believe in stuff like that, you know." There was a particular musical lilt to her voice that reminded Nate of why he was there. As if he needed reminding.

Nate smiled at her. "You go on believing that if you want."

"Yeah," Drennen said, balling his fists and taking a step toward her. "Believe what you want, you snitch. You snitch *whore*."

Nate raised the revolver and Drennen looked up to see the massive O of the muzzle. He stopped cold.

"You know her as Lisa Rich," Nate said softly. "I know her as Lisa Whiteplume. My woman's stepsister from the res. My woman was named Alisha. You two killed her."

Identified, Lisa thrust her chin in the air and put her hands on her hips defiantly. Proudly. Drennen stepped back.

Nate said to Lisa, "See what I told you about his type. He doesn't really like you. Even when you're in there thrashing around doing what makes him happy, he *despises* you for it. The more you please him, the more contemptuous he is of you, which is a pretty good indicator of what he thinks of himself deep down. Will you learn from that?"

She sighed, but she wouldn't meet Nate's eyes. "I guess."

"Oh, *shit*," Johnny repeated with even more emphasis than before. "Drennen, you need to shut up now."

"But, man," Drennen said to Johnny, "he can't prove anything. He says we did something to his girlfriend, but he can't prove it was us."

"You don't understand," Nate said. "I don't need to prove anything. It doesn't work like that with me."

Johnny asked, "Then how can you be sure it was us? What if it was somebody else?"

"Putting you two down is a net plus either way," Nate said. "Honestly, I'm insulted anyone would send a couple of mouth-breathers like you after me, and angry you got so close. And for the record, you left fingerprints and DNA at the scene. I got the beer bottle you left checked out by some friends in law enforcement. The name 'Drennen O'Melia' came back. And it didn't take long to find out he hangs with a loser named Johnny Cook."

Johnny turned on Drennen, accusatory, as if now remembering the beer bottle they left on the trail.

Then, squinting at Nate, said, "You're that guy, aren't you? How'd you get away?"

"I wasn't in the cave," Nate said. "But somebody I cared about was."

To Drennen, Nate said, "Looks like you got a faceful of that rocket launcher, pard."

"Please," Drennen said, pleading with his hands outstretched toward Nate and Lisa, "I didn't pull the trigger. It wasn't me."

Johnny listened with his face twisted in anger and betrayal. He thought of the gophers. He said, "It wasn't our idea. We were under the influence of alcohol and this lady we met in Saddlestring put us up to it. It was *her* idea. She hired us, and she drove us out there, gave us that rocket launcher, and paid us for the job. We were like"—he paused, thinking for the right word—"her *puppets*."

"Puppets," Nate repeated in a whisper. Then: "Was she tall, good-looking, mid-thirties? Chicago accent?" He reached up with his free hand and drew a line across his forehead with his left index finger just above his eyebrows. "Black bangs like so?"

"That was her," Drennen said quickly. "Told us her name was Patsy."

"Yeah," Johnny said, obviously still angry with Drennen but putting a priority on a possible new way to stay alive. "Patsy."

Nate said, "Like Patsy Cline?"

"Yeah!" Drennen said. "Like that. Whoever she is."

"Idiots," Nate grumbled. To Lisa, he said, "Her name is Laurie Talich. I had an altercation with her husband a couple of years back.

I'd heard she wanted to close the circle, so I've sort of expected to hear from her one way or other. But I still can't figure out how she knew where I was, or how to get to us."

"We don't know, either!" Drennen shouted, trying to bond with Nate and share his concern. "She never told us. She just drove us out there and said, 'Here's the rocket launcher, boys. The cave's down there on the trail. *Get to it!*' "

Nate shifted the weapon toward Johnny. "How much did she pay you?"

"Not a whole hell of a lot, as it turns out," Johnny said. "Barely enough for a week at Gasbag Jim's."

"How much?"

"Only fifteen grand," Drennen said, as if the lightness of the number somehow shifted the blame away from them to cheap Laurie Talich.

Nate took a deep breath and shut his eyes momentarily. He spoke so gently both Drennen and Johnny strained forward to hear.

"You killed my Alisha for only fifteen thousand dollars."

"We didn't know she was even there . . ." Drennen began to plead. "That Patsy told us you were some kind of badass dude—that the cops were after you but they didn't know where you were hiding out. She said you murdered her husband, and offing you was like doing something good for society, you know?"

"Fifteen thousand dollars," Nate said again.

"Look," Drennen said, "we can help you find her. We don't owe her nothing anymore. She obviously lied to us. Anybody can see you're a good guy. We'll even cut you in on our new business venture. Man, like Johnny said, we were just her puppets."

Nate let it just hang there. The shadows were longer now, almost grotesque in their length. The sun was directly behind him, and both Drennen and Johnny had to keep shading their eyes to see him.

"It's interesting how such small men cast such big shadows," Nate said. "I've heard enough. Now run."

"Oh, man . . ." Drennen said, his shoulders slumping.

"Run."

"We'll do anything," Drennen said. "I'll do anything . . ."

"Run."

Drennen was still moaning when Johnny Cook suddenly wheeled and took off. He was fast, and he put a quick ten yards between himself and Drennen. Drennen did a double take, glancing at Johnny then back to Nate, then started to backpedal. After five yards facing Nate, Drennen spun and ran away as hard as he could.

Nate watched them go. They kicked up little puffs of beige dust that lit up with the last brilliant moments of the sun. He could hear their footfalls thumping on the dry ground and the panicked wheezing of breath.

Drennen veered slightly to the left of Johnny's path, but was still twenty yards behind him. Nate could hear Drennen shout, "Wait up, Johnny . . . wait up!"

But Johnny didn't slow down.

After a minute, Lisa tugged on Nate's arm. "Aren't you going to chase them? You're going to let them *go*?"

The two figures were becoming smaller and darker as they receded; the sunlit Wind Rivers loomed over them.

Nate said, "Johnny's fast, but not Colter fast."

"What?"

He stepped quickly across her a few paces to the left. The two runners in the distance still had space between them. He walked a few more long strides to the left, until Drennen and Johnny closed into one form in the distance, despite the gap between them as Johnny continued to pull away.

Nate raised his weapon and cupped his left hand beneath his right, where he held the revolver. He looked down the scope with both eyes open, and thumbed the hammer back.

One shot. Two exit-wound balloons of red mist.

Both bodies tumbled down as if kicked by mules and lay still, more dust rising up around them from their fall. The fat clouds of pink hung in the light evening air.

Lisa stood there openmouthed and wide-eyed.

Nate peered through the scope to confirm there was no reason to walk out there. He said, "Like puppets with their strings clipped."

Nate spun the cylinder and caught the empty brass and dropped it in his pocket and fed a fresh sausage-sized cartridge into the empty chamber. He slid the .500 into his shoulder holster under his left arm.

"These shells cost three bucks each," he said to Lisa. "No need to waste more than one of 'em on men worth nothing at all."

She shook her head, unable to speak.

He said, "I'm going to go get a shovel and then I'm gone. I can drop you back home on my way to Chicago."

She started to argue, but when she saw the look on his face, she decided it wasn't a good idea.

SEPTEMBER 6

He who does not prevent a crime when he can, encourages it.

—Seneca

27

Joe hit the northern city limits of Cheyenne at dawn. He'd taken I-25 South all the way, stopping only for gas and a two-hour nap in his pickup outside Casper along the bank of the North Platte River. Radio activity during the night had been light, consisting mainly of sign-ons and sign-offs of law enforcement personnel, and he'd had plenty of time to think. He tried to connect the facts he knew about Earl Alden's death and Missy's arrest into some kind of logical scenario, hoping the disparate parts—the wind project, Bob Lee, the sudden appearance of Bud Jr.—would fall into place. He failed to make sense of it all, and he wondered to himself if he was chasing his tail.

He wondered if he, like Dulcie Schalk and Sheriff McLanahan, was stubbornly pursuing a theory at the expense of other plausible scenarios? Did he have blinders on? As he had since the discovery of The Earl's body, he felt uncomfortably disconnected. Joe was operating on the margins of a legitimate—if possibly too-narrow—investigation, trying to derail charges brought forth in good faith. He was used to operating without backup nearly every day he was out in the field. In this instance, his normal doubts were stronger than usual. He felt like he was operating without a net, and with spectators booing him.

But he'd promised Marybeth, and he wouldn't renege. He had no doubt there was more to the story of Earl Alden than he knew, and certainly more than the county attorney was aware of. Whether following his shaky instincts would shed doubt on Missy's guilt—who knew?

He needed coffee.

It was too early for the federal offices to open downtown, so Joe cruised by the new Wyoming Game and Fish Department headquarters—which were also still closed—and took Central Avenue past Frontier Park and into the heart of old Cheyenne. He'd found a Styrofoam cup of coffee and a microwave breakfast burrito at a Kum & Go convenience store helmed by an overweight Goth woman pierced a dozen places he could see and with full-sleeve tattoos. The coffee was bitter.

The golden dome of the capitol building was blinding with the opening salvo of the early-morning September sun. He took 24th Street and pulled over at a curb and was surprised to see Governor Spencer Rulon striding across the dew-sparkled capitol lawn toward the side entrance to his office. Rulon was alone and apparently deep in thought because his head was down and he was single-mindedly charging toward the entrance like an elk in rut. Joe checked his wrist-watch: six.

He got out of his pickup, clamped on his hat, and followed. The door the governor had used was unlocked and Joe entered the capitol building and let it wheeze shut behind him. *Only in Wyoming,* he thought, *would the governor travel around without bodyguards and the statehouse doors be open with no security personnel about.*

As he walked down the silent and poorly lit hallway, Joe took off his hat and held it in his left hand while he rapped on an unmarked door. "Good morning," he said.

On the other side, he heard Rulon curse under his breath, but a moment later the governor pulled the door open and stood there, larger than life and squinting at his visitor. Governor Rulon was big and ruddy with a head full of wavy rust hair turning silver. He was brash and brusque and barrel-chested. A former federal prosecutor, Rulon was halfway through his second term. He knew thousands of his constituents by name and they called him "Gov Spence" and often phoned him (his number was listed in the local phone book) at his home at night to complain or rant.

Joe owed Rulon his reinstatement and a small raise in salary, and despite the governor's sometimes-slippery methods and their clashes, he felt a profound loyalty to the man.

"Good morning, sir," Joe said.

"What happened to your face?"

"Someone hit me."

"I'll say.

"You're at it early."

"I'm up to my ass in alligators, that's why," Rulon said, motioning Joe to an empty chair across from his desk. "What the hell brings you down here into the heart of darkness?"

Joe sat down and nodded his appreciation when Rulon poured him a cup of coffee from a Mr. Coffee set on a credenza. "I'm here to interview a prisoner," Joe said. "Orin Smith. He's in federal lockup. The FBI and our friend Chuck Coon put him there. I happened to see you, so I thought I'd say howdy."

"Howdy," Rulon said sourly. "I hope this won't take long. I'm here early these days because Eastern Time is two hours ahead of us, which means those bastards in Washington have a two-hour jump on us in their never-ending effort to screw us or tell us how to live our lives. I need the extra time just to chew out federal asses. I can't afford to do it for just six hours a day anymore."

He flashed his teeth in a poor excuse for a smile to show he was kidding—sort of. "When the people of this state hired me, it was to go to work for them, not our federal overlords in D.C. But that's how it's turned out, and I'm getting damn sick and tired of it."

"Okay," Joe said. He'd heard Rulon on the subject several times before. Everybody had. It was one of the reasons the governor's popularity remained at record-level highs in Wyoming. That, and his penchant for challenging federal officials to bare-knuckle fights or shooting contests to resolve disputes.

"And you caught me on a particularly bad day," Rulon said. "A whole shitload of new federal rules just came down on our heads about set-asides and minority hiring and environmental crap. I've got to get on the phone and start yelling at these bastards."

"I understand," Joe said.

"I just want to govern my state," Rulon said. "I don't want to spend all my time yelling at those knuckleheads and suing them. Hell, I know what a minority is—they don't need to tell me. A minority is being a Democrat governor in Wyoming, goddamit! So why are they making my life a living hell?"

Joe chuckled, despite himself.

"Now what do you want?" Rulon said. "You know I didn't like how that deal went down last year with those brothers in the mountains. You know I didn't like how you handled that."

"I know," Joe said. "I did the best I could, given the circumstances."

"I know you *think* you did," Rulon said. "But it wasn't how I wanted it." Then, with a wave of his beefy hand, he dismissed the issue. "I need more yes-men," he said. "I *deserve* more yes-men." He grinned. "And fewer independent thinkers like you. Hell, I'm the governor."

He looked to the ceiling and opened his arms: "Where, Lord, are my sycophants? Do I need to run for U.S. Senate to get some?"

Joe snorted.

"You're going to have a new director at the Game and Fish soon," Rulon said, as always changing subjects with the lightning speed of a television remote control. "I hope you can get along with him. Or her. They may not allow you to operate with the kind of autonomy you seem to have. I mean, it's Tuesday morning and you're in Cheyenne. Shouldn't you be at work?"

"I just worked the whole three-day weekend," Joe said. "Last time I checked, the state owes me twenty-five comp days."

"That you'll never take," Rulon said.

"Except today and maybe a few more this week. I'm following up on something else right now."

"Right," Rulon said. "You're here for a reason. What is it?"

"Wind," Joe said. "What's the inside story?"

Rulon snorted and rolled his eyes. He said, "They're everywhere, aren't they? Those wind farms? I'm not against the idea in principle, and there are a few locations where they can actually be cost-effective and productive. But the wind energy people have got to play on a level field with everybody else. A lot of those guys are a thorn in my side, as if I need more trouble. They want to throw up those turbines on top of every hill and ridge as far as the eye can see. But they've got to *slow the hell down*," he said, "until we can get a handle on it." He shook his head.

"We used to think we were cursed with Class Five, Six, and Seven wind in this state," he said, "and now we find out we're *blessed* with it. But for Christ's sake, we've got to get some control. Not everybody wants to look out their window and see those things. In the last few years, we've all learned the word 'viewshed.' But what I need to be made to understand is why it is we're putting up all those turbines when right underneath them is all the oil, gas, coal, and uranium we'll ever need but *we aren't allowed to get.* If the reasons these windmills are going up is based on wishful thinking and policy and not need, what the hell are we doing?"

Joe shrugged his *I'm-just-a-game-warden* shrug.

"Is that what you want to know?" Rulon asked.

"Partly," Joe said. "But specifically I was wondering about the Rope the Wind project up in my neck of the woods."

Rulon sat back in his chair and laced his fingers across his belly, which was much bigger than the last time Joe had seen it. Rulon said, "Now I get it. This is about your father-in-law."

"Partly," Joe said.

"He was really chained from the blade of a turbine?"

"Yup. I found the body."

"Jesus," Rulon said, reacting as if a chill were coursing through him. "What a way to go. I hope it doesn't start a trend."

"Too much work," Joe said. "Most criminals don't want to work that hard."

"Give my regards to your mother-in-law," Rulon said, raising his eyebrows. "I'd hate to lose one of my biggest contributors on a first-degree murder charge. That kind of thing doesn't look good. Thank the Lord I'm nearly term-limited out and I won't have some jackass Republican using that one against me down the road . . . But I digress. From what I understand, it was going to be the biggest single private wind energy project in the State of Wyoming. *One hundred turbines!* But this murder has thrown it off track, maybe. And you think there is more to it than meets the eye?"

"Possibly."

Rulon cocked his head. "I didn't think you and your mother-in-law saw eye-to-eye on much. Why are you trying to save her?"

Joe said, "It isn't about her, although it is. My wife . . ."

"Say no more," Rulon guffawed. Then: "There isn't much I can tell you about it. The state hasn't been involved. It was done purely between the landowner, the power companies, and the Feds. There's no state land involved, so we've been kept out of it."

"I was afraid of that," Joe said. "You see, the murder trial starts next Monday."

Rulon sat back. "That's a *fast* trial."

"Judge Hewitt—"

"Hewitt," Rulon said, cutting Joe off. "I did a few trials before him back when I was a county prosecutor. Once he made me sing. Actually sing a song. But that's another story for another time. The guy is no-nonsense."

Joe said, "He drew a Dall sheep permit in Alaska. He wants the trial over before the season ends."

Rulon chortled.

"So I've got less than a week to figure out what's going on, if anything," Joe said sourly.

"This sounds like the whole wind energy rush," Rulon said. "It's out of control and moving so fast nobody can keep up with it. No one has stopped to look at what's happened in other countries when they decided to artificially change their energy policy to feel-good crackpot schemes. Jobs have been lost and their economies tanked, and they've completely backed off. But not us, by God!"

Rulon practically leaped across the desk. He said, "Wind energy has created some strange bedfellows. The traditional fossil fuel guys hate it, and they're partnering up with their traditional enemies, the greens. Some landowners love windmills, some hate them—it depends on who's getting paid. The Feds are going over our heads because it's new policy and they couldn't care less if it makes economic sense or if the states are players. And there's so much damned federal money involved . . . you just know things are going to get screwy."

"Thank you for your time," Joe said, standing. "I appreciate the background, but I know you're busy."

Rulon assessed Joe through heavy-lidded eyes. He said, "It's good to see you, Joe. I still think you're a man I can count on, despite everything."

"Thank you."

"You and me, we're not through," Rulon said. "I still have two years to go, and I may need to call on you again. I'll work it out with the new director when he's hired. Or she's hired. Will you respond if I ask?"

Joe hesitated, and said, "Sure."

"As long as it's within your boundaries," Rulon said sarcastically. "You ought to get a bumper sticker that says, 'What Would Dudley Do-Right Do?' Call it W-W-D-D-R-D. That has a ring to it."

Joe nodded. "That's the second time in two days I've been called that."

"Maybe there's something to it," Rulon said. "But hell, that's one reason I like you, Joe."

Joe shrugged.

"But like I said, I need more yes-men in the future."

"Sorry."

"Have a good day, Joe," Rulon said, "and my best to your lovely family." He always signed off that way, Joe thought. As if they'd just had a conversation about the weather.

"Yours, too, sir."

Rulon said, "Tell Coon to cooperate with you or he'll be hearing from me. And he doesn't like to hear from me."

"Thank you, sir," Joe said.

FBI Special Agent Chuck Coon said, "Yeah, we've got him. But why should I let you talk to Orin Smith?"

"I told you," Joe said. "He may be able to shed some light on a case

I'm working on. As far as I know, it's unrelated to why you've got him here in the first place."

They were sitting at a long empty conference table on the third floor of the Federal Center in Cheyenne. To get in, Joe had had to leave his weapons, phone, keys, and metal in a locker at the ground floor security entrance. He couldn't help but contrast the difference between getting in to see Chuck Coon and his morning meeting with the governor.

"What happened to your face?" Coon asked.

"I tangled with a motivated slacker," Joe said.

"I didn't know there were such creatures."

"Neither did I."

"When was the last time you saw Nate Romanowski?"

Joe stifled a grin because of the way Coon had slipped that in.

"I haven't seen him for over a year," Joe said. "In fact, I wish I knew where he was right now."

"Don't tell me *that*," Coon said. "Jeez, Joe. We're still after him, you know."

Joe nodded.

Coon had not lost his boyish features, although his close-cropped brown hair was beginning to sparkle with gray from running the Cheyenne bureau since his predecessor had been kicked up the ladder in the bureaucracy. Coon was incapable of not looking like a federal agent, Joe thought. He wore an ill-fitting sport coat over a white shirt and tie. Coon seemed like the kind of guy who would wear his credentials on a lanyard in the shower and while playing with his kids. In Joe's own experience and from what he'd heard from other law enforcement throughout the state, Coon was an honorable man doing a professional job. There was no doubt that he served a distant federal master, but in the two years he'd spent as supervisor, he'd built bridges between the myriad conflicting city, county, state, and federal agencies that overlapped confusingly throughout Wyoming. Joe liked him, and when they weren't butting heads, they discussed their families and Coon's new interest in archery.

"So why is he in lockup?" Joe asked.

"Ponzi scheme," Coon said. "I'm surprised you didn't hear about it. He's been running a good one for the last two years right here out of Cheyenne. Kind of a high-tech pyramid scheme, where he convinced investors who wanted to shelter their money from taxes to invest in his operation. He claimed he'd figured out a way to buy hard assets like gold and real estate through a legit offshore company. That way, he told them, they could shelter their cash so the government wouldn't get it and at the same time hedge their wealth against declines in the dollar. It was pretty sophisticated."

Joe nodded.

"There's a lot more of these kinds of scams these days," Coon said. "The rich are running scared. Some of them will do just about anything not to have to pay up to fifty percent of their income in taxes. So when they hear about an outfit like Orin Smith's, they get reckless when they should know better."

Joe said, "So he actually paid them dividends?"

"At first," Coon said. "It was a classic Bernie Madoff–like Ponzi scheme, but with a twist. The first few rich folks who sent him cash to shelter did receive dividend checks based on the increase in the price of gold or whatever. And they told their friends for finder's fees that Smith kicked back. But as more and more wealthy people sent him money, the dividend checks got smaller for the first investors and nonexistent for the later ones."

"What was the twist?" Joe asked.

Coon shook his head in a gesture that was part disgust and part admiration. "Unlike Madoff, Smith never even pretended to be aboveboard. He bragged on his website and in his emails that he operated outside the system. That way, he claimed, he and his investors were performing kind of a noble act in defense of free enterprise. He called it a 'capital strike.' The people who sent him money knew he wasn't going to report to the SEC or anybody else. The endgame was that when and if the tax rates ever went back down, the investors would ask him to sell off their assets and return the cash. For Orin Smith, it worked pretty well for a while."

"So how'd you catch him?" Joe asked. "If no one was willing to turn him in because they would be admitting they'd done something criminal."

Coon said, "Guess."

Joe thought for a moment, then said, "A divorce."

"Bingo. A trophy wife in Montana and her seventy-year-old husband split the sheets. They jointly owned a high-end ski resort where all the members were multi-millionaires, and she wanted half of everything. When she found out he'd invested most of what they had with Smith's company, she went ballistic and reported it to the Bureau in Montana. It was child's play for us to trace the IP addresses through all the firewalls right here to Cheyenne. And it didn't take us long to guess who was responsible, since Orin Smith has been running scams here for years."

Joe sat back. "I don't get it," he said. "This is the same guy who was the head honcho of a legitimate wind energy company worth millions? And he's been on your radar for a while."

"So," Coon said, "you want to meet him?"

"That's why I'm here."

"I'm going to sit in. If he says he doesn't want to talk, that's it. It's over. And he may want his lawyer present. If that's the case, you'll need to wait. And if your questioning goes anywhere it shouldn't, I'm going to shut you down. Are we clear?"

Joe winced, but he couldn't see that he had a choice. "We're clear."

28

Nate Romanowski pulled his Jeep into an empty space in long-term parking at the Jackson Hole Airport and checked his wristwatch: 10:30 a.m.

The sawtooth profile of the Grand Teton Mountains dominated the western horizon. It was a clear cool day with a bite in the air and there was a light dusting of snow on the top of two of the peaks: Teewinot and the Grand. River cottonwoods and mountain ash shouldering up against the Snake River in the valley were already turning gold. Out on the highway, a pair of bull moose were meandering from the sagebrush flats across the blacktop causing a backup in traffic that he'd simply driven around in the ditch. Since it was the only airport in the country located within a national park, getting there was a visual extravaganza, but he'd seen it all so many times and he had other things on his mind.

He flipped down the visor and looked at himself in the small mirror the way a painter inspects his work to determine if he's finished or more touch-ups are required. He hardly recognized himself. His hair was black and short-cropped, and his eyes were brown due to a pair of tinted contact lenses. He looked out through a pair of narrow black-framed hipster glasses. He wore a black polo shirt under a chocolate brown jacket (with an obligatory pink ribbon pinned to the lapel), chinos, and lightweight hiking shoes straight out of the box. Nate looked thoroughly Jackson-like, he thought. He'd look right at home on the streets of Jackson, Aspen, Vail, or Sun Valley. Like all the other politicos, hedge fund managers, and Hollywood players with second or third homes in mountain resorts across the West.

After hiding his .500 in a lockbox under the seat and slipping a new wallet into the back of his chinos and a black leather passport case into the breast pocket of his jacket, he topped himself off with an Australian-style brimmed hat and he looked so authentic, he thought, that he fought an urge to punch himself out.

The ticket agent behind the counter wore blonde dreadlocks and barely looked up when he said he wanted to go to Chicago on the next flight. She looked at his ID and said, "Mr. Abbey, there is one seat left on United 426 at 1:36 p.m. That will get you back home to Chicago at 7:14 p.m. with a change in Denver."

"Great," he said.

"Are you checking any luggage?"

"No. Just this carry-on."

"And will you be using a credit card today?" she asked.

"Just cash," he said.

She barely looked up as he handed over eight one-hundred-dollar bills. She gave him forty dollars in change.

The ticket printer hummed and she handed him documents for Phillip Abbey of 2934 West Sunnyside Avenue, Chicago, Illinois.

He strolled toward security and the white-clad TSA officers who seemed as bored with their jobs as the ticket agent. It was a common attitude he'd found in resort towns, he thought: Everybody who actually had to work couldn't wait to get off their shift and get outside and recreate in their chosen interest, whether it be hiking, mountain-bike riding, skiing, whatever. They were marking time, and their jobs existed solely to fund their time off. They had no emotional investment in the companies that employed them or the community where they lived. The ticket agent had no ambition to move up in the airline industry, and the TSA agents were there because all the post office jobs were filled.

No one cared who he was or what he looked like, and the elite crowds that washed through the airport daily had no desire to build lasting relationships with the low-level employees within. It was, he thought, the perfect airport in the area to arrive at or depart from without raising an eyebrow.

Plus, it would get him quickly to Chicago.

Phillip was for Phillip Glasier, the author of *Falconry and Hawking*, one of the ten books he'd once listed to take with him on a desert island. Abbey was for Edward Abbey, author of *The Monkey Wrench Gang*—another book he'd once have chosen but now that he'd seen more of the world would substitute with something else. Maybe the *Art of War* by Sun Tzu, although it wouldn't be the smartest name to put on a phony passport.

He reminded himself of two of Sun Tzu's rules:

Attack him where he is unprepared, appear where you are not expected.

And . . .

Bring war material with you from home, but forage on the enemy.

The West Sunnyside Avenue address belonged to the ex-governor of Illinois, Rod Blagojevich. That one made him smile.

Nate had not flown commercial since he'd been placed on the FBI watch list, and he'd vowed he never would again. He'd heard about the vaunted and annoying U.S. airport security measures, and made it a point not to pack metal objects or any liquid containers larger than three ounces. He breezed through security after they checked his ticket against his passport, a remnant of the old days that would expire soon. He'd been issued ten of them in different names and he still had two in reserve. He was curious if the agents would question him because he'd bought his ticket with cash, and was surprised they didn't. Fortunately, they were preoccupied with a woman in her mid-eighties traveling to visit her grandchildren who had tried to smuggle a large bottle of shampoo aboard in her makeup case.

He sat alone in the departure lounge with his carry-on across his knees and a Bluetooth earpiece in his ear because it seemed like the Phillip Abbey thing to do. He watched the sun highlight different aspects of the Teton Range. When the plane he was to take landed, he watched the incoming passengers as they filed through the doorway. They were wealthy, white, and woodsy folks chattering happily, pointing out to their seatmates through the massive windows where they lived in the valley, discussing the moose on the highway they'd seen in the distance as they landed. Several were already talking on their cell phones or into their Bluetooth devices.

He sighed, and continued to look like Phillip Abbey on this way to Chicago.

29

"I can promise you nothing," Joe said to Orin Smith, who sat across from him at a small table in a basement interrogation room in the Federal Building.

"Then why am I here?" Smith asked softly. "Agent Coon wasn't clear with me other than to say you thought I might know something about your case—whatever it is."

The room was small, close, institutional light green, and too brightly lit. Joe and Orin Smith were alone in it, although both were well aware of Coon's invisible presence on the other side of the one-way glass on the south wall, as well as two closed-circuit cameras with glowing red lights mounted in opposite corners of the ceiling.

Smith looked Joe over skeptically. "I've never hunted or fished in my life," he said. "I don't even like the outdoors. I don't see the point of going without a hot shower, a cold cocktail, and a flush toilet. As far as I'm concerned," Smith said, "camping is just nature's way of feeding mosquitoes."

"I'm glad we got that cleared up," Joe said. "But this has nothing to do with hunting or fishing."

"But you're what—a game warden?" Smith asked, after reading the patch on Joe's uniform sleeve.

"Yup."

"I think you may be in the wrong building," Smith said.

"Nope."

Orin Smith was in his mid-sixties and didn't have an aura that hinted at charisma or confidence, Joe thought. Smith was short and soft with a blade-like nose and wounded eyes that never remained in one place very long. His skin was thin and pale as if made of parchment. Ancient acne scars dimpled his cheeks and fleshy neck. He wore an orange one-piece jail jumpsuit, and boat shoes with the laces removed. Only two things set Smith apart from any other inmate, Joe observed. Smith's hair was long and swept back and expensively cut into layers designed to hide abnormally large ears, and his teeth were capped and perfect and reminded Joe of two strings of pearls.

"My questions have nothing to do with the charges you're in here for," Joe said. "I'm a lot more interested in your former life. Back when you owned a company called Rope the Wind."

The mention of the name created a reaction in Orin Smith that resembled a mild electric shock, although he quickly recovered.

"I owned a lot of companies," Smith said, finally.

"Let's start with that," Joe said, drawing his small spiral notebook out of his breast pocket. "What I can do, if you cooperate with me and answer my questions, is to put in a good word to the federal district judge. And, frankly, I can ask the governor to do the same. I'm not trying to incriminate you in any way."

"The governor?" Smith asked. "You know him?" There was doubt showing by the way he cocked his head slightly to the side, canine-style.

"I work for him from time to time," Joe said. "If you know him, you know there isn't a person in this state who can guarantee what he'll do or say, including me. But if you tell me the truth and help me out, I'll tell him just that."

"Interesting," Smith said. "Will you put that in writing and send it to my lawyer?"

"No," Joe said. "My word is my word. Take it or leave it."

"I should call my lawyer," Smith said. "I shouldn't be talking to you without him in the room."

"Suit yourself," Joe said, sitting back. "I'll wait until he gets here. But keep in mind I've got time constraints and I don't live here in Cheyenne. I can't guarantee the offer will still stand if you and your lawyer take your time making a decision to talk to me or not. I may not be able to come back here when you decide, and I may not want to come." Thinking: *Please don't call your lawyer and delay this.*

"I drove all night to get here," Joe said.

"That's your problem, not mine."

Smith assessed Joe in silence, looking at him in a detached and quiet way that reminded Joe of a poker player trying to guess if his opponent was bluffing.

"I'll have to get back to you on this," Smith said as he stood up. The man walked across the room and rapped on the one-way mirror.

"We're done here for now," he said.

Joe cursed to himself as a U.S. Marshall opened the door to let Smith out.

"He's wily," Coon said, as they walked down the hallway toward the elevator. "I wouldn't be surprised if he strung you along for a while and ended up saying nothing."

"I wasn't kidding about the time constraints," Joe said. "I can maybe stay tonight, but not longer than that."

"What're you going to do while you cool your heels?"

Joe shrugged.

"If he hasn't gotten back to you by tonight, you want to come over for dinner? I'll grill you a steak or a burger or something. You bring beer."

"Make it a steak," Joe said. "I know how much more money you Feds make than lowly state employees."

Coon snorted at that. At the door of the security entrance, Coon keyed the pad and the door whooshed open. "I'll give you a call if he decides to talk to you," he said. "Keep your cell phone on."

Joe nodded glumly.

His phone lit up while he was buying a fancy new wristwatch for Marybeth at a Western-wear store downtown. She'd accidentally dropped her last one in a water trough while grooming her horses. She liked Brighton watches. He stepped away from the counter and plucked his phone out of his breast pocket and saw it was coming not from Coon but from Marybeth.

"How's it going?" she asked.

He cradled the phone between his shoulder and neck while he dug his wallet out of his back pocket to hand the clerk a Visa card.

"Not well," he said. "I'm stymied in Cheyenne, waiting to talk to Orin Smith."

"Sorry," she said. "So where are you now?"

"In a store."

"A sporting goods store?"

"No."

"Joe, you don't go to stores."

"And I never will again, either," he said. "I need land, lots of land under starry skies above."

She chuckled, which was a good sound, but it ended abruptly. She said, "When my mother is cleared of this stupid murder charge, I think I want to kill her."

"Sounds good," he mumbled. He was distracted as the salesclerk behind the counter handed his card back and said, "Sorry, sir, but it's been declined. Do you have another card we can try?"

He knew his face was flushing as he replaced the Visa with a debit card. He didn't want to use the debit card because Marybeth kept close track of their checking account balance, and she might see he'd gotten her a gift before he had a chance to give it to her.

"Do you know why the Visa card won't work?" he asked her. "This is kind of embarrassing."

"I'm late paying bills this month," she said. "You know how it's been. I'm sorry. What are you buying, anyway?"

"Don't ask," he said.

"Joe, don't get me anything. I don't need anything, and we're tight this month."

"Don't worry about it," he said, trying to get her off the subject. He was relieved when the sales clerk swiped the debit card and it seemed to be processing.

"Did you even hear what I said?" she asked, annoyed.

"Yes. Let's kill your mother."

The sales clerk glanced up at that and Joe turned away, embarrassed again.

"She's sashaying around town like a school girl on Marcus Hand's arm," Marybeth said. "She's all giggly and silly and spending money like it was going out of style. Joe, she drove the Hummer—the very car they found the rifle in—and bought Hand an elkhorn chandelier display at the furniture store for fifteen thousand dollars. Just bought it outright and asked them to deliver it to the ranch. Then she took him to the country club and paid the golf pro to keep everybody else off the course while she and her lawyer played a round in private. She acts like she doesn't have a care in the world, and everybody's talking."

"Don't pay attention to them," Joe said.

"It's not about me," Marybeth said. "It's about her. She acts like she's just above it all—above the law with her big-shot Jackson Hole lawyer. If she deliberately set out to make a bad impression around town—to taint her jury pool—she couldn't do a better job."

He sighed. "I don't understand her," he said.

"I don't, either. But now even her country club set is turned against her. She's not thinking."

"Don't be so sure," Joe said. "Your mother never does anything that won't benefit her in some way. She's got something going—we just don't know what yet."

"That was a cruel thing to say."

"But true," he said. Then: "You know, I could just come home and, you know, let the chips fall where they may."

Silence.

He said, "I didn't mean that. I'm just frustrated. I drove all night and I've got nothing to do but wait for a call. Meanwhile, your mother is buying chandeliers for her lawyer."

"I know," she said. "She's her own worst enemy sometimes."

"I thought I was," Joe said, as the sales clerk gestured to him asking if he wanted the watch wrapped. He nodded yes.

"No," Marybeth said, "you're the one who is going to save her skinny old ass despite herself."

Joe thought about the forty-five miles over the mountains to Laramie from Cheyenne and looked at his watch. He didn't know Sheridan's class schedule, but he found himself driving south down Lincolnway toward an exit ramp to I-80 West. As he merged onto the highway he speed-dialed her cell phone.

"Dad?" She was clearly surprised. He could hear wind and other voices in the background, like she was walking along in a pack of students.

"Hi, honey."

"Dad, is everything all right?"

"Fine. You sound frantic."

"You never call me, okay?"

He started to argue but had to concede she was right. "I'm in Cheyenne. What's going on?"

He heard her tell someone, "Just a minute, I'll be right there." Then to him: "Ah, nothing. I'm still trying to figure out my way around. It's all a little confusing and I'm tired all the time."

"Are you getting enough sleep?"

She laughed, "What do you think?"

He dropped it. "What's your afternoon look like?"

The hesitation made him think for a moment the call had been dropped. "I've got class and then I'm meeting some friends for coffee. Why? Were you thinking of coming over?"

Joe said, "You drink coffee?"

"Daaad." She lengthened the word out.

"Of course you do," he said. His ears felt hot. He said, "No, I just had some time to kill so I thought I'd check on you. See how you were doing."

Another hesitation. When her voice came back it was soft, as if she was trying not to be overheard. "It's not like I wouldn't love to see you, Dad, but . . . it's hard. I'm just starting to feel like I'm really at college and not at home. It would kind of be tough right now to change plans and see you. It would set me back."

"I understand," he said. "Really."

"Remember what the orientation lady said. Six weeks. Try to go six weeks before seeing your parents and it will be easier."

"I remember."

"Are you on the way over?" she asked.

"Not at all," he said, pulling over to the side of the highway. He cleared his throat, and said, "So you're doing okay? Eating well? Getting along with folks?"

"Yes, yes, and yes," she said. She sounded relieved.

"You know what's going on with your grandmother?"

"Mom keeps me well briefed."

"We miss you," he said.

"I miss you guys."

"Remember," he said. "Keep in touch with your mother."

"I will, Dad. And thanks for calling."

He squinted and dropped his phone into his pocket, then drove slowly along the shoulder for a place to turn around to go back to Cheyenne. In his mind's eye he pictured her drinking coffee with students her own age.

His heart wasn't broken, he thought, but it was certainly cracked.

After steaks and three beers with Chuck Coon and his family, Joe sat at the desk in his hotel room and sketched out a time line from the murder of Earl Alden to the present time, bulleting each fact as he knew them. He hoped that by writing everything down, something would jump out at him.

He was wrong.

For the fiftieth time that day, he checked his cell phone to see if he'd missed a call from Coon or Orin Smith's lawyer. He hadn't.

As he was once again punching in the number for Nate's satellite phone, just in case, he had an incoming call.

Coon said, "Surprise, surprise. Orin Smith will talk to you first thing in the morning."

30

Nate Romanowski drove slowly down South State Street in a rental car on the South Side of Chicago with his windows down and his carry-on within reach on the passenger seat. The air was a warm stew of humidity: gasoline fumes, cooking food, and ripe garbage from Dumpsters. The sun had sunk and the last of it danced on the waves of Lake Michigan, igniting the sky and the west-facing sides of the downtown buildings, and now it was dark enough that the lights came on.

Simple things, he thought. Simple things that were so different. For one, it wasn't cooling down just because night had come. It was still as warm and sticky as it had been when he landed at O'Hare. And he'd lived so long in the awesome and immense quiet of Hole in the Wall canyon that the cacophony of pure urban white noise dulled his senses and pummeled his ears. There were still canyons, but these were walled by brick and steel and the sidewalks teemed with people. That, and when he looked up, the sky was muddy and soapy with city lights and he couldn't see through it to the stars.

Simple things. Like grabbing today's Chicago *Tribune* as he walked through the terminal and sitting down inside a crowded bar and flipping through the pages until he found:

Two Killed, Two Wounded in Drive-by Shooting at South Side Party

SEPTEMBER 6, 2010 7:13 P.M.

Two men were killed—one of them an expectant father—and two others wounded early Monday morning in a drive-by shooting in the South Side's Stony Island Park neighborhood, according to police and a family member of one of the deceased victims.

One person was being questioned in connection with the shooting, but no charges have been filed.

About 2:40 a.m., four men were near a party at East 84th Street and South State Street when they were shot from a passing vehicle.

J. D. Farr, 22, of the 9000 block of South Evans Avenue was hit and later pronounced dead at Advocate Christ Medical Center in Oak Lawn, according to the Cook County medical examiner's office . . .

So that's where he was headed.

And he was starting to get some looks. He could see them from the shadows behind buildings and grouped up in alleyways. As it got darker, they came out under the overhead streetlights, and there were knots of gangbangers gathered in certain places: twenty-four-hour convenience stores, eateries, bars. The sharp-dressed businesspeople in a hurry down on Michigan Avenue had been replaced by the people of the night in oversized shirts and coats and trousers on Nate's southern journey, and he wondered if they ever even encountered each other day-to-day.

Here he was, he thought, a white guy wearing Jackson Hole outdoor sports clothes driving a new rental very slowly, looking off to the side instead of through the windshield, windows down. He was sending a signal and some of them were picking it up.

The intersection of South State Street and 71st had the right feel to him, he thought. There was a well-lit BP station there, lights so bright and blazing in the dark neighborhood that it was hard to see anything else. Nate noted the young clientele inside the BP convenience store, and the high counters and Plexiglas that had been installed inside to act as a barrier between the clerks and their customers. He backed in on the side of the station, out of the harsh light. He couldn't see inside the station, and the employees couldn't see him. Nate scanned the light poles and roofs of adjacent buildings for security cameras. They were there, all right, but he knew as long as he stayed in the rental in the low light, he couldn't be identified.

It was a noisy intersection. Vehicles streamed below the State Street overpass, and he heard snatches of heavy bass from open windows. But on top it was a different level of darkness and mood.

Low-slung retail shops lined 71st: tattoo parlors, pawnshops, dollar stores, hair salons. Accordion-style security gates were up across the doors, and every window he could see was barred. Lights from inside the closed shops were dull and soft.

Across the street from the BP Station was a low square cinder-block building painted bright yellow. The facing wall of the building announced on the side that it was the State Street Grill and that it was open twenty-four hours a day. A list of items offered inside were painted on the side of the bricks:

T-BONE & EGGS $9.95

JERK CHICKEN WINGS

BBQ RIBS

BREAKFAST SERVED ALL DAY

The neighborhood just seemed right for what he was after. It was old, dark (except for the BP station), run-down, urban. The buildings weren't packed together tightly so there were plenty of places to gather, hide, or run. It would be hard to pin someone down here because of all the exits, and it would take someone in a car less than a minute to shoot down the off-ramp and join the stream of traffic going north toward the shining city center.

He was looking out at the street and the grill when he saw a flash of movement in his rearview mirror. They were coming up behind him on both sides of the car.

The passenger window suddenly filled with a pair of dull white eyes in a black round face. He said, *"What-choo-doin?"* as if it were a single word. Nate guessed he was fourteen or fifteen years old, maybe younger. A scout. He had close-cropped hair and big cheeks and a mouth that showed no expression. He was wearing big clothes under a down coat that was so enormous it reminded Nate of a frontier buffalo robe.

From inches away, at the driver's window, a girl said, *"What-choo-lookin-for, mister man?"*

Nate looked from one to the other. They'd approached his car in a rehearsed, cautious way—like cops. The girl was lighter-skinned, hair pulled back with beads in it, not unattractive despite her put-on street scowl.

"Wha-choo-*doin* here?" the boy asked, high-pitched, as if astonished by Nate's naïveté.

"I like that," Nate said to the girl. *"Mister man."*

"What about it?"

"I'm hoping you can help me," he said, keeping his voice low. "I'm looking for some protection. I was hoping you could steer me in the right direction."

"Pro-*tection*?" the boy said, still shrill and high-pitched and mocking. "Like rubbers? They inside." He thumbed over his shoulder toward the outside wall of the BP station. He laughed at his own joke and looked over at the girl, hoping she would laugh, too.

"You know what I mean," Nate said.

"Are you po-lice?" the girl asked. "You gotta tell me if you are. You look like po-lice." She said it *poh-lease.*

"No," he said.

"You lyin'," she said. "You a lyin' motherfucker, mister man."

Nate sighed. "Such language. Look, I need to buy a gun. If you two can't help me out, I'll find someone who can. I've got cash and I'm starting to lose my sunny outlook on life." He thought briefly of shooting his arms out and grabbing both of them by the ear and pulling them inside to make his point. He'd done worse.

The girl looked him over, her face as hostile as she could make it. He felt sorry for her, because her eyes told him she wasn't lost yet but was working on it. She said, "Wait here a minute," and was gone.

The boy shook his head at him, condescending, and started to say something and Nate gritted his teeth and whispered, *"Don't."*

The word struck home and the boy was gone.

Ten minutes later, Nate Romanowski steered his rental down the State Street off-ramp. The gangbanger the two had sent over had a thing for nines like most gangbangers, plenty of used pieces in stock, but Nate bought the only revolver he had: a five-shot .44 stainless steel double-action Taurus Bulldog with a two-and-a-half-inch barrel.

"That 'un 'ill make a big mother-fuckin' hole," the gangbanger cackled when Nate chose it.

"You don't need to tell me about guns," Nate said, and handed over eight one-hundred-dollar bills. The gangbanger threw in a half box of cartridges in the deal. Nate didn't spend much time speculating what the missing ten bullets had been used for.

As Nate cruised toward the city on the five-lane, he thought: *Simple things.*

Like how simple it was to buy an unregistered handgun in a city that tried its damndest to ban them. It meant he could pick one up just about anywhere—at any time. No hassle with gun stores, hours of operations, dealers, forms, ID, or criminal record checks.

As long as he had the desire, a purpose, and a brick of one-hundred-dollar bills, he was in business.

Twenty minutes on the computer in the business center of his hotel would give him the rest of what he needed.

Instinctively, he reached over and felt the heavy steel outline of the .44 in his overnight bag. He thought of Sun Tzu.

And he thought about going hunting in the morning.

SEPTEMBER 7

For they have sown the wind, and they shall reap the whirlwind.

—Hosea 8:7

31

Smith said, "What is it you want to know about Rope the Wind?"

As had happened many times when Joe interrogated people with a high opinion of themselves, it didn't take long for Orin Smith to open up. He explained how he'd come to own so many companies, and how he'd acquired them. While he explained the strategy and growth of his former enterprise, Joe nodded his head in appreciation, sometimes saying, "Wow—you're kidding?" and "What a smart idea," which prompted Smith to tell him even more.

Orin Smith was proud of his business accomplishments, and was grateful someone finally wanted to hear about them.

Smith explained how he'd—legally—taken advantage of a Wyoming initiative to encourage business development during the last energy bust of the 1990s. The state legislature had passed laws that made it very simple and inexpensive to incorporate in the state as a limited liability company. The idea, Smith explained, was not only to encourage new enterprises to start up in Wyoming but also to get existing firms to possibly move their headquarters for the advantage of low taxes and slight regulation. He said he learned the ins and outs of the process, and for a while served as a kind of broker between those wishing to incorporate and the state government entities that processed the applications and granted LLC status.

"I placed ads in newspapers and business journals all over the world," Smith said. "*Incorporate your company in Wyoming: it's cheap, easy, and hassle-free!*' For a fee, I'd make sure my clients did their paperwork correctly and I'd even walk the applications to the secretary of state's office on their behalf. You'd be surprised how many people out there took advantage of the new regulations."

But after serving as a facilitator for a few years, Smith said, he began to encounter more and more competition in the field. He realized there was a new market for turnkey companies that had already been created and were "established"—at least on paper.

"Think about it," Smith said. "Let's say you're an entrepreneur or you just came into some cash. What makes more sense—to put the money in a bank and declare the income so it can be taxed, or to 'invest' it into the ownership of a company with all the benefits a small business owner had at the time? Like expense accounts, travel, tax credits, and the like?"

Joe nodded and said, "*Exactly.*" He'd learned over the years in interrogations that using the word *exactly* seemed to encourage his subjects to keep talking.

"Then it hit me," Smith said. "Because it was so easy to create shell companies and bank them away, why not look ahead in the economy and create limited liability companies with names that investors and entrepreneurs might want to buy outright? I mean, wouldn't it be more valuable for a guy to approach the bank if he had just acquired a two- or three-year-old company with a paper track record than to go into the meeting with all kinds of highfalutin ideas about a start-up?"

"*Exactly,*" Joe said.

"So that's what I did," Smith said proudly. "I started coming up with company names that sounded great and applying for incorporation and filing them away. I tried to figure out what was hot and what was coming down the pike and tailor the names for that. I've always had a genius for names, you know."

Joe nodded.

"Some company names were plays on words: 'Nest Egg Management,' 'Green Thumb Growth,' like that," Smith said, getting more and more animated. "Then I realized how many of these folks out there liked company names that sounded cool and modern but didn't really say anything, like 'PowerTech Industries,' 'Mountain Assets,' 'TerraTech,' 'GreenTech, 'TerraGreen'—anything with *green* or *tech* in it was golden, man . . ."

Smith went through dozens of names and Joe recalled the short list Marybeth had read to him over the phone. He hadn't actually heard of any of the companies, but it *seemed* like he had. He conceded to himself that Orin Smith *did* have a way with names.

"So you were kind of like those guys who went out and bought all kinds of dot-com names in the early days of the Internet," Joe said. "You locked up common names so when folks came around to wanting to use them they had to pay you a premium."

"Right, but then it all came to a crashing halt," Smith said, his mouth drooping on the sides.

"What do you mean?"

"Apparently, some less-than-upstanding folks out there figured out how to buy and use these companies for unscrupulous means."

"Like what?" Joe asked.

Smith glanced toward the mirrored window, where Coon was no doubt listening closely.

"Apparently," Smith said, choosing his words carefully, "it's a lot easier to launder illegal money through a corporation than it is by other means."

"Like drug money?" Joe asked.

"Apparently," Smith said. "Or other kinds of cash. From what I hear, the Russian mafia and Mexican drug cartels discovered they, too, could set up cheap corporations in Wyoming and use them as a front for financial transactions."

"Not that you did that or knew anything about it," Joe said.

"Of course not," Smith said, acting hurt. "Not until the secretary of state started a campaign to shut me down and say that limited liability companies in Wyoming had to have all kinds of new restrictions, like street addresses and boards of directors and crap like that. It just wasn't fair."

"Exactly," Joe said.

"So I had to divest what I had, and fast," Smith said. "If the secretary of state would have just stayed out of my business, I'd still be doing it. I never would have gotten involved in this thing the Feds said I did. Not that I did it, you understand," he said with another glance toward the glass.

"Rope the Wind," Joe interjected.

Smith paused and sat back. "One of my best," he said. "It could be used for a dozen kinds of industries or products. I have to honestly say I wasn't thinking wind energy at the time I came up with the name. Nobody was."

"So that's how you met Earl Alden," Joe prompted.

"Not quite yet. That came later."

"Later than what?" Joe asked.

Smith squirmed in his chair, and rubbed his hands together.

"I saw the writing on the wall," he said, "a new president, a new administration. Their big talk about 'breaking our addiction to oil,' renewable energy, solar and wind. I could see it coming because it was right out there in front of us. They were talking about it all the time during the campaign.

"So by then," Smith said, "I couldn't create any more new companies without all the hassle, but I still had all the company names I'd already registered. I did a little research and figured out where the windiest places in the state were located. So instead of waiting for entrepreneurs to knock on my door, I decided to get proactive. To hit the road and talk to businesspeople and landowners about what was coming down the pike. You see, I could see it plain as day. Those fools in Washington earmarked eighty-six billion dollars for 'green initiatives,' including forty billion dollars in loan guarantees and grants for renewable energy projects. But convincing anyone—that's where I just . . . *failed*." He spat out the last word, and dropped his head to stare at something on the top of the table between his hands.

Joe shook his head, confused. "But Rope the Wind . . ."

"One guy actually showed some interest for a while, but he was just an ignorant rancher and he couldn't make a decision. He strung me along for months and then he stopped taking my calls. I hadn't heard anything from him for a couple of years and then he calls me a few weeks ago out of the blue and said he wished he would have done it. He tells me he was sick and going over what he'd done in his life and he realized not pulling the trigger on the wind project had been a mistake. *Now* he realizes, the dumb son-of-a-bitch."

Joe asked, "Was his name Bob Lee?"

Smith shook his head. "I remember Bob Lee. He wasn't interested at the time and told me to get the hell off his property."

"Who was it?" Joe asked.

"His name was Bud," Smith said. "Longstreet, or something like that."

"Bud Longbrake?"

"That sounds right."

Joe just shook his head. "Where was he calling you from?"

Smith waved Joe off. He said, "It was Calvin Coolidge who said the business of America is business. You ever heard that?"

Joe nodded.

"Not anymore," Smith said. "It's a thing of the past. That's what I found out when I took my concept out on the road. Nobody wants to take a risk or work hard. Nobody wants to own a business anymore because if they succeed they become a target of the politicians. Everybody's sitting back, scared, keeping their head down and waiting it out until the storm passes. If it ever does."

"So," Joe said, trying to get Smith to refocus. "No one was interested in investing in your companies?"

"That's what I'm saying," Smith said, annoyed.

"So why not do it yourself?" Joe asked. "Why not use Rope the Wind yourself? Or why not start your own business and provide something people want to buy? You seem to have a gift for all this stuff."

Smith simply glared at him. He said, "Don't be so simpleminded. Where have you been? That's for suckers. That's not how people make money these days. Owning a company is for suckers. Employing people is for idiots. Making money in the free market means you're a douche bag ripe for plucking."

Joe sat back, confused.

Smith said, "Today it's about winners and losers, determined by folks in Washington. The winners—God bless 'em—are cleaning house. If you're a winner, you get the money funneled to you and you can't fail. And if you do fail, they'll bail you out. But if you're a loser, well, you end up in the hoosegow wasting your time talking with a damn game warden."

"Bud Longbrake," Joe said. "The one who told you he's sick? Where did you say he was calling from?"

After the questions and answers continued throughout the morning—Earl Alden came up in a lot of them—Joe excused himself by asking Orin Smith to "hold that thought."

Joe found Chuck Coon in the hallway where he'd been observing the interview from a stool.

"Can I borrow a legal pad or something from you?" Joe asked. "I filled up my notebook."

"I've never heard him talk so much," Coon said, shaking his head. "You're actually pretty good at this."

"He's proud of his achievements," Joe said. "He wants someone to know about them. He's kind of a twisted genius in his way and he's done a lot, and it frustrates him that all anyone asks him about is the Ponzi scheme that brought him down."

"Are you getting what you need?"

Joe rubbed his temples with the tips of his fingers. "More than I bargained for," he said.

"This Earl Alden he keeps talking about," Coon said. "He's your murdered father-in-law?"

Joe nodded.

"I heard about that. Man, he really hated that guy."

"Nearly as much as the secretary of state," Joe said. "Were you aware of what he was saying, that it used to be legal in Wyoming to register companies by the dozen?"

Coon nodded. "Yeah. That's how Orin Smith got on our radar in the first place a few years ago. We kicked it over to the state since it was a state issue, but, yeah, we were aware of it."

Joe whistled. "This is going a direction I didn't anticipate."

"I take it you know this Bud Longbrake fellow?"

"My ex-father-in-law."

"Quite a family you've got." Coon whistled. "Let me get you a pad. But keep in mind Smith has a hearing this afternoon. You'll need to wrap it up after lunch. Speaking of . . ."

"Thanks," Joe growled, "but I'm not hungry."

"Okay," Joe said, reentering the interrogation room with a fresh yellow legal pad. "You were starting to tell me about your connection with the wind turbine remanufacturer in Texas."

At first, Joe didn't pay any attention to the rapping at the interrogation room door. He was busy scribbling, and trying to process what he was being told by Orin Smith. Finally, Smith quit talking and chinned behind Joe.

Coon and a U.S. marshal stood there. The marshal said, "Mr. Smith has an appointment upstairs before the judge."

"I think I'm through with him," Joe said. He thanked Coon for the opportunity and shook hands with Orin Smith as the marshal escorted him out of the room.

"I appreciate your cooperation," Joe said.

Smith nodded. "Just make sure to put in that good word—and to let Gov Spence know."

"I will."

As Smith left the room, he paused and turned. To Joe, he said, "If you get the son-of-a-bitch who did it, give him a big wet kiss from me."

Joe nodded that he understood.

Joe sat in his pickup outside the Federal Building and flipped through page after page of notes, rereading his shorthand and committing names, dates, and the players to memory. He shook his head and absently stared at his cell phone display. Marybeth had called twice but hadn't left messages. Her single text read, *"Is everything all right? Call when you're able."*

She answered on the second ring. He could tell from the hush in her voice that she was working behind the desk at the library and couldn't talk long.

"Joe—what's going on?"

"It's complicated," he said. "I'm sorting it all out in my mind and it'll take a while to get it straight. But I hope you're sitting down."

"I am. Just tell me one thing. Do you know who killed The Earl?"

"No," Joe said. "But the list of people who wanted him dead just got real, real long. That's if we can trust what this guy Orin Smith just told me."

He filled her in and she listened without comment. When he was through, she said, "Earl was a real son-of-a-bitch, wasn't he?"

"Seems like it. And if all this is true, everybody needs to rethink this whole trial."

Marybeth said, "Do you think Dulcie will drop the charges?"

"I doubt it," Joe said. "That would be too much to ask at this point. But she may want to ask for a delay in the trial so she can investigate this."

"My mother . . ." Marybeth said with a sigh. "She's going to be rewarded for her bad behavior. *Again.*"

"Let's not get ahead of ourselves," Joe said. "Nothing may work out like we think it will. For the time being, we need to let everyone know what Orin Smith claims. If you'll call Marcus Hand and tell him what I found out, I'll call Dulcie Schalk."

Marybeth paused. "Why both sides?"

Joe said, "Because, don't forget—I'm an officer of the law. I took an oath. I stretch it from time to time, but there's no way we can't inform both parties what we know."

"Is it that?" Marybeth asked. "Or are you playing both sides against the middle?"

"Maybe a little of that, too," Joe admitted.

"Are you on your way back home now?" she asked.

"Nope."

"Where are you going?"

"Believe it or not," Joe said, "Orin Smith claimed he knew where I could find Bud Longbrake Sr."

32

Laurie Talich pulled her Audi Q7 into the shaded lot of the dance studio in Oak Park, shifted into park so she could keep the motor running and the air on, raised her large sunglasses to the top of her hair, and turned in her seat to address her two girls. Melissa was twelve years old and Aimee ten. Both wore black leotards over pink tights and clutched their shoe bags. Melissa had dark hair and olive skin like her, and Aimee was fairer but had her father's light cruel eyes, if not his temperament, thank God.

She said, "I'll be back here in two hours. Don't dawdle this time. I don't know why it takes you two so long to change from your ballet shoes, but you need to hustle this time."

Melissa said, "It's Aimee."

"Is not!"

"It's Aimee," Melissa said, nodding her heard.

"I don't care whose fault it is. I don't want to have to come in and get you this time. I'll be right here."

Aimee was in Contemporary Ballet I, and Melissa Contemporary Ballet II. Neither was very good yet, and neither had shown any passion for dance, although Laurie held out hope for Aimee.

"Can we go to McDonald's for dinner?" Melissa asked.

"We'll see," Laurie said. It was always a hassle to drive home and start dinner after dance practice because the girls were starved and grouchy, so they usually went out. "It depends if you two hustle out here."

Laurie valued the two hours she got to herself while her daughters were at dance. She usually drove to a coffee shop and knitted or read while keeping an eye on the clock.

"Tell *her*," Melissa said, jabbing her little sister with a finger in the ribs.

"Ow! She's hurting me!" Aimee cried out.

"I barely touched her," Melissa said in defense.

"Girls!" Laurie said. "Go!"

The two unbuckled their seat belts as Melissa pushed the door open. Hot and humid air filled the Audi.

Laurie said, "Have a good practice, girls. Give me a kiss."

Melissa did a drive-by kiss because she saw her friend Sarah getting out of her father's car and she wanted to join her. Aimee kissed her mother good-bye, and said, "Melissa is the late one. She's always talking."

"Don't tell on your sister," Laurie said. "Now go. See you in two hours. And shut the door. You're letting all the hot air in."

She sat in the car to make sure both her girls went safely inside. It was a good neighborhood: leafy and prosperous. The children of the city's elite families attended the same dance school, and it was hard to get in. She wished her girls were better dancers and would stand out, but . . .

She gasped when the passenger door opened suddenly and a tall and rangy man swung in beside her and slammed the door shut. She instinctively reached for her knitting bag, but the big man placed his hand over hers and said, *"Don't."*

Laurie was paralyzed with fear and she went for her door handle, but the man pressed the cold muzzle of a large handgun under her right arm. He said, "Don't do that, either. Just drive."

"My girls . . ."

"Are fine," he said. His voice was deep and breathy and his eyes were slightly hooded. He was so calm it unnerved her. And he was familiar to her in a way she couldn't place at first.

He said, "Drive. Take us to the park in front of the Navy Pier. It'll take less than twenty minutes."

"I know where it is."

"Good. And don't think about anything but driving safely and calmly, and about the fact that if you don't, I'll blow you away."

He dug into her knitting bag and found the gun—a .38 Smith & Wesson Model 36 Lady Smith—while they drove past Columbus Park. He checked to see if it was loaded—it was—then snapped the cylinder home and slipped it into his waistband. He said, "You won't be needing this."

As she joined the flow of traffic on Dwight D. Eisenhower Expressway toward the lake and Navy Pier, he said, "Do you know who I am now?"

"Yes." She chanced a glance at him while she drove. "I thought you were blond."

"I was," Nate said. "Before I came out to find you."

"How did you . . . make it?"

"I wasn't there when your monkeys fired the rocket."

She could feel his eyes on her, picking up every flinch, every twitch. She knew she'd reacted to what he said.

"My woman was there. Her name was Alisha."

"My husband's name was Chase."

He was silent for several minutes. It made her more frightened than when he talked. But she found some comfort in the fact that he wanted to go to the pier. On a warm evening like tonight, she thought, there would be plenty of people around. It would be public. Someone might see them. Or maybe she'd have the chance to escape.

They approached the pier. He directed her toward the most remote parking lot. It was practically empty because it was the farthest away. She was dismayed to find that there weren't many people around.

"Here," Nate said.

She pulled into a space. Lake Michigan dominated the view of the windshield. The pier reached out into it on their right, and small waves lapped against the pilings. The city was behind them. She could see how simple it would be for him to shoot her in the car, leave her body, and just walk away. Maybe there were cameras—they were everywhere these days—but even if he was seen by them, she would still be dead. She thought about Melissa and Aimee, and pictured their faces when they came out of the studio looking for their ride to McDonald's. She couldn't stop from tearing up.

She said, "How did you find me? How did you know about dance practice?"

"Wasn't hard. Google," he said. "Your name is all over it. You're listed as a patron of the dance studio, and the hours and classes are posted. And there were a couple of newsletters listing the students in each class. Melissa and Aimee, right? I figured you'd be dropping them off or picking them up."

She stared at him. "But how did you know it was me?"

He said, "I killed your husband, but it wasn't personal. I didn't even know who he was at the time. He was just a man who turned on me, holding a weapon that a minute before he'd been aiming at an injured girl we were tracking. I had no doubt that he would have finished her off. I didn't think twice about it at the time and I'd do it all over again in the same circumstances."

She shook her head. "Chase wouldn't . . ."

"Of course he would," he said. "Don't be dumb. You know what kind of man he was and you're not a stupid woman. You married him, after all."

She tried to find the right words to establish some kind of connection with him so he might let her go. But he was inscrutable and impossible to understand. Kind of like Chase. She said, "Did you find Johnny and Drennen?"

"Yes," Nate said. "I can find anybody." And by the way he said it, she knew they were dead.

"They didn't tell me about your wife," she said. "They never mentioned there was anyone else down there."

"That's what happens when you work with amateurs."

"Professionals are hard to find."

"In Chicago?"

"I wasn't in Chicago. You weren't in Chicago. You were in Podunk, Wyoming."

"Careful there," he said. For the first time, she thought she saw a slight smile, an opening.

Then he shut it. "So it was an eye for an eye," he said.

"My father . . . my father said revenge is a cleanser. I needed . . ." She searched for words and he let her search. "I needed to show myself I wouldn't just take it. I wouldn't just let someone take my husband away like that and there would be no consequences. And if the law wouldn't or couldn't do it, someone had to."

He nodded as if he agreed. The gun was in his lap but still pointed at her, almost casually. He said, "But you understand that if you play at this level, the concept of mercy doesn't exist. You do understand that?"

Her mouth was suddenly so dry she couldn't speak. She clamped her hands between her thighs so they wouldn't tremble. She'd done well, she thought, up to now. But she was losing it.

"My girls . . ." she said, her voice a croak.

"You should have thought of them before you went west," Nate said. "That would have been a good time to think of consequences if you failed."

"I know," she said, and dropped her head. Tears fell from her eyes onto the inside lenses of her sunglasses and pooled there.

"There are people out there who want me gone," Nate said. "They've sent a couple of professionals out over the years, but I put them down. And I thought I was off the map so far they'd never find me. But you did. A nice mom from Chicago. If it weren't for what happened to Alisha, I could almost admire that."

She began to weep deep down from her chest. She couldn't help it and wished she could stop.

He said, "You obviously met someone in Wyoming who told you how to find me. And he or she probably helped you get your hands on a rocket launcher. I can't imagine you can buy them on the street here as easily as I can buy a gun in Chicago."

She said, "Yes. I met someone."

Nate said, "What was the name?"

She told Nate, but said she couldn't be sure he wasn't feeding her a line. After all, she'd told everyone her name was Patsy.

He described the man's physical features, and she agreed it was him. But it was hard to hear him through the roaring in her ears.

Finally, Nate said, "Keep your mouth shut. You never met me. *This is over.* We both lost our lovers. But always keep in mind that I found you and that I can find you again. This time, think of those two girls of yours."

And with that, he was gone.

When she was recovered enough, she got out and stumbled toward the front of the car, not sure her legs had the strength to keep her upright. She pitched forward and caught herself on the hood and the metal was so hot it burned her palms. Despite the heat and the humidity and the sun, she felt a chill race through her.

She raised her head, looking for him. She wasn't sure which direction he'd gone. The grassy hill between her and the city had a few couples on it sitting on blankets, oblivious to what had just happened. Or nearly happened.

Then she turned toward the pier itself. It was crowded with tourists, but one tall man with dark hair was among them. He paused at the railing, and she saw two objects drop and splash into the lake. The guns.

She looked at her watch. An hour before she needed to pick up the girls. Enough time for a drink, or maybe two. She needed them like she'd never needed a drink before.

Nate leaned against the railing on the pier away from the crowds. He didn't throw the weapons into the water, but let the weapons drop out of his hands so his movements wouldn't be obvious to anyone.

The name she'd given him had shocked him at first, but the more he thought about it the more sense it made. The dots connected.

He checked his watch. He had time to return the rental and catch a red-eye back to Jackson Hole, to his Jeep, to his .500.

He wasn't through, after all.

33

Driving north on I-25 approaching Chugwater, Joe scrolled down through the call records on his cell phone, looking for a number from several weeks before when Dulcie Schalk had called him from her cell to ask questions about a poaching case. He highlighted the number and pushed SEND. She picked up on the third ring.

"Joe?" she asked, her surprise obvious.

"Since it's after hours I didn't know whether to call the office, and I couldn't wait until tomorrow," he said.

"We're neck deep in work, Joe," she said. "Getting ready for opening arguments next week. I really don't have much time right now, I'm afraid."

"I'm sure," he said, "but there's some new information you need to know. I'd never call otherwise."

"So this *is* about the Alden case." It was a statement, not a question, and she sounded disappointed in him.

"Yup."

There was a heavy sigh. "Joe, you know the situation. You're personally involved in this whole thing, and it's inappropriate to contact me after hours to lobby for your side."

Joe eased his pickup over to the shoulder of the highway and parked. The few lights of Chugwater were in his rearview mirror. To the west, three heavy-bodied clouds sat suspended over the bluffs of the horizon, their rose-colored bellies lit by the setting sun. When he turned the key off in the ignition, the sweet smell of desert sage filled the cab. "I'm not calling to lobby," he said evenly, "and I don't have a side."

The tone of his voice seemed to jar her. She said, "But I thought . . ."

"I need you to listen to me for five minutes. If you think I'm lobbying you after that, I'll hang up and wait for you to lose the trial. Is that the way you want to go here?"

"No," she said, with a slight hesitation. "Okay, I've got five minutes."

He filled her in on his conversation with Bob Lee and what Marybeth had found online about Rope the Wind, which had led him to Orin Smith.

"He's in federal custody," Joe said. "I interviewed him at the Federal Building in Cheyenne."

"Under whose authority?" she bristled.

"Under mine," he said. "But for the record, both the governor and the federal agent in charge knew I was there and what I was doing. In fact, the FBI listened in to the interview."

He could tell by her silence that she had no foreknowledge of Orin Smith or his connection to Rope the Wind, and therefore Smith's previous efforts to get a wind energy company started in Twelve Sleep County among the landowners. He wasn't surprised, since the sheriff's investigation had taken them no further than Missy. He hoped she wouldn't get defensive and territorial and shut him down before he heard him out. Joe knew Schalk didn't like surprises, and he'd seen how she bristled when others offered speculation with nothing to back them up. And like every county attorney Joe had ever worked with, she hated it when investigators struck out on their own.

She said, "This man, Orin Smith, he's in federal custody? And I assume this testimony might help him out at sentencing? Why should I think he's a credible witness?"

"Good point," Joe said. "You have no reason to believe anything he says right now. He's up for eleven counts of fraud, after all. I'm not sure I believe everything he told me. But please jot down what I relate to you and check him out on your own and make your own decision. And keep in mind Sheriff McLanahan wants a big simple win over a rich woman nobody likes. He's never wanted to look any further than her, and he's never focused on anybody else. Dulcie, neither have you."

"Continue," she said. Her tone was ice cold.

Joe said, "The other night, I heard Earl Alden described as a skimmer. I wasn't exactly sure what that meant at the time or why it would matter. But now I have a better idea.

"Alden was connected politically and professionally," Joe said. "And that seems to be the way it works these days. Success has nothing to do with ideas or inventions or hard work. It's about who you know and which politician may pick you to succeed. The Earl was a skimmer with no personal ideology. He gave big money to folks in both parties and made sure they knew it. That way he was always covered no matter who won. For The Earl it was like investing in research and development: He was never sure who would pay off. If there was an opportunity, he was right there with his hand out. And when it came to this big push for wind energy development, The Earl was right there ready to rock with the new administration in Washington and all their green initiatives."

She said, "Are you getting to the point soon?"

Joe said, "Believe me, I don't like to talk this much, either. But you need to know Alden's background before you can understand what he did and who was affected by it."

"Okay," she said, unconvinced.

"Anyway," Joe said, "with this wind energy deal, he saw a way he could cash in. The money was phenomenal, and he figured out a way to keep it coming from all sides.

"First," Joe said, "he heard about Orin Smith and Rope the Wind. I don't know who told him, or if Earl figured it out on his own. You know how fast word spreads in the county, and no doubt some of the ranchers Smith approached talked to each other over coffee or at the feed store. He might have even heard something from Missy or Bud Sr., for all we know. However he found out, The Earl met with Smith after every other rancher in the county had turned Smith down. Earl saw the value in a three-year-old wind energy company even if the three years was nothing more than incorporation records sitting in a file at the secretary of state's office. So Earl offered not to buy Rope the Wind for cash, but to make Smith a partner in the effort. In effect, Earl told Smith he'd get forty percent of the profits once the wind farm was built and producing electricity. Since Smith had struck out everywhere else and he knew Earl Alden was this legendary cash-generating machine, he agreed to the deal."

"I don't get it," Schalk said. "Why would Earl want to cut Smith in on the profits? Couldn't he have just bought the name on the cheap and done it all himself? Or just started his own company without this Smith guy?"

"He could have," Joe said, "but he was ten steps ahead of Smith and everybody else. See, Smith also had contact with a firm down in Texas he'd help incorporate several years before. The Texas company wasn't all that big, but they specialized in buying old or malfunctioning wind turbines and remanufacturing them into working units. There's been a market for legitimate wind turbines for years, I guess. These guys down there were sort of scrap dealers who fixed the turbines and put them back on the market. But because of the big money suddenly available for new wind farms, the new companies that went into the business didn't care about buying old turbines at a discount. You've got to forget about things like supply and demand, and free markets, when it comes to wind energy. All the incentives were designed for *new* companies building *new* turbines and putting people to work so the politicians could crow about what they'd done for the economy and the planet. So this Texas company was floundering and sitting on over a hundred pieces of junk they couldn't unload."

"O-*kay*," she said, drawing the word out, making Joe feel like a crank.

"Listen," he said, "you don't know all the pieces to this yet."

"Go on. So when do we get to the Cubans on the grassy knoll?"

Joe ignored her. "With the information Smith had given him about that big ridge where the wind blew all the time that bordered Earl's ranch, Earl bought the acreage from the Lees. Those poor Lees got the short end of the stick in every regard. So Earl owned the windiest place in the county and the one perfect spot for a big wind energy project. That was the first piece to fall into place.

"Once he had that ridge secured, Earl locked in the agreement with Orin Smith for the company, and suddenly Earl Alden had a three-year-old wind energy operation and land with almost constant Class V to Class VII winds. The reason that was important was because those two things were essential to start working the system—to kick-start a skimming operation on a big scale."

Schalk said, "Skimming whom?"

"You, me, all the other taxpayers," Joe said. "Here's how it worked, according to Smith. Like I said, The Earl was connected. He knew which banks across the country were going to receive federal bailouts because certain politicians didn't want them to fail. Earl approached those banks with the package for financing a massive wind farm called Rope the Wind. He knew at least one of them would go for it because the banks were being encouraged to lend to renewable energy schemes with bailout dollars, and they knew that even if the deals went bust, they'd be taken care of by the federal government. So no need for caution for these bankers—just open the floodgates to federal money, take their fees, and funnel it right back out the door to the right kind of company. In particular, and you may want to write this down, Smith said Earl got almost all of his financing through First Great Lakes Bank in Chicago. Heard of it?"

"You're kidding," she said. "Everybody's heard of it. This is the one they call the Mob Bank? The one with all the questionable loans that just disappeared? Haven't they been shut down?"

"They have now. But not before everybody got paid off in fees," Joe said. "They were connected, too."

"But that's not The Earl's fault," she said.

"No, it isn't. But that's how he financed his company. And he was just getting started."

He heard her take a long breath on the other end. He said, "Earl took the loan—which was backed by the Feds—and bought a hundred old wind turbines from the Texas remanufacturing company. He paid a million dollars each, Smith said, but applied for tax credits and incentives for new turbines, which run four to five million apiece."

"Jesus!" Schalk said. "That's outright fraud. That's what, three or four million per turbine? Or four hundred million dollars in the clear?"

"You bet," Joe said. "But who is checking on these things these days? There's so much of it going on, and so much bureaucracy in the process, no one knows what's what. I mean, how likely is it the Feds would send out an inspector to make sure the wind turbines were brand-new? And keep in mind, the profits are all paper profits at this point. They're on a balance sheet, but that's all. That's how a guy like the Earl skims. Everything is under the surface."

"I see your point."

Joe consulted his notes and said, "So The Earl doesn't stop there.

He's like a junkie when it comes to skimming. He got a fifty-million-dollar grant in federal stimulus funds from the Department of Energy because his project was about wind. That's why he bought Rope the Wind, because it had been around for three years on paper and that was one of the criteria for receiving the grant—that the company have a track record. Then he has his people go out and secure power contracts with a bunch of cities and states who have passed laws that mandate that certain percentages of their power must come from renewable energy. With the farm going up and the contracts in place, Earl now owns a genuine electric utility, which gives him the right to condemn the private land owned by the Lees to create a corridor for transmission lines. Even though these places are buying power at a loss and there wasn't any way of getting the power to them yet, it makes them feel good. So The Earl takes advantage of *that.*"

"I'm getting lost," she said.

"Here's how Smith explained it to me," Joe said, looking at his scribbles. "It's like Earl figured out a way to have someone dig a gold mine for him using their money and mining equipment, but he gets to sell all the gold he produces to others at an inflated cost that's guaranteed by the government. Then he uses grants and new federal programs to guarantee that the mine will always make money or at least never lose it. Then he signs deals with people to buy his gold at a preset price, because they're do-gooders and market prices don't matter to them. He used all the grants, subsidies, incentives, and tax credits to bail out the losses of all of his other interests."

"Joe . . ." she said, objecting, he thought, to the enormity and complexity of what he was telling her.

"I know," he said. "But in order to understand this, you've got to throw out everything you know about how real capitalism works. That's how The Earl thought. It was all a big poker game where the chips were free to him because he was one of the favored players. And with all those chips, he was able to create a multi-layered corporate entity that was completely cushioned against any kind of risk or loss. He could now protect all of his other assets like big ranches or homes all over the world, because the contracts, tax credits, and guarantees tied to Rope the Wind to offset all his losses and limited his liability."

Joe paused to review his notes and let her take it all in, and to see if he had left anything out.

She asked, "But why would Orin Smith dump on his partner like that if he stood to make a killing? Why tell you all this?"

Joe said, "I wondered the same thing, but the fact is all these transactions and technicalities benefitted Earl personally, but the wind farm won't show any real profit for years on its own. It's designed to suck up subsidies and provide tax credits, not to create power in the real world for real people. It'll take years to get transmission lines to that ridge to actually move the power to the electrical grid. And remember—there are no true profits until all the overhead is paid for, and that will take decades. Building those things is expensive, even with used turbines they got on the cheap."

"So Smith is cut out," she said.

"That's what he claims," Joe said. "He says he'll never live long enough to see a penny. And I have to believe him, because the guy got so desperate for cash that he created the Ponzi scheme that landed him in federal custody."

"Do you think he had something to do with Alden's death?" she asked. "Is that what you're driving at?"

"No," Joe said. "I don't think he was involved, even though I'm sure he wouldn't have stopped it if he'd known about it. But what you should consider, now that we know all this, is how many people would benefit from Earl Alden's death. I mean, besides Missy."

"Who do you mean?" she asked cautiously.

"Think about it," Joe said. "If this scheme was made public—which it might now be—the whole house of cards would fall and dozens of people would be implicated in the fraud. You want me to name them all?"

"No need," she said sullenly. "You've got the owners of the Texas company, who likely knew what Alden was up to because no one had ever bought their entire inventory before. You've got the officers, shareholders, and regulators of Great Lakes, who all benefitted from the financing of a crackpot company. You've got the mob in Chicago, who's suddenly lost their own personal bank that doesn't ask questions. You've got the cities and states that signed contracts without investigating whether or not Rope the Wind could actually produce the power they claimed it could produce. You've got other wind farm companies—legitimate ones—who didn't get all that stimulus money because Earl was there first. You've got the Lees, who were cheated out of their land. And you've got the politicians in Washington, who designed the mechanism to allow for and encourage fraud at this level."

Joe said, "That's a start."

"But you don't have a specific villain, do you?" she said. "You don't know who in that cast of characters was desperate enough to shut him up that they took action?"

"No," Joe said. "It's like a big locked-room mystery. There are maybe forty, fifty, sixty people out there who were taken advantage of, but who wouldn't want the scheme exposed because it would hurt them. So the only way to prevent the thing from blowing up would be to kill the king."

She paused for a long time. He could only imagine what she was thinking.

He said, "I really don't know who could have done it. And it will take time and a lot of investigation to find out. I'm not thinking it's the city, state, or government people involved. They wouldn't solve it this way. I'm thinking either the mob, or an angry shareholder out there. Maybe even someone local who realized how The Earl had taken advantage of them, or someone crazy with rage because they'd been cut out. We should definitely get the Feds involved, and Chuck Coon heard this stuff and may be starting to make some calls as we speak. But given the stakes and the suspects, I don't think it's out of the realm of possibility to think that someone figured out a way to off Earl and frame Missy."

She said, "This is so far-fetched."

He sighed. "I know it sounds that way. But what about the method of death? Why would anyone go to all that trouble of shooting him and hanging the body from a wind turbine blade except to send a message of some kind? If it was Missy on her own, why didn't she just cut the gas line on his car or poison him or something? Why didn't she smother him in his sleep?"

She said, "Unless she wanted to steer us away from her."

Joe thought about it. "She is pretty crafty, all right. But I don't know if she's capable of that kind of premeditation." As he said it, he thought about how Missy, over the years, had lined up the next rich husband well before the soon-to-be-discarded one had a hint of dissatisfaction. And how she'd mastered the fine art of hidden but definitive language in her prenuptial agreement with Bud Sr., which had gained her his third-generation ranch.

Joe sat back in his seat. The rose-colored clouds had lost their light and now looked like heavy clumps of dark steel wool set against a graying sky.

"Well," Schalk said, "this is all very interesting."

"This stuff I just told you," Joe said, "it's new information, right?"

"Most of it," she said.

"So it may be worth looking into?"

"Except for one thing," she said.

"Bud Longbrake," Joe said.

"And as far as that aspect of the case goes, it's still solid," she said. "You can throw all these conspiracies at me and watch the implications of what Alden did fly all over the country, but the fact still remains that we've got a man who claims your mother-in-law tried to hire him to kill her husband and he's willing to testify to that fact. We've got phone records to prove that they were talking, even though Missy claims she hadn't seen Bud or heard from him since she filed a restraining order against him. And, Joe, we have the motive. I've got people who will testify to the fact that Earl Alden was seeking a divorce."

Joe winced. "But still . . ."

"Facts are stubborn things, Joe," she said. "And I can promise you a jury will be able to understand Missy wanting to kill her husband much easier than a wild-eyed conspiracy involving wind energy, tax credits, the mob, and so on."

He said, "You're probably right about that. But is it worth it? Would you do your best to convict a woman who may be innocent because it's easier than expanding the investigation?"

Her voice had a sharp edge to it when she said, "Don't you ever question my integrity again. If I didn't believe she did it, we wouldn't have brought the charges against her."

"I apologize," Joe said, flushing. "I went over the line."

"Yes, you did."

No words were spoken for a full minute. Then Joe said, "But you've got to be thinking of what Marcus Hand will do with this."

"I'm thinking about that, Joe," she said. "No doubt he will use it to muddy up the case and confuse the jury."

"He'll find a juror or two—maybe more—to buy his theory," Joe said. "We both know that. So given what he'll do with this information, you might want to consider delaying the trial until you can make sure you can counter it."

She said, "So, when did you get your law degree? When was it you were elected by the voters in Twelve Sleep County to enforce the law?"

Joe said, "I've seen Marcus Hand in action. I've seen him win with less than this."

"Besides," she said, her voice lightening in tone, "who says he needs to know all this ahead of time?"

Joe looked suspiciously at his cell phone before raising it back up. "Dulcie, you didn't just say that."

She was silent.

"Dulcie, now I'm questioning your integrity."

"I was just speculating," she said, a hint of desperation in her voice.

"He knows," Joe said. "Marybeth is talking to him."

"Joe, you're a son-of-a-bitch."

He was speechless.

"And the same goes for your wife," she said.

Joe took a deep breath. He said, "Dulcie, this isn't you. This is somebody who wants to beat Marcus Hand so badly they've lost their judgment. Dulcie, I need to talk to Bud."

Silence.

"You still don't know where he is, do you?"

She said, "See you in court, Joe."

"Dulcie, please—"

She hung up on him.

"You may not know where he is," he said to the dead phone, "but I think I do."

As he pulled back on the highway, he tried to call Marybeth, but his call went straight to voice mail. No doubt, she was speaking to Marcus Hand or her mother, or both. Telling them what he'd told the county prosecutor.

He said, "I'm headed back, but I'll keep my phone on. I've got a stop to make on the way."

Then: "I'm really disappointed in Dulcie. But she's probably going to put your mother away. The women's prison is in Lusk, by the way, if you ever want to visit her."

Glendo Reservoir shimmered in the moonlight to the north and east of the highway. There were a couple of boats out there in the dark, walleye fisherman Joe guessed, and a few lights across the lake from a campground.

After his conversation with Schalk, he got angrier with each mile traveled. He was angry with Dulcie Schalk, Sheriff McLanahan, Bud Sr., Bud Jr., Orin Smith—the whole lot of them. But he traced most of his anger to his own frustration with himself. He couldn't crack this thing, he might never be able to crack it, and he wasn't sure, deep down, he wanted to.

What Smith had told him about The Earl and the way business was done in the country these days had instilled a deep and hopeless strain of melancholy. There was no right and no wrong anymore.

34

After filling his Jeep with gasoline in Jackson, Nate drove north and east toward the dark Gros Ventre Mountains via Togwotee Pass.

He pulled over on the two-lane highway before he reached the Togwotee Mountain Lodge. He got out and kept the engine running. There were walls of lodgepole pines on each side of the road and a channel of sky above his head like a river carrying fallen stars. The high mountain air, piney and cool with oncoming fall, helped place him back where he needed to be. Behind him, through the narrow clearing in the trees due to the road, he could see the tops of the Teton Range silhouetted on the horizon like the teeth of a frozen buzz saw. He reached down beneath the seat and checked to make sure his .500 hadn't been stolen. It was there.

He shed his Jackson Hole clothes and threw them into a pile in the back and pulled on jeans and a heavy shirt. He laced his boots on tight.

Nate swung himself back into the cab of the Jeep and eased off the shoulder onto the blacktop. He hoped he could make it over the summit to Dubois before all the restaurants closed. He hadn't eaten since breakfast in Chicago.

He planned to drive all night until he found and killed the person who'd given him up.

Nate leaned into the switchback turns coming down off the mountain. He drove fast and kept his lights dim so he could see beyond the orb of headlights for the eye reflections of elk or cows or mule deer on the road.

He thought about Alisha, how he hadn't yet allowed himself to really mourn her. Even when he'd built the scaffolding for her body, he'd concentrated on the construction of it, the materials, the timbers, the sinews holding the joints together. How he'd hoist the body up without letting it fall apart on him. And he'd left her without looking back.

Still, though, he hadn't wrapped his mind around the fact that she was really, truly gone.

He just knew he couldn't do it, mourn her, until he'd avenged her first. In a strange way that made him feel increasingly guilty, he knew the journey to Eden and Chicago and back had been done with such a murderous single-mindedness that he'd used it to justify pushing his feelings away.

After it was done, he would slip onto the res and talk to Alisha's relatives and the little girl she was taking care of and allow his focus and rage to turn into something else.

He wasn't sure how to do it when the time came, what to say, or what words to use.

For the first time since it had happened, he gave it some consideration. Joe could help, he knew. Joe and Marybeth, especially. They were in the mainstream of sorts and Nate's only real connection to the world of loving couples, growing children, mortgages, pet dogs, lawns, and social mores. It was a world he wished he understood and hoped he could enter some day, but it was still as foreign to him as daily life in Outer Mongolia. But because Joe and Marybeth were his only true connection to that world, he wanted to nurture them and protect them and keep them away from what he knew to be out there. Not that Joe wasn't capable of protecting his family—he was, and in surprising ways—but Joe still seemed to believe in his oath and duty and in innocence and the law's brand of justice. Nate didn't want to be there if and when Joe learned otherwise, because it wouldn't be pretty.

Marybeth could help him with the words, Nate thought, and Joe could stand by with nothing but his own kind of humility and decency that would be like an anchor or a wall for Nate to attach himself to.

There was nothing open in Dubois except a convenience store with shelves filled with processed food in plastic packaging. Nate bought a large paper cup of weak coffee (because there was no strong coffee), beef sticks that weren't much more than stringy black muscle tissue laced with sodium and preservatives, and a package of string cheese.

It had been years since he'd eaten such things. He couldn't wait to get this all over and harvest an elk and an antelope and grill the back straps.

What Laurie Talich had told him shouldn't have been such a surprise, he thought. It all made sense when he thought about it and connected the dots. He was grateful his location hadn't been determined by The Five, but through local channels.

He once again pushed the particulars of mourning out ahead of him and concentrated on the task at hand.

There was a compound to enter, and it was guarded. There might be motion detectors and no doubt there'd be cameras. Not that they'd stopped him before . . .

SEPTEMBER 8

Letting the cat out of the bag is a whole lot easier than putting it back in.

—Will Rogers

35

Joe rolled into Saddlestring at 12:30 a.m. and drove straight to the Stockman's Bar. There were several cars and trucks parked diagonally outside, and he was grateful it was still open. The Coors, Fat Tire, and 90 Shilling neon beer signs lit the small windows on the side. He knew Timberman often shut the place down before 2:00 a.m. if he had no customers or if the drinkers who were still there had stopped drinking.

Joe pulled into a space out front and killed the engine. He recognized a few of the vehicles and was pleased to locate the one he was looking for: a 1992 Ford pickup with a cracked windshield that had primer painted on the top of both rear fenders.

He got out and strode toward the bar and instinctively patted himself down to make sure he was geared up. Cuffs, pepper spray, bear spray, digital camera, digital recorder, notebook, pen, citation book, radio, cell phone, .40 Glock with two extra magazines in a holster. Not that he planned to pull his service weapon or, God forbid, try to hit something with it.

He paused outside the door of the bar, took a couple of deep breaths to calm himself down against anticipation, and pushed his way inside.

Timberman looked up, his eyebrows arched slightly, which meant surprise. Joe hadn't been in the place so late at night for eight years or so, and it was obvious the barman wasn't expecting him.

Joe nodded to Timberman and took in the customers. He recognized all of them. The one he was looking for avoided his eyes.

He walked down the length of the bar and took the stool once occupied nightly by Bud Longbrake Sr. Keith Bailey, Bud's friend and drinking partner and the gatekeeper for the Eagle Mountain Club, leaned slightly away from him, putting space between them. Bailey slowly rolled a can of Budweiser between his big hands and there was an empty shot glass sitting on the bar next to Bailey's glasses and a copy of the Saddlestring *Roundup*. Bailey turned his head a quarter toward Joe, just enough to see him warily with both eyes. His expression was stoic. *Cop eyes,* Joe thought.

When Timberman approached, Joe said, "A bourbon and water for me. Maker's Mark. And whatever Keith is having."

"We got Evan Williams," Timberman said.

"Fine."

"None for me," Bailey said. To Joe, he said, "You're out late."

"Past my bedtime," Joe said.

When Timberman turned and went for the bourbon bottle, Joe said to Bailey, "I bet you wonder what took me so long."

Bailey's response was a slight beery snort.

"All this time I've been looking for Bud and I never even thought of asking the most obvious guy," Joe said.

Bailey shrugged.

"Where have you let him stay up there? One of the maintenance buildings, the club itself, or did you give him the keys to one of the members' houses?"

Timberman delivered the drink, and Joe took a sip of it. It was cold and smoky and good.

When Timberman turned around, Bailey said, "He's under a shitload of pressure and pain right now. He needed some time away.

There's no law against helping a buddy out unless he's wanted for something. You got charges on him?"

"No," Joe said. "I just need to talk to him. I've been trying to find him for days and you know that."

Bailey turned away from Joe and turned his palms down on the bar. He stiffened. "You never asked."

"No, you've got me there. So are you hiding him from the sheriff as well?"

"So you're freelancing?"

"Yup."

"I'm not hiding him from anyone," Bailey said. "He's hiding himself. I've got no stake in this thing that's going on, other than helping an old friend. Back in the day when Bud owned the ranch, before that witch took it from him, he was a big man around this country. He helped out a lot of people, and he wasn't a jerk about it." He seemed to want to say more, but like so many men Joe had encountered of Bailey's age and station, he didn't feel the need to go on.

"He's struggling," Bailey said, ending it at that.

"With what? With what he's about to do?" Joe asked.

"I'm not getting into the particulars. That's not my business. I'm not sure it's yours."

Joe sipped his drink again and shook his head at Timberman when Timberman raised his chin with a *"Want another?"* look.

Joe said, "I'm not going to hurt him in any way. You know me. I used to work for him, and we always got along. I shouldn't even have to say that."

"I'm not worried about you," Bailey said. "But Bud seems to think there might be some other bastards after him. Trying to get to him before he testifies."

Joe said, "Who?"

"Don't know," Bailey said. "We don't talk all that much. He asked for a place to stay and I helped him out. We don't sit around and *share feelings.*" He said it in a way that made Joe smile and like Keith Bailey more than he'd thought.

"He fades in and out," Bailey said, "but you know about that."

Joe nodded. He recalled Bud Sr. showing up in his backyard a year ago, waving a gun, looking for people who were out to get him. For some reason, he thought one of them would be Nate.

"He's worse than that now," Bailey said. "On account of his condition."

"What condition?"

"You really don't know?"

Joe shook his head.

"I'm not going to be talking out of school here. He can tell you what he wants to tell you. All I'll do is let you know how to find him," Bailey said. Then: "On one condition."

"Shoot."

"If you're caught up there, you didn't get the keypad code from me. I don't care where you say you got it from—a member, maybe. Or that someone gave it to you so you could check out the wildlife on the place or something. But if you say I gave it to you, I could lose my job."

Joe agreed, and Bailey tore off a corner of the Saddlestring *Roundup* and scratched out a seven-digit numeric code.

"You aren't going to call him and tell him I'm coming, are you?" Joe said, taking the scrap of paper.

Bailey didn't say yes, didn't say no, but signaled Timberman for his check.

In the daylight, the Eagle Mountain Club overlooked the Bighorn River valley from its massive perch along the contours of a rounded and high eastern bluff. The club had a thirty-six-hole golf course that fingered through the foothills of the Bighorn Mountains, as well as a private fish hatchery, shooting range, airstrip, and about sixty multimillion-dollar homes that had been constructed long before the economy turned sour. Because of the airstrip, most of the members could arrive and depart without ever venturing beyond the gates. Built in the 1970s, the club was separate and apart from the moods, rhythms, and culture of blue-collar Saddlestring below it, although a handful of its members ventured into the community and some were great patrons of the museum, library, and other civic groups. The Eagle Mountain Club had only two hundred fifty members, and new people joined only when old members died, dropped out, or were denied privileges by a majority of the members.

The locals who worked at the club signed employment agreements to keep quiet about who the members were—CEOs, celebrities, politicians, magnates, a few trust fund moguls—and what went on inside. Still, most people in town seemed to know both, including Joe. What had always impressed him was how un-awed the locals were about the famous people who ventured down from the club and shopped and dined among them. There were never any public scenes of gasping recognition or autograph requests. Joe attributed the phenomenon to a wonderful mixture of proprietary pride—*These rich folks could live anywhere in the world and they choose to live here with us!*—and a stubborn independence and the optimism that perhaps, someday, they'd be members, too.

Joe had been within the boundaries of the club only a few times in his career. During his first year as district game warden, he'd located a rogue colleague holing up with a rich wife whose husband was away on business. Since then, he'd been on the grounds on calls where game animals had been found killed or local trespassers had been spotted. While he was there, he'd been shadowed by private resort security vehicles whose occupants had watched what he did and where he went through spotting scopes.

Access to the resort was via a guardhouse manned during the daytime hours by Keith Bailey. At night, members gained entrance by calling the security people at the front desk of the clubhouse. Closed-circuit cameras were hidden in the brush along both sides of the driveway and throughout the massive compound.

Joe drove up the driveway and punched in the numbers Keith Bailey had given him. The iron gates clicked and swung away. He eased his pickup past the empty guardhouse, looking both ways for security personnel who might swoop down on him any second. No doubt his entrance was being captured on videotape. Joe chose to believe that no security people were watching the monitors live, since it was September and most of the members had already left.

As the gates wheezed shut behind him, Joe crept along the banked blacktop entrance to the heart of the club. The road ran along the rim of the bluff, and the lights of Saddlestring were splayed out below to his right. Subtle lights marked both sides of the road.

He crested the hill and turned left, past the turnoff for the main clubhouse up on the hill. There were a few lights up there, but no activity he could see. The road dipped slightly, with large set-back houses on both sides, and he strained to see the plaques with the names of the owners in the grass marking each driveway.

He looked for a sign that read SKILLING. Kimberly Alice Skilling, heir to Skilling Defense Industries of Houston. She owned not only a large house on the grounds but also two guest cottages.

And she'd asked Keith Bailey to keep a special eye on her place, especially one of the cottages where the pipes had burst the winter before.

Joe gave some credit to Bud Longbrake. Hiding in plain sight all this time.

36

Nate nosed his Jeep into a thick stand of tall willows on the riverbank, making sure his vehicle couldn't be seen from the road. He spooked a cow moose out of her resting place as he drove up, and she scrambled to her feet, all legs and snout in his headlights, and wheeled away from him and high-stepped off.

He killed the engine and the lights and climbed out. As he strapped on his shoulder holster and darkened his cheeks and forehead with river mud, he could hear the moose grunting and splashing and crashing downstream. He'd hoped to proceed soundlessly. He hadn't counted on the demolition derby–like grace of a wild moose in the same area.

When his eyes became adjusted to the darkness and the only ambient light was from the stars and the fingernail slice of moon, he stepped back away from the vehicle and surveyed the terrain all around him. The river was in front of him: inky and determined, lapping occasionally at pale, round river rocks that rimmed the bank as he passed by. Behind him were swampy wetlands created by beavers damming up the fingerlike tributaries of the river. He was lucky, he thought, to have found this dry spit of land to drive on.

To his east was a sudden rise. The cliff face was striated and pale in the starlight. Small, dark forms shot across the flatness of the face, either starlings filling up on an evening insect hatch or bats doing the same thing. On the lip of the cliff he could see brush and bunched thick grass.

Nate took it cautiously as he crossed the river. The water was cold and surprisingly swift and it came up to his knees. He stepped from rock to rock and sometimes couldn't tell what was beneath him. It was shallow and wide here, but there might be hidden deep holes. He aimed for smudges of tan or yellow beneath the surface, hoping they were rocks, hoping he wouldn't slip on them.

He made it to the other side, but found himself walled in by twelve-foot-high brush that was too thick and tight to get through. He paralleled the river for a while, but couldn't find an opening. Then he dropped to his knees and crawled through the brush on a game trail. His presence spooked low-bodied animals that squealed and ran out ahead of him.

After thirty yards, the brush thinned and he was able to stand. He found himself closer than he thought he would be to the cliff wall. Hands on his hips, he leaned back and scouted a route to the top. There were lines of dark vegetation zigzagging up the face. Since the seams were level enough to host weeds and grass, he assumed they would be flat enough to climb up.

But before approaching the wall, he stood stock-still and simply listened and looked around.

It was a familiar quiet, like Hole in the Wall Canyon. But he'd learned how treacherous that kind of quiet could be if he wasn't fully alert and engaged.

He saw no other people anywhere. No fences. But as he concentrated on a pair of tall cottonwood trees between him and the wall, he saw an anomaly. Nothing in nature had perfect lines, and he'd seen perfect lines. He squinted, and recognized two box-shaped pieces of equipment secured waist-high to the trunks of the trees.

Hunters called them scouting cameras. They were battery-powered digital cameras designed to be mounted near game trails. The cameras had motion detectors and either flashes or infrared nighttime capability. They could take up to a thousand 1.5- to 5.0-megapixel images from a single set of four D batteries.

The usual range of the cameras was forty to fifty feet. He was beyond that. But how could he possibly bypass them or get close enough to destroy them without having his photo snapped with every step?

He stayed still and thought about it.

There were so many moose, deer, elk, and antelope in the river bottom that no doubt the cameras got quite a workout at night. But was someone actually looking at each shot live?

He shook his head. This was the Eagle Mountain Club, not the Pentagon. What probably happened was some intern or maintenance guy was sent down the hill every few days to retrieve the shots and see if trespassers had entered the grounds, and who they were. Individual digital photographs stayed inside the camera and weren't transmitted to a central control room.

Additionally, the trail cameras were mounted high, not at ground level. It was probably so the security guys wouldn't have to stare at hundreds and hundreds of photos of rabbits and grouse.

So Nate once again dropped to his knees and simply crawled through with his head down. He didn't hear a single shutter snap.

Climbing the cliff face wasn't difficult. In less than fifteen minutes, he slid through the strands of a barbed wire fence and he was in.

Joe drove into the driveway of the Skilling guesthouse, turned off his headlights and the engine, and looked for signs of life. He sat for a moment, studying it. If someone was inside and heard him drive up, Joe expected to see a curtain edged back or a light switched on.

The guesthouse was small but well tended. It was beige, one level with three curtained windows facing out, and a railed porch leading up to an extra-large wooden double door. An attached double garage was on the right side. Tall twin cottonwoods flanked the walkway up to the porch. A second guesthouse to his left was an exact mirror of the one he was facing—including the trees—but Joe barely glanced at it because Bailey had said this was the one. In the center of the large picture window on the left side of the door was a faint vertical stripe, and Joe guessed it came from the living room. There was a light on.

Joe climbed out of the pickup and slid his shotgun out of the scabbard behind his seat. He checked the loads—five rounds of double-ought buckshot—but didn't pump a round into the chamber. As he made his way up the walkway, he pondered whether to slink around the house and see if he could see anything inside or bang on the front door. He thought about the fact that he had no warrant and no real authority for being there. If Bud was inside and decided to start blasting away at an intruder, he would be justified in doing so.

Joe rapped sharply on the front door with his knuckles and stepped aside. He called, "Bud? It's Joe Pickett. Open up. I need to talk to you."

He paused to listen, but heard nothing from inside. He knocked hard again and repeated his words, this time louder. After all, it was two in the morning. Joe didn't expect Bud to be up and around and wanted to give the man time to throw some clothes on.

Joe reached down and tried the door. Bolted. He banged on it again and shouted. Nothing.

He went down the porch steps and sidled up to the picture window where he'd seen the vertical slash of light. He removed his hat and cautiously leaned across the glass, suppressing a flash vision of Bud inside aiming his .45 at Joe's face. Joe could feel his pulse race as he leaned and looked.

The space between the curtains was less than half an inch, so he had to move his head back and forth in order to see the whole of the room inside. It was a living room, after all, and there were signs of clutter. A coffee table was covered with empty beer bottles, some on their side. A stout liter bottle of Jim Beam lorded over the beer bottles.

Joe said softly, "It's Bud, all right," although this was a Bud he wasn't sure he knew anymore.

Clothes had been thrown over the backs of chairs, and on the couch were several take-out containers he recognized as coming from the Burg-O-Pardner in town. As Joe moved right to left and elevated onto his toes, he could see the carpeting and a single cowboy boot on its side, sole facing out from the corner of the couch. Just the sole. The shaft of the boot was hidden from view by the furniture. Joe felt his insides contract. Was Bud's leg connected to the rest of the boot? Was his body back there?

Probable cause for entry. Joe recalled Bailey saying Bud was sure someone was after him.

In normal circumstances, Joe would alert the Eagle Mountain Security office or the sheriff's department, so they could go in together. And he would call them, eventually. But he wanted to see the inside for himself before they took over the scene. To document the PC for entering, he took three photos of the boot by the couch with his digital camera.

He got his Maglite from his pickup and returned to the front porch and felt around at the obvious places for a spare key—the top of the doorframe, under the mat, beneath several flat river rocks on the side of the walkway. No key. Then he jogged back to the front door, propped the shotgun against the railing, paused while he took a breath, and rushed the door hard, smashing into it with his shoulder. It didn't give at all, and the blow caused pain to shoot through his entire body. He stepped away from the solid door, rubbing his shoulder, wondering if he'd broken something.

Joe considered smashing through one of the windows with the butt of his shotgun and crawling inside, but decided to try any other doors first. There had to be one in back. He retrieved his shotgun—*man, his shoulder hurt*—and paralleled the front of the house to get to the corner. He glanced again through the slit in the curtains, saw the boot hadn't moved, and ducked a cottonwood tree branch. His boots sounded loud on the concrete driveway, and as he walked past, he grabbed the handle and jerked, even though he assumed it was powered by an electric garage door opener.

It gave. Joe stopped, surprised. Then he rolled it all the way up.

Bud Longbrake's F-150 pickup was inside. Joe looked up and saw that the manual catch on the garage door opener had been clicked back, and it made sense. Bailey had given Bud a key to the house, but the remote control for the garage was probably in Kimberly Alice Skilling's car, wherever that was. In order to hide his vehicle, Bud had had to disengage the opener and slide the door up and down the old-fashioned way. After parking inside, he'd forgotten to slide the bolt home.

Joe swung his Maglite up and held his breath as he reached for the knob of the door to enter the house.

Unlocked as well.

Nate shouldered through thick, seven-foot-high mountain juniper bushes until he stood on the manicured grass of the club lawn itself. He stopped for a moment with his back to the brush to see if there were any vehicles on the roads or obvious cameras or sensors ahead of him.

Satisfied, he crouched down and crab-walked from tree to tree toward the homes in front of him. The one he was looking for was right there ahead: a three-story Tudor with a couple of guest cottages.

He approached the main house and went straight for the back of the garage. No one ever put curtains on garage windows, and he peered inside. Five stalls and not a single vehicle inside. The floor looked polished and it reflected a beam of moonlight.

He stepped back and assessed the main house. It felt big and empty to him. All the curtains were closed tightly and there wasn't a single leak of light from inside. He turned toward the guest cottages and moved from tree to tree, bush to bush, until he was behind them. As he'd moved, he'd noted the outline of a pickup truck parked in the driveway of the first structure, and now as he paused, a light clicked on inside at the far-left window, closest to the garage.

Nate slid his .500 out of its holster, hoisted it up near his right ear, and as he leveled it his left thumb cocked the hammer back. The scope gathered all the available light, and Nate rested the crosshairs on the center of the window.

Joe couldn't help but think that Bud should have taken better care of a house in which he was a secret guest. Like in his apartment above the Stockman's Bar, wrappers, empty bottles, reeking cartons, and bits of debris were everywhere. The door from the garage led into the kitchen, and Joe noted the stack of dirty dishes in the sink and the overflowing garbage can against the wall across from the stove. A scrawny gray cat fed among a pile of chicken bones it had pulled from the garbage can. The cat looked up at Joe with no fear at all.

"Bud, are you here?" Joe called out. "It's me, Joe."

As he passed the kitchen window, Joe leaned over and patted the cat on the head.

Nate saw a glimpse of a head and a hat through the window. He put the crosshairs on it, and as he began to squeeze the trigger, the head was gone, as if the man inside had fallen through a trapdoor. He cursed, kept his weapon up, and waited for the target to reappear.

But it didn't, and another light clicked on behind the curtains of the middle window. He'd moved on.

Nate wondered how he'd known to duck at that precise moment, but dismissed it as happenstance.

And now Nate would have to go inside. It would be better that way, he thought, as he jogged toward the back door. Face-to-face would be best.

He wanted Bud to see his face, know Nate Romanowski had found him, before Bud's head exploded.

The back door was locked, but it gave slightly when Nate leaned his shoulder against it. He opened his knife and slid it down through the crack between the door and frame. No bolt. Which meant it was locked at the knob set. He pushed the knife farther in, slid it down until the blade rested against the pawl, and chopped back.

He was in.

With his shotgun out in front of him, Joe entered the living room. More clutter. A table lamp was on with a lampshade that had been knocked cockeyed, the orb of light throwing out a yellow pool on the carpeting like a side glance.

A high-backed lounge chair blocked his view of the side of the couch so he moved to his right, weapon ready. Joe girded himself to see a dead body.

It was a single boot lying on its side with no Bud attached.

Joe sighed, and yelled, *"Bud!"*

"Joe?"

Although Joe recognized the voice instantly, he still racked the pump and wheeled and raised the stock up to his cheek. The voice came from a darkened mudroom at the back of the house. "Nate? What the *hell*?"

He heard Nate chuckle drily at the use of the curse.

"I've got the same question for you," Nate said, emerging from the mudroom into the light, rotating the cylinder on his big revolver until he could rest the hammer back on the empty chamber, holstering the weapon beneath his arm. Nate had cut and darkened his hair and he looked serious and severe. He asked, "What are you doing here?"

"Trying to find Bud Longbrake," Joe said, lowering the barrel of his gun.

"Me, too," Nate said. "I'm here to kill the son-of-a-bitch."

"Really?"

"Really."

Joe saw the black braid attached to the barrel of Nate's handgun and he recognized its color.

"Oh, no," Joe said. "You think Bud was responsible?"

Nate said, "He set me up."

Joe was puzzled. "Why would he do that?"

"Why did he do anything the last couple of years?" Nate said. "I don't know whether it was the alcohol, or his paranoia about me coming after him, or what happened to him when he lost the ranch, or whatever. But something made him go crazy. And Alisha died because of it."

Joe said, "You've got me on that one. I was just thinking how he'd become a different person than the one I used to work for. Like his personality changed."

"It doesn't matter what caused it," Nate said. "He still has to answer for his big mouth."

Joe said, "I wanted to talk with him because he claims he has the goods on Missy murdering her husband. That's why *I'm* here. I've been trying to find him because the trial starts on Monday."

"You could have shot me," Nate said, looking at Joe's Remington Wingmaster.

"Yup," Joe said. "Sorry about that. You scared me."

"So where's Bud?"

"He's not here, but he hasn't been gone long. His truck is in the garage, so either he caught a ride or someone got here just ahead of us and took him."

"Too bad," Nate said. "Who could have taken him?"

Joe said, "I've got so many suspects in this case, my mind is boggled. I'll fill you in if you want to hear it all. How long have you been here?"

"Two minutes," Nate said. "I just came in the back door and heard your voice. A minute before, I nearly shot you in the head."

He said it in such a matter-of-fact way that it took Joe a second or two to grasp the import. *"You nearly shot me in the head . . ."* Joe repeated, trailing off.

Nate shrugged. "Wouldn't it have been something if we'd drawn down on each other by mistake? That would be a hell of a thing."

Joe stifled a smile. It wasn't funny what they'd almost done to each other, but the way Nate said it was.

Joe said, "It's good to see you, Nate."

"Likewise."

"I'm sorry about what happened in the canyon. I found the scaffold."

"Did you tell anyone?"

"Marybeth and Alice Thunder. Both have kept it to themselves."

Nate nodded, grateful. He said, "I found the guys who did it, and the woman who put them up to it. I put the guys down, but I let the woman off . . ."

"No details," Joe said, putting his hand up to stop Nate from saying more.

Silence hung in the air.

Joe said, "Nate, can we get past what happened last year?"

Nate nodded. He said, "I've had plenty of time to think about it, as I'm sure you have. It boils down to this: You were wrong, but you had no choice."

Joe said, "I think I agree."

"Then we don't need to talk about it anymore," Nate said.

Joe liked that.

"So," Nate said, "where did that son-of-a-bitch Bud Longbrake go?"

Before Joe could speculate on an answer, he heard the sound of motors outside and the quick whoop of a siren that blew open the quiet night. Flashing red and blue lights filled the window and danced across the walls and made the living room seem like an unlikely party scene.

Joe stepped over and parted the curtains with the back of his hand. "The sheriff is here," he said. Two department vehicles: Sollis' SUV and McLanahan's pickup. There were two heads in Sollis' unit, but the sheriff was alone in his.

"You want me to take them out?" Nate asked, reaching for his .500.

"Jeez, Nate."

"I'll catch you later then," Nate said, retreating toward the mudroom. Joe watched him. He doubted the sheriff had sent anyone around the back to block the back door since he'd arrived with such fanfare at the front.

"My house," Joe called after him, and Nate was gone.

Joe laid the shotgun on the couch and cautiously opened the door before McLanahan could bang on it. He wanted to show himself in the open, and that he offered no threat.

The sheriff looked purposeful and self-satisfied in the flashing lights of the vehicles. Sollis stood smugly behind him and to the left, with his hand on his holstered weapon. Deputy Reed was farther back, looking solemn.

"Hello, Joe," McLanahan said. Then to Sollis, over his shoulder, "Arrest this man for breaking and entering and attempting to tamper with a witness. Maybe trespassing as well, if the club wants to charge him."

Joe sighed. "Except I didn't do any of those things." He pointed out the boot on the floor, the reason he had probable cause for entering without a warrant or notice.

"I've got photos of what I saw," Joe said. "I really did think Bud Longbrake was dead or hurt, so I entered. The garage door was unlocked."

"Anybody with you?" McLanahan asked, peering over Joe's shoulder.

"No." Thinking: Nate should be sprinting across the lawn out back toward the edge of the property. Still, he felt guilty for misleading the sheriff.

McLanahan rocked back on his heels and hooked his thumbs in his belt loops so he could lean back and look down his nose at Joe. McLanahan twitched his mustache from side to side, and said, "Not sure I'm buying it."

Joe shrugged. "I'm not trying to sell you anything."

"How'd you get access to the club, anyway?"

Joe caught himself before he looked away. "I know the keypad combination."

"Right," McLanahan said, snorting. Joe thought he was caught, and he felt cold dread in his belly.

"Probably got it from your dear mother-in-law," McLanahan said, sure of himself.

Joe felt the dread dissipate. He said, "Rather than screw around with me, I'd suggest you put out an APB on your star witness, Bud Longbrake. He's gone."

The sheriff grinned and looked over his shoulder at Sollis, who smiled back at him. Reed found something interesting to stare at on the top of his boots. They knew something he didn't.

"No need for that," McLanahan said. "Bud's safe and warm in sheriff department custody, but I ain't sayin' where. He's probably enjoying a cocktail to calm his nerves. He called us because he heard you were coming after him. He said he feared for his life."

"That's ridiculous," Joe said. "I'd never hurt Bud."

"Poor old guy," McLanahan said, ignoring Joe. "He's under so much pressure, and you make it worse. He's a sick man, you know."

Joe shook his head. He recalled Orin Smith saying something similar. "I don't know about that," Joe said. "I just need to talk to him."

"Not before the trial," McLanahan said, shaking his head. "Not unless he tells me to let you in. Even then, you'd have to get through Dulcie Schalk, and I don't think you're real popular with her right now."

Sighing, Joe said, "You're on the wrong track, McLanahan. You've been wrong since the murder. Bud wants revenge on Missy and he's using what happened to get back at her. I don't blame him, but this crime . . . there's a lot more to it. Things you've never even considered or looked at."

"Yeah, yeah yeah," McLanahan muttered, dismissing him. Then to

Sollis, "Take this yahoo in and get his statement. Then we'll decide if we want to arrest him and on what charges. Reed, you drive his truck down to the county building. I'll call Dulcie and see how she wants to proceed."

Joe said, "You don't have to do this."

"Sure I do," McLanahan said, turning aside to spit a stream of tobacco juice onto the lawn. To Joe, he said, "Why aren't you out there trying to catch poachers or something? Shouldn't you be doing your job instead of mine? You ever think about that?"

"I do," Joe said. "I just figure one of us needs to do your job."

Reed snorted a laugh and looked away quickly.

McLanahan froze, and Joe saw something ugly pass over his face. Joe squared up, ready if McLanahan swung.

The sheriff took a deep breath and said to Sollis, "Cuff the son-of-a-bitch."

On the way through the grounds of the Eagle Mountain Club, handcuffs biting his wrists, Joe thought that he was pleased to have hooked back up with Nate. But he couldn't help thinking it might be too late to affect the outcome of the trial. And he'd never imagined spending a night in a county cell.

He thought of his daughters. Their grandmother up for murder, their father in jail.

April's words mocked him: "I guess maybe *I'm* not the only one in this *perfect* little family who makes *mistakes.*"

SEPTEMBER 14

Justice has nothing to do with what goes on in a courtroom; Justice is what comes out of a courtroom.

—Clarence Darrow

37

On Wednesday morning, the day Bud Longbrake was to take the stand to testify against Missy Alden for the murder of Earl Alden, Joe sat next to Marybeth in the eighth row of the Twelve Sleep Country Courthouse and dug his index finger into his shirt collar to try to loosen it against the tight cinch of his tie. It didn't give much, and he felt that he was slowly strangling to death.

He surveyed the room. Everyone seemed to have taken the same seats they'd occupied the previous two days since the trial began.

Judge Hewitt's courtroom was full and warm and close. Family members, local gadflies, civic leaders, Bud's drinking buddies from the Stockman's including Timberman and Keith Bailey, law enforcement personnel, the all-male morning coffee crowd from the Burg-O-Pardner, and local, state, and regional press took every seat. There was a low murmur as everyone waited for what the *Roundup* called "pivotal Day Three" to begin. All the players were in one place, Joe thought. He whispered to Marybeth that if Stovepipe's metal detector was malfunctioning again and a bomb were to go off inside, Saddlestring might as well close down and sell off the fixtures.

Marcus Hand and Dulcie Schalk were at the bench discussing the schedule and rules for the day with Hewitt, who stood and leaned down toward them so the conversation could be kept confidential. Hand wore a dark charcoal suit, white shirt, bolo tie, and his pointy cowboy boots. A silverbelly Stetson sat crown-down on the defense table, but Joe never saw Hand actually put it on. It was solely for effect.

Schalk was dressed sharply in a dark pin-striped business suit and skirt with a cream-colored bow at her throat. Her hair was pulled back so she looked severe and serious. And older.

Monday had been spent selecting a jury. Like everything that took place in Judge Hewitt's courtroom, it had gone like lightning. Twelve local jurors and two alternates were selected out of a pool of thirty. Joe knew most of the jurors: seven women and five men. All were white and middle-aged except for a Shoshone woman who lived outside the reservation. Although Hand had worked to challenge as many of the blue-collar types as he could, apparently assuming they would more easily convict a nasty woman of means like Missy, Marybeth observed to Joe that Hand seemed to do it halfheartedly, more for the show than from determination. Like he had something up his sleeve, and the makeup of the jury didn't matter.

Marcus Hand only needed one juror to nullify a guilty verdict, Joe replied. He couldn't determine which one or two who'd been selected met Hand's satisfaction. Maybe the unemployed city worker who couldn't find a job in the bad economy hated the world and would love to stick it to The Man? Or maybe the Shoshone woman, filled with years of resentment and the existential burden of her white layabout husband, could finally get back at the system?

Joe had spent most of previous Thursday in the sheriff's department interview room after being taken from the Eagle Mountain Club. Deputy Sollis had checked in on him from time to time with a grin on his face, explaining that they were waiting for Sheriff McLanahan to return for the questioning to begin. Joe knew it was a stall and an attempt to humiliate him, and conceded that it was working pretty well. No charges were filed that he was informed of.

Finally, mid-afternoon, Dulcie Schalk blew into the room. She was angry with Joe for trying to contact Bud Longbrake and with the sheriff for holding Joe without questioning him or pressing any charges. Right behind her was Marcus Hand in his black turtleneck and fringed buckskin jacket.

She said to Sollis, "Let him out of here *now.*"

Joe thanked her, and she snapped, "Do not speak to me."

On the way to his pickup after retrieving the keys from a very sheepish Deputy Reed, Hand draped his arm around Joe's shoulder and whispered, "You hate us until you need us. That's the way it works."

The past weekend with Marybeth and Nate was interrupted only by a call into the break lands east of town from a citizen reporting a wounded antelope staggering around on the road. Nate had gone with him in the truck, and Joe spent hours filling him in on the murder, the investigation, and what Joe had learned from Smith about Rope the Wind.

"I'd put my money on the boys from Chicago," Nate said, after listening to Joe and after the game warden had dispatched the suffering animal. "I could see them sending someone out here to shut up The Earl once and for all. They came, shot him, and hung him from the windmill, and they were on a plane back to O'Hare by the time you found him."

"It may be what happened," Joe said, "but it's speculation at best. Marcus Hand sent two of his investigators east, and they may come back with something before the trial is over. But they may not. What

I have trouble with in that scenario is how this Chicago hit man would know to frame Missy."

Nate said, "They had an insider."

"And who would that be?"

"The same guy who told Laurie Talich where she could find me."

"Bud?"

"Bingo," Nate said. "It took a while for me to figure it out and there are still some loose ends I'd like closed, but it makes sense. Missy knew vaguely where I was living because she talks to her daughter, and last year she tried to hire me to put the fear of God into Bud, remember? She might have let it slip to her ex-husband that if he didn't stop pining over her, she'd drive to Hole in the Wall Canyon and pick me up. Somehow, Bud found out where I was. And by happenstance, he meets a woman in the bar who has come west for the single purpose of avenging her husband. Bud has contacts with the National Guard who just returned from Afghanistan, and he was able to help her get a rocket launcher. Then he drew her a map. He must have been pretty smug about how it all worked out. He thought he was able to take me out of the picture without getting his own hands dirty."

"Bud—what's happened to him?" Joe asked, not sure he was convinced of Nate's theory. "Why has he gone so crazy on us?"

"A man can only take so much," Nate said, "especially a good man. His no-good kids abandoned him. His new wife cuckolds him, and then cheats him out of his ranch. And to add insult to all this misery, the new husband figures out how to make a killing on the land Bud had in his family for a hundred twenty years. They took away most of his dignity, and then they stomped on what was left. And for no good reason, because Bud was a good man who only wanted to support the community and pass along his ranch to his children. I can see where he went crazy. No one deserves what they did to him."

Nate placed his fingertips on the grip of his .500. He said, "Not that I forgive him for it, or what he set in motion."

Joe thought about it as he patrolled. "He seems to have gotten his kids back, though," Joe said. "Bud Jr. and Sally. So there's something."

"I wonder," Nate said.

On Tuesday, Day Two of the trial, Dulcie Schalk and Marcus Hand gave opening arguments. Schalk pointed her finger at the defendant and outlined the prosecution case against with cool and unadorned efficiency:

Missy's record of calls to Bud Longbrake begging him to help her take care of Earl Alden;

Her lack of an alibi for the approximate time of the murder;

Her motive—the fear Earl would soon divorce her;

The murder weapon found in her car;

Missy's history with husbands and her pattern for ruthlessness;

Her apparent lack of remorse that included a brazen shopping spree just days after the tragedy.

She concluded her argument by softening her voice and addressing each member of the jury in turn. "This is not a complicated judgment. The defense will try their hardest to make it complicated. We'd like to welcome Mr. Hand and his team. They've come all the way from Jackson Hole to spend time with us in our little community, and to try and convince you that you really can't believe your own eyes or your own ears. But don't fall into that trap. Be wary of it. This is a very simple case. We'll prove that Missy Alden is guilty. We'll prove her motive, her opportunity, and her premeditated plan to execute her own husband. We'll show you the murder weapon and prove that it was hers and that she used it on her husband. Don't let all the smoke the defense will create in this courtroom confuse you. Sometimes, things are what they are. Simple as that. And you're being asked to help us punish one of our own who has always considered herself above and beyond the law. Let's show her she isn't."

"Wow," Joe whispered to Marybeth when the opening argument was done. "Dulcie's more brutal than I am when it comes to your mother."

"Joe . . ."

"One thing, though," he said. "I thought they had tapes of the calls between Missy and Bud, but she didn't say anything about that. Apparently, they just have records of the calls being made."

"Still . . ." Marybeth said, and let the rest of her thought trail off. Joe thought how tough it must be on his wife to see one of her friends indict her mother with such surgical precision. He wondered if she was getting doubts, but he didn't ask her. Instead, he put his arm around her and kneaded her shoulder. She didn't respond. Her muscles beneath her jacket were as tightly coiled as steel springs.

Hand's opening was surprisingly short and breezy, Joe thought. He conceded to the jurors that Missy was "kind of hard to like until you got to know her," but that he'd prove to them beyond a reasonable doubt she'd been framed. He alluded to other explanations for the murder that would be revealed. Hand spoke smoothly, but with a lack of slickness that impressed even Joe. He gestured to Missy and urged the jury to put themselves in her place.

"Think about how you would feel," he said to them, "if your ship finally came in and you were able to raise yourself out of your humble beginnings to a place you'd always dreamed of. And imagine if, when that finally happened, you were framed for a murder you didn't commit. Imagine how you'd feel if the full force and weight of the government had decided to persecute you not only for what they say you did, but who they think you are?"

Hand stood in silence for a full minute, as if he'd choked himself up and couldn't continue.

But he did. "Gentlemen and ladies of the jury, what you are about to see is the most classic case of tunnel vision I've ever encountered in a courtroom. The prosecution decided within minutes of the crime that my client was responsible. They didn't look left. They didn't look right. The government didn't look *up* to see what other forces may have led to this tragic crime. They started with the conclusion and worked backwards, picking out every little thing they could find to fit the story they believed and didn't even consider anything that didn't fit into their perfect little box. The government wants my poor client's head as a trophy on their wall, and they want mine right next to it. Nothing else matters to them. This isn't smoke, folks. Just because we'll introduce evidence that doesn't fit into the prosecution's perfect little box doesn't mean it's smoke . . ."

Joe watched Hand work. He felt the pendulum rock from the prosecution to the defense. And he noted that every time Hand said the word *government* he seemed to be talking directly to the unemployed city worker, and the juror, probably unconsciously, nodded in agreement.

Hand said he agreed with the government that the entire prosecution's case rested on the testimony of one man—Bud Longbrake—even though Schalk hadn't exactly said that. Joe noted that Hand didn't even try to dispute the motive, the record of phone calls, or the rifle.

Then Marcus Hand thanked the jury for taking time out of their busy lives to see that justice would be done, and sat down.

Joe had been the first witness called for the prosecution. Dulcie Schalk led him through the discovery of the body and dismissed him before they got to the arrest of Missy. Sheriff McLanahan had followed Joe and walked the jury through the rest of the day, culminating with Missy's arrest. McLanahan was smug and countrified, but well rehearsed. A state forensics examiner was next, and Schalk prompted him through a PowerPoint presentation tying the murder weapon to the fatal wound, the ownership of the weapon to Earl and Missy Alden, and the fingerprints on the rifle to Missy.

A county clerk employee was the last witness called on Day Two, and the PowerPoint screen showed the jurors Earl's official filing for divorce proceedings. Joe noted that Missy slumped to the side, head down, during that part of the presentation.

Marcus Hand declined to cross-examine any of the opening witnesses except for McLanahan, and he asked only one question: "Sheriff, did your investigation extend any further than my client?"

When McLanahan said there was no need to broaden the investigation, Hand rolled his eyes so the jury could see him and sat down, anticipating an objection from Dulcie Schalk and a rebuke from Judge Hewitt for his body language. Both complied.

The day ended as Hand asked Judge Hewitt for permission to recall both Sheriff McLanahan and game warden Joe Pickett to the stand later in the trial. Joe's stomach clenched because he knew where Hand was headed.

Hewitt granted the request.

The morning of Day Three, Missy sat small and prim, with her back to everyone, next to Dixie Arthur, one of Hand's law partners from

Jackson. Joe assumed Hand had chosen her to be at the table because she looked friendly, small-town, and approachable. The kind of woman who would never have been there if she honestly believed Missy was guilty. Arthur had a quick smile and a round empathetic face and she seemed to have become fast friends with Missy because the two whispered to each other with great frequency and familiarity. So far, she hadn't asked any questions of the witnesses but seemed to be the keeper of the defense playbook, and she'd conference with Hand from time to time to, presumably, keep him reined in.

At the prosecution table was Assistant County Attorney Jack Pym. Pym was tall, solid, boyish, and not quite thirty years old. He was a Wyoming native from Lander who had played tight end for the Wyoming Cowboys football team prior to law school. Joe liked him, and since Pym was a fly-fisherman like Joe, they'd made plans several times to float the river but it hadn't yet worked out. This was Pym's first murder trial, and it showed. He seemed anxious and, like his boss, overly eager to take on the legendary Marcus Hand. Joe had observed Pym attempting to stare Hand down, as if he faced him across the line of scrimmage.

Bud Longbrake Jr. sat in the very back row with several of his colleagues whom Joe had seen outside the Stockman's Bar that day, and his sister, Sally, was broken and shriveled in a wheelchair placed next to him in the aisle. Joe hadn't seen Bud's daughter for years and not since her accident, and he barely recognized her. She didn't look back, and Joe assumed she was under medication. Shamazz did look back, defiantly, and Joe turned around.

"Odd they're here," Marybeth said, echoing his thoughts.

Both attorneys returned to their desks and shared the result of the conference with the judge with their co-counsels, and Hewitt returned to his seat. Joe could see a stack of papers on the judge's bench off to the side of his microphone. He recognized a manual deep in the stack as a copy of the Alaska hunting regulations. Joe smiled grimly, reminded that the trial would proceed quickly since the Dall sheep season would close in just over a week.

He noticed Marybeth, like the other spectators, kept turning and looking over her shoulder toward the double doors manned by the bailiff, Stovepipe. She was waiting for the first appearance of Bud Longbrake.

Dulcie Schalk prolonged the anticipation by calling a technician from the local phone company as her first witness instead of Bud. As she did, the air went out of the room. Joe half listened to the technician as he explained a call record list that was being shown on the screen, detailing the dates Missy's phone called Bud's phone and vice versa, and allowing himself to be led to the conclusion that the telephone conversations increased in frequency and length on the days leading up to the murder.

When the doors opened, even the phone company technician paused to look up.

Joe turned as well, but instead of Bud Longbrake, two of Marcus Hand's investigators eased into the courtroom, surprised at the attention they'd drawn to themselves. Although they wore sport coats and ties, Joe thought both of the men looked rumpled and tired. Like they'd been traveling nonstop to get there.

Judge Hewitt was obviously annoyed and glared at Hand but didn't admonish him. He waved at Schalk to continue questioning the technician, and as she did, the two investigators went silently up the aisle, heads down, trying hard but failing to be inconspicuous. Joe watched as they took seats directly behind the railing separating the defense table from the gallery, and leaned over the railing to whisper to Marcus Hand. The attorney rocked back in his chair, presenting his ear but not turning to them, and Joe tried to read Hand's face as he heard the results of their trip to Chicago. Hand displayed no emotion but stared vacantly at a spot above the jury box while he listened. Joe couldn't recall seeing anything like it before while court was in session, but then again he'd never been a witness or participant in a trial where the defense lawyer had a team of underlings to send out on the road. Jack Pym glared at Hand and the investigators, and Dulcie Schalk shot angry glances at them while she went through her list of questions for the technician. Joe saw a few members of the jury, the ex–city employee in particular, watch the exchange with interest.

When they were through, Hand turned to one of them and mouthed, *"You're sure?"*

Both investigators nodded. And for the first time, Hand let go a little smile before he settled back around and pretended to pay attention to the telephone company expert.

After Marcus Hand told Judge Hewitt he had no questions of the witness, Hewitt called for a twenty-minute break.

Behind them, Joe heard one of the Stockman's Bar group tell another, "Bud's here. Somebody saw him being taken into a room down the hall. He's going to be called next."

"How's he doing?"

"He looks like hell."

Marybeth left Joe to be with her mother during the break. Joe milled around in the hallway with a dozen other spectators, listening with one ear to the speculation being offered and texting Sheridan that Bud was about to testify.

He pushed through the front doors and stood with the smokers for a few minutes, wrapped up completely in his own thoughts.

It was a crisp day, cool and clear, and he could see the peaks of the mountains had been dusted with snow overnight. The top of the stairs afforded a good view of the trees in town, most blushing with gold and red. The smokers on the steps were talking to each other about which areas they'd drawn deer and elk tags for, and how they were looking forward to hunting season. Someone joked about not saying too much in front of the game warden, and Joe smiled cryptically.

He was trying to imagine what the investigators had told Hand, and why Hand seemed so self-assured in court. Maybe that was simply his way of putting the jury at ease, bringing them along on his river of charm and self-confidence.

As the smokers looked at their watches and stubbed out their smokes, Marybeth appeared on the steps. She looked slightly stunned.

"What happened in there?" Joe asked. "Did you hear what they found out in Chicago?"

"No," she said, obviously distracted. "Nothing like that."

"Then what?"

"Joe," she said, looking up into his eyes. "My mother took me aside and said she wants us to move out to the ranch. She wants us to live in the old house and she'd like you to manage the operations."

"What?"

Marybeth shook her head. "She said she's gotten to the age where she realizes she wants her family around her and she wants to show her appreciation for our support in this. Joe, she said she wants us to eventually inherit the entire place."

Joe stepped back. He said, "Your *mother* said that?"

"She did," Marybeth whispered. "She said she wants to make sure we never worry about money or our future again for the rest of our lives."

"What did you say?" Joe asked. His head was reeling.

"I didn't know what to say. I told her we could talk about it when the trial was over. I thanked her, of course."

"The whole damn thing?" Joe said. "The biggest ranch in northern Wyoming?"

Marybeth simply nodded.

"How can she do that?" Joe asked. "If she's in prison, the whole place will go into probate or something. We have no idea who will actually own it. Banks or trusts or whoever. It won't be hers to give away."

"Joe, think about what she's offering."

"I am," he said. "But she can't offer anything unless she's free and clear."

Marybeth shrugged, as confused as Joe was.

When Joe helped guide her toward the doors, he noticed that her arms seemed to have turned into jelly. As had his legs.

They sat in their seats. Joe could barely concentrate on the proceedings.

But he heard it when Dulcie Schalk said to Judge Hewitt, "The prosecution would like to call Bud Longbrake Sr. to the stand."

Bud *did* look like hell.

Joe found himself grimacing as his old employer and ex-father-in-law slowly made his way up the center aisle of the courtroom. Instead of sixty, Bud looked eighty. He was stooped and drawn, and his suit, which Joe remembered from Bud and Missy's wedding six years ago, hung loose and baggy on him. The collar of Bud's Western dress shirt gaped at least an inch. He peered out of it like a turtle looking out of its shell, Joe thought, and Bud's pants hung around his legs. Bud held his Stetson in his right hand, and reached out with his left from chair top to chair top for balance as he proceeded toward the bench.

"My God," Marybeth whispered. "Look what's happened to him."

Joe was surprised when Bud glanced over as he passed. His eyes were rheumy and unfocused, but for a split second Joe could see the man he remembered somewhere in that shell. Bud seemed to acknowledge the spark of recognition.

Joe nodded his head slightly. Bud nodded back.

It took a minute for Bud to get settled into the witness stand. He didn't seem to know what to do with his hat. Schalk gently took it from him and put it on the prosecution table. Now there was a cowboy hat on both tables and it looked, Joe thought, like Wyoming.

After he'd been sworn in, Schalk asked Bud to state his name and address.

"Bud C. Longbrake Sr. I live at 2090 Main Street, here in Saddlestring. Apartment A. It's called that on account as it's the only apartment above the Stockman's Bar." His voice was familiar but tinny.

Joe heard a titter among the bar regulars behind him.

He leaned over to Marybeth. He whispered, "It's more than the Jim Beam and hard living. There's something really wrong with him."

Marybeth nodded in agreement. Unconsciously, she was lacing and unlacing her fingers on her lap. Joe couldn't tell if the reason for her anxiety was because of Bud's appearance, her mother's trial, the offer just made, or all three.

For the next ten minutes, Schalk patiently referred to her legal pad and established Bud Longbrake for the jury. His history in the county, the marriage to Missy Vankueren, the divorce and the loss of his ranch, the restraining order Missy had placed on him. Bud answered each item simply, but the time it took him to respond to each question dragged on longer each time. The long silences seemed to add to the tension in the courtroom. Joe noticed spectators glancing at each other, wondering if Bud was up for this. Joe wondered the same thing.

Schalk signaled to Jack Pym to cue the PowerPoint projector, and once again the list of phone calls between Bud and Missy was shown.

She said, "This document was produced by the phone company. It lists a series of telephone calls between your cell phone and the main landline at the Thunderhead Ranch or from Missy Alden's private cell phone. Do you recall the telephone conversations that took place?"

Joe noticed that Bud hadn't turned his head to look at the screen.

"Mr. Longbrake?" Schalk asked gently. "Can you please turn your attention to the screen?"

As if suddenly awakened, Bud jerked on the stand and swung his head over at the list, squinting.

Judge Hewitt cleared his throat and held up an outstretched palm to Schalk to wait on the next question. Hewitt said, "Mr. Longbrake, are you all right to continue? You seem to have a little bit of trouble focusing on the proceedings here. Do you need a glass of water or a break before we continue?"

Bud looked dolefully at Hewitt. "Nah, Judge, I'm okay," he said.

"You're sure?"

"Yep," Bud said. Then: "I'm real sorry, but sometimes I kind of fade in and out. I think it's getting worse. It *is* getting worse. You see, Judge," Bud said, reaching up and tapping his temple with the tips of his fingers, "I got this inoperable brain tumor the size of a baseball in my head."

Marybeth gasped and dug her fingers into Joe's knee.

Dulcie Schalk stood her ground, but she was clearly shaken. She shot a murderous look to Sheriff McLanahan that Joe caught. Either she wasn't aware of the tumor, or McLanahan—who had supervised the depositions—had downplayed its effect on Bud to her.

"I have good days and bad days," Bud continued, "and believe it or not, this is one of the good days. I'm okay. Sometimes I just need things repeated, is all."

Hewitt's face softened as Bud talked. He said, "Then let's continue." To Schalk, he said, "Please keep Mr. Longbrake's condition in mind as we proceed."

"I will, Your Honor," she said.

"Please repeat the question," Hewitt said.

She asked him again if he recalled the phone conversations.

He said, "Yep. Every damned one of 'em."

Joe, despite himself, sighed with relief. Bud seemed to be back, at least temporarily.

Schalk was also visibly relieved. She looked down at her pad for her next question. As always, she was faultlessly prepared and her questions scripted to elicit a clear narrative in the mind of the jurors.

Marybeth prodded Joe with her elbow, and when he looked over, she chinned toward Missy at the defense table. Missy had tears in her eyes, and she dabbed at them with a tissue. When she looked up at Bud, her face was not angry but sympathetic.

Joe was surprised. Didn't she *hate* this man? He thought about the offer Missy had made Marybeth minutes before. He looked at his mother-in-law in a sudden new light.

And under that light, other things fell into place. The reason for Bud's mood and personality changes now made sense. Joe recalled the collection of medications in Bud's bathroom over the bar, and kicked himself for not noting the names of the drugs. Then there was the fact of Bud Jr. and Sally coming back. Plus, Orin Smith's reference to a rancher who was ill. And Keith Bailey saying Bud was "under a shitload of pressure and pain right now."

He wanted to punch himself for not putting it together.

Dulcie Schalk said to Bud, "Let's begin with this first phone call back on July 2 that was placed from the Thunderhead Ranch phone to your cell phone. Can you tell the jury who called you and what was discussed during that call?"

"Yep."

Joe, like the jury and everyone else, waited. Bud just sat there.

"Mr. Longbrake," Schalk said, "can you tell the court the subject matter of that July 2 call?"

"I can."

"Well, please tell the court, Mr. Longbrake."

Bud rotated his head as if stretching out a stiff neck. He said to her, "Miz Schalk, can I just cut to the chase?"

Behind Joe, one of the bar regulars chuckled at the response.

"I'd rather we do this methodically, Mr. Longbrake," Schalk said, gesturing with her legal pad filled with questions.

Bud squinted at the pad and said, "I might be dead by the time we get through that whole damn list."

Several people in the galley laughed at that, and Hewitt looked up in warning. The judge turned back to Bud and seemed to assess his condition, then said to Schalk, "Given the circumstances and Mr. Longbrake's condition, let him cut to the chase. The prosecution can follow up with background questions later if necessary."

Schalk said, "Your Honor, in order to establish—"

"I know how much you adore your lists," Hewitt said, cutting her off. "But if we can move along here, we might avoid a very uncomfortable situation."

His meaning was clear: *Let's get this over before the old man dies right here on the stand.*

"Cut to the chase, Mr. Longbrake," Hewitt said.

"Thanks, Judge," Bud said. He took a moment to gather his thoughts, then cleared his throat. Joe found himself holding his breath waiting.

"Here's the deal, Miz Schalk," Bud said. "I'm dying. I knew I was sick, but I didn't know how sick. I know I shoulda gone to the doctor years ago when I started getting headaches and blacking out, but I just thought I was hung over. Now it's too damned late and nothing can be done. My brain is being replaced by a damned orange. But I can't go to my grave knowing what I know without coming clean."

Dulcie Schalk stood there helplessly, with her arms at her side, pleading with her eyes to the judge.

Bud said, "I shot that son-of-a-bitch."

Joe felt Marybeth dig her fingers into his leg so hard it made him cringe.

Bud said, "I planned it for a while, and I got madder every time one of those god-awful turbines went up. I started calling McLanahan there telling him Missy was up to no good. Setting her up. I knew McLanahan would fall for it because he's dumber than a box of rocks and he needs to get reelected somehow.

"I knew how to get into the house through a basement window that didn't lock and I took that Winchester out of my old gun case. I drove right up on old Earl and shot him in his goddamned heart, which was so small I shoulda used a scope. Then I threw him in the back of my pickup and drove him to his goddamned wind farm and hoisted him up and chained him to the blade of that windmill. And to get back at all Missy done to me, I hung it all on her by putting the rifle in her car and calling the sheriff."

Joe was stunned. He wasn't alone.

Bud turned to Missy. He said, "I'm so sorry, Missy. I wanted to make your life as miserable as mine was. But something changes when you find out you've got maybe a few weeks to live, and that's what the doctor told me this weekend. It tends to focus the mind, and I figured that if I can't savor my revenge, then what's the damned point of getting it? Plus, if I'm meeting God in a few days, I don't want to have to explain what I done, because there's no way He will let me off the hook. So I was gonna say you asked me to kill him, and when I said no, you did it yourself. But now I just can't.

"Don't get me wrong," he said directly to her. "I don't feel bad about Earl. He was a prick. But damn, I never shoulda blamed it on you."

Schalk stood stock-still, her mouth open. Hewitt was frozen behind the bench, his eyes blinking madly. Sally Longbrake suddenly shrieked a long, mournful wail.

Missy sat back in her chair with her fists clenched at her chin, her eyes streaming tears.

Behind Joe, one of the Stockman's regulars said, "It's like fuckin' Perry Mason!"

Bud Longbrake wiped his mouth with the back of his sleeve. He looked pale and spent. He said to Judge Hewitt, "Judge, I said what I wanted to say. But right now I'm not feeling so good all of a sudden."

Marcus Hand stood up slowly and said, "Your Honor, I move for an immediate acquittal."

Dulcie Schalk seethed. She strode the courtroom floor and slammed her pad of questions on her table, her eyes boring holes into Sheriff McLanahan, who looked away.

Joe sat astonished. It *was* like Perry Mason. All that buildup and a last-minute courtroom surprise? He was happy for Missy—well, happy for Marybeth, anyway—but something loomed just beyond the peripheral vision of his mind's eye.

Why did he feel like a large rock was about to drop on his head?

SEPTEMBER 15

Entia non sunt multiplicanda praeter necessitatem.

(Occam's Razor: "The simplest explanation is usually the correct one.")

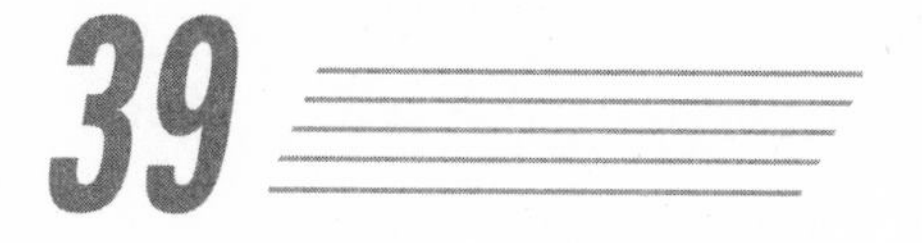

The rock fell the next day.

It was the season opener for pronghorn antelope in the rest of the hunting areas throughout Twelve Sleep County, and Joe called to Tube and they were out of the house two hours before dawn.

As he rolled down Bighorn Road in the dark, he called dispatch. "This is GF53 heading out."

"Morning, Joe," the dispatcher said.

He ate his sack lunch of a peanut butter and jelly sandwich and an apple on the same sagebrush knoll he had used weeks before when he discovered Earl Alden's body. He tore off small pieces of bread crust and fed them to Tube while he looked over vistas of sun-drenched terrain complicated by sharp draws and hidden arroyos. The mountains filled his rearview mirrors.

He could be seen for miles. His presence on the perch, his green Ford Game and Fish pickup, was enough to remind most of the hunters to keep their noses clean and follow regulations.

All the work that had once been going on at the wind farm had ceased. He saw no Rope the Wind employees or vehicles out. The

Tinkertoy assemblage of wind turbine parts sat where they had when he first saw them. And the assembled turbines turned slowly in the wind, generating empty power that went nowhere.

He'd spent the morning checking hunters and inspecting their harvest, but he'd done it by rote and felt disconnected to his task the entire time. Joe's mind was still in the courthouse, if his body wasn't.

Cars and pickups were scarce on the two-lane blacktop of the state highway leading up to the mountains. He paid no attention to them unless they slowed and left the pavement and turned into the hunting areas.

For some reason, though, he noticed the yellow van towing a trailer on the highway, and swung his spotting scope toward it. It was the same van he'd seen leaving Earl Alden's funeral. The back of the van was covered with bumper stickers. The van was moving slowly, as if the driver were looking for something. Joe zoomed in on the plates: Montana. Then he focused on the driver.

Bud Longbrake Jr. was at the wheel. His sister, Sally, sat next to him, slumped over. Joe sighed and sat back, assuming the vehicle would continue on. But then it slowed and turned onto the gravel road and under the elk antler arches to the Thunderhead Ranch. Were the siblings out to take a last look at the place they grew up? And why take a trailer?

The van stopped at the gate, and Bud Jr. got out and worked the keypad. It swung open.

He watched the van roll down the distant gravel road until he could confirm that it took the road that led to the former Longbrake ranch. He watched it through his scope until all that was left of its appearance was a long trail of settling dust.

He was wondering how Shamazz knew the keypad combination when Marybeth called on his cell phone.

"Mom called," she said. "They're having an acquittal party at the Eagle Mountain Club tonight."

"An acquittal party?"

"That's what she called it. She wants to know if we'll come."

Joe winced.

She said, "If she asks us about her offer, what are we going to say?"

"You mean, do we want to take over a multi-million-dollar ranch and never have to worry about financial difficulties ever again in our lives?" Joe said.

"When you put it that way . . ." Marybeth said, but didn't finish her sentence. "Did you hear about Bud?"

"No," he said, expecting the worst.

"He's in a coma. No one expects him to come out of it."

"I'm sorry to hear that," Joe said.

"It's awful. It's just awful. I suppose I should feel good about all this—not about Bud, of course, but about how the trial went—but I guess I can't wrap my mind around it yet."

"Me neither," Joe said, thinking about Bud Jr. and Sally driving to the ranch with a trailer attached.

When it hit him, he felt something cold and sharp shoot through his stomach and chest. The calls between Missy and Bud. The rifle in her car. Bud's last-minute revelation and recanting. Missy's odd behavior from the arrest to the end of the trial. As if . . .

He said, "I've got to go now. I've got to check something out."

"So what about tonight?"

"I may not be able to make it. I'll let you know," he said, closing the phone.

He tossed the rest of his sandwich out the window, put his pickup in gear, and nosed the vehicle off the knoll in the direction of the wind farm.

Joe parked next to the wind turbine where he'd discovered Earl Alden's body. He got out and called for Tube to follow him.

His dog was ecstatic to be out of the truck on such a fine clear day. He wasn't as pleased when Joe looped a chain around his middle and started hoisting him up inside the tower.

40

A few minutes before midnight, Joe saw a sweep of headlights across the interior walls of the house and heard the crunch of gravel outside in the ranch yard. The garage door opener growled, and he stood up in the dark, approached the window, and parted the curtains to see Missy's Hummer enter the open door. She was alone, it appeared. Good. He doubted she'd been able to see his vehicle, which was hidden behind the shop.

He checked to see if anyone was right behind her, but there were no other headlights on the entrance road. Yet. He sat down on a plump leather couch burned tastefully with Thunderhead and Longbrake Ranch brands, checked the loads in his shotgun, and waited.

In a minute, sounds came from the kitchen; the clinking of glass and the scuffling of cabinets being opened and closed. As he approached, he could hear her humming lightly to herself.

Joe stood at the threshold of the kitchen in the dark hallway, watching her fill the coffeemaker with grounds and water and pull down a half dozen mugs and set them on the counter. She held a full glass of white wine and sipped from it as she worked. She looked stunning, Joe thought, in a snug dark blue dress and oversized pearls. She'd kicked her heels off on the floor and padded around on small bare feet.

When she saw him standing there, she gasped and let out a squeak and dropped the glass to the floor.

"Joe!" she said, hopping back from the broken glass and spilled wine. "What are you doing here? You scared me to death."

He said, "I assume Marcus Hand and his crew are on the way. How long before they get here?"

She looked up at him, quickly regaining her composure. Her brows furrowed and her face became the porcelain mask she'd perfected. "They won't be long. Everybody had plenty to drink, and I wanted to have some coffee ready. You missed the party."

He nodded and entered the kitchen and put the shotgun on the counter next to him, letting her see it.

She shook her head, then let some anger seep through the mask. "Does Marybeth know you're here? What are you doing, measuring the drapes? Checking out your new office?"

He tried to smile, but couldn't. He said, "I saw Bud Jr. and Sally today on their way to move in to their new digs. You don't actually expect them to live there and work it, do you?"

A flash of terror—*finally!*—shot through her eyes and her nose flared. She didn't breathe for a moment. Then, almost as quickly, she raised her chin and set her mouth with bitter resignation. "No," she said, "I expect them to sell it back to me after a reasonable length of time. The old place was appraised at six million dollars, you know."

Joe said, "You probably could have bought their silence for less than that."

"Probably," she said. "But Bud told them the price, and I suspect they'll hold me to it."

Joe nodded. He said, "It's just you and me here. You can't be retried for murder, and we both know it. So walk me through how it all worked."

She looked at him as if she was determined not to give an inch.

He said, "When you decided to make your last upgrade, your last trade-up, and get rid of Earl, you contacted Bud. You knew he'd take your call because for some reason he still loves you, despite everything. And you offered him his ranch back if he'd take Earl out of the picture. After all, you still had this place and all the other property holdings you and Earl combined when you got married. You probably even hinted that the two of you could get back together someday. Am I right so far?"

She rolled her eyes.

Joe said, "And Bud said of course, he'd do it. But he was sick. He didn't know at the time how bad off he was, and it turned out he wasn't sure he was physically capable of pulling it off. But he sure wanted that ranch back, if not for him, then for his kids. He always wanted them to have it."

She shook her head and said, "Even though they shit on him all their lives, he still wanted them to have it."

"That kind of selflessness just doesn't work for you, does it?" Joe asked.

Her eyes drilled into him. "Some children these days can be so ungrateful. They feel entitled to things they didn't earn."

Joe ignored her and continued, "So you and Bud talked it over, back and forth, for a month or so. He wanted to help you out with your Earl problem and get the ranch back, but you were running out of time. Was it at that point you figured out Earl had consolidated all his assets and put everything into the wind farm? I bet that didn't make you very happy."

"It was reckless and irresponsible," she said, her anger palpable. "Taking everything we had together and leveraging it to build that idiotic *thing* out there on the ridge. He was not only risking everything he had, he was risking everything I've spent my life trying to get—and had finally achieved. And for what? He had no right to do that."

"Plus he wanted to get rid of you," Joe said. "That must have hurt."

"It did," she said simply.

"You found yourself in a dilemma, though," Joe said. "Bud was in it with you, but he couldn't perform. And you couldn't risk him talking about it, either. So you told him you'd let him set you up with the sheriff and you'd have it done as long as he'd wait until the trial to take the rap. He agreed to that, but you could never be absolutely sure he'd follow through when crunch time came. In the back of your mind, you must have worried that Bud might screw you the way you screwed him. That must have made for some sleepless nights."

She didn't react, but stared at Joe with ice-cold eyes.

"In the middle of your discussions with Bud, you both realized that you'd tried to contact Nate to work for you along the same lines, but Nate refused. Which meant there was another person out there who knew what you were capable of. You urged Bud to tell that woman Laurie Talich where Nate lived to get Nate out of the picture. It almost worked, too. But Alisha Whiteplume was killed instead of Nate. I hope that's on your conscience, too. If you have one."

"I had nothing to do with that," she spat back. "Bud did that on his own. He thought it would please me, I guess."

Joe shrugged. He said, "Nate would have never talked, so what you did was pointless. And right now, he is at my house. He still wants revenge."

Her eyes got large. "But . . ."

"All I have to do is tell him," Joe said. "Unlike the court, he has no rules about double jeopardy."

"Please don't," she said. "Think about what I've offered you."

"I don't want your blood money," Joe said, dismissing her. "Back to where we left off. You drove right up to your husband and shot him in the heart. Then you drove his body to the wind turbine. I tested the hoist system today with my dog and found out how easy it is to crank a body up to the top. I figured it would require a lot more upper body strength, but it's easy. Easy enough for you. So why did you hang him up there, anyway? Out of spite, or to throw everyone off?"

She sighed and looked away, apparently deciding it wasn't worth it to pretend any longer.

Joe said, "The one thing I can't quite wrap my mind around is how you hung the body from the blade. Earl was heavy."

She pursed her lips. "I admit nothing," she said, "but I can tell you when you're a small person all of your life, you learn how to use leverage to get what you want. You learn to use the power of objects to work in your favor and to use people's superior strength against them."

Joe whistled and shook his head. "So you looped the chain around the body and threw the loose end over the blade while it was turning. You let the spinning blade lift him out of the nacelle."

Missy arched her eyebrows, acknowledging Joe's theory. "I suppose it could work like that," she said coyly.

"But why the wind turbine at all?"

She said, "Admitting nothing, one might have thought the sheriff or Miss Schalk would pursue the wind angle. One would assume Marcus would go that direction and come to find out about Earl's dealings with unsavory people and his fraud. Once that information was out, there would be people on the jury Marcus could convince. But it couldn't come from me—that would have been too obvious."

Joe shook his head. He said, "So you set yourself up. You made it plain and simple. So simple, that people like your daughter and me would automatically assume there was more to it. That you'd been framed."

She was quiet, because there was no need to say anything.

"Hand's investigators learned there had been a contract put out on Earl in Chicago," Joe said. "That's what they told him in the courtroom yesterday. If you'd just waited, it would have all been taken care of without you even getting involved."

She said, "That came as a surprise, but what if they'd botched it?" She looked squarely at Joe. "I don't count on people to take care of me, I never have. I'm the only one who will take care of me, Joe, and I trust no one but me. If my daughter had learned that lesson, maybe she wouldn't be what she is today: a part-time librarian in a crappy little town with you as a husband."

"I know," he said. "And against my better judgment, I was burning up the miles and my reputation trying to get you off."

Nodding, she said, "I knew I could count on you, Joe. I knew you'd dig into the wind farm scheme and lead Marcus to it. So even if Bud died or forgot about our agreement or went back on it, I was covered. There would have been reasonable doubt."

She paused and looked at her hand, assessing the shade of red on her painted fingernails. She said, "I've spent my life working simple men like you and Bud."

Joe reached over and wrapped his hand around the shotgun and pulled it up.

She looked at him with disbelief. "You'll never do it."

"I might surprise you," Joe said through clenched teeth.

"The offer still stands," she said, suddenly shaken. "If you do this, you get nothing. Your family gets nothing." Then: "Does Marybeth know?"

"Not yet. But we talk to each other. Imagine *that*."

"So you'll tell her?" Missy said. "You'd tell her that her mother is a murderer after all? You'd tell my granddaughters?"

"I haven't decided yet," he said. "It depends on you."

"What do you mean?" she asked, tears in her eyes. "What do I have to do?"

He couldn't determine if the tears were authentic, and he didn't care. He outlined his proposal.

When he was done, he said, "If you don't do the right thing here, you're dead. And in the future if you try to go back on what's right, I'll let my friend Nate know who was responsible for Alisha."

The porcelain mask was off. She said, "You're such a bastard, Joe Pickett. You're as conniving as I am."

"I wouldn't say that," he said. "You're in a class all your own."

The sounds of motors rose outside. Headlights flashed in through the windows as Marcus Hand and his associates arrived.

"They're here," she said.

"And I'm gone."

Joe slipped into bed as quietly as he could, but Marybeth reached over and put a warm hand on his thigh. With a voice drugged by sleep, she said, "You're really late."

"Openers," he said. "Lots of hunters out there. I also stopped by the hospital to see Bud."

"How is he?"

"Dying."

"Mmmmmm, that's so sad. I'm glad his kids came back, though. That probably made him feel good."

"He was a simple man," Joe said. "He took care of his family."

She yawned and said, "I'm exhausted. This has been a long couple of weeks."

"Yup."

"Dulcie called," she said, more awake now. "She feels terrible how this all went. She said she let her competitive nature get the best of her. It was kind of an apology and I told her we were still friends. That seemed to make her feel better. And she is a good person, Joe."

"I agree."

He reached over and pulled her to him. She was wide awake. "Mom called, too," she said ominously.

"Really?"

"She said she's thinking about going on a long cruise around the world, then selling the ranch and moving. Something about how everything around here reminds her too much of Bud and Earl. She sounded a little drunk."

"That's probably a good idea," Joe said.

"She said she's creating a college fund for our girls and a trust fund for Alisha's ward," Marybeth said. "She's going to talk to Marcus Hand about setting them up before she goes. I'll tell you all the rest in the morning. I'm too tired now. I guess that means her offer for the ranch is off the table, but this is better and she sounded very humble. Even thoughtful."

"That's great." He buried his face in her hair. "I'm tired, too," he said.

"She was very sweet," Marybeth said in a whisper. "It was an odd conversation, because it seemed like she had a lot more to say. And it almost seemed like she was saying good-bye."

Joe didn't respond.

"I might even miss her a little," Marybeth said.

"Yeah," Joe said. "Me, too."

SEPTEMBER 20

Therefore pride compasseth about as a chain; violence covereth them as a garment.

—Psalm 73:6

Epilogue

Nate Romanowski once lived in the stone house on the banks of the North Fork of the Twelve Sleep River. Across the river, to the east, a steep red bluff rose sixty feet into the air. The morning sun lit up the red face of the bluff. The river was so low that it was no more than a series of pocket water pools kept on life support by an artery of underground springs. To the east was a long flat dotted by sagebrush. A two-track cut through the flat from the highway and was the only road to the place.

Nate awoke in his blankets near the trunk of the single ancient cottonwood on the side of the house to discover that the peregrine had found him during the night. The falcon sat high and silent above him on a branch of the same tree. The bird didn't look down and acknowledge him, and Nate didn't call to it. It was just there. That was the nature of their partnership.

He kicked off his blankets, hung his weapon from a peg in the bark of the tree, and stood up naked and stretched. Although the stone walls of his house still stood, the rest had been vandalized over the years he'd been gone. The windows had been kicked in. There were two dozen bullet holes in the front door and a few shotgun blasts. Someone had entered the place and started a fire on the floor, which had burned down through the joists. A family of skunks now lived under the floorboards, and an owl nested in the chimney.

Nate walked down to the river and lowered himself into one of the deeper pools. The water was icy and bracing, and he washed his skin and most of the black out of his hair.

Shivering, he dressed in his best shirt and jeans. Then he pulled on his boots. He cleaned and roasted a sage chicken he'd killed the night before. He ate all the meat and tossed the bones aside for his falcon.

Joe and Marybeth were due anytime. They'd agreed to go with him to the res and to help him find the right words to use with Alisha's mother. He was curious to hear more about the trial, too. He already knew the result. And he knew that Bud Longbrake Sr. had died three days before. He'd never come out of the coma, and to Nate it was a bittersweet ending. An incomplete ending. He was not satisfied.

When Nate heard the sound of a car motor coming from the west, he wasn't alarmed. He squatted and repacked his things into his duffel bag. When he returned, he'd begin rebuilding his stone house, making it habitable and secure for the winter ahead. He'd need to lay in meat and wood, and repair the well that had been knocked over by yahoos.

Although he couldn't see the vehicle yet, he recognized the particular sound of the motor. It wasn't Joe's pickup or Marybeth's van.

Squinting toward the sound, Nate took his holster down from the peg and slid it on and strapped it tight.

Large Merle's 1978 Dodge Power Wagon ground over the top of the distant western rise, and the cracked windshield caught a brilliant flash of morning sun. Nate stepped behind the trunk of the cottonwood tree and waited. Merle drove slowly, and swerved from side to side, the front wheels climbing out of the two-track and wandering away a few feet before being turned back in.

Was Large Merle already drunk so early in the morning?

Slowly, the old 4x4 drew closer. Nate could see Merle's unmistakable woolly profile through the windshield. There was no passenger. Nate expected Merle to brake to a stop next to his Jeep, but he drove slowly right by it. As he did, Nate could see Merle's head slumped forward, chin on his chest, eyes closed.

"Merle!"

The vehicle rolled over Nate's old vegetable garden, headed straight for the stone house.

"Merle, wake up."

And he watched the Dodge drive head-on into the side wall of his house with a heavy crunch. The wall was solid, though, and didn't collapse. The motor coughed twice and died.

As Nate approached the rear of the Dodge with his hand on his .500, ready to draw, Merle's door opened and the big man tumbled out and landed sloppily and heavily on the dry grass. His feet remained in the car and he lay on his back, his mouth open and gasping, his blood-soaked hands clutching his belly.

"Jesus," Nate said. "Merle?"

Large Merle rolled his head over toward Nate. His face was ashen. He spoke through gritted teeth. "That girl . . . that Montana girl. She was a scout."

Nate didn't understand at first. Then he did. The girl who'd seduced Merle, who'd asked him to come to Montana with her. She had been sent out to find him. And to find Nate as well. And she'd succeeded.

He winced as he got closer to Merle and could see that his friend was clutching at his huge belly in an attempt to keep slick yards of blue-colored intestines from rolling out. He'd been gutted.

"The Five," Merle said. "They've deployed."

Acknowledgments

The author would like to thank everyone who assisted in the research, reading, editing, promotion, and publication of this novel, including Tim Curley, Lonie Hardenbrook, Ryan Lewis, Bob Budd, Max Maxfield, Karen Wheeler, Sherry Merryman, Doug Lyle, M.D., Roxanne Box, Molly Box, Laurie Box, Mark Nelson, Terry Mackey, and Bob Baker.

Kudos to Don Hajicek for cjbox.net and Jennifer Fonnesbeck for the Facebook page.

Special thanks and recognition goes to the wonderful Ann Rittenberg as well as the champion Putnam team of Ivan Held, Michael Barson, and the legendary Neil Nyren.